WOULD HE PROMISE HER ANYTHING?

Brandt shook himself. These soft feelings for Rowanne could ruin him. The way he felt when she looked at him was more powerful than a sword, more deadly than poison. Brandt had never known fear, not since his eighth year of life. But when he looked at Rowanne and felt the thump of his heart, something akin to terror seeped into his bones.

It unmanned him. *She* unmanned him. And yet . . .

Her eyes were so full of pain and loneliness, 'twas nigh unto impossible for him to shut her out of his mind. Brandt cursed himself silently, calling himself a weakling, a mewling pup, and worse. He reminded himself once again of the good and true men that called him lord. Men like Desmond. They should not be forgotten in favor of a winsome maid who warmed his blood and touched his black, benighted soul.

He could see her now inside the cart, applying a dampened scrap of cloth to the injured woman's head. She had courage. She had spirit and mettle, and in spite of her pain, all she had suffered, she had compassion.

" 'Tis a foolish man who grows soft with his enemy," Brandt muttered to himself, hearing the ghostly laughter of Gervais echoing through his head.

He looked at Rowanne once more. He wanted her body. He wanted her birthright. If he took one, then he could not have the other.

Dear Romance Reader,

In July of 1999, we launched the Ballad line with four new series, and each month we present both new and continuing stories set everywhere from medieval England to the American West—the kind of passionate, romantic stories you love best, written by the most gifted authors. At the back of each book, we tell you when you can find subsequent books in the series that have captured your heart.

Getting this month off to a dazzling start is **The Bride Wore Blue,** the debut story in our charmingly romantic series *The Brides of Bath,* from award-winning newcomer Cheryl Bolen. In the most picturesque of cities, the *ton* lives by its own rules—until, that is, love breaks them all! Following her much acclaimed *Bogus Brides* series, beloved author Linda Lea Castle sweeps us back to the spectacular atmosphere of medieval England in her newest keeper, **Promise the Moon.** This is the first story in her compelling series *The Vaudrys,* in which three long-lost siblings rediscover each other against a backdrop of passion and intrigue.

Also this month, Lori Handeland returns with **Nate,** the highly anticipated fifth book in her sexy, compelling *Rock Creek Six* series, in which a pastor's daughter and a gun-for-hire discover how love can overcome even the most difficult obstacles. Another one you won't want to put down! Finally, Kathryn Fox begins *Men of Honor,* a stunning new series on the danger-filled lives of the Royal Canadian Mounties. In this first book, **Reunion,** she takes us deep into the snowy wilderness—where tenderness and passion are challenged by the hardships of life on the northern frontier. Enjoy this extraordinary selection!

Kate Duffy
Editorial Director

THE VAUDRYS

PROMISE THE MOON

LINDA LEA CASTLE

ZEBRA BOOKS
KENSINGTON PUBLISHING CORP.

http://www.kensingtonbooks.com

ZEBRA BOOKS are published by

Kensington Publishing Corp.
850 Third Avenue
New York, NY 10022

All Kensington titles, imprints and distributed lines are available at special quantity discounts for bulk purchases for sales promotion, premiums, fund-raising, educational or institutional use.

Special book excerpts or customized printings can also be created to fit specific needs. For details, write or phone the office of the Kensington Special Sales Manager: Kensington Publishing Corp., 850 Third Avenue, New York, NY 10022. Attn. Special Sales Department. Phone: 1-800-221-2647.

Zebra and the Z logo Reg. U.S. Pat. & TM Off.

First Printing: January 2002
10 9 8 7 6 5 4 3 2 1

Printed in the United States of America

The Vaudry series is dedicated to my sons, Brandon and Logan.

Promise the moon is for you, Brandon. Thanks for exploring the castles and customs of England with me. I hope you enjoy this one.

Love, Mom

CHAPTER 1

He came before dawn without warning.

The studded door of the icy chamber swung inward. It hit the stone wall behind it with a thud. Rowanne flew from her bed trembling. She clutched the neck of her gown in one hand and her small eating dagger in the other.

The dying coals in the brazier provided a weak light. Suddenly a candle flared to life. Lady Margaret, Rowanne's fellow captive, held it in one hand and a smoldering stalk of straw in the other. Her eyes were hard as she focused on the intruder.

Thomas DeLucy scanned Rowanne with one quick glance. He stood in the open doorway, the hall behind him yawning dark as the gates of hell.

"I have brought news, Rowanne. Your father has died."

"My father?" Rowanne's heart skipped a beat. Sensations of pain and regret tugged at the corners of her mind. She had waited, locked in this accursed tower for years for her father to come. She had prayed he would rescue her. But he had not.

"Died?" Rowanne repeated. Now there would be no

chance for him to come—no chance for her broken heart to heal.

"Aye, Etienne Vaudry is dead, and I have arranged for you to wed anon."

"Nay, Thomas," Lady Margaret, wrapped in her heavy velvet robe, interrupted. "She will not be a pawn in your game. I will not let you bring misery to her as you have done to me."

Leopold, Thomas's one-eyed henchman, stepped through the arch of the open doorway. He grinned evilly at Lady Margaret. The blade of his dagger hummed a high-pitched tune as it left the leather scabbard.

"Milady Margaret, 'tis a fine day to see you again," Leopold said. "Do ye plot mischief against my lord?" The lid of his sightless eye pulled taut across livid scars as his grin widened. "My lord said the wench will marry."

Rowanne shrank back from the gleaming blade and Leopold's hideous one-eyed stare. She hated herself for showing fear, but she could not forget—could never forget—what he had used that dagger for. It was the most vivid and horrific memory of her youth. That and her mother's dying screams.

"As I was saying, Rowanne. Your father is dead. He passed nigh onto twelve months past. Sadly, we only just received word from a traveling monk."

"Was he murdered at your order like my brothers and my mother?" Rowanne was strengthened by a simmering rage. She felt a chill in spite of the fur-lined robe she had pulled around her.

Thomas glared at her. "You have no proof of any treachery." He adopted a belligerent stance. "Have I not provided the best food and cloth? Even books, and Lady Margaret for your companion. Are these the actions of a murderer?"

"You have kept both me and Lady Margaret prisoner because it suited you. Prithee do not paint it otherwise."

"I have kept you both alive up to now, Rowanne. That is a fact you would do well to remember." Thomas's eyes glittered with malice. He reached out as if to touch her, but she recoiled from his bejeweled fingers. He frowned but did not attempt to touch her again.

"I would never marry you," she said with disgust.

"Me? Me? You think *I* want you to wife? I have no use for wives, isn't that so, Margaret? Nothing is quite so troublesome as an unwanted wife. Is that not so, Meg?" His gaze flicked to Lady Margaret, but she did not answer.

"Who would you have me wed?" Rowanne asked. Her knees were trembling with a combination of fear and foolish hope.

Thomas tilted his dark head like some great butcher bird about to strike and studied Rowanne with intense scrutiny.

"Rowanne, you are leaving Sherborne Hall this very morn. You are returning to Irthing Keep with all possible haste."

Rowanne's heart fluttered within her breast. "Irthing? I am going home? Finally you will set me free? Why?" Hope suddenly lived in a room where hope had long since died.

"Because it is time."

"And Lady Margaret may come to Irthing as well?"

"Nay. My offer is for you and you alone, Rowanne," Thomas said with a grim smile. "With your father's death you are now the heiress of Irthing. You must wed quickly so your position will be secure."

"This is the reason you have kept me here all these years? You have been waiting for me to inherit Irthing?" Her mind could not wrap itself around the extent of his greed, or his patience.

"Aye. Any man who takes you to wife will have wealth and power."

Thomas smiled wolfishly, his dark eyes twinkling with cruel delight. "For nigh onto two years my own son and heir, Geoffroi, has bided at Irthing with your sire. He has by now surely learned all there is to know about managing the holding. You will wed my son, Geoffroi DeLucy.''

"No!" Rowanne and Margaret screamed in unison.

"Thomas, you shall not force her to wed. King John will surely hear of this outrage. He will not allow it." Margaret was shaking with rage, her usually serene face lined with emotion.

Thomas beetled his brows together and shook his head. "John Lackland is no longer on the throne. And that most gallant of knights, William Marshall, is no longer regent.

"Being locked away here has certain disadvantages, does it not?" Thomas grinned cruelly. "Lackland's sickly son wears the crown now. Young Henry III is but a boy. He is content to listen to his advisors and amuses himself with building like a child plays at blocks. Think you he will care about the fate of one insignificant maid who has a marriage settled upon her?"

The stone floor seemed to shift beneath Rowanne's feet. Now she knew why she had remained alive when her family had been put to the sword. She was the key to power and lands. Irthing and all the Vaudry wealth could be taken now. Her mother and brothers had bled and died so this day could come for Thomas.

"I will not marry the son of the man who butchered my family. I hate you—I hate your bloodline. I would sooner die." Rowanne took a deep breath.

Thomas studied her quietly for a moment, greed and ruthless calculation gleaming in his dark eyes. "Perhaps you would prefer death, Rowanne, but I wonder, would you be so willing to offer up someone else's life? Were you not satisfied to have your brothers and your mother die? Must another innocent perish so you will see that I am in earnest?"

"What mean you?" she whispered. A chill of foreboding rippled through her.

He turned to Leopold. "Take Lady Margaret up to

the battlements, and have a care, the edge is crumbling. It would be a pity if she fell."

"No. You cannot." Rowanne took a halting step toward Lady Margaret, but Leopold was quicker. He had the blade to Lady Margaret's throat, pricking her skin as he dragged her against his body.

"If at the end of one hour Rowanne Vaudry of Irthing has not readied herself to travel, cut off Lady Margaret's fingers, one by one," Thomas said softly as if he were ordering up a new cloak. "If Rowanne still does not concede after another turn of the hourglass, then you may slit pretty Meg's throat and throw her body to the hounds."

Rowanne's blood turned to ice. She searched Thomas's face for some sign of humanity. There was no mercy, no kindness, no spark of compassion. Nothing but his hard-willed determination to see her bent in obedience showed in his features.

"You devil," she hissed. "You *DeLucy*. How I hate you and your spawn."

"I care not what you like or dislike, Rowanne. You will journey to Irthing Keep, and once there you will be wed. You will be obedient and breed well or Lady Margaret will suffer for your lack."

"I vow to you now, Thomas DeLucy. My dead brothers will rise from their graves and walk this earth before I will wed anyone with DeLucy blood in his veins."

"We will see, Rowanne, we will see."

CHAPTER 2

Give up your body if you must, Rowanne, but never, ever give up your heart. Lady Margaret's oft given advice trilled through her head.

Rowanne clutched the dagger secreted within the folds of her clothing and made a silent vow. She would see both Leopold and Thomas die, and when their blood seeped into the cold English soil, she would hear them beg for forgiveness for taking her family's lives.

Somehow, some way, she would escape from Geoffroi DeLucy, and then she would return to Sherborne and see Lady Margaret free. She took comfort in that thought as she clung to the side of the cart in silence. With Leopold as her guard and a weeping maid named Betta as her companion, she finally left the gates of Sherborne.

Patches of snow clung to the northern faces of stone outcroppings and blended with chalk. A leafless copse of larch and towering sweep of evergreen yew lined the track on which the wooden wheels bumped over frozen ruts.

Though her heart was heavy with sorrow because Lady

Margaret was now hostage against her behavior, she could not ignore the majesty of life around her.

Harsh bird cries drew Rowanne's gaze to the ebony rooks that flitted beside the cart like a winged escort. High above a falcon floated motionless on a warm current of air. Suddenly it folded its wings and began to dive, disappearing behind the bare branches on the horizon.

After years of living behind cold stone walls she was nearly giddy with so many sights to behold. Outside the walls of Sherborne, serfs readied the earth for spring planting. Rough-coated curs barked while ragged, barefoot children scampered beside the cart until Leopold and the guards Thomas had provided chased them away.

For hours they traveled. Rowanne braced herself against the jarring of the wagon. She forced her thoughts inward. She alone could save Lady Margaret. But how? Time slipped by while she considered and discarded many foolhardy plans.

Without warning an arrow bit deep into the side of the cart not a hand's span from Rowanne's face. Then another and two more. Men on horseback flew from the weald beyond the cart. Rowanne shrank down into the cart, hiding behind the domed chest containing her clothes. Weak sunlight played along halberds, swords, and pickaxes. The wintry forest sounded like the din of hell.

"By the Rood! 'Tis bandits. They lief slit our throats and leave us for the ravens," Jonathan cried. "Hold fast." He whipped the cart horse to a gallop.

The chest containing Rowanne's small clothes strained hard against the rope holding it. Suddenly the cording snapped. Rowanne gripped the side of the cart to keep from falling, but Betta did not. She and the chest tumbled into the icy road. The leather hinges of the chest gave, and the lid popped open like a ripe melon. Some of the thieves halted their mounts and set upon the broken chest like hungry wolves upon a bleeding stag. Others fell upon the serving wench.

"Milady!" Betta screamed. Rowanne stared in horror as the girl's clothing was ripped from her body. She was stripped bare and taken by more than one. Rowanne saw it all—saw the girl ravaged, raped, and finally killed.

It took only minutes. It was the second time in her life Rowanne had witnessed such unspeakable carnage.

The wheels of the cart hit another rut. Rowanne's teeth met with a painful snap. An image of her mother, Rowena, came unbidden. From the darkest recesses of her child's memory she saw a flash of her mother— bloodied, raped, and violated. Her stomach rolled, and she gagged. Surely death would be preferable to dying like her mother and Betta had died.

The cart reached a hill. No longer able to gain any speed, it halted. Leopold and the guard turned and met the thieves in pitched battle.

Metal hit metal. Horses screamed, men shouted and groaned. The scent of blood wafted on the breeze. Rowanne didn't want to watch, and yet she was powerless to look away, though she surely had already seen too much death and blood in her young life.

A Sherborne soldier swung his blade. A bandit fell, screaming in agony as his body crumpled like a tender sapling beneath a woodsman's ax. Rowanne nearly retched, and yet she could not look away.

An arrow hissed from a bandit's strong yew bow. The DeLucy soldier stiffened and clawed at his throat. Blood gushed from the wound like a crimson fount, covering his fingers, and then he slowly slid from his horse and moved no more. His mouth was open in a silent scream.

Magpies, rooks, and butcher birds began to gather in the barren branches of the gloomy forest surrounding the road. Rowanne wondered if they knew the end was at hand.

One bandit gave an exultant roar and cleaned his gory blade on the headless but still quivering body of another Sherborne man. Rowanne sagged over the edge of the cart and was ill.

'Twas too much horror, too much death. She had seen death on the day before she entered the gates of Sherborne, and now here it was again, waiting to greet her as she left Sherborne. And if she did not do as Thomas commanded, then Lady Margaret would be butchered.

The trapped feeling nearly splintered the thin veneer of her control. She wanted to scream. She wanted to take up a sword and draw blood.

She watched Leopold, swinging his sword from side to side as a clutch of thieves closed in. He deserved to die. She anticipated his death with an almost unnatural fervor, and yet she could not ignore the truth. When he fell, the bandits would surely take their pleasure upon her as they had on Betta. And when she was dead, Thomas would have no reason to keep Lady Margaret alive.

She drew forth the small eating dagger she carried in her belt. It was a pitiful weapon but better than no weapon at all. She held the blade low, the hilt braced against her hip.

"I will not be ravaged." She was prepared to take her own life rather than submit to an ignoble death.

One bandit shot an arrow at Jonathan, grazing his arm. The cart veered sharply left, throwing Rowanne into a tangle of arms and legs and heavy cloak. The wheels bounced over thick tussocks of half-frozen grass before it came to a shuddering halt.

"Milady, they are on us!" Jonathan cried. "Mother of God, protect us."

A savage, blood-chilling roar rose from the woods. Rowanne turned toward the forest in search of the source of the unholy sound, preparing to plunge the blade into her breast.

A single armored knight thundered from the dense cover of leafless elm and larch. His sword was drawn and ready. He rode a powerful destrier, dark as the night. The stallion's hot breath threaded 'round his head like mist over an open grave. But he rode not toward the cart—rather, toward the bandits.

Rowanne blinked, expecting the apparition to vanish like brume in the sun. But the knight did not disappear. He was closer now—solid, real, and grim. Rowanne's pulse matched pace with the rhythm of the animal's pounding stride. She allowed herself to leave the corner where she cringed, moving to get a better look at the solitary knight who thundered down upon the bandits.

In what appeared to be slow-measured time, he used both hands to raise his great blade. A brigand's body fell in twain on either side of the terrified mount.

One blow. One powerful slice of the sword had cleaved a man in half as if he were no bigger than a spitted spring lamb.

Rowanne was repulsed, yet at the same time she offered a prayer of thanksgiving for the brutal knight's prowess. He had saved her and by doing so had saved Lady Margaret.

Screams of torment filled the air and rippled over Rowanne as one by one the thieves fell before the avenging knight.

She could not breathe, or move. She could barely think. The sound of her heartbeat was loud as thunder in her own ears.

"Mother of God." She heard her own harsh whisper.

The knight in the crimson surcoat was as deadly as the archangel Michael. He wheeled his great, dark horse. Several bandits were making for the trees. The knight paused. Leopold saw him and spurred his horse toward one straggler. He dispatched the hapless thief with a thrust to his retreating back.

For a moment there was no sound, no movement. Even the wintry air was still. Men lay scattered like dead leaves on the forest floor. Blood congealed in black pools. Then the forest came alive. Crows, magpies, and butcher birds took flight. Scores of wings flashed blue-black and white as the carrion eaters gathered about the slaughtered men to feast, to pluck out eyes and rend raw, warm flesh.

Rowanne released the breath she had been holding. Her savior sheathed his sword and raised his visor with a gauntlet-covered hand.

His eyes were dark, his face lean. He was young, not more than five and twenty, a little older than herself, and yet there was an ageless appearance to him. His eyes were those of one who has seen torment, misery, and despair.

Though many paces separated them, Rowanne felt the burn of those hard, merciless eyes as he took her measure. Prickly flesh skipped up her arms and down her spine. Her heart beat heavy and weighted in her chest.

She squeezed her eyes tight and gulped in air. He was as terrible as God's own avenging angel and yet this man of death had saved her. A mingling of fear and fascination flowed through her veins.

"You are well met, sir," Leopold chirped as both he and the knight galloped toward the cart. Leopold laughed as if the morning had been spent hunting woodcock. He paid no heed to the gore clinging to his poleynes and sollerts. "You have the good fortune of saving the life of Rowanne Vaudry, heiress to Irthing Keep," he said with a proud smile.

The knight's eyes narrowed. Now there was more than simply a knowledge of pain in his eyes. They were canny, hard, and shrewd as they skimmed over her face and form. As foolish as it seemed, Rowanne wished she were not so disheveled, that her bliaut were not tattered and stained from the cart, that a fresh wimple covered her hair. She called herself a curdle-brain and worse. After all, she was alive and still chaste. And she must remember that the task of saving Lady Margaret and herself from Thomas's machinations yet loomed.

Abruptly the knight swung his head toward Leopold. His sword was still in one gauntleted hand.

"Your name, good sir?" asked Leopold.

"I am Brandt le Revenant."

"Le Revenant . . . one who returns from death?" Leopold made a face. "A most unusual name."

"I earned it in the Holy Lands," Brandt le Revenant said shortly.

"Well met, le Revenant. And since you have done us this good turn, you have my thanks. Come, ride with us to Irthing or as far as your path will allow. We will be safer together as at least a handful of the knaves got away before you came."

"You journey to Cumbria, to Irthing castle on the border?" Once again Brandt turned to stare at Rowanne. His expression was unreadable, but something about it made her shiver. It was foolish for her to be both attracted and fearful, but that was the right of it.

"Aye, to Irthing. Do you know it?"

"I have heard of it. I will ride with you, but tell me true, who is yon maiden?" he said to Leopold.

"As I say, she is Rowanne Vaudry of Irthing."

"A fine jest, put pray do not continue to beard me thus. Even in the far reaches of the kingdom the sad tale of the children of Irthing is known. No Vaudry remained alive after that night of treachery and slaughter. 'Tis a tale oft told around fires."

Leopold bristled at being challenged. His face turned a mottled crimson. " 'Tis no jest, sir, but the truth. The maiden Rowanne goes to claim her birthright—and to wed. Her new husband will be the new Lord of Irthing and the Black Knowe."

Though he made no move, nor said a threatening word, the knight's eyes shrank down to dangerous slits. His jaw became harder than stone. Rowanne shrank back in fear.

"I know not what game you play, or what plot you hatch but I know truly that all of the Vaudry line lies dead and buried since good Etienne went to God. There is no heiress to claim the keep. If this baggage says otherwise, then she is an imposter. Do you plot with her, old man?"

Leopold unsheathed his sword. "By the Rood, I shall have your blood for that insult."

Brandt le Revenant's lips kicked up in a humorless smile. He did not raise his blade as he spoke. "You would challenge me? I am half your age and have two good eyes. Do not be foolish, I would not take advantage." His voice rang with amusement.

Leopold seemed to be digesting that information. Rowanne hated him even more in that moment, for he was truly a coward—he was the child-killer of her nightmares.

"Since you have done me service this day, I will let your insult slide, le Revenant, I have no desire to draw your blood. But I tell you truly, 'tis no lie. The maiden *is* Rowanne Vaudry, daughter of Etienne and Rowena of Irthing." Leopold pouted. "I am in service for my lord to be her escort until she reaches her betrothed in Cumbria."

"As I have no desire to draw your blood, old man, let us say no more—for now," Le Revenant said coldly. He slid his sword into its sheath while his thoughts rattled inside his head like stones in a wooden bucket. Young King Henry had placed a deed to the lush forests of Black Knowe and all of Irthing into Brandt's own hands. He had not mentioned any maiden with claim to the keep. Knowing the caliber of advisors that had surrounded the boy king since William Marshall died, Brandt could not believe they had made a mistake on so serious a matter.

No. This pretty maid was false, an imposter, a changeling. Perhaps she had been hired to try to steal the keep. But Leopold swore her betrothed awaited her there. Brandt glanced at the one-eyed man-at-arms. The entire situation was unbelievable.

Who could the betrothed be? What noble would be so bold or so foolish as to attempt such a ruse? Or was this some jest put into motion by Desmond and Brandt's men? 'Twould be like them to play such a game.

Brandt shifted his weight on Clwyd's wide back and glanced at the maiden, just visible within the tattered leathern cover of the cart. His journey thus far had been boring and ordinary, but now he had been provided with a little mystery and spice.

Keep your enemies beneath your gaze, Brandt. Gervais Monfort's ghostly voice rippled through Brandt's head. Gervais had brought him from orphaned guttersnipe to squire, and finally to an honorable knight's spurs. Though Brandt could scarce consider a broken-down warrior and winsome blue-eyed maiden as worthy enemies, he decided to follow Gervais's advice. It would be an interesting diversion for him until he met with his men in Chester. And perhaps he could find out if this was a poorly thought out deception or some humor perpetrated by his own men

Brandt focused on Leopold and managed a smile. "Let me journey with you, for I, too, am bound for Cumbria."

Leopold blinked his solitary orb, then he glanced at the bodies being rent by butcher birds. He shivered visibly. "With all my guard lying dead I would be glad of it, Brandt le Revenant."

Rowanne did not miss the unmistakable tone of relief in Leopold's words. He was no doubt thinking of the long road ahead and his solitary sword. It gave her some small amusement to see how quickly Leopold could overlook an insult when his own hide was in jeopardy.

"Good. Then we are of one mind," Brandt said smoothly. "Allow me to offer my sword arm to you and your *heiress*."

CHAPTER 3

Brandt le Revenant was by far the biggest man Rowanne had ere beheld. His hands, his legs—everything. She was certain that when he dismounted and stood, he would tower over Leopold, who was no small man himself.

A strip of leather bound his left wrist, a wrist thick as a good-sized branch. The hard muscles of his thighs bulged when he flexed his legs or moved his spurs against his war-horse.

She was fascinated—enchanted—by the look of him.

Rowanne drew in a deep breath and wondered why she felt a quickening of excitement and fear each time she looked at him. Had her years of confinement left her crippled in some way? Was she unable to be in the company of men without having ill humors?

She chewed the inside of her lip and raised her gaze, only to find Brandt le Revenant watching her with the same rapt attention she had been giving him. Her cheeks flamed.

Feeling foolish beyond measure, Rowanne turned away from him. She focused her gaze on the hawk soaring above them. The bird had kept pace with them since they left the scene of the battle.

"What an odd bird that is. It seems to be flying with us as we go north," Rowanne said aloud.

Suddenly Brandt whistled a strange shrill call.

"Come, Glandamore," he said in his deep, melodious voice. "The lady wouldst see you closer, methinks."

Rowanne's gaze darted to him. Then her gaze returned to the sky. Although there was no reason to expect the bird to obey, she found herself waiting for it to do so. The knight seemed magical—capable of doing anything.

He whistled again, a long, high trill. The bird of prey hung in the sky for half a heartbeat. Then it dived toward the earth. With amazing grace it tucked its wings and came to light upon the leather strip lashed to Brandt's left wrist.

"She is yours?" Rowanne asked in breathy excitement. "She is lovely. What is her name?"

"This is my lady Glandamore. She is the female that holds my heart." As if the bird was pleased to hear her name, she made a trilling sound and her razor-sharp talons curled into the leather. The bells on her jesses tinkled like raindrops as she settled herself.

"Vainglorious creature. I will have no peace until you are hooded, I see." He chuckled. He slipped a tiny hood constructed of cow-skin and bells onto her head. Each time she moved, the bells tinkled merrily.

"She is magnificent. And somehow she seems a fitting companion for one called the ghost," Rowanne said, feeling shy and yet too curious to be silent. "Does she always come to your call?"

"Aye. She is an obedient female." His eyes twinkled.

"Where did you get her?"

"I brought her back from the Holy Lands. She was my payment for saving a high-born Saracen. I had my choice: either the hawk or a harem. I took Glandamore, for I would rather have a bird who can hunt and fill my cooking pot than a pack of shrewish wenches good only for warming my bed."

Heat climbed into Rowanne's cheeks. Just looking at him made her warm all over. Hearing his voice, hearing the things he said, made her skin prickle. Jesu, she had never imagined that a man's converse could do such things. What would happen if he ever touched her? She ducked her head and tried to school her thoughts and emotions.

"Ah, I have made you blush. Pray forgive my coarse tongue, lady. I spend too much time in the company of men."

"And I, evidently, not enough," Roxanne mumbled, trying hard to tame her confused emotions.

Brandt watched the pretender. She was like a child in her innocence. It oozed from her soul like sweet nectar from a flower. What fool would be so thick as to believe *this* maiden could pretend to be an heiress? God's tears, every thought, every emotion blazed across her face in full view of anyone with wits enough to look. She lacked the jaded polish of a high-born lady. She was too pale, too thin—too eager. She lacked the hard-edged polish of a true heiress, though with her fair hair and pale eyes she could pass for one nobly born. But only a dullard would think this green girl and an aging knight could wrest Irthing from Brandt le Revenant. No man living would take what he had fought so hard to gain.

Rooks and magpies chattered and swooped by the cart, as if to tease hooded Glandamore. Brandt found his attention not on the hawk but on the maid calling herself Rowanne Vaudry. If she had tried to win Brandt's regard, he would simply have ignored her, hardening himself against a practiced whore's tricks. But this innocence—this joy at the simplest events—unmanned him. He found himself unnaturally curious.

When a flock of pigeons took flight from a copse of chestnut trees she giggled like a young girl. A childlike purity shone in her every glance, expressed itself in every graceful gesture as she braced herself to keep from tumbling against the hard oaken sides of the poorly sprung cart. The maiden surely must be close to twenty, Brandt decided finally, much older than most betrothed females. And yet, like one much younger, she looked upon every small detail as if seeing it for the first time. Perchance this was all part of the deception. Could it be this maid was more treacherous than she appeared because she was able to feign such virtue?

"A practiced deceiver, to be sure," he murmured beneath his breath. If that was true, then by heaven she would make a formidable foe. But he found he could make no firm judgment on the matter.

Was she a tender joint that a man of Brandt's appetite could swallow whole in one bite? Or was she a lovely flower that hid poison in its petals?

Later in the day they took a rest. The maiden slipped into a willow hedge for privacy. Leopold went into the woods to relieve himself. Soon the cart driver did the same. Brandt lounged against the cart waiting for Rowanne to return. When she made as if to climb into the back of the cart, he was upon her. She was trapped like a leveret between his outstretched arms. He leaned near, widening his nostrils, inhaling the musky scent of her femininity.

"I've been waiting for you," he said in a low growl guaranteed to frighten virgins and milksops.

She was terrified. He was glad. It was her fear he wanted. Perhaps he could intimidate her into telling him the truth and spare him the trouble of ferreting out her scheme.

"Tell me, vixen, what do *you* hope to gain by this thin deception?" He kept his voice to a husky whisper. He lifted one hand and brought it near her face. He saw her flinch. Was it fear or anticipation that made her taut as a longbow?

He did not touch her, yet his hand hovered near the smooth column of her throat. He watched in satisfaction as her pulse quickened, fluttering beneath the thin flesh.

"Who are you?"

"Sir, I don't understand your words." For all her terror she tried hard to appear unflummoxed by him.

He leaned nearer and drew in another breath, filling his nostrils, burning her scent into his senses as Clwyd would do with a mare in season.

She shuddered, the tremor flowing the length of her body.

He nearly let her go—he nearly kissed her. With a growl Brandt pushed any kind or merciful feelings aside. Innocent or no, she had set herself in his path. Nothing and no one was worth losing Irthing—his Irthing.

"I speak of this vain attempt to foist yourself off as the heiress of Irthing. 'Tis a foolish jest and one that may well stretch your pretty neck across a block. What do you hope to gain?" He finally gave in to the temptation to touch her. He ran one finger down the ivory column, stopping at the hollow in the middle of her throat.

She trembled violently but she did not try to flee. Her pulse was visible, fluttering like the wings of a captured bird just beneath her satiny flesh. He wanted to sip her skin, to see if it tasted as soft and sweet as it appeared.

"You are mad."

He grinned at her response. "Mad, am I? Then tell this mad man, what is your name, your *true* name?"

"I—I truly am Rowanne Vaudry. I do not know what has made you think I am anything but who and what I claim to be," she answered in a thready voice.

"The facts, sweet liar, the facts." Brandts finger trailed back and forth along her delicate collarbone. "The story is well known. Due to treachery the Vaudry family was all killed, all but Etienne. He mourned his family for the rest of his days."

"Then you do not know the true story. I am Rowanne, but I do not think my father grieved so very hard or else he would not have left me to the mercy of my captors." She slipped beneath his arms and darted out of his reach. She was breathing hard, and her blue eyes were round as bowls. Her breasts rose and fell in a steady rhythm. How delicious it would be to swive an untouched virgin.

Brandt shook himself and tamped down his lust. "Breathe, little deceiver. Just breathe."

She dragged in a ragged breath. Tears welled in her eyes. Her bottom lip began to quiver. She managed to stare at him without blinking—until the first tear spilled over and trickled down her cheek. Then she blinked rapidly as if to stem the tide of salty tears.

"I am no deceiver. I care not if you believe me. What difference would it make to me?" She turned, and like a doe fleeing a hunter she ran back into the woods.

The mystery, Brandt decided, was becoming thick as pottage. The little vixen was a clever pretender, acting as if his doubt and suspicion actually offended and frightened her when more like 'twas the threat of exposure that made her quake.

He was now even more determined to ferret out the truth and find out who she really was. He would play out their silly charade to the very gates of Irthing if needs be. Then when he was established fully as Lord of Irthing, he would mete out justice.

Leopold rode in front of the cart, Brandt beside it. It made conversation with him inevitable for Rowanne.

"Sir Brandt?" Rowanne scrambled to the edge of the cart and peered up at him. Her bliaut and cloak tangled clumsily, and for a moment he caught a flash of soft, tender calf.

"Aye?"

"I would speak with you."

"Ah, I thought you were still angry with me." He gave her a half smile.

"I was not angry, I was frightened. And that was exactly what you meant me to be."

"You were also angry. So now I must call you little liar as well as little deceiver," he said softly.

Her eyes flashed blue fire, but she kept her temper. "In your travels have you ever hired your sword to right a wrong—to redress and bring justice to an issue?" Her voice had dropped low, and Brandt realized she did not want the cart driver or Leopold to hear over the creak and thump of the wheels.

"What injustice do you seek to rectify, lady?" Brandt asked coldly, trying to banish the image of that slender ankle and creamy calf.

"Perhaps there are certain victims that need help. A knight such as yourself would offer his sword—for a price—would he not?"

"Perhaps. If the cause or the price was worthy."

She frowned and bit her bottom lip. He could see her working that out. Finally she said, "What would your price be?"

"Ah, now that would depend upon the task. I would need to know more before I could say."

"Of course, that is only sensible," she said with a nod. "We will speak of this again." And with that she moved back to her former position. Soon her brow was furrowed and she was deep in thought.

She was a strange female, and though Brandt called himself a coddlepate for it, he wanted to know more about her. While he watched her unaware, Clwyd picked his way carefully over the tangled track. But suddenly the cart lurched. And in the blink of an eye Rowanne was dumped through the splintered boards at the back into the muddy, rutted track.

"Have a care lest you break your stupid neck and spoil my lord's plans!" Leopold shouted. "I would hate to take the news of your death to him, for you know how hungry his hounds are."

Brandt saw the blaze of pure, white-hot hatred in Rowanne's eyes as she rose from the ground. She swiped at the mud clinging to her gown as she glared at Leopold.

If Brandt had not known they were in league, he would surely have warned the one-eyed fool. For in the maiden's eyes was the cold sting of murder.

CHAPTER 4

Thatched cots sprouted like mushrooms in the long shadows of Castle Cary's curtain wall. There was not an inn or a common house among the collection of wattle huts, but a few coins Leopold grudgingly produced from his purse induced a robust villager and his wife to provide bread, meat, and a dry place by the fire for Rowanne and Leopold. Brandt preferred the company of Glandamore and Clwyd where he could sleep more soundly and not have to worry about getting his throat slit in the night.

Brandt led Clwyd into a tumbledown byre where an aging ram and two shaggy ewes chewed dried twists of winter grass. He settled Glandamore on a post nearby and tugged off his heavy helm, grateful for the wash of cool air against his scalp. He tunneled his fingers into his sweaty hair to separate the thick, damp strands. Flexing his neck first right then left, he heard the pop and snap of his bones. Each battle remained with him in the collection of aches and pains and scars he carried. It was the wage and due of a successful mercenary. He wondered how the maiden fared after her hard day's journey.

He was taken aback when he realized his thoughts

were running in the direction of the little imposter. What cared he if she was covered with bruises? She was, after all, a liar, bent on taking his rightful holding from him. And yet he had perceived threats in Leopold's words to her.

Clwyd nudged his arm and brought him back to the present. Brandt yanked the heavy saddle and padding from his back. With a handful of clean straw he brushed the dirt and sweat from Clwyd's sleek body.

"Ah, you and I are aging bags of bones, Clwyd. What we need is a squire and a groom to see to our comforts." Brandt chuckled. It was a source of some amusement to Brandt's best friend, Desmond, that even after Brandt was given the title of baron he could not find a squire who would endure his bad temper and spoiled steed.

He grinned at the thought of seeing Desmond and his men-at-arms. Brandt had gained one or two warriors after each successful battle while on Crusade. One day he had waked to find he possessed an army; a host of fighting men composed of adventurers, landless second sons, unacknowledged bastards, and even a few high-born noble knights. He loved them one and all. Now with Irthing he could offer a warm hearth and a permanent demesne to one and all.

"Unless by treachery I lose Irthing," he mumbled the unthinkable. "Nay. I vow a score of men cannot take what I have fought and bled for, eh, Clwyd?" Brandt whispered grimly. But deep in his heart the question burned: Could a winsome maid do what armed men could not?

Brandt nearly scalped himself on the low oaken lintel when he entered the croft. Rubbing his forehead and cursing himself for a clumsy oaf, he waited for his eyes to adjust to the dim interior. The only light was from the fire in the hearth where Rowanne sat on a stool. The damp smell of winter clung tenaciously to the inside of the dwelling, mingling with the tang of unwashed bodies and sour beer, but it was warm.

For the first time since Henry had handed Brandt the rolled and sealed parchment, the full weight of his new responsibilities hit him. There would be peasants in Cumbria who needed food, clothes, and wood to see them through winter. Those peasants and villeins would look to Brandt, their new lord, for protection and prosperity. As the lord of a holding flourished, so did his people.

Brandt squared his shoulders and resolved to be a worthy lord, to see that all his people, from the highest to the lowest, including outcast bastard children, were as well off as he could make them.

"Have a joint." Leopold shoved a trencher of greasy and overcooked meat toward Brandt.

Brandt frowned suspiciously at the meat but finally picked up a piece of brawn and took a bite. He had certainly eaten worse. He resolved to leave a few extra coins for the crofter before he departed on the morn.

"You look like a thirst is upon you." Leopold held a jackmug. " 'Tis weak and sour but 'tis wet. Come share my cup. Drink."

"As you say," Brandt replied absently. He sipped the watery brew and listened to Leopold.

"Our meeting today was fortunate." Leopold slurped loudly and cleaned his mouth on the back of his hand. "I am pleased you have consented to ride with us."

Keep your enemies in striking distance. Gervais had warned Brandt this while he taught him the ways of a knight.

"Aye, I will journey with you, mayhap all the way to Cumbria."

"If you can remain until I have replaced our escort, I can ask no more than that," Leopold said, taking back the jackmug for another drink.

"Tell me about yourself, le Revenant. Are you nobly born?"

"I am the unacknowledged bastard son of a minor baron."

"Ah, so half noble," Leopold said knowingly.

"Aye, on my mother's side," Brandt said without a trace of humor.

Leopold blinked his one eye and asked no more questions along that line. Rowanne sat by the crude, poorly vented hearth and tried not to stare at Brandt through the haze of smoke. She had been mentally rehearsing what she would say to him. She wanted to appeal to his sense of justice, but 'struth, did he care about justice, or was coin his only inducement? And another thorn nettled her. How could the simple task of removing bits of armor so change a man?

She had not been prepared for the sight of Brandt le Revenant without his helm and gauntlets. His thick, dark hair tumbled around his shoulders like a wild mane. Without his mail coif she could see all of his jaw and his chin, even the parts where a dusky shadow of beard grew along his strong, angular jaw. And each time he turned to look at her his wide-spaced brown eyes shone with shrewd discernment and quick intelligence.

She realized that even when he seemed not to be listening his ears were pricked as a woodland fox's. He was strong and sleek as a well-tempered blade.

And just as deadly. Brandt le Revenant was beautiful and terrible. God's own avenging angels could not have been more perfect.

He shifted on his stool, and she realized that she had been staring—intently. She snapped her head around, afraid he would catch her studying him. Busying herself with the bread and cheese the housewife had provided, Rowanne nevertheless tasted little of what she chewed. Her throat was dry as sand, and her heart beat a heavy cadence in her chest.

Brandt le Revenant, *the ghost*, was just the kind of man she needed to thwart Leopold and Thomas. And yet she knew so little about him. She closed her eyes and listened while he spoke.

"You have a knight's spurs, le Revenant. Tell me who trained you."

"I earned my spurs in service to Gervais of Monfort."

"Your sire helped you by placing you with him?"

"Nay, unless you call being tossed out the gate of his keep in the dark of a stormy night placing me." Brandt's eyes were hard and Rowanne shivered.

"And yet you remember your sire well. Surely 'twas not so bad."

"Oh, I remember him well. I have vowed never to forget his cruelty. I pray to the Holy Rood I will be given a chance to repay all his deeds in kind."

Rowanne smiled to herself. She would and could appeal to this hard knight, for he was a mercenary with a taste for revenge.

Rowanne marked the passing of time by watching the logs in the hearth burn to ash. Now the only sound was the rhythmic breathing of those within the cottage and the rush of her own blood in her ears.

She was terrified, but she was ready.

Holding her breath, Rowanne rose and crept toward the door of the croft. She skirted the snoring Leopold as carefully as she would an adder, trembling like a newborn fawn when she swung open the door of woven reeds.

Moonlight illuminated the path, painting the ground silvery white. Her thin slippers made no sound on the hard-packed, frosty earth. When she reached the byre she soundlessly slipped inside the crude shelter. The smell of the animals triggered a long-ago memory that choked her with emotion.

She would make Thomas pay.

At the threshold she hesitated. Would the mercenary

sleep on the ground? If she startled him, would he draw
his sword against her and slay her in the dark?

Rowanne thought of Lady Margaret's unflagging
courage and kindness through the years of captivity.
When Rowanne had been plagued by nightmares, it
had been Margaret's hand that soothed her. When she
sickened, 'twas Lady Margaret who nursed her. She took
a breath and stepped inside the yawning blackness.

She walked slowly with her hands extended in front
of her. Her fingers met the warm bulk of the war-horse,
Clwyd. She flattened her palms and ran them along his
warm body.

Rowanne worked her way 'round until she was standing at the front of his head. It was a bit alarming that
he was so large. " 'Twas not my intention to disturb
your sleep, oh, mighty steed."

He snorted a gust of warm, hay-scented breath upon
her forehead. From her tower prison she had always
admired the way horses looked.

"Would you be here to slip a blade betwixt my ribs,
little deceiver?" Brandt's hard-edged voice brought her
spinning around awkwardly in the darkness.

She could not see him, but she could feel him there
in front of her, a wall of heat and suspicion. "I mean
you no harm."

"Now why should I believe that when you have come
stealing into what passes for my bedchamber in the dark
of night?"

Brandt's body tightened with awareness. In the dark
she was even more enchanting, with her soft, lilting
voice. He fought the desire heating in his groin. "Speak,
little pretender. Tell me why you are here."

"I have came to ask a boon." Rowanne wished her
body would stop prickling with heat. "I wish to strike a
bargain with you."

"I trow I am intrigued. What could a little imposter
such as you want from me?"

"You make this difficult, sir." The darkness was thick

with mystery. She found her thoughts scattered, her body too aware of him as a man.

"Ah, you are expecting chivalry from me? I am but a lowly mercenary, lady. If I had any soft manners, they were left in the blood-soaked sand of the East." Jaded disillusionment rang in his voice.

"You have killed many men?" she asked softly.

"I have earned my crusts by killing. You saw the proof of it when I chanced upon the bandits."

He heard her shift uneasily at the reminder of the carnage.

"You handled your sword well."

"There is an art to killing, I suppose, if one has the gorget to appreciate that sort of thing. But I grow weary of this. Speak plain, what is it you desire? I wish to gain my bed before the sun rises."

"I would have you slay a man for me," Rowanne blurted.

A rustle of sound. A flare stung her eyes. A tallow stub glowed within the grasp of Brandt le Revenant's strong fingers. Light limned his face, creating satanic shadows along his high cheekbones.

"God's blood, what manner of creature are you?"

"I had intended to explain . . ." Her voice trailed off uncertainly.

"Indeed." His eyes skimmed her face as if seeing her for the first time. "Do so now."

She straightened her spine and her resolve. She was about to bargain with the devil. "I do not go willingly to my betrothal and wedding."

He shrugged. "I have heard it said few maidens truly do."

"No, you don't understand. It is more than maidenly shyness. Leopold must die."

He jerked his chin back as if she had struck him. "Slay Leopold? Your man-at-arms, protector, and escort?"

"He is not my protector. He is a fiend. He must die. He *must*. The sooner the better."

Her heart thudded three hard beats before the knight exploded like a lightning-struck yew.

"By the saints' blood! First you lie about who you are, and now you want your accomplice slain." He dragged his open hand down his face. "Gervais always vowed there was no honor shared among thieves. Now I see he spoke true. I'll not be drawn into this deception. I'll not kill Leopold because you have a falling out over shared portions."

She took a deep breath and tried again. "I have stated my suit badly, sir. You do not understand. I must help someone, but I see no other way to do that but to hire your good sword arm."

The only indication he had heard was the sudden arching of one brow. It added to his hellish countenance, that peak of dark hair, tufting slightly in the middle as he glared down at her. She would have backed away from that unyielding glare if the destrier had not been breathing hot air down the back of her bliaut.

"Hire my sword?" He repeated each word deliberately. "That sounds too gentle. Say it for what it is. You want an assassin."

"I will see you are well rewarded. I promise you will benefit greatly. I must be free of this one-eyed watchdog. I must help someone," she added hopefully.

"I am no damn assassin," he said with disgust. "Do your own murdering if you must."

"But, but you said—you are a *mercenary*." Rowanne found herself coming a half step nearer to him. The heat of his muscled body in the close confines of the chilly byre warmed her. "You wield your sword for the highest price, is this not true?"

Brandt's scowl deepened. "I am a mercenary, not an assassin. There is a difference. I do not kill men because of a woman's whim." He shook his head to deny her.

"If you have had a falling out with Leopold, settle it yourself."

" 'Tis no whim that makes me wish Leopold dead. 'Tis injustice that I must right."

"What would a little deceiver such as you know of injustice?" Brandt sneered bitterly.

"More than you think." Rowanne gulped down her fear and took another step. She tilted her head at an uncomfortable angle to see his face.

"It is important to me—vital to another. A life hangs in the balance. Won't you please aid me?"

His mouth twitched at the corners. "Is this about a lover who is too much a coward to put the knife between Leopold's ribs himself?"

"Nay." Anger stiffened her spine. "It is justice, I say."

"My answer is still nay. I am no assassin."

She could not stop herself. With trembling fingers she reached out and grasped hold of the front of his surcoat. He was so tall she didn't even reach his chin. Desperation and the image of Lady Margaret spurred her to recklessness.

"Oh, but you must *kill* him. He has to die, he *must* die. It is the only way. First Leopold must die and then—"

"What? Jesu, what manner of bloodthirsty creature are you? Who else do you wish dead?"

"I wish no more to die, but I must have a hostage—" she blurted, still clinging to his cloak. "My betrothed."

Both brows arched. He gently, with great precision, took hold of her hands and removed them from his surcoat.

"You are a cold and unnatural female. I wonder if you are quite mad. First you claim to be an heiress. Now you beg me to kill your escort. Then you plan on taking your betrothed hostage. Is this all a perverse fantasy? Or is this some elaborate jest? Did Desmond set you on this course?"

"I know no one named Desmond."

"As you say. Then please do not think me impertinent, my *lady*," he said sarcastically, "but in view of the fact you wish me to kill Leopold, may I have the full story of why?" Let her play the innocent maid in need of a champion, let her try to deceive him with this unbelievable story, he would not be taken in by her soft skin and wide eyes.

"Prithee, enlighten me, little temptress," Brandt continued harshly. "I am waiting. Tell me what makes you so bloodthirsty," he said.

Rowanne was not sure she could trust Brandt. If she told him about Thomas, he might recognize the name and think to barter more coin from Thomas to betray her. And then Lady Margaret would suffer.

"Why must you have the story now? Can you not kill Leopold and then I will tell you?"

"You speak freely of murder and death but cannot say why. 'Tis a great deal you expect of me on faith alone, Lady Rowanne."

"Is it not enough I am willing to pay?"

"Nay. I know not what your game is, but you surely play one with a plot and intrigue."

"I have learned of such from the master of deception. He has betrothed me to his son. He plans to force me to wed, but I will not. You need know nothing more than that, you *mercenary bastard!*"

Brandt stiffened. Suddenly he was back at Sherborne, only a child, ten years old, hungry and alone. He was struggling to overcome the taint of his father's blood and the shame of his father's cruel actions.

Bastard. The name stung like the fangs of an adder.

Brandt's pain was as raw and fresh as if he had just suffered the first insult moments ago instead of more than two decades past.

"By Saint Brigid, you have surely misthought yourself."

"Nay, I have not." Rowanne jerked her arm free and stepped back, tears blurring her vision.

Brandt grabbed hold of her again. He dragged her

against his chest, his strength more than sufficient to hold her with one hand. "Then you have misjudged me. I will slay no man. Go."

"If you will not do what I ask, I must find a way to do it myself." Her voice trembled with emotion.

Brandt studied her face. He could not ignore the pain in her eyes even though her words were full of venom. He unconsciously eased his grip on her arm and allowed his palm to slide down her slender forearm. Then, in an impulsive gesture he was powerless to control, he gently wrapped his fingers around her wrist and brought it to his lips. He kissed the spot where her pulse beat. He felt her heart beat faster. He longed to put his lips to hers and see if they were as sweet as he imagined. Brandt fought his lust and shoved her gently from him. Before he released her, though, he nipped at the tender flesh of her throat.

She drew in a sharp breath.

"Prithee, little imposter, lie no more. Methinks this is another plot you have hatched, another story to make your claim of being the long dead heiress more believable. Your attempt to gain my sympathy will not work. I believe you not. Now go. Get thee to your bed and speak no more to me of this web of lies.

"Get thee to your bed before I forget you are posing as a highborn lady, and slake my lust upon you here in the straw like a common-born whore."

She ran from him, her shame of cowardice fluttering around her shoulders like the ghosts of her past.

CHAPTER 5

Morn arrived cold and gray as Brandt's mood. The events of the previous evening had robbed him of sleep and left him with both an ache in his head and a sour belly.

The little deceiver had managed to make him feel sorry for her in spite of his better judgment. How she had done it, he didn't know, but she could spin lies quicker than any spider.

"And methinks the whole mad performance was a lie. She surely does not wish Leopold dead."

Muttering curses on the heads of all winsome blue-eyed maids and greedy half-blind soldiers, Brandt roused himself from his bed of straw. He saddled Clwyd and saw to Glandamore's needs, taking his time with his own morning ablutions. Piece by piece he donned his padded gambeson and armor, and with each item he spewed another epithet about the enchanting imposter who had blundered into his life. And even though he took his time he was still finished before the straggly red cock crowed in the muddy yard outside the byre.

Brandt's breath hung in front of his face like dragon's smoke when he led Clwyd outside. And though it was early, a thready tendril of smoke curled from the chimney of the croft, barely visible in the graying dawn. He broke his fast in the company of only Clwyd and Glandamore, standing in thick muck and chicken droppings, which he found preferable to breaking bread with liars and deceivers. And while he choked down the dry bread and ale he had pulled from his own pack, he puzzled over how one so sweet and innocent looking as Rowanne could be mired up to her pretty blue eyes in intrigue.

King Henry's deed to Irthing was safely in his pack and his men scheduled to meet him in Chester with wagons of plate, rugs, and furnishings. His position was secure. He had nothing to fear from Rowanne, so why did he give a second thought to her honeyed lies? Why didn't he just ride on alone?

Brandt fancied himself a hard man. He had to be, growing up as he had, and the years plying his sword had only made his skin thicker, his heart more immune. Yet the little fraud's request to do murder had managed to shake some sleeping part of his soul.

Gervais had often told Brandt that he was not so hard as he pretended. But this *softness* toward a female who was obviously bent on destruction disgusted him.

She claimed she was an heiress. She claimed the son of her worst enemy was waiting to take her to wife. She claimed she wanted Leopold dead to right an old wrong.

Was any of it true?

"Ah, if good Desmond were here he would laugh in my face and tell me to swive the wench and clear the cobwebs from my head. And 'struth I would not be opposed to showing her the pleasures of the flesh."

But Desmond, his truest friend, the man who had taught him to cipher and read, was not here. Brandt was alone with his ghosts and the strange woman with claims that could not be taken seriously.

"Alas, I cannot decide if she is a liar or a would-be murderess. 'Tis a poor wage for one so fair."

By the time Leopold appeared, rubbing sleep from his eye, Brandt's mood had darkened farther.

Leopold's hair bristled about his head like an angry hedgehog. He grimaced openly with each stiff step, clearly pained by old wounds. How could a man so near to his dotage dare to become embroiled in a scheme to steal a rich keep like Irthing?

Clearly, whoever was behind this plot was a halfwit and a dullard. Not only was the maiden a poor substitute for a haughty highborn lady, which the lost heiress of Irthing would have to be, but her man-at-arms was only half a man at best.

"Good morrow." Leopold skirted Clwyd when the stallion bared his teeth and snorted a warning.

"Whether it be good or ill, I cannot say. The day is yet young," Brandt grumbled in response.

Yawning, Leopold untied his codpiece. He relieved himself into a pile of straw, the pizzle splashing up to stain the toe of his own boot on his blind side. His gnarled, knotty knuckles made retying his hozen a difficult chore.

Rowanne came from the croft, pulling her fur-lined cloak tight around her. Fury smoldered in her eyes. She was clearly holding a grudge about his refusal to be her assassin. Or was her hatred because Irthing was her goal and he was not the soft sot she had been expecting?

It was a mystery that grew with each passing moment. In one breath Brandt was resolved to ride on alone, in the next he was determined to stay and see his curiosity satisfied.

"The ground inside the croft was hard as a witch's heart. I slept not a wink before dawn. How fared you?" Leopold asked Brandt as he readied his horse.

"I rested well enough," Brandt mumbled absently. If Leopold told the truth then he must've known that Rowanne wandered abroad in the darkness. Or was he more incompetent than Brandt perceived? Had she managed to creep from the cot undetected?

Rowanne was studying Leopold with burning intensity. Brandt had decided to mount Clwyd and leave them to stew in their own broth of lies when the flash of a blade within her cloak stilled Brandt.

By all the saints in heaven, is she going to plunge the dagger into his ribs right here in broad daylight? Leopold, blind as he was on one side, would see nothing coming until the blade had done its work. None would know of her deed.

"Except for me," Brandt whispered.

None would gainsay her when she turned those innocent-looking eyes upon them and sweet lies rushed from her moist lips. Rowanne continued her stealthy advance toward Leopold. Like a cat stalking a dormouse. It was as if she was ensorcelled, mesmerized by the sight of the aging man's back. She was no more than a rod from him, approaching silently on his blind side. The old man was unaware, grumbling about his lack of rest.

Rowanne's hand was trembling like a leaf in the wind.

Leopold bent to check the front hoof of his destrier, providing a wide target.

Brandt smelled the stink of death on the wind. Something about the pitiful shaking of her hand made Brandt almost pity her determination. What would make a maid be so intent to kill when it was obvious she took no pleasure from the effort?

Brandt had little knowledge of the workings of a woman's mind, but the expression in the winsome pretender's eyes was full of sorrow, and yet she was as resolute any crusader he had ever ridden beside.

A river of conflict opened inside his chest. Women did not kill in cold blood. Surely she would not *kill?* But even as he thought it, he saw her eyes narrow. He could see the pulse spot in her neck thrumming. She trembled so much he was surprised she could hold the knife.

God's teeth, was she mad? He had thought her claim of being Rowanne Vaudry was born of greed, but mayhap she was moonstruck, demented, ensorcelled. Mayhap she truly believed all her lies.

Brandt thought of her words in the byre. He told himself it didn't matter to him if the foolish baggage got her neck cleaved from her head on the ax-man's block. In fact, it would save him the trouble of refuting her claim if she did indeed show her face at Irthing with this preposterous claim on her lips.

And yet . . . it was not the way of a knight to see a man cut down blindly. And there was that look of trapped desperation in Rowanne's eyes. It had been there last night. It was there now.

The morning sun glinted on the point of the blade as she lifted it high. Her hand shook violently, but she did not falter.

Brandt was moving in spite of his decision not to get involved. He grabbed her trembling hand in his own.

"Milady, *Rowanne*, allow me to assist you into the cart." It was the first time he had openly used the name she claimed as her own. It sounded right, but he pushed that thought aside and focused on the moment.

"What are you about, knight?" She stiffened and tried to jerk free, but he held her fast. "Are you mad?" Her voice was little more than a whisper. "Loose me at once."

He bent her wrist until the knife was tucked beneath the folds of her cloak once again. She could not match his strength and 'struth she was trembling so much he was afraid she might collapse. Her furious gaze flew to his face. His hold tightened. Pain, rage, and a mixture of violent emotions flashed in her eyes.

"You dog-hearted knave," she whispered harshly. "Why did you stop me? God's tears, if you won't help me, then let me do what needs be done."

"If I leave you to do this you will find your pretty little head on the chop." He forcibly turned her and guided her toward the leather-covered cart. The crofter's wife was giving Jonathan a small wineskin and round of cheese.

"You have no right. You don't understand. I have to free myself from Leopold."

He took the opportunity to speak plainly. "Lady, you are a dangerous woman. Shall I take the dagger from you, or may I have your word you will make no more attempts at murder?"

"Have you been sent by Satan himself? When you said you would not help me, I never dreamed you would take a hand against me in this."

Brandt ignored her temper. "Answer me. Shall I take the dagger?"

"Try it, you churlish cockerel, and you shall feel its sting for your trouble."

He nearly laughed. "It is too early in the morn for the sight of blood. But mark me, if you make any more foolish attempts, I will relieve you of your *weapon*," Brandt quipped.

He put his hands tight around her waist, lifted her up, and deposited her into the cart. Her eyes were like bolts of crackling blue light.

"Fie, sir, for a man who cannot stomach the sight of blood in the morning you seemed more than capable of spilling it yestermorn. You are a craven hedgepig."

"A well-placed barb, but you cannot draw blood on me, lady. My skin is thick as leather."

He tightened his fingers against her waist, savoring the feel of her slender form, marking the tensing of her muscles, somewhat surprised at the satisfaction he felt.

"If you let me go now, I may still be able to kill him."

"You have a bold tongue, madam, to speak so plain. I wonder, little assassin, are you bold in other ways?"

"You offer me insult upon injury. I begged your aid last eve. You refused me. Now you stop me. I will pay you well for this—mark me."

Brandt frowned. "At our first stop you and I will speak

more of this, and by heaven I will have the truth from you—plain or fancy, I care not as long as 'tis truth I hear from your lips."

"I have told you no lies. It is plain you haven't got the wit to know it. I swear to you, Brandt le Revenant, you will regret this day's work when you stayed my hand."

"Little minx, I find your wrath oddly pleasing," he said with a twisted smile, and for some mad reason he leaned down and brushed his lips across her own. Her hands came up and she shoved hard at his shoulders, but the thing was already done—the kiss stolen. And he was stunned by his own reaction.

"You knave." She jerked free of his hands still encircling her waist.

"The only thing I regret is that I cannot have another taste of your sweet lips."

Brandt had little experience in dealing with temperamental women, but he had come to wonder if Rowanne Vaudry was mad as a stoat.

There were times when she was soft and seductive. A woman worthy of warming a highborn lord's bed. She could breed a brood of lusty boy children. "But lief they would all be hanged or locked away by the time they reached seven and ten if they took after the mother," he muttered to himself.

Though his good sense told him move on, he was like a moth caught in a spider's web. He could not drive Rowanne from his mind. Surely no man would want her to wife.

Unless she is the heiress to Irthing Keep. Brandt shifted his weight uneasily in his saddle. 'Twas a sad fact that many men would be more than willing to overlook baldness, a lack of teeth, and even heredity madness if their bride would bring them ample property. Irthing was more than ample property.

She cannot be the legal heir to Irthing. By Henry's pleasure,

Brandt had been deeded Irthing. No living heirs were known. No close relation laid claim after Etienne Vaudry died. Doubt crept into Brandt's mind like slow poison. A nagging and persistent sense of foreboding nipped at his mind as he held out his wrist for Glandamore to fly from the hawking glove.

Rowanne sat rigid, so angry she no longer felt the jolts of the cart. She had never felt such anger as she did now. Aye, she hated Thomas DeLucy, but that sentiment was akin to falling into a frozen pond—icy, numbing. Brandt le Revenant had spawned a white-hot wrath within her.

How dare he interfere? And how dare he kiss her as if she were some common trull? Even now she could feel the touch of his lips. Strong, demanding, his kiss made her weak with a strange kind of longing. Her stomach had done flips and flops and her heart had beat so hard she thought it might fly from her chest.

The kiss had been different from what Lady Margaret had told Rowanne to expect. Indeed, she had made a kiss sound somewhat disgusting with much slobbering and groping. There had been none of that, only Brandt's firm grip on her waist and his body drawing her near as if he were a wizard's lodestone.

"But he shall rue the day he spared Leopold's life," she mumbled.

Le Revenant had gone too far by his interference. By now she could have been on her way to make a plea to the king himself for help in bringing Thomas down. Surely not even Thomas would be so foolhardy as to harm Margaret if the king were to take an interest.

"But that chance is now gone. And Brandt must have his dose of truth," she hissed. "I hope he chokes upon it."

They stopped by a gurgling beck where pink cowslip grew in great abundance. Rowanne waited until Leopold was busy berating Jonathan for some new offense. Thomas's bootlicker filled the air with epithets. He was a small man who felt adequate only when tearing others down. But at least while he was occupied thus her words would be for Brandt alone.

"You bloody, meddling lack-wit." She spat the words out so fast even she was surprised by their fury.

Brandt le Revenant rocked back on his boot heels, his eyes narrowed, flinty and cold. "Have a care, madam, men have died for giving less insult." His voice was soft and dangerous.

Rowanne had worked herself into a fine spit of temper and would not be silenced now. She thrust out her chin and met his gaze with courage and indignant outrage.

"Oh-ho, do you threaten to open my gullet? I think not. You wanted truth; now you shall have it, all of it, and I hope it hangs in your gorge. Your fine morning's work may well cost the life of one I hold dear."

The words sizzled through Brandt's consciousness like summer lightning. He wanted the truth but not to hear about some milksop of a man that she was trying to save.

"—the dearest person in all the world is still behind those walls—"

"What has all that to do with me?" He demanded, interrupting her, hearing little of what she had said.

"If you had not stayed my hand, he would be dead by now. I could go to the king—I could appeal for help. He could send an army."

A frisson of nagging doubt sizzled up Brandt's back. She would go to the king? No imposter would go to the royal court with a false plea for aid.

"You should have let me kill him."

"He is a half-blind fool and not worthy of you staining your soul with his blood," Brandt said softly. He was torn between his own selfish need to protect Irthing and himself and the pain in her eyes. He wanted to fold her in his arms, to whisper honeyed words of comfort.

"Perchance we do not see the same creature when we gaze upon Leopold the butcher. I see the man who slew my mother and brothers. What do you see?"

Brandt turned to look at Leopold. He tried to imagine him younger, with the vigor of youth upon him. While he was watching, Leopold roughly grabbed the front of Jonathan's tunic and hauled the driver toward his twisted and scarred face. The metal rings on his brigandine vest strained across the muscles of his chest. Hard sinews corded in his arms. Aye, even now there was cruelty and strength, if one had eyes to see. Leopold was not the toothless serpent Brandt had first thought. A niggling shame for not seeing what was right before his eyes started at the base of his spine and worked its way upward. His temples began to throb as a bitter truth revealed itself.

"Have you not guessed? Leopold bragged about doing his master's bidding. Do you think I am under his *protection*? He is not my escort, he is my keeper. I was Thomas DeLucy's prisoner; now I am his pawn. I will have no more of it."

Thomas DeLucy.

"Thomas is determined to have Irthing through me. I have only recently learned that is why I was spared when the rest of my family was not."

The name hit with the power of a mace. Brandt's brain refused to process the information, but every fiber of his body knew she did not lie.

Thomas DeLucy.

His own hated father? The man who refused to acknowledge his by-blow? He was the man who commanded Leopold?

"Are you telling me Thomas DeLucy is behind a mad scheme to foist you off as the heiress of Irthing?" Brandt took hold of her shoulders. His gauntlets bit into her flesh. "You are in league with Thomas DeLucy?"

"Are you such a dullard and lack-wit? I *am* Rowanne Vaudry, you beef-witted fool. Thomas murdered my family. He kept me prisoner. Why else would he be wedding me to his coxcomb of a son, Geoffroi? Think, Brandt. Open your eyes and see the truth."

Something hot and bitter bubbled in the back of Brandt's throat. His eyes slid over her face. There was no deceit in it, only pain and hatred and a desperate need to be believed. The words she uttered assaulted him. She had known Thomas's son—his legitimate son—was named Geoffroi.

"Geoffroi wants to wed you?"

"Whether he wants it or not, I cannot say. His sire wishes it," she said bitterly. "I have sworn an oath. I will see my own dead brothers walk the face of the earth before I will wed any man with DeLucy blood in his veins. And I will do murder to see that vow kept."

"I believe you," Brandt said softly. His gauntlets slid from her shoulders. "I believe you are Rowanne Vaudry. I believe you were Thomas DeLucy's prisoner." A thousand half-formed ideas of retribution and revenge swam in his brain.

"At last," she said softly, a sheen of tears forming in her eyes. Her shoulders slumped. For a moment he nearly wrapped her in his arms. Then he straightened his shoulders and hardened his heart.

"So you are in need of a champion to thwart the house of DeLucy? To foil *Thomas* DeLucy?"

"Aye." Rowanne saw something in Brandt's hard eyes that drove all the weakness from her. "I will see you rewarded. If you will save me from this marriage, I swear you will have your heart's desire if it is in my power to give it."

The image of Geoffroi, his own whey-faced, golden-haired brother, flashed through Brandt's mind. Thomas would be in a fine rage if his plans to wed Geoffroi to an heiress went awry. Then another thought raced through Brandt's head.

Rowanne must never be allowed to marry. He held a sealed deed that gave him Irthing, but the only way he could be sure his claim would stand was if Rowanne was set aside.

"My sword arm is yours until Thomas DeLucy is defeated."

After that, Brandt would have to decide what to do with the woman who unknowingly threatened his future.

The harsh caws of rooks rose on the wind. Glandamore tilted her hooded head to listen intently as a vee of ducks flew overhead. Flocks of starlings and jays took flight from a leafless tree, kiting in perfect unison.

" 'Tis time for you to teach the noisy buffoons a lesson, methinks." Brandt slipped the little leather hood free from Glandamore's noble head. "Be off with you. Find yourself some sport and bring back something for tonight's sup." With a lift of his wrist the hawk gained the sky.

"We have not the time for hawking," Leopold grumbled. "I would have us make better time. Our pace today has been too slow."

Brandt smiled grimly. Anything that annoyed Leopold and would ultimately displease Thomas was well worth a bit of his time. He actually pulled Clwyd to a slower pace and turned to Leopold, smiling.

"Surely we have no need to rush. We fellow travelers should learn more about each other. Tell me of your lord, Leopold."

Leopold yanked his horse to a standstill, his previous desire for speed all but forgotten. He drew himself up like a proud little rooster and crowed proudly. "I am in service to a mighty baron. Rowanne is to marry Geoffroi, only son of Thomas DeLucy of Sherborne. The combined power of Irthing and Sherborne will rival the crown."

"Have a care, Leopold, lest the knight think you speak treason," Rowanne taunted.

Brandt's gaze slid to her for only a moment. As much

as he hated to admit it, he admired her spirit. 'Twas the whimsy of God, or mayhap the old goddess Mab herself that had brought him to ride the same road with Rowanne of Irthing. How it would curdle Thomas's gorget if he knew that King Henry had deeded the demesne of Irthing to his own unacknowledged bastard. And that Brandt would stop the wedding anon.

He turned to look full at the fair Rowanne. No longer did he see her as a little deceiver. Her profile was now more noble, her eyes more genteel. Now he saw her for who she was. The true owner of Irthing.

His rival.

A grim and hateful thought crept into Brandt's mind. He had to remove the threat of Rowanne.

Murder?

No, he could not take her life. But he could forever alter it. He had the means to buy her a place at a well-appointed convent. Once she was secure behind high walls he would be free from the threat of her ever claiming Irthing or ever breeding a son who could threaten him in the future.

That was it. His way was clear. Now that he had decided he had no more to worry about, why did he feel as if someone had plunged a dagger into his heart? He had been weaned on bitterness, raised up on hatred. Why should this day's decision leave him feeling bereft?

Since leaving Sherborne on a cold, dreary night he had survived in order to show Thomas that his bastard son was better than Geoffroi. So now that his goal was within reach, why did it taste bitter as poisoned dragon's blood?

Revenge was finally at hand. Both Thomas and the legitimate son who bore the name of DeLucy would be brought low. All Brandt had to do was kill his half brother and then lock Rowanne away to live the remainder of her life in seclusion. She could never know any man's touch—not even his own.

It was the only way.

CHAPTER 6

"I think I love the rain," Rowanne chirped. She had her fingers out, watching the droplets run over her fingers, like a child at play.

Brandt guided Clwyd through the morass of mud. For two days the unpredictable English spring had dumped cold, drizzling water on his head. He was tired and damp. Leopold had driven them hard, urging speed for Thomas's sake, which made Brandt wish he were drinking mulled wine at a warm abbey or common house. He had insisted on a short respite at St. Michael's on the Tor, but 'twas too soon over. He was mean-tempered and spoiling for a fight. How did Rowanne smile through all this?

"Tell me, Leopold, was the upcoming marriage of Geoffroi arranged by Rowanne's father?" Brandt asked in an attempt to turn his attention away from the beguiling water nymph.

"Nay." Leopold shook his head from side to side. "My lord Thomas informed Rowanne after the death of Etienne Vaudry."

"Is that not queer?" Brandt asked mildly. "Should the bargain have been done before her sire went to God, or is that what your lord Thomas waited for?"

Brandt took satisfaction from the white-rimmed discomfort in Leopold's one eye. " 'Tis not for me to say. My lord's designs are his own. He wishes that his son be aligned with the maid for reasons old and new."

"Ah, I see. And how does the maiden herself view the wedding and bedding?"

Leopold bristled with indignation. "She is most fortunate, for she wilt likely find no better alliance than with the house of DeLucy."

"Oh, indeed you are right, and yet . . ." Brandt said thoughtfully. "Since she is an heiress of some wealth and property one would expect she would have a gaggle of suitors vying for her hand."

Leopold's expression closed and shuttered. "Mayhap. I am but a soldier with little knowledge of such things. Her betrothed awaits. Nothing must delay the wedding."

Brandt suppressed a smile. Leopold was a wily fox, but he was easily tempted to rise to the bait. Brandt was sure that the one-eyed man knew much more than he claimed. He had to be aware of all the intrigue surrounding Rowanne. He also knew that if the world learned she lived, there would be no shortage of knights willing to take up her cause or her lands. Irthing was a plum that would tempt any man.

In a perverse way, Brandt's position would benefit by reaching Cumbria as quickly as possible. Yet he was loath to reach his destination. Not because he had any compunctions about slaying his half brother, but because he found himself enjoying the time spent in Rowanne's company.

He was torn. One part of him reveled in the notion of challenging his brother to combat but at the same time he realized that once that was done he would have to send Rowanne to a convent.

No matter how many times he told himself to forget her, she remained in Brandt's thoughts. His eyes were drawn to Rowanne, lovely, vulnerable Rowanne.

She looked up at him and smiled. A small, tentative curling of her lips. The cloth wimple covered her hair but a tendril of palest gold curled around her forehead. A hot flash of pure desire shot through him.

But he could never taste of her sweet lips, nor could he allow any man to know her. She must remain a virgin so his claim to Irthing would be secure. Through no fault of her own she was his rival.

Brandt was growing weary of Leopold's cruelty. Only this morn the brute had knocked Jonathan into the mud for being slow in hitching the horse to the cart. He needed a lesson in manners, and with each passing day Brandt yearned to be the one to school him.

"If you are so concerned with speed, why do we not find a village and purchase a horse for Rowanne? With the trunk gone there is no more need of a cart. Jonathan can walk faster than this constant bogging down in the mud will allow," Brandt suggested.

Rowanne's laughter could be heard from her perch just inside the leathern cover. She leaned out, her eyes sparkling with defiance as Leopold swung his head to stare at her.

"Leopold would sooner cut off his sword arm than see me mounted on my own horse," She said with a taunting gleam in her eye. "Isn't that true?"

"I'll not waste good coin on a horse for you. And my lord Thomas bid me bring you to your betrothed by cart," Leopold said sullenly.

"Or are you afraid the timid bride will bolt?" Brandt challenged.

The blood drained from Leopold's face. Brandt knew it was exactly what Leopold feared.

"She would not leave," Leopold said with a sly grin. "There are reasons why she would stay fast, but the maid cannot handle a horse properly. She must stay in the cart for her own sake."

"Hold the wagon," Brandt commanded in a tone that brooked no argument. Jonathan swung his head around to stare gap-mouthed as he yanked the horse to a stop—which maneuver required little effort since the cart was barely creeping through the black muck. Clwyd snorted whilst he danced nimbly on his iron-shod feet, sucking noises accompanying each movement.

"What are you about?" Leopold stared at the leafless forest, his hand tightened on the hilt of his sword.

"You may be at ease about her safety. I am of a mind to have the maiden ride pillion, and I will keep her from harm."

Leopold's expression altered. First, disbelief washed across his features, then a slow, simmering anger.

"Nay. You have no leave to do so. The maiden will remain in the cart—'tis the proper place for a betrothed woman."

"Even when you urge more speed? Even when the cart is poorly sprung and the maiden will be black and blue by the time we see Cumbria's borders?" Brandt asked slyly. He would have Rowanne with him if it meant drawing Leopold's blood to do it. "I doubt her betrothed will say gramercy to you when she is too battered to receive his attentions." Brandt would see Geoffroi in the earth before that eventuality, but Leopold did not know his plan.

Brandt let his gaze linger on Rowanne. Jesu, she was lovely, with her alabaster skin and innocent eyes. She was almost as surprised as Leopold by his bold suggestion, he could tell by the way she searched his face. He wondered if she might refuse to ride with him. There had been that implied threat in Leopold's words again. Brandt began to wonder what kind of a hold the devil had on Rowanne.

"Will it please you, lady, to ride pillion with me for a march of time?" Brandt's heart was beating hard and his hands itched to touch her skin. He could not bed her, but he could allow himself the pleasure of her company for a short while. "Clwyd is obedient. You need not fear."

"I am not afraid of your war-horse." She smiled, and it was like the sunshine of a summer's day.

"Nay, I say," Leopold croaked impotently. "I will not allow it."

"Will you gainsay me in so innocent and simple a matter?" Brandt's voice was low and soft. His gauntlet-covered hand rested lightly on the pommel of his sword.

Leopold's tongue darted out to wet his dry lips. He swallowed hard. "Nay. I will not gainsay you, le Revenant, but I hope the maid does not waggle her tongue and drive you mad with her chatter."

Rowanne and Brandt glanced at each other. There it was again . . . an unspoken warning. Brandt was glad a bargain was already struck, but he intended to gently question Rowanne, for it was obvious there was more she was not telling him.

Brandt held out his hand. She hesitated, unsure if she should take it. There was a magic and mystery about him that her body wanted to explore, but she was suddenly timid and shy.

"Lady?" le Revenant's voice jarred her. "Will you not ride with me?"

She looked up into the flint-hard eyes of her new champion. Her insides drew and warmed. There was a compelling strength in his face. She was no longer alone in her fight against the DeLucys.

Brandt smiled. Her heart fluttered within her breast. Jesu! Could any living man be more beautiful? Could the thought of being near him make her any more giddy?

"I will." She gathered her fur-lined cloak and the skirt of her kirtle in one hand and reached out to Brandt with the other. It was like clasping live coals in her palm. Heat sizzled up her arm straight to her heart.

The moment his metal-clad fingers folded over hers, she knew. He would bed her. She wanted him to bed

her. She wanted to learn all the secrets of the flesh in
Brandt le Revenant's arms.

"Not since I was a child have I felt so lighthearted. I
have been remembering bits and bobs. I think I remember riding with my—my father."

"Did you truly spend all your time at Sherborne in
the tower?" Brandt whispered so that only she could
hear. A little voice warned him to ask no more questions—to learn no more about the maiden who was
melting the ice around his heart. Nevertheless, he
waited for her answer.

"In truth I was pampered. I had books, threads, all
the things to fill my days. In good weather I could climb
the stair to the battlement, but the stones and mortar
are old and crumbling. It frightened me, and it made
me melancholy to look down on a world I had no part
of. I was happier in my tower prison."

"You make it sound a bleak existence," Brandt said
softly.

"Enough prattle about me. Tell me of yourself,
Brandt. Do you have happy memories of your childhood?"

"In truth I have no happy memories until I was well
past a child."

"Then tell me how you got your name, 'the ghost,' "
she said boldly, as if she wanted to turn her thoughts
to something less somber. "I would wager there is a
story to your name."

"Ah, so you have the heart of a gambler." Brandt
chuckled. "The man who persuaded me my salvation
might be found in the Holy Land gifted me with it."
Brandt grinned crookedly when he remembered.
" 'Twas my first successful battle, but just when I
thought the fray won, I took a blow to my helm that
knocked me senseless. All thought I was dead. Yet at
nightfall I roused, rose from a pile of corpses, and stag-

gered like a drunkard to my fellows. More than one
man pissed their braies while falling to their knees in
prayer."

"Oh!"

"Pardon, Lady, I forgot myself," Brandt apologized.
He could not take his gaze from her face. She was
angelic, with her prim white wimple framing her flushed
cheeks.

"Gervais thought 'twas a fitting name for me for I
appeared to have returned from the dead."

"You've had a hard life, I trow," Rowanne said, as
though she understood the demons that drove him.

"No more so than you," he responded gruffly, oddly
uncomfortable with the acceptance glowing in her eyes.

"I did not suffer. As I say, Thomas made sure I never
hungered or knew cold. If a jailor can be kind, then he
was."

A sharp pang of conscience stabbed at Brandt's soul.
Suddenly he had a vision of her behind cloistered walls,
her lovely pale hair shorn, her knees bruised from kneel-
ing in prayer. Would she consider that life a prison as
well?

Brandt kicked Clwyd till the big horse eased into a
rocking canter. He was determined to shove aside the
disturbing thought of Rowanne finding herself imprisoned once again when he put her in a convent. He told
himself he wanted no more than was his due. But while
his mind was busy making excuses, his body tightened
in awareness. She held herself close to him, pressing
her body against his as she sat before him on the horse.

He had never shared his horse with a woman before.
He found it extremely erotic and almost as personal a
thing as bedding would be.

Clwyd hopped lithely over a tussock of grass. Rowanne
gasped and grabbed a greater portion of Brandt's clothing. Her hand was near his tarse and stones. His blood
heated, thickened, and slowed.

"I never dreamed 'twould be like this," she said. "To

ride, I mean. I could never do this alone, but I feel safe with you, Brandt le Revenant.''

"Have you never felt safe with a man before?''

"Oh, nay. I have said I was not allowed from my tower except to walk the battlements.''

If that was true, Brandt wondered how she had met her beloved. Was he some member of Thomas's guard—a man who had succumbed to her charms as the days of her confinement wore on? Or mayhap some lowly castleman who had been kind to her, and she in gratitude had given him her heart.

Brandt squirmed uncomfortably. His possessiveness congealed into a tight, hard ball in his lower gut. He did not understand why he was so curious about the man Rowanne sought to protect and free from Thomas.

"Tell me, Rowanne, and let there be no mistake betwixt us. Speak plain, and tell me how it is that you came to bide at Sherborne and be lost to your father, Etienne.''

"After the murder of my mother and brothers, I was taken to Sherborne,'' she said in a voice so flat and devoid of emotion that it conveyed years of pain and sorrow.

"At Thomas's order?''

"Leopold brought me by night.''

"Was no effort made to ransom you home?''

"Thomas said my father never tried.''

"And you believed what Thomas of Sherborne told you?'' Bitterness tinged every word.

"I believed that until recently. Now . . . I wonder. But even though Thomas is a master liar, the truth is I remained at Sherborne. So either my father did not care, or he did not care enough to meet the ransom.''

"And now Thomas has decided you will wed Geof-froi,'' Brandt mused, more to himself than to her.

"Aye, but you will prevent that wedding,'' she said softly. "You will save me. I will not wait in vain as I did for my father.''

"Aye. I have given my word as a knight, Geoffroi DeLucy will never take you to wife."

Nor will any man.

"And then I will return to Sherborne," she said with a breathy sigh. "I will see Thomas undone. I will see my dearest friend free."

The image of a youth, soft and useless, flashed through Brandt's brain. What kind of milksop waited for a maid to rescue him? Brandt did not wish to hear of him, or think of him. The more she spoke of her beloved, the tighter the knot in his stomach drew and twisted.

"Gramercy, Brandt. As I have pledged, my dead brothers will walk the earth again before I willingly give myself to any man bearing DeLucy blood. You have made it possible for me to keep my vow."

CHAPTER 7

The farther north the group traveled, the more winter still clung to the land. Leopold kept them to the roads, and Brandt knew he feared the bandits that had escaped. One day, when the damp fog enveloped the ground and their breath hung, vapory and white before their faces, they came upon a man, and beyond him, barely visible in the thick brume, a leather-covered wagon. Brandt unsheathed his sword and quickly slid Rowanne to the ground.

"Jonathan, keep her near the cart. If she comes to harm, you will not see the sunset," Brandt bellowed. Glandamore circled overhead, screeching at intervals, while Brandt rode toward the wagon.

"Thank the saints. I am Waltham of Grendaville." A portly man with blood smeared across one jowly cheek spoke. "Oh please, sir, my lady wife received a blow to the head—she lies insensible. Have you any among you skilled in the healing arts?"

Like a faery sprite, Rowanne appeared from the mist. "Mayhap I could help. I know little of healing, but . . ."

"Lady Rowanne—" Brandt dragged her to his side. "Have a care. It is a fine way to spring a trap—by feigning injury and claiming that a gentlewoman lies

within. I would not like to see your pretty throat slit."
He was stunned by the ferocity of his feelings to protect
her. He saw a smooth-faced lad leaning against the rich
wagon. The driver? Or a decoy?

"Oh lady, pray come quickly." Waltham said.

"Where are your guards?" Brandt did not let Rowanne pass.

"I had none. I thought I would be safe so short a
march from my own hall."

Brandt rode forward and lifted the leathern cover of
the cart. Blood soaked the thick, rich hangings on the
side of the conveyance.

"Prithee . . . my wife." The bedraggled man wrung
his hands, his eyes filling with tears.

Brandt sheathed his sword with a whine of steel
against leather. The woman inside was pale as death, a
terrible wound on her head, caving inward. He had
seen such wounds while on Crusade. They were usually
mortal.

"Oh, would that I could turn back the hourglass,"
the merchant moaned. "Only this morn 'twas I advised
to hire a guard, but I thought it folly to part with my
coin. Now my purse is gone and my good wife lies near
death."

The misery in his voice made Rowanne grimace. She
wondered what it would feel like to be loved so intensely
by a man. But if a woman were loved by such as Brandt
le Revenant she would be safe from the perils of the
world.

"Set upon by thieves less than a day's walk from Chester." The man continued weakly.

"Prithee, sir, allow me to tend your wife while we
travel. As I say, I have little skill with injury, but I will
do my best to see her comfortable," Rowanne offered
from inside the wagon.

"Aye, pray do what you may'st." The merchant staggered aside, looking dazed.

Rowanne settled herself beside the lady. The interior

was filled with soft furs and plump pillows. Other than the harsh breathing, there was no sign the lady yet lived.

Outside the wagon the men had gathered to speak. Rowanne could hear their muffled voices through the covering.

"What is this about thieves?" Leopold asked.

Aye, you boot-licking dog, you are only brave with babes and children, Rowanne thought in disgust.

"A band of brigands—may God rot their benighted souls—took my wife's serving wench and before my eyes used her cruelly. 'Twas horrible. But I am a merchant, not a soldier." The man began to sob. Rowanne could feel his anguish as she went about making the lady as comfortable as she could. When she was sure she could do no more, she climbed out the back of the wagon.

"Drink this." Brandt thrust a new skin of wine at the merchant. "It will give you a bit of courage to face what you must."

Slowly, like a man moving through a dream, he took the skin and tipped it to his mouth. A little color began to stain his flabby, pale cheeks. Waltham swallowed noisily and drew his hand across his mouth. Flecks of drying blood remained on his hand.

"I was told the best fighting men in the kingdom can be found in Chester. I would journey to Chester and hire an army of mercenaries. I will see those thieves found."

Leopold cast a fearful look at the hills ringing the clearing. Brandt could almost see his mind working. He took the skin of wine and gave it to Rowanne. She did not argue, but tipped it up and took a healthy swallow.

"The king's roads to Northumberland are a brigand's dream and a traveler's nightmare. Forests, glens, and sheltered valleys aplenty lay betwixt here and Irthing. Attacks can be launched in secret from a hundred places," Brandt told them all.

"Waltham, say you are going to Chester?"

"Aye, for a healer." The man looked near to collapse.

"Then we best make haste, for I would reach that good city anon. We will travel together," Leopold barked suddenly.

Rowanne did not miss the feral smile that flashed across Brandt's chiseled face. She wondered why he looked so satisfied.

"Do you know a common house or inn where I might hire men?" Waltham asked, his eyes now brighter, whether from the wine or his desire to have justice, Brandt did not know.

He thought of his own rowdy troupe. They had likely pinched and swived every round-bottomed wench and drained every new wineskin on the high street of Chester.

"The Crown, or mayhap the Blue Bull. Both are favored by men who earn their crusts by their swords and their wits."

"I am most anxious to leave these accursed woods and find men who will travel with us to Cumbria." Leopold turned to and fro, scanning the countryside.

Brandt glanced at Rowanne, catching her eye before she climbed back into the wagon with Waltham's wife. Her eyes glowed. She was enjoying Leopold's fear. He shook himself. This was not a line of thought he would be wise to follow. When he woke in the night his first thought was of her and how she had suffered. If a noise drew his sight while they traveled, his first impulse was to rush to her side and protect her. It was more than lust, more than their bargain. He felt responsible for the maiden and far too possessive.

They were not emotions he wanted. These soft feelings for Rowanne could ruin him. The way he felt when she looked at him was more powerful than a sword, more deadly than poison. Brandt had never known fear, not since his eighth year of life. But when he looked at Rowanne and felt the thump of his heart, something akin to terror seeped into his bones.

It unmanned him. *She* unmanned him. And yet . . .

Her eyes were so full of pain and loneliness, 'twas nigh unto impossible for him to shut her out of his mind. Brandt cursed himself silently, called himself weakling, a mewling pup and worse. He reminded himself once again of the good and true men that called him lord. Men like Desmond. They deserved a hearth and home. They had bled and hungered and fought at his side for nigh onto a decade. They should not be forgotten in favor of a winsome maid who warmed his blood and touched his black, benighted soul.

He could see her now inside the cart, applying a dampened scrap of cloth to the injured woman's head. She had courage. She had spirit and mettle, and in spite of her pain, all she had suffered, she had compassion. Once again the ribbon of protectiveness wrapped tight around his heart.

" 'Tis a foolish man that grows soft with his enemy," Brandt muttered to himself, hearing the ghostly laughter of Gervais echoing through his head.

He looked at Rowanne once more. He wanted her body. He wanted her birthright. If he took one, then he could not have the other.

The sky darkened as if covered by a gray burial shroud. Wind blew through the leafless branches, creating an eerie refrain of clattering wood as one bare bough struck another. Not a single creature stirred except for the weary travelers on the road.

Waltham sat with his wife, so once again Rowanne rode with Brandt. She held herself tighter against Brandt's body, snuggling into his mail-covered chest. At her touch the fine hairs on the backs of Brandt's hands and his arms stood on end. An energy filled the air, fierce and potent. It was not the elements that affected him, but the seductive power of Rowanne.

"I am frighted," Rowanne said softly.

The first ominous rumble shook the earth beneath

Clwyd's feet and traveled up to vibrate the saddle 'neath Brandt's rump. The war-horse snorted and blew, anticipating the fury of the storm about to hit. Though Glandamore was hooded, securely riding on Brandt's wrist, she screamed her displeasure at the change she felt in the air around her.

Brandt shrugged deeper into his surcoat and gambeson and in the process, settled Rowanne closer to his groin. Jesu, he never imagined a winsome maiden would be settled in front of him so saucily that his tarse stiffened each time she moved.

" 'Twould be wise to wrap more tightly, milady." Brandt advised. He felt her shift and squirm in a most delicious fashion as she drew her rabbit fur–lined cloak more tightly about her body.

"Mayhap you should return to the cart for protection." *Nay, stay with me. Let my body cover you, shield you, pleasure you.*

"Mayhap you are right. The rain is coming, and we shall both be soaked." She agreed so quickly that he died a little inside.

Within moments she was in the cart. Rowanne reminded Brandt of a young tercel, not yet able to fly or hunt but ready to face any danger with a steely eye and valiant heart—and the slender blade she kept hidden in her cloak. It had not escaped his notice that she kept the dagger close at hand, and though she had made no more attempts to kill Leopold, he had seen her knuckles turn white on the hilt each time the one-eyed man was near her.

"Gramercy, Sir Brandt, for letting me bide awhile with you and grand Clwyd. It was wonderful to be in the fresh air." Rowanne's voice floated on the strengthening breeze. She peered up at him from the leathern cover of the cart. A small smile tickled the corners of her mouth.

"I'll never forget your kindness on this journey. You

shall be well rewarded. Whatever is in my power to give you, I shall."

In that moment something hot as molten silver enveloped Brandt's soul. Would she feel such gratitude if he knew his true motives? Would she instead turn her blade upon him if she knew he intended to take her birthright? And that he was the bastard son of Thomas DeLucy? And that he vowed to see her put into a nunnery?

Or would she shrink from him if she could read the lust, see how he yearned for them to be entwined in splendor, tasting each other's passion, learning each other's secrets? Would she turn away in shame and disgust that a bastard mercenary lusted for her?

"Take yourself inside. The rain is coming and you would do better to move farther inside the cart lest you take a chill." His voice was gruff and husky with pent-up desire. Brandt felt the veriest cullion. She was an innocent, unaware of her seductive power over him, as she was unaware that he was other than he seemed.

" 'Tis true and yet, I find I would risk the rain. There is a certain comfort being able to speak with you. My bruises will fade soon enough when we reach Irthing."

Could she be unknowing of what her words did to him? Just the mention of her body made his own burn with need and want and the desire to take her, plunder—possess her.

For the first time in his life, Brandt wished. He wished things were different. But even if he did not covet Irthing and all that was hers, there was no way for them to ever come together. For the moment she learned that Brandt was Thomas DeLucy's by-blow she would hate him with the same ferocity that she now gave Geoffroi. Brandt had not the DeLucy name, but he had DeLucy blood coursing through his veins. And she had sworn an oath that she would never give herself to any who had DeLucy blood.

The sting of icy rain and Glandamore's unhappy

screech broke through Brandt's reverie. The hawk reacted violently to the cold rain, screaming her displeasure while she flapped her wings against Brandt's head and shoulders. He hunched lower into his surcoat and helm, both for shelter and to spare himself from the bird's short-lived burst of temper. Glandamore cried out twice more before she slipped into unhappy silence, rain sheeting off her wet feathers, the very image of misery.

"There be no dry haven for either of us here, Glandamore." Brandt clucked his tongue in sympathy. The hawk tilted her hooded head, focusing on the sound of his voice. The little bells of her hood tinkled with each droplet.

"Push on, push on. Let us naught tarry here!" Leopold's harsh shout floated on the wind. "We will find shelter up the road a ways."

"As you say, Leopold. We are all anxious to reach Cumbria. The sooner, the better," Brandt agreed. He hunched lower, feeling every bit as miserable as Glandamore as he put his spurs to Clwyd. The sooner he saw this journey finished, the best it would be for them all.

A man could not change the blood that flowed in his veins or the destiny that awaited them all in Irthing.

Near Shropshire they passed over Offa's Dike. On this day Leopold was clearly preoccupied, his thoughts troubled. He was not paying attention to the path his mount chose. Suddenly his horse stumbled badly, going hard to one knee on the greening verge where a scatter of pebbles made the going uncertain. Leopold yanked sharply on the thick leather reins to help the horse right itself, but when the gray regained its footing it was limping, favoring a front leg.

"Is it broke?" Brandt drew Clwyd to a halt beside the gray. For the first time Clwyd did not back his ears and threaten to bite Leopold's destrier.

Leopold slid from the saddle and picked up the stallion's hoof. "Nay, 'tis not broke. He has but thrown a shoe." Leopold held up the studded iron shoe and broken chunk of hoof. "Bloody hell." He tossed it into a hedgerow. A fat brown hare sprang from the hedge. Brandt released Glandamore's jesses and let her take wing in pursuit of the rabbit.

"We are but a few leagues from Chester." Brandt scanned the horizon with a frown as if he could will the walled village nearer. "Waltham will find a healer to see to his wife, and I am certain there would be a smithy in the hamlet."

"By my beard, we have had one blight after another on this benighted journey. 'Tis as if we were traveling under a curse," Leopold growled with another oath.

"Or perhaps in the company of ghosts," Rowanne said, drawing that strange, far-off look from Leopold. She was riding in the cart today while Waltham tended his failing wife.

"I will tether my stallion to the back of the cart and ride with Jonathan at the front," Leopold said to Rowanne.

Brandt frowned. It had been in his mind to offer Rowanne the pillion seat behind him just to keep her far from Leopold, but he fought the impulse. He grimly congratulated himself, on his self-control. But if he had such steely mastery over himself, why then did his gaze return again and again to the object of his distress?

CHAPTER 8

"Oh how wonderful the spring is," Rowanne said to nobody in particular. She had no memory to rival this. If these colors and flowers and birds existed before she went to Sherborne, then time had wiped them from her mind. A swan floated silently in the water that meandered like a serpent beside the track.

The battered cart was unusually steady this morn, rolling over a short carpet of turf, barely swaying on the padded surface. Now Rowanne was rarely flung against the sides, she could almost feel her bruises fading as the distance between her and Irthing became smaller and smaller.

With her fingertips draped over the edge of the cart she stared wide-eyed at the green-leafed limbs swaying overhead in the gentle, soughing breeze of English spring.

"Are you well today, lady?" Brandt asked as Clwyd cantered beside the cart.

"Exceedingly well," she said, suddenly feeling shy beneath his questioning gaze. Her nipples peaked and rubbed against the cloth of her shift. She felt a drawing heat in her lower body whenever Brandt looked at her thus.

"Ah, I see you are still doing aught you can to curry favor. You are a sly one, le Revenant," Leopold interrupted rudely from his perch on the seat beside Jonathan. She looked up into the smug face of the one-eyed man-at-arms. Hatred lodged deep within her breast as the memory of her dead mother washed over her.

Laugh whilst you can, old man. I will see justice done.

"Of course, Leopold," Brandt replied smoothly. "You have the measure of me." A humorless smile twisted his lips, and the note of sarcasm in his voice was sharp as a dagger blade.

Leopold's smile melted away. "Have a care, Brandt. I understand ye and yer mercenary's heart, but then I have had to make my way in the world without benefit of title and rank. Geoffroi is a young lordling, unaccustomed to the ways of commerce. Perhaps he will misread your intentions. Have a care that in your efforts to further your position in the DeLucy household you don't misstep and gain yourself an enemy. Rowanne is a comely maid and Geoffroi could well be jealous of your attentions. It may come to pass he calls you to do combat for your offense."

Brandt bowed his head as if cowed. "Ah, well, then I needs must tread carefully lest I have to face the mighty Geoffroi in combat. I am fair quaking in my sabatons at the thought."

Rowanne nearly giggled at the gleam in Brandt's eyes. She could see he was as fearful as a wolf. In that moment a burst of pure admiration surged through her. He was a man who knew his strength and worth. It was a magical aphrodisiac to look upon him.

The cart lurched violently. Rowanne was so surprised she did not have time to grab the side to brace herself. Leopold leaped from the seat. She saw a flash as the cart-horse sprinted ahead, dragging the split tongue of the cart in his wake.

" 'Tis going to turn over!" Jonathan bellowed over his shoulder as he jumped clear of the toppling cart.

Rowanne stood up and tried to climb free, but the cart kept sliding down the steep embankment toward the crystalline water below. With a snap, the tether on Leopold's gray gave. Now nothing held the cart back.

"Rowanne!" Her name erupted from Brandt's lips at the moment his spurs touched Clwyd's sleek body. The destrier was airborne like a great mythical beast with wings. He landed hard and skidded down the pebble-strewn slope on his hocks. Every manner of waterfowl splashed and squawked, filling the air with the sound of wings and cries of fright as they fled only seconds before the mighty horse crashed into the water.

The earth and sky blurred into a smear of blue and green. Rowanne could no longer distinguish grass from cloud. Her stomach lurched and roiled from the impact of each new revolution.

"Rowanne!"

Brandt's rugged voice penetrated her terror. He was coming for her. He would always come for her. And then she was in the water, sinking among the broken boards and tattered leather of the ruined cart. Water closed over her head, and she felt the compression of her lungs as the heavy cover pushed her down—down into moss and darkness.

Down. She had no breath left in her body.

Down. She was drowning.

Down. She was not fearful.

Down. Brandt would come for her. He would always protect her.

Brandt plunged Clwyd into the icy burn and drew his sword. Praying he did not cleave Rowanne in twain he made one mighty lunge. The sharp blade sliced the leathern cover. He snagged it on the tip. The weight of it nearly unhorsed him as he gathered it to him and with two hands flung it away.

There she was, unmoving, pale as death beneath the clear water. Was he too late?

Brandt leaped from the saddle. He took a last gulp

of air and dived. The temperature of the beck was only slightly warmer than ice. His padded gambeson drank in the liquid thirstily, drawing him down to Rowanne.

Down.

His hands closed around her. Her leg was caught beneath a shattered plank. He kicked hard and the plank gave way. A sense of relief near unmanned him. With one mighty kick he surged to the surface, sucking in air when his head broke through, pulling her face up for air . . . for life.

"Quick, fetch my cloak from my pack," He yelled. Mayhap it was the tone of his voice, mayhap it was because Leopold feared what would happen if Rowanne did not reach her betrothed—whatever the reason he scurried to Clwyd without a moment's hesitation. Luckily the destrier did not try to kill him as he yanked the pack from the saddle.

"Rowanne. Can you speak?" Brandt laid her on the verge, rubbing her chilled face betwixt his rough hands, willing her to wake, bargaining with God to spare her life.

Her eyelids were tinged purple. Her lips were nigh unto blue. She looked as dead as any fallen knight on a battlefield.

"Do not die!" Brandt bellowed at her. "Do not dare die on me, little deceiver."

Brandt grabbed her shoulders and shook her—hard. He was desperate. There was something hard and cold and sharp in his heart. He could not bear it.

He shook her and shook her.

Rowanne sputtered and coughed, sending a rivulet of water from the corner of her mouth.

"Brandt . . ." she whispered.

The cold, sharp pain eased. Now a strange constriction gripped Brandt's chest as he looked at Rowanne. She was drenched and half frozen but to him there was no more lovely sight on earth. The impact of that knowledge sent his heart hammering a painful tattoo.

"At least I will not have to endure another moment in that thrice damned cart." Rowanne whispered. She awkwardly levered herself up on shaky elbows. "God has finally answered my prayers."

Mine as well. Thought Brandt. *Mine as well.*

Brandt cradled Rowanne between his forearms. Leopold now rode with Waltham, and his stallion walked with Jonathan beside him. From time to time Glandamore would peer down at Rowanne and make her strange trilling noises. Brandt told Rowanne they were welcoming sounds, rather than the jealous scolding they truly were.

"I feel like a caterpillar in a cocoon," she murmured. Her voice was soft, muffled, like a woman waking from sleep. That made him think of closed bed-curtains, smooth, bare flesh, and his own throbbing erection.

"Poor Jonathan," she said. "When we reach Irthing and all is put right, I will offer him a place in my household."

Brandt allowed his gaze to wander to Jonathan. His cheek was swollen and had turned a shade of blue-green where Leopold had cuffed him.

"Leopold had no reason to chide Jonathan," she said. "The cart was poorly made, poorly sprung, and no doubt that was the reason Thomas sent it. I can well imagine him deriving satisfaction knowing each mile in that thrice damned conveyance left me with more black and blue marks."

Brandt squirmed as another image of her without clothes sizzled into his mind. Every step Clwyd took was exquisite torture.

"I am glad it is now at the bottom of the beck. 'Twas not Jonathan's fault the axle broke but Thomas's own greed."

"You could have died." Brandt looked down at her,

seeing the silken hair turning a hundred shades of gold in the sunshine.

"I knew you would save me," she said with complete confidence. "Oh, look, hollyhocks and gillyflowers are blooming."

"Spring has come at last," Brandt said absently. He was trying to school his thoughts and failing miserably.

"Lady Margaret wouldst fancy a nosegay of those blooms."

"Lady Margaret?" Brandt asked.

"Mmmm."

"Who, pray tell, is Lady Margaret?"

"She is—was—my companion whilst I was held at Sherborne. My dearest friend."

Companion. Dearest friend. The words sizzled through Brandt. He had not allowed himself to think any more on the nameless, faceless lover, but now a niggling doubt shot through him. Her words were the same ones she had used before.

"Your companion—at Sherborne?"

"Aye. 'Twas only we two. My only friend. She is like family now, like my own blood."

"Thomas holds her hostage so you will do his bidding."

"Aye. That is why I wanted to kill Leopold." Her voice cracked and broke as the memory of her mother's death shot through her. "Why I *must* prevent him from returning to Sherborne. Leopold—"

"Will not live to carry any tales to his master at Sherborne." Brandt finished the thought for her while a million new emotions bloomed inside him. She loved no other man. There was no milksop, no youth, no cowardly man waiting.

A strange, warm satisfaction seeped into Brandt's soul. He shifted his weight, settling Rowanne more fully against him.

Rowanne looked up at him while he glanced down at her. Something hot and possessive arched between them. 'Twas palpable, potent, and fraught with promise. Brandt shifted his weight again, trying to accommodate the swelling flesh of his tarse. Lust surged through him like a rain-glutted river overflowing its banks. Rowanne had laid claim to him in some indefinable way that he could not explain.

"You have my pledge, little seducer, upon my life, Leopold will take no tales to Thomas."

She narrowed her gaze on the one-eyed man-at-arms and allowed herself to think of his death. Perchance she could find an herb to put in his food—something that would turn his bowels watery and give him a slow, lingering, painful death. She was savoring the prospect when she realized Brandt had spoken again.

"Chester, milady. Look you upon the last city that lies 'twixt us and Irthing Keep."

The spires of Chester's cathedral came into view, silhouetted by the setting sun. Brandt urged Clwyd across the bridge spanning the wide river Dee. The eastern gate of the city was under the watchful eye of well-armored guards, attesting to Chester's richness as a trading city. A clutch of people engulfed their cart as they approached the gate.

A hum not unlike a hive of busy bees filled Rowanne's ears as merchants and patrons poured over the street. Stalls and barrows lined every avenue. She bit down on her lip. Having so many people near seemed to squeeze the air from her lungs.

"Oh, look," Rowanne said excitedly. "So many colors, so many wares."

Clwyd's iron-shod feet rang out a tune on the cobbled road that wended its way past weaver's stalls, baker's shops, and fine-timbered Guild Halls of weavers, goldsmiths, and tanners.

Rowanne covered her ears. The noise was deafening, but it was also like water to a thirsty person. All the years she had stood upon her stone perch and stared down at the activity in Sherborne she had wondered what it would sound like being in the middle of a tournament or a fair.

The reality swept over her in a mighty wave of emotion. Tears stung her eyes. A great lump crowded the back of her throat. Animals squealed, squawked, and brayed. Fowls of every variety were jammed into small wooden crates, and makeshift bowers had been constructed to hold oxen, sheep, and goats. Hoarse-voiced merchants held up clay pots. Fresh-caught eels, whelks, and fish filled the air with a pungent aroma.

" 'Tis wondrous." Rowanne whispered as if the fishy odor were the finest scent. She drew in a breath and felt the energy and life of the teeming market fill her up to overflowing. She had never attended a fair, never eaten a plump pasty purchased from the hands that made it. She had never argued price with a vendor for a bit of ribbon or lace.

Leopold leaped from Waltham's cart and untethered his stallion. Jonathan took the reins. Leopold rudely grabbed a passing merchant and inquired about the smith.

"There on yon hill," the merchant told him, obviously anxious to be on his way.

"I lief he will want a pretty pence for this day's work," the one-eyed man grumbled to Brandt. "But s'truth I will happily pay twice to get us on the road again."

Brandt shifted Glandamore upon his arm as Rowanne twisted this way and that to get a better look. "Hopefully he will not be so busy you have to wait."

"If so, then I will offer three times the coin!" Leopold said as he turned and tugged his steed up the hill.

"I will leave you now as well," Waltham of Grendaville said. "You have my thanks." And with that he turned away. His wagon was soon part of the tide of the city.

Rowanne pitied the man, hoping that with God's help his wife would recover. But she could not remain sad for long, not with all there was to see.

"Brandt, whilst I see to my horse I leave Rowanne in

your keeping. Remember, a fat reward awaits. Where shall we meet up?"

"The Hart and Hind." Brandt wondered what Desmond would say when he saw Rowanne.

"So it shall be. I will meet you by sundown." Leopold and Jonathan then set off in the direction the merchant indicated.

As soon as the men blurred into the crowd Rowanne looked up at Brandt. "Now he is gone I am going to look at everything."

"I must keep you safe."

"And so you shall," she said, sliding to the ground beside Clwyd.

"There are cutpurses and thieves aplenty on market day. They would lief slit your throat for a single groat. Give me a moment to see Clwyd and Glandamore settled."

"I will wait, but not for long," she teased up at him. His heart hammered in his chest. He wanted to kiss her.

He understood her excitement. How she must have craved a day of frivolous merriment while she was Thomas's prisoner. A shaft of bitter hatred pierced Brandt's heart. His own benighted sire had used her cruelly; now he himself was bound to set her aside and lock her away in a cold convent. He felt the taint of DeLucy blood more acutely now than ever before, and a niggling worry that he was indeed imprinted with his sire's poisoned spirit never left his mind.

"If you are bent on a tour of the town on market day, then I shall accompany you," Brandt said, sighing in resignation. "Together we will have a look at Chester's fine wares." He dismounted and placed Glandamore on the pommel of his saddle. The bird would be safe from thieves and cats, for Clwyd would soon dispatch any who came too near.

"Make haste," Rowanne said, while her eyes skimmed over the stalls. She could not take it all in. There were gypsies and crones, beggars and lords. It was a wonder.

She took a step nearer one stall to look at rows of gloves. They were crafted from the finest of leathers and smelled sweet.

"We have all sizes, milady," the glovemaker said. "And my leather is sweetened with petal perfume." He held up a pair near Rowanne's nose, and she smelled a light, delightful fragrance.

"How do you do so?"

"After the tanning the leather is layered with petals for a half year," he said with pride.

"Truly a wonder," she said and ambled off a little farther. There was so much to see.

"By God's Teeth!" Brandt returned to the spot where he last saw Rowanne, expecting to see the golden-haired sylph waiting for him. There was only empty space.

He slammed his open palm against the armor on his thigh. "When I get my hands on the little cabbage head, I will—" Spewing oaths that fair blistered the ears of any unfortunate soul who happened to hear, Brandt began to shove his way into the crowd.

He was tall enough to be able to see some distance over the milling crowd. But he searched for that distinctive silken crown in vain. A stab of unease came into his heart. His anger quickly gave way to anxiety, which shortly melted into fear.

He had never known fear in battle, but he was paralyzed with terror now for Rowanne. She was like a newborn lamb among wolves. He had to find her before she came to harm.

Rowanne's pulse was thrumming with excitement as she was jostled, shoved, and carried along on a tide of humanity. Ragged beggars limped, impatient merchants shoved. To a man, whether high-born or the low, they all breathed the same air, thick with the scent of damp wool, hot tallow, unwashed bodies, and the unique attar of market day. Never had Rowanne imagined such a barrage of smells, sounds, and colors.

"Have a sweetmeat, milady. Two a pence." A young boy with rusty-colored freckles hawked his wares.

Rowanne handed over a coin. With a happiness she had never before known she took the sweetmeat in her own hands. It was the first thing she had ever purchased. Closing her eyes, she bit into it. It tasted light on her tongue. The blend of spices and honey awoke her hunger. She promised herself to savor the moment, but she soon ate it, and then a second one greedily. After they were gone she stood licking her fingers, surveying the landscape of foodstuffs and wares.

Bright silk cloth and vibrant wools caught her eyes. Crimson and a hue of blue, even rare black cloth.

The instantaneous roar of the crowd sent chills dancing up Rowanne's arms. A motley jester in gaudy green struck his fellow with an inflated pig bladder. Crowds of children and their parents clustered around, cheering and jeering, entranced by the skill of the entertainers.

Rowanne was shoved along on the tide of humanity. She was unmindful of where she was headed. Freedom, she was learning, was a potent draught indeed.

Brandt searched through the crowd, his heart hammering inside his chest. He cursed himself for not having watched her more closely. She was headstrong and defiant—and enthralled by all that was new to her.

He stepped around a pile of fish heads and walked beyond a stall where cockles, whelks, and mussels lay in huge woven-reed baskets lined with sea grasses.

"Eels, good sir? Fresh caught with me own hands."

"Nay. I am searching for a maid with golden braids and eyes of blue." Brandt craned his neck to see over the sea of heads, searching for the flaxen crown of hair.

"Oh, aye. Eyes the color of a summer's sky, skin like morn's fresh cream?"

Brandt swung around to look at the fishmonger. "Aye,

the very one. Which way did she go?" A sense of urgency nipped at Brandt's heart.

"Down yon lane, though I warned her 'twas naught wise to wander from the market square. Cutpurses and thieves are thick as fleas on a dog during market day."

Brandt rushed from the booth, the fishmonger's words drifting away behind him. By brute force alone he parted the throng of people. The air was thick and stank of fish, flesh, and his own despair.

And then he saw her. His heart stilled.

She stood at the end of a darkened alley cornered against a lichen-covered wall by three brawny men. In one glance Brandt registered the terror in Rowanne's eyes and the flash of a blade. A dirty hand grabbed her throat, rough fingers an obscenity against her pure, white flesh. Brandt drew his sword from his scabbard as he ran.

She screamed. The sound was absorbed by the stone walls that surrounded her. She screamed once more and then fell to the cobbles in silence.

"Rowanne!" Her name erupted from Brandt's lips.

CHAPTER 9

The brigand busy untying his braies was unaware or uncaring that death stood only a heartbeat away. The cutpurse shoved Rowanne's legs apart with his foot. Then he grabbed her bliaut and ripped upward, exposing her pale, creamy thighs.

Brandt lunged forward. A hot tide of possessive instinct drove him.

"Stand aside or die," Brandt ordered.

"There be three of us an' only one o' ye." The poxy pair faced him boldly.

"Soon there will be nothing of you but bones for the dogs," Brandt said through clenched teeth. The tip of his sword left a trail of crimson down one thief's shoulder. The scut atop Rowanne glanced up, the glaze of lust leaving his eyes in a cold tide.

"The others may live if they go now, but you will forfeit your life for laying hands upon her," Brandt promised. "I am looking forward to opening your belly and watching your entrails spill out into the dirt."

"Run, Cob!" One of the men shouted. "He be a madman! Run!"

The sound of footsteps behind Brandt told him all he needed to know.

"Ah, so they have found their brains and left you deserted, to die alone." He stalked closer, the bloodlust thick in his veins. "I shall kill you slow. With each breath you will beg the lady's forgiveness, you poxy bastard."

" 'Twas only a bit o' sport. She ain't hurt. Look, she be right well." He was fumbling with his braies and easing himself off Rowanne.

"Let me go—I beg o' ye."

Cold rage filled Brandt. "Nay. Your life was owing and forfeit from the moment you touched her." Brandt was only two paces from him now. Then, like a cornered animal, he bared his teeth and drew a pitifully small dagger from his sleeve.

"Ye'll not cut me without a fight."

With a guttural yelp he lunged at Brandt, swiping blindly, leaving his belly open. One quick upward thrust and the thief's eyes went round with shock.

"Ye've done me to death. My innards ha' been pierced," he whispered.

Brandt yanked his sword free, and a wash of crimson spewed along the length of his blade. The man made a feeble attempt to hold his guts inside. Two bright bubbles of blood left his lips before he crumpled to the dirty lane in silence.

In one movement Brandt was beside Rowanne, lifting her head, touching her cool cheek with his knuckles. "Rowanne? Speak to me, little temptress, tell me your wounds are not mortal," he murmured as his hands searched her body for blood.

Rowanne heard a familiar voice and it all came back to her in a throbbing rush.

Brandt. As the men had closed in, blocking her way from the alley, her last thought had been of Brandt le Revenant. Slowly, as if waking from a long sleep, she focused on his face. "You came for me," she whispered. "I knew you would."

A hot, liquid rush surged through Brandt. He *had*

come for her. Not because she was the weak link in Thomas's armor. Not because he needed her for vengeance. He had come for her because he wanted— *nay*—because he *needed* to keep her safe. In that terrible moment when the cullion was trying to violate her, Brandt had known a fear that turned his knees to water.

"Aye. I will always come for you," he said gruffly, fighting the terrible feeling of helplessness that had ripped through him when he first saw her in the alley. He was shaking. It shamed him to be so weak before her.

"You are trembling, Brandt le Revenant." She reached up and laid her palm along the contour of his jaw. She was trembling, too.

Never in his life had anyone touched Brandt with such tenderness.

"You are my champion."

"Say no more." Brandt choked on his shame. He scanned her face, the clear blue of her eyes, the upturned nose, the graceful column of her jaw.

She was the heiress to Irthing, and by that fact alone he should not allow tender feelings for her. He was the son of Thomas DeLucy, her most hated enemy. There was no future for them. Even though he had learned it was a woman she had sought to rescue and not a lover, nothing had changed.

He had to set her aside. He had to put her in a convent for his own security. He could not have her. He kept repeating that litany as he laid claim to her soft lips.

Tentatively her hand left his jaw. Slowly, by the merest inches, it came round his neck. She kneaded the flesh beneath his sweat-dampened nape.

Would she be offended by his maleness? Would she be repulsed by his sweat and the great knotted muscle of his war-hardened neck? Her fingers were smooth, cool, and fine against his heated flesh. She was a lady and he a baseborn bastard. They were different as hot and cold, love and hate, and yet slowly, seductively, she twined her fingers in the strands of his hair. 'Twas a gesture of claiming and acceptance.

A low, needful moan escaped his chest. He deepened the kiss, wanting to know more of this enigma that he held in his arms.

There was a potent sweetness to her kiss. She had eaten cinnamon and sweetmeats, he could taste the flavors on her tongue. They intoxicated him, drew him ever closer. His tongue swept her mouth. He knew he was playing with fire, but he slid one hand to her thigh, nudging her stained and torn bliaut aside.

The yearning desire to put his fingers against the hot core of her womanhood taunted him. Brandt fought himself for mastery. Jesu, she had just been treated basely, he could not do the same. She was an innocent. He was a bastard by birth, but he had never been a cullion who tumbled virgins in dirty snickleways.

Though it took more will than he thought he possessed, Brandt broke the kiss. The sultry veil of passion clouded Rowanne's eyes. Her lips were softly bruised and swollen from his kiss.

His heart lurched hard within his chest. His sac, already heavy and thick with lust, grew ever more heavy in his braies. In fact, the more control he exerted over his passion the deeper it became, until it clawed at him from the inside like a living, breathing demon.

"You saved my honor and my life as you did in the woods. As you did in the cold beck. Once again I am alive because of you, Brandt le Revenant."

"Aye," he choked out, feeling the hammering of his own pulse in his ears. "It would seem to be my destiny to keep you safe."

"I have never been kissed by any man before you," she said with a shy smile. "I think I like it." One of her fingertips rubbed along his bottom lip. "Pray, may I have another? My champion, would you kiss me again?"

"Rowanne, you know not what you ask."

"I ask to be kissed again ... by you ... by my champion."

Passion, hot, raw and wild flared within him. The voice of reason screamed to stop this madness now, to halt while he had his honor and his soul. All Brandt could hear was the pounding of his own pulse, roaring like the ocean in his ears.

In the end he knew he would give her what she asked for at the peril of his own blighted soul.

Brandt carried Rowanne through the streets and grinnels of Chester, ignoring the curious glances and bawdy remarks they gained as they came nearer the market square where the crowds thickened.

"What will you say happened?" Rowanne asked, giving voice to Brandt's own mind.

"I shall say I escorted you to the market and we became caught up in some rowdy disagreement over the price of a swine."

"A swine?" she repeated doubtfully, humor in her voice. "A swine could cause all this disarray to my person?"

"Aye, 'tis the way of markets and fairs to sell pigs in a poke. We shall say that a canny buyer had the good sense to look at his pig and discovered a slat-thin cat in the bag. It is reasonable that your gown would have been torn and soiled if by mischance you had fallen in the middle of the ensuing struggle."

"As you say, good knight," Rowanne said with a sigh. She allowed her eyes to roam freely over the wares flashing by. Embroidered linens and beautiful cloth of the softest wool held her gaze.

"Do you fancy a length of wool? Could you fashion yourself a new gown?" Brandt peered down at her with his thick brows furrowed. She realized he had been watching her, following the line of her vision as she turned her head.

"Nay. I will make do with this one gown until I reach Irthing. Once there I will reclaim what is mine."

The mention of Irthing made Brandt's jaw tighten until it pinched. Why did she have to remind him of all he was powerless to change? For when they reached Irthing's gates *he* would claim the keep, not her. And then he would see this lovely maiden sent to a nunnery.

Rowanne was forbidden to him. More forbidden than anything he could imagine. For in her veins flowed Vaudry blood, and Irthing was rightfully a Vaudry holding. Brandt could not, *would* not become a slave to his lust. The maid was going to a nunnery as soon as Geoffroi had breathed his last. Brandt would take no chance that she might snatch Irthing from him.

Once again he cursed Thomas. For if not for the DeLucy blood in his veins perhaps there would be a chance. He and Rowanne would make a fine pair, holding Irthing, raising up sons and daughters loyal to the crown.

Every disparaging word she had ever uttered about the DeLucys rang sharp and loud in his head. And the bitter hell of it was, he did not disagree. Thomas was a scoundrel and worse. Geoffroi was the spoiled, mewling son of a petty lord.

And Brandt? Brandt himself was greedy and harsh. He was doomed to hunger for a woman who was destined to hate him. The inner voice that hammered at Brandt was neither meek nor soft. It called him knave, churl, and worse. And though Brandt wished it otherwise, in his heart he knew 'twas true. He might want the maid, might even steal her kiss, but he had been able to do that only because she did not know he carried DeLucy blood. In the end he knew there could be only one outcome to this tale. She would go to a nunnery, for he could do nothing to change the fact he was Thomas's by-blow.

A half hour later Brandt had settled Rowanne at the Hart and Hind, Clwyd and Glandamore in a rented byre with a hostler that appeared to be both sober and competent. Now he hurried off to find his men, having contrived to place them in Leopold's path and thereby insure 'twas his men that were hired as escort to Irthing.

His prick spurs rang out on the cobbled streets as he made his way through garbage-strewn grinnells to a cluster of public inns. The first two were empty, but the third, The Silent Woman, boasting a sign of a headless wench, yielded fruit.

He lingered in the door watching his men, feeling a frisson of relief and manly affection at the sight of familiar faces. *Now,* he told himself, *I can put aside these foolish notions about Rowanne.* For he was sure the staid company of Desmond would banish whatever mysterious thrall had possessed him. The company of his fellows would wipe away the guilt he *might* feel about seeing her in a nunnery. *He was almost certain of it.*

Smoke and the attar of seasoned fighting men filled the air of the public room. Jackmugs and tankards lined the rough plank table where his men lounged, a host of weapons in easy reach in front of them. 'Twas the sign and measure of their worth that they kept weapons close at hand even while they took their leisure. A surge of pride swept through Brandt's chest as he gazed at them.

Most were bastards or landless second sons with little hope of inheriting even a hide of land. The occasional nobleman was thrown in the mix for spice and the roaring good fight their presence oft brought to men of lower birth. All were brave and restless souls, all men Brandt could count on for their loyalty and ability to wield a sword or broadaxe.

He loved them to a man, just as he loved his king and his country, his horse and his hawk and the hold of Irthing. For though he had not yet seen it, the place had sent roots deep into his soul. 'Twas a part of him now, as surely as this rough group of fighting men 'twas his family.

"I tell you we should go searching," Desmond du Luc roared, slamming his closed fist to the table to garner attention.

"And let Brandt know we thought him unable to care for himself? Methinks you are daft. Not on your bloody life would I take such a course!" Harold Potts challenged with a shake of his shaggy mane. "I'll naught give insult to my overlord by doing that which brings him shame."

Edward and Blaine put their dark heads together, discussing the wisdom and hazards of both actions, as they were always wont to do.

Brandt drew his dagger and flung it to the center of the table. It stuck fast, tip first, vibrating a dull song. In the blink of an eye metal hissed on leather as daggers were drawn. His men rose up from their seats to vanquish the as yet unseen foe. To a man smiles split their faces.

"My lord!" many voices rang out.

"Is this how you spend your time when your lord is not around?" Brandt scowled, feigning anger. A smile tickled his lips but he tamped it down and continued his mock attack as he yanked his blade free of the scarred oak plank.

"Soft and lazy, that is what you are. Who is your careless overlord so that I may tell him what a lot of slackards he has in his service?"

Desmond waggled his dagger toward Brandt. "Have a care when you speak of *my* overlord, you churl." His face was grim but his eyes twinkled with boyish mischief.

"Would you draw your blade and my blood for him?" Brandt asked as he adopted a bored stance. "Such loyalty for a churlish cur who deigns to leave you cooling your heels in this poor excuse of an inn?"

"I would draw my blade and the blood of any man foolish enough to defame him," Desmond replied. "Have a care . . . lest your liver and gizzard are served up to you raw."

" 'Struth, sir," Harold Potts shook his shaggy red head back and forth, grinning broadly. "Our overlord is the veriest rogue in Christendom, but we are honor bound to defend him and, 'twould be a great hardship to have to train another lord to *our* ways when we only just got this one broke in."

The table exploded in laughter. Brandt slapped Desmond on the back, then jerked him into a hard, brotherly embrace.

" 'Tis good to see you—all of you."

"Aye, and you as well, my lord," Desmond agreed in a baritone growl. "Where have you been? What has delayed you?"

"Ah, so you were worried." Brandt grinned at each face, remembering the specific battle where they had met, counting the years between, the wounds, the scars, the lost ideals. All that spilled blood and disappointment had bonded them closer than most families.

"A more pertinent question 'twould be the location and condition of my goods while you worthless curs are filling your bellies with ale." Brandt swung a leg over the bench and sat down, glowering good-naturedly.

A buxom serving wench appeared from the taproom with a tankard of brew. Brandt looked her up and down, then he turned to Blaine with one brow arched in accusation.

"And you, Blaine, have you been finding your pleasures in the arms of willing women such as this one?" Brandt nodded toward the smiling wench. "Is all that I struggled for already lost on chance-met wagers and swiving? Am I a pauper yet?"

"Never say so, milord," Harold Potts said with a stricken expression.

"Aye, my lord, twenty of your best men guard the wagons at all times." Edward Renat, serious and somber as a Cistercian monk, gave Brandt his solemn promise.

Brandt's smile widened. "And I thought this lot the best, but now I have your admission that twenty others are your betters." He sighed heavily with great relish. "Such a pity."

All seated around the table exchanged a shocked and chagrined glance. Then another burst of hearty masculine laughter exploded from them. For long minutes the room echoed with their mirth. By fits and starts the noise finally died away.

"What *has* kept you, milord? We have had a moment of concern," Desmond du Luc said sheepishly.

"So I heard when I entered. We have time to discuss that later, but for now I have a task for two of you." Brandt swept an assessing gaze over the table as all his men drew themselves up to their full height. His eyes came to rest on two eager faces that begged to be picked.

"Coy and Desmond," Brandt said, smiling grimly. "I have a mission of deception and intrigue for you."

Both men gained their feet in a nonce, squaring their shoulders with pride. "We are at your service, my lord," Desmond said.

"Go you to the ramshackle tavern called the Hart and Hind."

"Aye, I know the very one." Coy nodded eagerly.

"There you will find an ugly one-eyed brute, drinking—most likely alone, for his fist is tighter than that of a Scotsman and his humor more ill than a poxy whore's." Brandt leaned closer and lowered his voice. "Buy him a jackmug of the best ale the tavern can offer. Let him draw you out. Say you are in need of a new lord and would employ your sword arm with great zeal. Take whatever amount he offers without argument—though brace yourselves, for I trow the offer will be miserly indeed."

With solemn purpose the men clapped their hands over their hearts. "As you will, my lord Brandt."

"And one more thing . . ."

"Aye?" Coy asked, halting his step.

"Make no mention of me in any way. When our paths

cross again, act as if we are the veriest strangers. Make
no slips.''

"You can rely upon us, my lord.'' Then, without questions or hesitation, both men turned on their heels and
quit the alehouse.

"I am most curious.'' Renal leaned back and fingered
his small, pointed beard. "What manner of intrigue
have you ferreted out now? First 'twas that incident in
Acre, then young Henry's court, and now—?''

Brandt heaved a sigh, puffing out his cheeks as he
did so. "I have rescued a damsel in distress.''

A collective *ah* went round the table as elbows were
placed in ribs and knowing winks were exchanged
amongst the warriors.

"A damsel, is it?'' Will rolled his eyes toward the
smoke-stained ceiling. "Since when has any maiden, in
distress or no, ever caught your eye?''

Brandt signaled the serving wench to bring another
strop of ale, for as his thoughts settled on Rowanne his
mouth went dry as dust. "This one is—unique.'' Brandt
drummed his fingers on the scarred surface of the table.
"Before I say more I have a task for another of you.
Will, go forth and find a fine gown of wool. Take it
to the Hart and Hind and see it is taken to the Lady
Rowanne.''

"And who shall I say sends it?''

"Say it comes from—her champion.''

A spat of whistles and whoops went round the table.
Soon Will was off in service to his lord.

"Now tell us about the maid,'' Renal said.

"By a strange twist of fate she is journeying to
Irthing.''

"To Irthing?'' Harold Potts asked as more ale was
brought and placed before his lord.

"Aye, to attend her wedding and claim her birthright,'' Brandt said.

"Does this woman of mystery have a name?'' Harold
asked.

Brandt continued to drum his fingers idly. "She is Rowanne Vaudry, heiress to Irthing."

Harold Potts gained his feet. He placed both palms on the table and leaned near to Brandt. "I believe it naught, my lord," Harold said with complete conviction. "It cannot be."

"And yet it is," Brandt replied.

Harold frowned and drew himself up under Brandt's hard gaze. "Someone is having sport with you my lord. The children of Irthing died in a raid—'twas said to be Scots reivers that slew them. Nay she cannot be. The maiden is an imposter."

"Aye, that's what I thought. 'Little deceiver,' I called her, but I was wrong. She *is* Rowanne Vaudry, though I would give all I have if she were not. Or if by magic or sorcery I could change who I was born to be."

CHAPTER 10

Brandt was deeper into his cups than he usually allowed himself to be. Whether 'twas because of the taut passion coiled within him, or the sheer delight in once more being with his trusted companions, he did not know, but ale, beer, and wine flowed freely at the warriors' table well into the night.

The tension of the last fortnight was winnowed away in the smoky attar of the public rooms. Bragging, singing, and displays of strength were interrupted by farting, belching, and more loud drinking.

"Milord Brandt, when we reach your demesne we shalt open a cask of that fine Norman wine and stay drunk as stoats for a sennight!" Robert Claire announced.

"I have not enough wine to keep *you* drunk for two days much else a sennight," Brandt said, chuckling, then quaffed deeply, hoping the wine would banish the image of Rowanne that plagued him yet.

" 'Tis deep into night, milord," Corman said, jutting his chin toward the open doorway.

Brandt craned his neck, willing his vision to right itself. "So 'tis. I must be off." He lurched to his feet but swayed unsteadily.

"Milord, let me go along—for company," Harold Potts offered.

Brandt squinted at him, then shrugged. "As you will, good Harold. As you will."

Several times on the way to the Hart and Hind Brandt miscalculated in the dark and stepped into horse apples or rotting refuse. Other times he wound up in a close that went nowhere. At length he leaned against the stone facade of a building and scraped his sole on a paving stone, trying to free the muck and get his bearings.

"Here we are, my lord," Harold announced cheerfully, pointing at a crooked sign that showed a stag with an impressive rack of antlers, "the Hart and Hind."

Brandt blinked and glanced up. He was in a narrow, dark, snickleway below the inn. While he stood there, trying to get his bearings, a window swung open and spilled a bright bar of light into the alley. A chamberpot was dumped. He and Harold staggered back before they were splashed. Brandt looked up, ready to deliver a blistering oath.

Then he saw Rowanne.

She was clad only in a blanket wrapped round her torso. Her hair was sleek and wet. Lusty heat, searing and molten, jolted Brandt to complete sobriety. He swallowed, and swallowed again.

He thought of her in the plain gray-brown habit of a nun. He thought of that luxurious mane of hair shorn, covered by a wimple. He thought of her at endless prayers, never to know the touch of a man. Never again to know his kiss or the ecstasy they might share.

"My lord—the maiden yon is a great beauty," Harold mused. "And by my beard, she is the image of Rowena of Fontmell—the mistress of Irthing."

"Eh?" Brandt asked, never letting his gaze leave Rowanne's creamy shoulders. "You saw Etienne Vaudry's lady?" His stones felt thick and heavy between his legs. His tarse leaped to life, nudging at his braies.

"Aye. I saw her. My father's burgage and smithy was nigh to Irthing. Now I understand why you are certain the wench is no imposter," Harold whispered harshly, his eyes wide.

"She is no imposter but a practiced thief." *She has stolen my heart.*

"What think you? Does the king decree she is the heiress? Will there be a marriage?" Harold asked.

What does the king decree? The question ripped through Brandt's lust-filled fog. For the first time he thought of the king. He turned to face Harold.

"Ye gads, Harold. You have the right of it. I needs must send word to the king." Brandt frowned and allowed himself one last look at Rowanne—lovely Rowanne, forbidden Rowanne—before he pulled Harold round to his chamber in the Hart and Hind.

Harold watched his lord with a combination of wariness and interest. Brandt's shoulders were stiff, his body rigid with lust—and had been so since they gazed upon the maiden in the window. 'Twas the same kind of primal agitation that Harold's destrier exhibited when around a mare. He had never seen Brandt behave thus around any woman, even the cloying females at the king's court, who were expert at attracting a man's eye, had never tempted Brandt. They had teased him, called him a Templar, said he had taken a secret vow of celibacy, wore shearling braies, had been castrated, any manner of things to explain Brandt's indifference. But now—Jesu.

Harold was not sure what gave him the most pause. The fact that Rowanne Vaudry was alive and well, or the fact that his lord was clearly smitten with the lass.

"I have a task for you, Harold," Brandt said as he put quill to a sheet of vellum he had wrangled from the innkeeper—a man who was less than happy to be roused from his warm bed at so unholy an hour. Brandt sanded the ink on the skin, then read the message to be sure it correctly relayed the facts for the king and his advisor,

Hubert de Burgh. Then Brandt cut a length of ribbon from the deed Henry had given him, melted some wax from the tallow candle, and used the ring Henry had given him to seal the ribbon shut. He rose and strode across the plank flooring, shoving the vellum roll into Harold's hands.

"My lord, Brandt?" Harold's eyes were round as a cod's and his face whiter than snow—as if he had seen a ghost—a ghost with creamy skin and long strands of golden hair. "I can barely credit it, my lord. If the maid lives, then what of the brothers? 'Twas it all a lie and ruse? Think you the whole family survives?"

"I doubt it, for if the brothers did live, then surely the maiden would know of it. Or someone who wanted Irthing would know of it. 'Tis too much to expect the Vaudry family to have been the recipients of three miracles." Brandt clapped his hand on Harold's forearm.

"Ride to the city gate, tell them you are about the Crown's business. Go with all haste to King Henry's court and put this directly in his hand. Wait for him and de Burgh to make a decision." Brandt smiled grimly. "And hold your tongue about all you have seen and heard; I want no word of this reaching the ears of my enemies at Sherborne."

"Aye, my lord." Harold nodded. He was one of a handful of men who knew the details of Brandt's bastardy. Only a few friends knew Thomas of Sherborne was Brandt's father.

"Bring the king's reply to Cumbria. You will be able to make good time riding alone and should, with luck, be able to overtake us on the road to Irthing."

"Aye, my lord." Harold nodded his assent. "Have no fear, I will find you long before you reach the gates of Irthing." Harold took a step then hesitated. "Do the rest of the men travel with you?"

"Nay, only the two deceivers, Coy and Desmond. I have sent the rest to travel another road. Better that the wagons and carts of my household goods do not arouse suspicion in Thomas's man until I learn the king's mind about this mystery—and learn his wishes about Rowanne Vaudry."

"Aye, my lord, Brandt." Harold turned on his heel.

Brandt went to the open window and stared out into the salmon-colored morn. Harold's spurs rapped against the cobbled stones of the empty street as he made his way to his horse.

Brandt told himself that he was doing what any sensible and loyal subject of the king would do. He told himself that he had not sent word to Henry in order to delay consigning Rowanne to a life of prayer in a nunnery. He told himself one lie after another, but in his mind's eye all he could see were her bare shoulders, her sweet neck, and her lips the color of a pomegranate.

In his heart he knew. He had set the wheels of his own destruction in motion.

Now the king would set aside Brandt. He would surely decree Rowanne the heiress. By his own hand Brandt would have lost his title and his demesne. Castle Irthing, the Black Knowe, and all that he had coveted was slipping through his fingers like desert sand.

And he felt a great sense of relief to know she would not be wearing the habit of a nun.

"Rowanne, you must keep your brothers safe. Run. Run deep into the Black Knowe and hide. Hide, child! Gruffudd will find you, but you must keep my sons safe from the DeLucy swine."

In her dreams Rowanne was a child again, running along the Roman wall. Her brother's small hand was clutched in her own, and the nursemaid ran behind them with the younger babe in her arms.

Memories swirled in her mind, scattered in the dark corners of the past like autumn leaves in a gusting wind. Ghosts from the shadowy nooks of the Roman ruin had come to haunt her this night on the great wall that ran the width of England. Once again she was a child in Cumbria.

A profound and lingering sense of guilt fogged Rowanne's senses and caused her heart to ache within her breast. Even in sleep the pain was sharp and ragged, her guilt undulled by time and distance. The nightmare, which had been held at bay by Lady Margaret's care and nurturing, had returned with the icy fury of a winter storm.

She was trapped inside the terror ... running ... pursued. If Rowanne and her siblings could but reach the woods beyond the keep, they could hide until the murderers were gone.

Run! Her mother's pleading voice echoed in the memory of her mind. Rowanne's lungs burned. A sharp pain gripped her side, but she ran—ran as fast as her watery legs would carry her. Her brother stumbled and fell, nearly dragging her down with him. Rowanne risked one glance over her shoulder as she scooped him up. He was heavy, but she ran on into the night ... toward the safety of the Roman wall.

A man loomed up before them like a demon from hell. His face was hideously torn. One eye bulged from its socket. Gore and ruined tissue hung in strips. Deep bloody grooves, scored into his flesh by a woman's fingernails.

Her mother's nails. He had killed her mother! Oh, her mother was dead. Rowanne screamed and fought as the man grabbed her. She kicked and hit and screamed again.

"Milady?" A strong, warm hand gripped her shoulder, stilled her body. Though she wanted to leave the horror, she could not break the jaws of terror as she was trapped in that place between sleep and waking.

"*Rowanne?*" Brandt's rough, concerned voice parted the veil of time. The sound of her name on his lips fully woke her.

She blinked and came once again into the present.

His tunic hung open to the waist in the front as if he had been roused from his bed. His hair was tousled. He was staring down at her, dying embers from the brazier in her chamber casting long shadows and an unholy glow over his lean face. Concern was etched across his noble brow.

"I—I—" Confusion and fear clung to her mind. Where was she? "Brandt?" she asked around her thick tongue.

"Aye, 'tis me, little temptress. You have naught to fear now. I am with you." His scarred knuckles lightly grazed her cheek. 'Twas the hand of a warrior that touched her, a hand that could wield a sword, snuff out a life. Yet there was infinite gentleness in the light scrape of his worn and callused flesh against her own.

Something hot and liquid burst inside her chest. She wanted him to be untouchable, fearsome, terrible in his wrath—she wanted to be strong and independent. And all the while she wanted to fold herself into his strong arms and let him keep her terrors at bay.

"Where are we?"

"At the inn in Chester. You had an unpleasant dream. Tears glisten upon your cheek like jewels." He reached out as if to capture something from her cheek. " 'Twas a piteous whimper that brought me awake and to your side. What plagues you so, little temptress?"

"I—I—Memories from the past. That night," she stammered, suddenly feeling stripped bare by the softness of his voice.

"Memories? Or ghosts?"

"They are all much the same, I fear." She glanced away, suddenly loath for him see her thus—to know her weakness—to see her vulnerable and afraid. She had to be strong for Lady Margaret.

"Did I rouse any one else?" she asked as she drew the blanket up to her chin as if the thin fabric could shield her from an unwanted truth.

"Nay, the house slumbers yet." He nodded toward

the shuttered windows. "Dawn is not yet come. I hear what others do not."

"Do you see what others are blind to as well?"

He scanned her face for a long minute as if he actually could see something deep within her—something hidden. "I see a maid tired onto death. I see a maid that needs sleep so she will be strong and fresh when she sees her home."

Rowanne saw something in Brandt's eyes that made her blood thicken and slow in her veins. She could not speak, could barely breathe as her heart marked the passage of time.

"Rest now, little temptress." He stroked his knuckles on her cheek.

His words and his touch paralyzed her. She could not move, or breathe. She thought of her home, so old and solid and waiting for her to walk through the portcullis and claim it. A nagging voice in the back of her mind asked why she should be anxious to reach Irthing when it would surely mean the departure of the mercenary.

With a shake of her head she forced herself to the present. The door to her chamber was shut—Brandt was gone. But now she found herself thinking once again of Irthing. Features that had been lost to her were now clear and crisp, a result, she supposed of the nightmare.

In her mind's eye she could see the keep, built of large rough-hewn stones scavenged from the massive Roman wall that stretched the breadth of England. By the hundreds the blocks had been carted away and refashioned into the curtain wall, donjon, buttery, stables and barracks of Irthing. Even beyond Irthing's walls those great stones had been employed for more godly purposes than a heathen like Hadrian could have imagined.

The legend was well known, worn smooth by years of retelling. Even as a child Rowanne had taken pride in her noble ancestor, Robert Vaudry. The first of her line, in 1166 he had founded Lanercost Priory, laying the first stone; a block hewn by the Romans in a futile effort to hold back the fierce Scots bandits. Nestled in the richly wooded valley of River Irthing, the priory had been mystical and enchanting to Rowanne. She well remembered the baritone harmony of the brothers' voices as they sang their prayers. There was a bond betwixt that holy place and all Vaudrys, forged first by Robert de Vaudry with the laying of the cornerstone, and kept alive through the generations.

But some said the bond went deeper than that. There were those who whispered about the old ones, Queen Mab and the priests who worshipped in oak groves across Britain. And there were the ogham stones—older than memory, etched deep with crude precision—that held the prophesy of the Vaudrys. The stones said the Vaudry offspring would rise from the dead when a ghost walked among the stones. It also said the Vaudry children were destined to love only once. But those legends were not spoken of openly, not since the church took power and the abbey had been built near those pagan stones.

Rowanne's lips twisted into a forlorn smile. She had always felt comforted by the gentle Augustinian brothers and the solid stones of Irthing and Lanercost Abbey. She had roamed among them, listening to gravelly voices that spoke of contemplation and sacrifice while she traced letters etched deep in stone by Roman soldiers who had once stood as lonely sentinels along the wall.

Those stones and men had taught her the meaning of sacrifice—and honor—and the sanctity of keeping one's word.

Irthing would give her strength when she reached it, but she also faced the fact that 'twould be a place of haunted memories. And without Lady Margaret at her side, who would soothe Rowanne when the crushing failure of her past loomed before her? Who would smooth her brow and tell her that she had been only a child, the pleading of her dying mother too heavy a burden for her slim shoulders? When she walked the cold corridors of Irthing, who would keep the ghosts of her guilt from dragging her into the shadows?

Brandt le Revenant is strong enough to hold them back, a spectral voice whispered on the wind. And for a moment she allowed herself to consider such a possibility.

CHAPTER 11

Brandt urged Glandamore onto the cantle of his saddle. He had drunk too much and that, coupled with Rowanne's dream, had left him feeling cranky. He should be full of good cheer—after all, each day drew him closer to his revenge against Thomas. The odd thing was that it no longer gave him a sense of pleasure to think about slaying his half brother. The only reason he was intent on killing Geoffroi now was to protect Rowanne, to keep their bargain. He no longer lived to settle old debts with his sire but only to see Rowanne safe.

He thought of this puzzle as he waited by the Hart and Hind's stairs. He saw Leopold headed in his direction, a wide smile splitting the hideously scarred face.

"Ah, Brandt. Good news." Leopold grinned up at him. "Last eve I hired men for the rest of the journey. We are now four swords instead of two."

"Indeed?" Brandt focused his attention on Leopold, trying to keep his expression bland. He had not doubted his loyal men had accomplished their task.

"Aye, two stout knights that have need of ready coin met me last eve." Leopold leaned close, his fetid breath taking Brandt's breath away, making his stomach churn. "And I got them for a quidding amount of coin."

"Of that I have no doubt, Leopold. You squeeze a coin until it slips from your fingers," Brandt replied.

Brandt's own men stepped forward at Leopold's signal. They gave no indication they knew him.

"This is Coy and Desmond, both recently returned from the Holy Lands."

"Indeed," Brandt croaked out again. His head was beginning to pound, his stomach rolling and tossing like a cork on the open sea. Whether it was from too much ale or being around Leopold he was not sure.

"Aye," Leopold said. "These good men will journey with us as far as the border, and a good thing too, for you look as green as a lizard's spleen this morn, Brandt."

Brandt nodded and swallowed again. He did feel quite green, and the mention of a lizard's spleen nearly sent him running for a garderobe or the nearest gutter.

" 'Tis a comfort to have two more sword arms. Bandits and outlaws are on every road these days. We were set upon, as well as a fool of a merchant." Leopold's brow was furrowed.

"I will sleep better for having two more to guard the lady," Brandt said, wishing for nothing more than to find a dark stall in which to curl up and sleep the day away.

Leopold turned, casting about. "Now if that churl Jonathan has found a palfrey that 'twas not too dear . . ."

"A palfrey?" Brandt repeatedly stupidly. "Why are you buying a palfrey?"

"Ah, here they are now," Leopold said, smiling again. "I have thought and decided it bodes ill for the lady to ride pillion with you. I'll not risk my lord Geoffroi's wrath by us arriving with her on your steed."

Brandt looked up, but it was not a nimble-footed palfrey that captured his gaze but a vision in blue wool.

Jonathan rushed toward Leopold. "I hurried like ye ordered, sir."

But Brandt no longer cared about the horse, or that Rowanne was being allowed to ride. Suddenly the ache in his head was gone, his stomach forgotten. Now his discomfort 'twas only the insistent throbbing in his loins. His eyes, traitors that they were, skimmed over the slender bow of Rowanne's back, marking each luscious curve within the blue fabric. He memorized every delicate sinew until his gaze stopped on the golden mantle of her hair.

In his agony this morn he had forgotten about the impulsive order for Will to get her a new gown. He had forgotten that he wanted to see her smile by having something more suitable to wear to Irthing. Now he regretted that order, for his eyes were drawn to Rowanne's figure, her enticing body.

He flicked a glance upward to her face, but that was also a mistake. The blue wool made her eyes light as if illuminated from within. Perchance they were. Perhaps a warm fire burned inside her, and Brandt's cold soul could do little but seek out that sweet heat, searching for the warmth that had the power to thaw his frosty soul and free his icy heart.

He clung to the newel post of the cross-timbered building like a drunkard seeking support. His body tightened and tightened again. Why could he not remember his plan for vengeance and let all this foolish fancy go?

Rowanne walked with her chin up, her clean, unbound hair flowing over her shoulders like a golden stream, a shimmering pennon. Her face was scrubbed pink, her flawless skin perfect except for a few small bruises and scrapes from the cart accident and the ruffian's attack.

Jewels, she needs jewels to caress her lovely throat, Another rebellious thought ripped through Brandt's mind.

The soft blue wool skimmed over Rowanne's willowy body. The simple braided leathern girdle that held a plain almsbag drew his lust-stung eyes to her incredibly tiny waist. His hands could span that girth easily.

The strange hot coil inside his gut tightened. The ice around his heart began to melt, trickling downward, where it pooled in his loins. It heated until 'twas molten with desire, boiling him from the inside out. His sac and tarse drew taut as a longbow string. He was itchy, hot, restless.

She was a beauty. Nay. She was a goddess.

Regret, lust, and sadness for what could never be between them threatened to swamp him. Would that he were another man's bastard son—*any man's* bastard but Thomas DeLucy's.

Leopold made a choking sound that drew Brandt's tortured gaze. The one eye was wide and staring, his jaw was open and slack. A small stream of spittle ran down into the stubble that dotted his chin as he stared, pale and unmoving at Rowanne.

"Leopold?" Brandt spoke his name but 'twas like speaking to a corpse. Then the one eye blinked slowly.

"God's mercy, 'tis Rowena," Leopold whispered.

"Leopold?" Brandt glared into that one bloodshot orb. "What ails ye? This is Rowanne."

"What?" Leopold blinked again. Then he looked at Brandt and swallowed hard while he rubbed the back of his hand across his lips. "Not—not Rowena?"

"Nay. Are you fevered?" Brandt frowned and looked at Leopold's shaking hand. "Do you need a leech? I can send Jonathan to fetch a leecher."

"Nay, 'tis only that, for a moment with the light—" He leaned a bit and looked back again at Rowanne. "For a moment—but then it is not possible. The dead do not walk, no matter what the simple folk say." He looked at Brandt. "Do they? Can they rise again from the grave, Brandt? Do they *haunt* people? You carry the name of a walking spirit, *le Revenant.* Tell me, do the dead walk?"

"I have never seen a dead man walk, but in battle I

do not usually tarry to watch. As far as being haunted, I believe our deeds haunt us, not the dead. Are you certain you do not need me to fetch a leech?''

"Nay. Here is Jonathan with the palfrey. Get you mounted, Rowen . . . I mean, Rowanne. You will ride to Irthing for we must hurry.'' Leopold's voice was harsh. "Let us make good time for I am most anxious to turn you over to the care of Geoffroi. I would be done with this task anon.''

"I am ready. With Clwyd nearby I pray the mare will be sweetly docile,'' Rowanne said. She took the reins in her hands and smiled sweetly. All Brandt could do was grieve for a future that could never be.

The expression in Brandt's eyes 'twas more than hunger . . . but what was it? Rowanne wondered.

When he slew the bandits on the first morn she met him, she had seen a terrible wrath in those depths. When he found her and saved her, she had seen relief simmering in eyes the color of polished agate. And each time he kissed her his eyes had gone smoky with passion.

The look in his eyes now was raw, stripped bare and full of unspoken promise—but there was sorrow behind his gaze. What was he thinking? What emotion simmered below the surface? Did he not find her comely in the very gown he had secretly purchased for her?

"Sir, I want to—to say gramercy,'' Rowanne said as he readied himself to ride. "For the gown.''

His eyes narrowed down to slits and his mouth became a thin, taut line. Above his padded gambeson she saw his Adam's apple work up and down as he swallowed.

" 'Tis not necessary to give me thanks, milady.''

"Are you pleased with the results? It fits well.''

Brandt swallowed hard again. "Aye, most agreeable fit.''

"Mayhap if we come upon another market you can get a tunic for yourself.''

He froze. "I have tunics enough.''

Her cheeks flamed as she realized he had taken insult.

"I did not mean to imply that your wardrobe was in any way lacking, sir. 'Tis only that you have been all that is kind and generous to me. I wilt not forget it."

Something lurched deep inside him. Jesu, if she knew his heart, then she would be less than grateful for his company and attention. But for now he would await to hear the king's pleasure. It gave him a grim satisfaction to know his hands were tied and his own actions had bound them.

Until then—in this small march of time she still admired him, thanked him, thought him a worthy knight.

He allowed his hungry gaze to skim over her winsome body again. By Saint Cuthburt, he wanted to confess all to her, to tell her that he was deeded Irthing by the young king. He wanted to unburden his soul and tell her that he had in mind to use her as a weapon of revenge. He wanted to confess he was Thomas DeLucy's bastard. But more than that, he wanted to drag her against him, to feel her skin, to taste her mouth. He wanted to possess her. And that was why his heart felt as if it had been pierced by a crossbow's bolt. For on the day he told her all, he would no longer see kindness in her blue eyes, but contempt and well-deserved loathing.

She hated all with DeLucy blood, she had said so often.

He was a coward, he knew, for wanting to keep that day when she discovered his lineage at bay for as long as possible. Brandt closed his eyes and inhaled two long gulps of city-fouled air. 'Twas only a few more days to the border. A sennight at most. Surely Brandt could keep himself in check for that long. And he would have two of his men along, even though they pretended to be strangers, he would glean strength from their presence.

Aye, he could keep himself in check. He had to keep himself in control. He could not have Rowanne of Irthing.

CHAPTER 12

Glandamore cried out, swooping over the first blooms of heather in a great circle. She flew back and forth over a hedgethorn that slashed like a dagger's edge through a rolling hill of new green. Beyond, a fielder was sowing barley in dark, tilled earth. Rooks and songbirds circled, waiting to get their portion.

Glandamore cried out.

Brandt frowned. Glandamore 'twas not given to calling to him while she hunted. Now he trained his attention on her, wondering what she was about. The hawk went into a deep dive but instead of skimming near the earth and coming away with a hare or a woodcock grasped in her lethal talons, she settled on the verge, walking in her strange awkward gait toward something that held her attention. She tilted her noble head this way and that, walking 'round and 'round a tiny nubbin of brown that lay near the boxwood hedgerow. Brandt spurred Clwyd up the hill to investigate. He dismounted and stared at the creature that held Glandamore in thrall, amusement kicking up the corners of his mouth.

"Prithee, what will be in our cooking pot this eve?" Leopold shouted from his vantage point along side the cart. "I grow tired of grouse, mayhap the bird has found a plump hare."

" 'Tis too small a joint for the pot," Brandt said.

He took a step toward the small thing, curious about why Glandamore had bothered with it. 'Twas a pitiful creature, in need of a mothering hand and not even an adequate snack for the hawk.

Brandt turned his back and stared to walk away, but something halted him. He turned. The pitiful beast was helpless. An uncharacteristic tug of sympathy pulled at his heart.

It was too small to live alone. He glanced toward the fielder. Perhaps the plow had killed its mother—if so, it would be sup for some hawk more hungry or less choosy than the pretty Glandamore.

Brandt glanced toward Rowanne. Even at this distance he could feel her eyes upon him, could almost read the vexation in her gaze. She no doubt thought him to be a ruthless brute. All she wanted from him was the vengeance he could bring her with his sword.

And yet she had said she liked his kisses. He had felt her respond to his ardor. She liked the blue gown he had given her.

Brandt frowned across the tilled field. Rowanne Vaudry wanted him because he could bring a swift death to Geoffroi. But there was more to him, he had learned recently, more kindness and soft humors than even he had known. Could he show her a different side of himself? If he did show her his heart, could she perhaps look beyond his mercenary's body and his tainted blood to see him—the man?

As he stared at the orphaned creature in the shade of the boxwood the last chunk of ice broke away from his heart, and he bent down and scooped up the animal. After putting it inside his tunic, he launched himself into his saddle. Glandamore took wing and followed a little above his head as he spurred Clwyd toward the palfrey.

She will never know 'tis a DeLucy that wants to claim her heart, his guilty heart said. His armor creaked and clanked as the destrier slowed beside the palfrey. She was a sweet, biddable creature.

"Pray hold out your hands, milady," Brandt's voice sluiced over her like slow honey. His nearness made her flesh prickle, her heart beat heavy in her chest. She felt naked beneath his penetrating gaze—wanted to be naked beneath him. With those provocative images burning into her mind, she became shy and uncomfortable. She wanted to do his bidding, and yet her desire to please him made her feel strange. She was embarrassed by the visions she could not banish from her imagination nor understand.

"I must hold my horse, sir, lest she bolt." He laughed at her reply. The sound was like sunshine on her skin.

"I will keep her steady. Pray, hold out your hands. 'Tis not something that should be in the pot, lady. Hold out your hands . . . I pray thee, Lady Rowanne."

The deep, melodic sound of his voice skipped over her flesh and made her skin prickle with an itchy awareness. Her body betrayed her with a sensation of hunger—hunger for him.

"Rowanne." The masculine sound braided itself with magic and removed her hesitance. "I vow, I would never do you harm. I promise, it is no bloody leveret I wish to put into your keeping but a small gift." There was no smile on his face. "Trust me, Rowanne—if you are able to trust such a man as I."

Trust me, Rowanne. Surely Lucifer spoke so sweetly in the garden when he enticed Eve into sin.

A strange and dreadful battle waged within her. Jesu, she wanted to do as bid—wanted to do *whatever* he bid, but a stubborn streak in her soul fought against submission. There was something fearful and threatening in giving in to him. He was asking her something more, something greater than to simply hold out her hands, and she knew it.

But had she not already put her complete faith in the hands of a cold-eyed mercenary who spilled men's blood without care? And had he not justified her faith by saving her life more than once?

She held out her hands to him.

Brandt grinned boyishly at her. The edges of his even, white teeth gleamed against his bronzed flesh. He looked years younger—he looked playful—seductive. He shook her to the core of her womanhood with that beguiling smile.

"It is a foolish fancy, but I thought you might'st make a pet of it." He inclined his head toward her hands and let something fall, gently, into her waiting palms.

Rowanne looked down. There, curled protectively into a small, prickly ball of spines, rested a helpless baby hedgehog.

"Is it alive?" She gasped.

"Aye." Brandt laughed again. "Glandamore would not deign to waste her time on such a pitiful creature as a half-dead hedgehog. Like as naught, the tilling of the fields has made it an orphan."

"Oh, the poor tiny thing." Empathy poured through Rowanne along with the strange and exhilarating knowledge that Brandt had once again given her something. He had given her gifts—her life, her gown, and now, if a baby hedgehog could'st be considered a gift, this tiny pet.

" 'Tis near frighted unto death." She gingerly stroked her finger along the erect spines.

"Aye. 'Tis likely terrified." Brandt looked sympathetically at the animal for a moment, then he raised his wrist. The hawk landed upon his cuff immediately. "Glandamore 'twas more curious than intent on doing it injury. Weren't you, my fine lady?" A dimple appeared in his left cheek as he spoke softly to the bird, stroking her breast with one finger. For a heart-stopping instant Rowanne could not draw any air into her lungs. Her head felt light and fuzzy.

Jesu, I am dying. Brandt's beauty and power and her own wanton desire conspired to squeeze the air from her body. Her fevered mind cried out for surcease.

He was too brilliant, too manly, and, by the saints, he was far too dangerous for a girl who had spent her life imprisoned. His magnificence was disturbing, like one of God's host. Aye, that was it. Brandt le Revenant was a mortal archangel fallen to earth.

"If you want it not, I will release it," he said softly, shattering her fantasy and drawing her attention. She blinked and tried to clear her head. He was watching her with a curious look in his eyes.

"You were frowning," he said. "If you want it not—"

"Nay. I will keep it." She drew her cupped hands closer to her body, suddenly overcome with the desire to shield and protect the homely little orphan.

His eyes narrowed in silent speculation, but after a time he nodded and said, "As you wish. When you tire of it I will set it free in a hedge."

"I will never tire of it—not ever," she declared in a whisper. "He will be my pet. The first I have ever possessed. And I will call him Thorn."

Slowly the little animal began to unroll itself. It peered up at her with tiny, bewildered black eyes.

"Thorn will be safe with me. And I will treasure the gift, Brandt." She smiled and cooed to the hedgehog. In her eyes 'twas the finest hedgehog, the most handsome of creatures, the noblest beast because it had come from Brandt.

Brandt looked at her, sitting pertly on the palfrey, petting the prickly meadow pig as if it were a fine, silky alaunt hound from the king's own kennels. Her hair shimmered down her straight, slim back like a golden fount.

Brandt's tarse and stones tightened in a hot contraction of lust. How she would look in his bed, with only her glorious hair to cover her body—to cover them both in a bower of carnal bliss. The image made his blood burn hot.

The flickering light leaped from logs Brandt had hacked with his own sword. Deep shadows danced and capered on Rowanne's face. The shifting, writhing image of her golden hair taunted him, teased him until his blood burned with lust.

Coy and Desmond sat across the fire, and he could feel their secret gaze upon him. Several times during the day he had seen a knowing smile on Desmond's lips.

He rose from his crouched position, pretending to ease a cramp in his leg. Glandamore had provided grouse for the pot. Jonathan was still sucking noisily on the bones. Leopold had lapsed into a strange silence. He had not even cuffed Jonathan once today. He kept himself apart, staring at Rowanne, muttering and whispering to himself.

Rowanne cooed to her hedgepig, and like a hound on a short leash, Brandt was pulled to her side.

"You are a prickly little man, Sir Thorn."

"Too lofty a title by half, I should think." Brandt stepped out of the dark, drawn to her as surely as a moth is to flame. "Allow me to provide sup for your pet."

She looked up in surprise as Brandt dropped three fat, pale grubs beside the hedgehog. The little orphan nosed his way toward the grubs. With astounding alacrity and fierceness he ate one, then another.

"The beast is hungry as well as prickly," he commented dryly.

"So it would seem." Rowanne wrinkled her nose as the third disappeared head first into Thorn's maw. The hedgepig began to rub its nose, evidently cleaning itself after supping.

"Sir Thorn, allow me to introduce you to Brandt le

Revenant, your rescuer and benefactor," Rowanne said as she petted the tips of the spines gingerly with the end of her index finger. Sir Thorn stopped and arched his back as if to roll up in a ball again. But then he lifted his head and peered upward. Whether 'twas at Rowanne or simply the night sky, Brandt was unsure but the ugly little brute appeared to look at something.

"I am honored to make your acquaintance, Sir Thorn," Brandt said seriously. He squatted down on his haunches beside Rowanne, pretending to be interested in the animal when all he wanted was to be closer to her, to feel her sweet heat, to smell her woman's musk. The moment he took a deep breath, inhaling the scent of her, his throbbing tarse reared to life, nudging insistently inside his braies.

Jesu, can I not even be near her without lusting like a stag in rut?

"Sir Thorn, lord of the hedge," Rowanne said softly, "Le Revenant is my most ardent protector and champion."

The sound of the word made his heart skip a beat. She said it with such an expression of intimacy he was afraid he might shame himself right there in the twilight. While he struggled to regain his composure, she turned her head and looked up at him.

The firelight made her face a palate of shadow and muted light. He could not speak, could barely breathe.

Rowanne stared at le Revenant. She felt a powerful tug on her heart. There was far more to him than just his sword arm—or his wide shoulders—or his well-filled hozen. She swallowed the thought and tried to keep her heart from hammering inside her chest.

'Struth there was a side to him that was deadly; she had seen the proof of that when first she met him, but there was more. So much more.

He was deeper, more mysterious than one would think on first meeting. In fact, as she watched him now from the shelter of her downcast lashes she thought he was much like the icy burns of her homeland. He might appear to be clear and shallow, but when the foolhardy stepped off the bank, 'twas to find themselves immersed in water way over the head.

Rowanne was that unwary fool who had ventured far out. She was over her head. She was drowning in the riddle of Brandt le Revenant—mercenary, rescuer of women and orphan hedgehogs. If she allowed herself, she could fall into the depths of his agate eyes and lose herself entirely.

She could love this man. The thought came from nowhere.

A melancholy chill settled over her. Her avenging angel was capturing her heart. And that she could not allow. As long as Geoffroi and Thomas yet lived and Lady Margaret was still a prisoner in Sherborne, Rowanne needs must keep her mind—and her heart—set upon her goal. She had not the luxury of finding love while the old debt was still owing.

"I know little of you, Brandt. Tell me of your family," she said softly.

"Family is not a word I would use when speaking of my life." He picked up a stick and broke it in half. "I have a half brother. My clearest recollection of him is the day he gave me a longbow. When our sire found out, he put me in a pillory and laid a whip across my back. My half brother watched."

"Have you no other family—no one to care for?" Rowanne wondered if she were speaking of Brandt or herself.

"Nay. I am the unacknowledged bastard of a petty baron. I have no kith nor kin." His guilty gaze flitted across the fire to Coy and Desmond. They were watching him.

"Perhaps when we are done," she said, flicking a telling glance toward Leopold, who was staring into the fire as if ensorcelled, "perhaps then you can find a wife and begin your own family."

Brandt's head snapped up. "I think the fates have destined me to live my life alone, lady. For any woman I should want would never settle for a bastard like me."

Brandt finally found the strength to rise. He moved away from Rowanne and brought a new skin of wine from his pack. He quaffed deeply of the grape, determined to keep his body from thrumming to the sound of Rowanne's every breath. She lay down on her side and pulled her cloak around her. The glow of firelight danced along her unbound hair. Golden tresses lay like a mantel over her body, spilling down onto the falding and soft fur of her cloak.

Brandt's tarse throbbed, his stones ached with desire, his mouth dried out. It was as if he were once more being parched by the relentless sun of the Holy Lands.

Brandt wanted to lie beside her. He wanted to feel her soft hands upon his belly, upon his tarse. He wanted her to cup him, to take him in hand, to make cooing noises and smile at him until he plunged himself deep inside her.

He *wanted* with a fierce hunger that consumed him.

He tore his gaze from her and took another long pull on the wineskin. Why should he persist in torturing himself? As soon as his vengeance was complete upon Thomas he *would* either see her in a nunnery or the king would see her settled as heiress of Irthing. Either option left no way for them to be together.

He narrowed his eyes and gazed at Rowanne over the barrier of leaping flames. There was life and strength and robust vitality in her. For a wild and reckless moment Brandt prayed to all the angels in heaven for some way to wash the DeLucy blood from his veins. For some way to turn the mad topsy-turvy world a'right so that he might have his surcease from battle and the winsome maid as well.

Sunlight broke like a beacon over the top of the budding forest and shone upon Brandt's hair, igniting it to a fiery torch. Roxanne lay on her side watching the burnished lights appeared among the dark strands that hung to his shoulders and wound themselves into the links of his mail. With each passing moment he looked less like a bloodthirsty warrior and more like a comely seducer of maidens.

He turned over. Their gazes caught and held, simmering, burning with barely hidden desire across the frost-tipped grass of the fell. Rowanne's breath came to her in heavy, slow drafts. 'Twas strange, this feeling she had each time she allowed herself to gaze upon Brandt le Revenant—her warrior, her champion.

She wanted to talk to him, to tell him of all the things that plagued and frightened her. She wanted to fold herself into his strong arms and let him soothe her fears, carry her burdens, take charge of her life and destiny.

I want him to be my lover. A tingling began in her belly, driving back the cold, hollow sadness of a few moments ago. Hunger and a newfound awareness raced across her flesh from head to toe. Along with that awareness came the memory of Brandt's gentle touch, his concerned waking of her on the last eve. The memory came unbidden and unwelcome.

She wanted to accept all he offered, but she would not. Lady Margaret's fate lay in the hands of this man— this mercenary. Rowanne wanted no softness in him. She wanted no mercy, no pity, no caring, and most especially no confusion betwixt them. Rowanne wanted his blood-lust hot. She needed him to wield his deadly blade.

"He must prevail. He *will* prevail," she whispered to herself. "I cannot consider otherwise. And I wilt not let myself think of tender thoughts and a future that cannot be until Geoffroi DeLucy lies in his grave and Lady Margaret is free."

CHAPTER 13

Brandt shifted in his saddle and smiled smugly to himself. He had hoped Desmond would keep Rowanne occupied until he was able to break the potent enscorcellment of her charms. And it seemed his friend was content to do that very thing without being asked.

Brandt watched his most trusted man and heaved a great sigh that he told himself was surely relief. From the time of breaking their fast this morning Desmond had taken charge of Rowanne. Leopold was even more odd today. His single eye was red-rimmed and he spoke in low murmurs as they rode.

Desmond rode close beside Rowanne's gray palfrey. He smiled, showing a dazzling number of straight white teeth whilst he kept a steady stream of questions coming her way. She had no time to do aught but ride and answer.

No time to cast sweet glances Brandt's way.

It did not escape Brandt's notice that Leopold had chosen to stay a goodly pace from Rowanne, giving Desmond ample time to work his charm. 'Twas as if seeing Rowanne in a the new bliaut had awakened some curious and unseen terror for Leopold. He had called her Rowena—could it be she so closely resembled her mother? But why should that fact have such a queer effect on Leopold?

"Tell me more of your home, lady," Desmond asked in a milk and honey voice that seemed to thoroughly capture her attention. Brandt found himself riding nearer so he could better hear their converse.

" 'Tis windblown. Irthing sits on a sweet, fresh beck that flows from the river. My father enlarged it, had it dug wider and deeper to use as a moat, but it is not the usually stinking, brackish water that flows by Irthing. The flow is fresh and sweet as rainwater. In springtime water plants bloom and their scent is carried up the ramparts." Rowanne closed her eyes.

Brandt sat a little straighter in his saddle. He was pleased that Desmond was now the object of Rowanne's attention. Or was he?

They were of a kind, both gilt and slender. What a picture they made, their golden hair gleaming in the sunshine, their pale eyes twinkling with interest at what the other had to say.

"And tell me, lady, what canst you see from your chamber? I have heard there is naught but mountains and sheep and rough Scot reivers in Cumbria," Desmond said with the most innocent of expressions on his face, but something about the way his blue eyes twinkled made Brandt scowl.

Brandt's breath lodged in his throat. Could it be that Desmond truly *liked* Rowanne? He had thought his man was doing what needs be done for his lord—but what if . . .

Nay, it did not signify. Desmond had just met the maid and he was ever the silver-tongued seducer of maids. Nay, it could not be.

Her tinkling laughter brought Brandt's chin up with a jolt. He watched as she smiled, coyly, *flirtatiously*, at Desmond. Something cold and wicked twined around his heart.

"Is it not true that only barbarians and growers of wool reside in Cumbria?"

"Nay, sir, you have been most grievously misled, for there is much in Cumbria besides wool and rocks and border bandits," Rowanne promised with a smile. "There is much more."

Something hot and bitter flowed through Brandt's chest. What had only moments before seemed his salvation, was now appearing more and more threatening. He did not like the thoughts running through his mind, nor the fact that he was on the verge of riding to Desmond, ordering him to follow at the rear. With the order poised on the tip of his tongue, he realized he could not even do so if he chose. For by his own word and design Desmond now was a stranger to him. And by his own devious scheme, Desmond was taking orders only from Leopold.

Brandt had been so clever; Desmond now played the part of a freelancer—a man who owed no allegiance to Brandt or any lord. And as such he was free to make bold with a beautiful maiden.

"Indeed, Sir Desmond, the aspect from my chamber is most breathtaking," Rowanne said with a saucy tilt of her head. "On a winter's night, when the air is still, I trow I can hear the monks chanting their prayers from Lanercost Abbey."

"An abbey, say you? Tell me of it, for as you speak of your home I find the light in your eyes most comely," Desmond said and followed his brazen compliment with a wink.

Rowanne ducked her head and blushed crimson. She held the palfrey's reins a little tighter.

Could it be that Desmond was trying to seduce Rowanne? Was she succumbing to his charms? Did she find his golden looks so enchanting that a morning of sweet words had captured her heart?

Brandt put his spurs lightly to Clwyd's sides, drawing nearer to Rowanne. He told himself he only wanted to hear more of their conversation in order to learn about his holding, but Gervais's long dead and much scornful laughter echoed in his ears.

Glandamore stretched her wings and made the trilling noise that signaled she would like to hunt.

"Later, Glandamore," Brandt mumbled impatiently as he drew close to Desmond. "Mayhap after our nooning meal."

Brandt gripped Clwyd's bridle and scanned the horizon. His eyes burned from searching the vista for Harry. And though he told himself 'twas because he was a loyal subject and a staunch man of the king, inside he knew the truth. For two days he had been burning with jealousy. And he feared that his friend Desmond had become intoxicated by the sight and sound of Rowanne.

Each day when they stopped for the nooning meal, the ever gallant Desmond would spread his cloak for Rowanne. In the sunshine they were a striking study, the sunlight bronzing two heads of gold. Their gentle converse and laughter spoilt Brandt's appetite before he had taken two bites of the bread and cheese.

Compared to the dashing, mannered Desmond, Brandt was the roughest cullion. The truth of his coarse breeding burned him, seared him, made him crazed with envy. He loved his friend truly and well, but the feeling he had for Rowanne was something beyond friendship.

He glanced at Leopold. The man-at-arms had become almost insensible. In truth, had Rowanne tried to run off, he would barely have noticed. He had become more and more ill-humored. When he looked at Rowanne the color leeched from his face and he mumbled strange prayers and incantations under his breath and frequently spoke the name of Rowena Vaudry.

Brandt wondered if Rowanne even noticed. She had eyes for only one person now. And that person was

Desmond. Rowanne had a new companion that made her smile and laugh.

Brandt was being split in twain with jealousy and confusion. He loved Desmond best of all his men, like a brother or even a son. The first time he heard Rowanne's trilling laughter in response to Desmond's voice, it had sounded as sharp and painful as the quarrel of a crossbow rending his flesh. Now it opened the wound wider every time he heard it. He hovered between anger and despair while a tide of unknown, unruly emotions swept over him.

He was *not* jealous. Rowanne was happy. Desmond was his friend.

Rowanne laughed again. Her soul sighed in contentment. For the first time in so very long she found herself laughing, giggling, and feeling light of spirit. She cradled Thorn in her hand and listened to the wonderful, melodious sound of Desmond's voice while he relayed yet another improbable tale. Just having the strong, blond knight near her was a comfort.

"Desmond, your stories are most entertaining, but methinks you are a bold-faced liar," she said between giggles.

He clasped his hand to his breast in feigned agony. "You wound me, for I swear upon my honor all 'tis true."

"Then tell me more, good knight."

"Have I spoke of the time a friend of mine stormed into the brothel like a bull and jerked a knave up by the neck?"

Rowanne's gaze slid to Brandt. Her happiness would be complete if he would only ride nearer and participate in their foolishness. But he had turned cold lately. It broke her heart to see him so sullen.

"He did not. There is no mysterious friend, Desmond; you have made it all up. I do not believe you have such a friend," Rowanne challenged.

"Aye, milady, there is such a man. He is a man with

no past, but he does exist," Desmond said with chuckle and a conspiratorial wink at Brandt, who seemed to grow stiff and stern.

Brandt silently willed Desmond to stop, but he was not to be quelled. Desmond was at his best with an enthusiastic audience, and Rowanne was indeed eager to hear.

"My mysterious friend is a gallant rogue," Desmond continued. "In the Holy Lands he rescued a Sultan's two youngest daughters from bandits."

Rowanne drew in a breath. Her eyes grew wide. Brandt felt a surge of annoyance and pride.

"Say 'tis naught so, Desmond. What a brave man he must be."

"Ah, 'tis true, milady. Single-handed, with his sword singing through the air like a well-tuned lute, he saved the damsels' lives and honor."

"Your friend sounds like the veriest hero from a troubadour's lay." She laughed and her lashes swept down over her eyes. Brandt thought he would die from beholding the beauteous image.

"Aye, he is that, my lady, he is all that and more," Desmond said with another wink in Brandt's direction.

Rowanne found herself swiveling in her saddle to cast a curious gaze at Brandt. His jaw was rigid, held taut and immobile. Her heartbeat quickened when their gazes met.

"Leopold tells me we should reach your home by the morrow, lady," Desmond said, drawing her attention once again.

"Aye. The morrow, I trow." Rowanne felt little joy in the prospect. Suddenly the thought of having Geoffroi killed paled. Her thoughts were only on Brandt. She wondered if he would choose to leave the moment he had seen their bargain done.

She knew she must endeavor to find a way to keep him with her, in order to see Lady Margaret freed. Or was the reason because her heart contracted painfully at the thought of him leaving?

Brandt loosed Glandamore to hunt. She soared over heather blooming in shades from white to mauve among the coarse gray green bracken, flushing feathered game and four-footed creatures alike. Geese, ducks, cranes, and all manner of waterfowl rose from the mist-shrouded becks while ground-nesting birds exploded into the sky as she kited by.

With a clatter of antlers against the branch of an ash, a brocket sprang from the thicket and bounded across the glen. Fleet as a wisp of smoke, he vanished into the dense cover of an aspen grove. Coy, who had been as silent as Desmond had been vocal, swiftly nocked an arrow from his quiver. He held his longbow ready in case the hawk startled another hart into the open.

"Milady, you have turned your alms bag into a hedge-pig's home," Desmond said in his usual honey-smooth tones as he eyed Thorn peeking from the bag at Rowanne's waist.

Coy glared at him. "If ye would keep yer voice down I could get us meat for the pot," he said sharply. "If ye keep blathering ye will startle all the game."

" 'Tis gone by now," Desmond said with a chuckle and a careless gesture of his gauntlet-covered hand. " 'Tis said the young king favors his hedgepig baked and spiced."

As if he knew he was being discussed, Thorn nudged the leather flap up and stuck his head out of the alms bag. He blinked his obsidian black eyes against the brightness of the sun.

Rowanne smiled. "I cannot imagine eating such as Thorn. He is a sweet creature, but his aroma is most pungent."

"And what shall you do with our aromatic friend?"

"I will treasure him," Rowanne said, and nodded in Brandt's direction.

"An odd sort of token to receive from a mercenary, would you not say?" Desmond observed with a grin. "He doth look like a man who would give grief to a maiden and not gifts."

"I believe he saw a certain similarity between us."

Desmond's brows shot up. "Lady, forgive me, but unless I hath been blinded by your beauty, I see little resemblance betwixt you and the hedgepig."

Rowanne giggled. There was something so winning about Desmond, he could say anything and she would never be offended or grow weary of his foolishness. "We are of a kind 'neath our skins. We are both orphans in the world and 'struth we both have prickly and secluded ways."

"And yet it would seem you both have found a measure of safety with the stern knight who glares at me," Desmond observed dryly, his gaze flicking in Brandt's direction.

"Both Thorn and I have been fortunate to cross paths with Brandt le Revenant." Rowanne spoke softly, as she stared at Brandt's hard, unyielding jaw. She both dreaded and anticipated the moment she would see Irthing's gate—when he would slay Geoffroi and Leopold and free her from their evil hold.

Would he make another bargain with her? Could she tempt him with gold and promises of wealth? Or should she try to strike a bargain with Desmond du Luc? He was far more congenial than Brandt ever was. In fact, he acted almost eager to be in her company. Perchance he would be willing to help her save Lady Margaret.

But saving Lady Margaret is not the only reason I want to strike a new bargain with le Revenant. Even though it made her squirm in her saddle to admit it, she did not want to see Brandt le Revenant ride out of her life. When she looked at him her heartbeat quickened. When he touched her a strange, drawing hunger entered her body.

She wanted him to kiss her again. She wanted him to stay with her—to help her explore these newfound and barely understood feelings. She wanted . . .

Desmond trilled out romantic lays and troubadours' ballads as they rode. Coy had complained there would be no hunting, but Brandt was very near to drawing his dagger and doing violence upon his oldest friend. Desmond graced them with every conceivable bawdy alehouse rhyme. Each new limerick brought a mixture of embarrassed laughter and puzzlement to Rowanne's face.

Brandt wanted to throttle the knight with his bare hands. Desmond had a fine, strong voice, but Jesu, did he have to sing now? And to Rowanne?

And where was Harry? Brandt was near to madness wishing for Harold to bring word from the king. In fact, he was desperate for his liege to give him guidance about Rowanne and her fate. He wanted—needed to be prevented from putting her in a nunnery.

CHAPTER 14

Ye God, if only Desmond would shut his pie hole. Brandt cast what he hoped was his fiercest look in Desmond's direction, but the chortling knight had his mouth wide open and his eyes shut. He failed to see Brandt's fury. Then, to make matters all the more unbearable, Desmond began to trill out a ditty using Brandt's own name in place of the customary "Rab of Avinaunce."

"There was a knight named Brandt . . . who earned his living with sword and lance . . ." Desmond sang in his deep, melodious voice. "He traveled the yird with horse and hawking bird . . . and he gave no brigand a chance."

Even Leopold, who was listless and dull-eyed, chuckled low in his throat. Rowanne giggled behind her hand, then suddenly she laughed freely, her eyes twinkling with merry mischief. The sound was like water to a thirsty man.

Normally taciturn Coy even took a turn at rhyming, then Jonathan managed a verse or two.

"It appears the task now falls to you, Sir Brandt, to finish the lay," Rowanne challenged Brandt as she brought her palfrey abreast of Clwyd. "Or do your manly talents lack in the area of witty verse?"

She tilted her head and looked at him with a flirtatious expression. It made Brandt itch and burn to pull her into his arms, to kiss her until she was breathless, senseless. Or until she no longer smiled at Desmond.

"I fear so, milady, and my voice is naught so pleasing as our new companion's," Brandt grumbled. The more she smiled, the more his body tightened with longing. Having her soft eyes upon him was doing potent things to his entrails. His tarse hardened rapidly, making him shift awkwardly in his stirrups. Brandt accidently jabbed Clwyd with a spur, nearly sending him into a defensive rear as if in battle.

"Hold, Clwyd," Brandt commanded. The stallion's muscles bunched as he tried to obey Brandt's confusing signals. 'Struth, Brandt's own body was just as confused, just as perplexed as that of his horse. His mind fought to maintain control, to deny the attraction he felt for Rowanne, while his body craved her. His blood pumped hard and hot in his veins.

Jesu, all it took was a word or look and his body responded to the comely maiden. What would happen if she actually reached out and touched him today? Would he go up in flames like so much dry tinder?

An errant breeze brought a hank of Rowanne's hair blowing across her chin. Brandt longed to reach out and move it away, to rub the silken strands between thumb and forefinger, to feel her breath upon the back of his hand.

"Brandt?" Her voice ripped him from his delicious fantasy.

"Pardon, milady, I—" He glanced away, shocked by the intensity of his desire, chagrined that he was no longer master over his own flesh.

"Sir, le Revenant," Rowanne leaned forward slightly as she spoke, using his battle name. The soft blue wool pulled taut across her bosom. " 'Tis a matter of honor—

you *must* finish the ballad or be shamed before these men."

"Honor?" Brandt repeated dumbly. "Shamed?"

"Aye. All the men have rhymed—save you," She said softly.

"God's wounds, Brandt, finish the bloody tune so we may have some peace!" Leopold bellowed from his position at the back of the troop, his eye looking wide and fevered. He glared once at Rowanne and then looked away as if the sight of her turned his blood to water.

"Fie, I will do my best, lady, because you ask it, but you will doubtless be disappointed by my skills." Brandt tried to think of words that rhymed and not of the way the sun kissed Rowanne's flesh. He cleared his throat and fought the rising tide of lust.

"There was a woman of York, who was overly fond of pork," He mumbled.

"Louder, Brandt, we cannot hear ye!" Jonathan bellowed. Desmond and even quiet Coy sniggered behind their hands at the clumsy wit of Brandt's first line. Brandt fairly shouted the next line. "So she married a swineherd from Leithenrawn and—and—"

He searched his mind for words while a hot flush crept up his neck. "And now at dawn and nooning she eats brawn," he finished in a quick rush while his throat and face flushed with heat.

"That was the worst rhyme I ever heard!" Desmond crowed. "I have no fear that your skill is with a sword and not with your tongue. Though I have heard those with Norman blood are like to know what a tongue is for when with a wench."

Brandt flushed hotly. "Let us hear no more of my *blood*," he said, glaring at Desmond and making himself a promise that when he reached Irthing and settled himself in as baron—when the ruse of being strangers was gone—he would gift Desmond with a fortnight of

cleaning the garderobes to atone for his disrespect to
his overlord.

"Have a care, sir, that you do not anger my champion," Rowanne said. Then Brandt made the mistake
of glancing at her. His anger dissolved as his belly drew
tight. She had tilted her head back as she laughed. Her
eyes were shut, her long lashes rested on her cheeks.
The long, smooth column of her throat was bare—
inviting his hands to stroke it. Her lips were parted.

Exactly the way she would look if she were being
bedded.

Jesu, I want her, he thought in a sweaty rush of lust. *I
want the one maiden I cannot have.*

"Come, lady, ride by me and I will find more pleasing
rhymes to make you smile," Desmond said smoothly.

Rowanne nodded and put her heel to her palfrey's
side. Brandt watched her slender back whilst jealousy,
hot and bitter, flooded through him, almost crushing
the desire of a moment before . . . almost but not quite.

"Milady, since our traveling companion has no liking
for songs and stories, let us speak once again of your
home," Desmond said in his warm-honey voice. "Tell
me, what do you miss the most about the wild borderlands?"

Brandt narrowed his gaze and studied his oldest and
closest friend with a bitter sense of betrayal choking
him. Was Desmond deliberately baiting him—pushing
him to anger?

"I remember the way the wind felt blowing through
my hair," she said softly. "The wind does not come
gentle from the north, Desmond. It tears at Irthing's
walls and howls with a mournful sound, but I loved it
all the same."

Brandt shivered. Was it the wistful note in her voice
or was it the image of those molten tresses being kissed
by a north wind that made him feel hot and cold?

"In the springtime I would climb along the old
Roman wall and pick wild gillyflowers and thistles.

Father would be angry, fearful that Scots raiders would carry me off."

"Ah, 'tis a lonely job to be the father of a lovely maid," Desmond said with a winning smile that hinted of babes and years to come. The very thing Brandt dared not let himself want.

"Less than a league away from Irthing's large bailey lies a stone cairn. There are words cut deep in the stone. I spent hours as a little girl trying to understand them."

"And did you divine their meaning?"

"Nay. Only the old houndsman, Gruffudd, could divine the meaning. He told me it is the old legend of the Vaudrys."

Another cold and bitter thought came into Brandt's head. Could it be even remotely possible that Desmond was trying to usurp Brandt's claim to Irthing? Brandt could not credit the notion. After all, Desmond was the only child, an adopted son, of a rich baron, Basil du Luc. He would have all the du Luc lands and a fine fortune soon enough. Surely he did not covet Irthing.

But what about Rowanne? Did he covet a maid sweeter than wine and warmer than sunshine? Who could blame him if he did? He was a man, and Rowanne was the embodiment of feminine temptation.

Rowanne studied the two knights from under the fringe of her lashes. Brandt was all darkness, shadow, and barely restrained power. Desmond was golden light, smiles, charm, and compliments. 'Twas like looking at the nooning sun and the midnight sky. Where one man was shuttered and mysterious, the other was clear as a fast-running beck. Which one would be the better choice to save Lady Margaret? The question rolled over and over through Rowanne's mind.

Each time she looked at Brandt her pulse quickened and her stomach knotted with unsoothed desire. But when she was with Desmond there was a sense of something being made whole—there was a *rightness* in his presence that she could not explain but could not easily ignore.

Each man had qualities that made her wish to select him as rescuer of her friend. The choice she made would likely determine whether or not she would be victorious over Thomas and Geoffroi, or whether she would once again have to bear the burden of failure. She could not afford to let feelings of desire cloud her judgment.

Without meaning to, she let her gaze fell upon Leopold. The very air around him seemed to crackle with madness and a dark portent of events about to unfold.

I wilt be forced to choose. For Lady Margaret I needs must pick the right man—the right knight to see DeLucy slain. And with that thought running through her head, Rowanne lapsed into silence, lost in thought and contemplation.

"Tell me, sir, have you been in the Holy Lands?" Desmond asked Brandt with a bland expression on his face.

Brandt glared at him, disgusted with the ruse of pretending to be strangers. "Aye," he bit out the word, wishing that Desmond would stop drawing him into these conversations. And did he have to smile so much—especially at Rowanne?

"I too have fought in the Holy wars," Desmond said lightly, as if Brandt truly had no knowledge of him.

"Indeed." Brandt nearly snarled his response.

"Sir, you are fair stingy with your words," Rowanne said pleasantly as she cantered up beside them.

Brandt looked at her and felt the air rush from his lungs. He wanted to drag her from her rouncy, to kiss her again. He wanted to show Desmond and Leopold and Rowanne herself that she was . . . his?

But she was not his. She was the heiress to Irthing, the betrothed of his half brother. Rowanne Vaudry was many things, but she was not now, nor would she ever be, his. She would never belong to the bastard son of Thomas DeLucy.

With one last look at her face and form, a look he prayed would last him a lifetime, Brandt put his spurs to Clwyd and galloped north, toward his destiny, with a new and frightening sense of the unknown. For somewhere in the depths of Rowanne's azure blue eyes and the road to Cumbria, Brandt had lost his craving to use Rowanne for revenge.

The first glimpse of the Cumbrian hills awakened something in Rowanne that had been sleeping. Emotions crowded her chest, made it tight and hard to catch her breath. She stared across the rolling hills and sparkling burns, and beyond, where the country began to flatten out. Verdant hedgerows dwindled and disappeared until they were completely replaced by harsh, dry stone walls. Pine, copper beech, and old-growth oaks dotted the landscape. Pale yellow flowers bloomed among the thorns of the gorse.

Cumbria. The country of her birth. This was the wild, rolling vista that fed her soul. Its memory had kept her alive while she was imprisoned, after hope for her father to rescue her finally died.

Her heart beat harder inside her chest. Memories that had lain buried rushed to the surface like air bubbles through the water. Hot tears stung the backs of her eyes, and for some reason she wished Desmond to tell her a bawdy tale, to comfort her turbulent thoughts.

Her soul hung betwixt and between, on one side euphoria, on the other despair as she realized that her dream of coming home was nearly fulfilled.

Why? Why the torn emotions? Was she miserable because her mercenary, her warrior, her sword of vengeance would do as he bargained and then disappear from her life? Or was it the knowledge that a choice lay before her.

She could feel it, smell it on the crisp air. The time was coming nigh when she would look at Desmond, all bright light and smiles, and then at Brandt, clothed in shadow and secrets, and she would choose.

She would have to choose. Which knight would she have as her champion? She turned to look at Brandt, momentarily stunned by how proud and impossibly handsome he was. Glandamore perched upon his pommel, looking almost as arrogant as her master-knight. Brandt's dark eyes and nostrils flared as he returned Rowanne's gaze. He was all male, strong and virile as the stallion he rode. He was wildness embodied.

Then she glanced at Desmond and a feeling of kinship—of loyalty and friendship swept through her. He was light and kind words. He offered comfort and stability in a way that Brandt could not.

She closed her eyes against them both. How could she choose? How? They were different as hot from cold, light from dark. She could not choose, but choose she must.

CHAPTER 15

Castle Irthing was near. She could feel it, sense it deep in her core. Her destiny awaited. She thought of the gown she wore, of the hedgehog Brandt had rescued, and of the way his eyes skimmed over her face and made her pulse quicken. He was strong and fine, but he was a wandering knight—as lief to be kept in one place as the wind.

And then she thought of Desmond. He was all courtly manners and teasing smiles. He had a calming effect on her. Where Brandt made her pulse quicken, her heart pound, her blood rush through her veins, Desmond made her think of peaceful hearths.

"Fear naught. You have my pledge of protection," Brandt's voiced rippled over her, and she realized that he was riding no more than an arm's length away. "No harm will befall you as long as there is breath in my body. You may trust your life to me, lady."

She sucked in a shuddering breath. She struggled to find words to tell him that she had to choose.

"Smile for me, lady. Lift my heart and soul with your beautiful smile. Give me this gift, for it may be the only one I shall ever have from you," Brandt said, his eyes sad.

She tried, truly she did. She managed to lift the corners of her mouth, but no joy was in her heart. And Rowanne's strange, melancholy gesture clawed at Brandt's soul. He had allowed himself, like a fool, to hope that upon their arrival at Cumbria some magical change would happen and that somehow, some way, he could have a future with Rowanne. But now he faced the folly of such a hope.

"I wilt see you safe and well settled," he announced, a myriad of conflicting emotions sizzling through him. It no longer mattered what the king's decision was. Brandt could not allow himself to usurp Rowanne's position at Irthing Keep.

Besides, since she was a great heiress, Henry was probably even now naming her a husband, a powerful baron who would be worthy of her. Mayhap Desmond du Luc himself, though that thought brought equal portions of fury, sadness, and frustration ripping through Brandt's mind.

He had no one to blame but himself. By the very action of allowing himself to believe Rowanne was truly Rowanne Vaudry, and by sending word to King Henry, Brandt had sealed his fate. He told himself that he did thus because he was a loyal subject of the king's will. But in his heart he knew the truth. He had sent word to the king hoping secretly that Henry would stop him from committing Rowanne to a nunnery, would command him to give all to Rowanne and be her champion until a man worthy of her was selected to be her betrothed.

A part of Brandt still tried to hope it would be him, but he knew that the only way he could be truly worthy of her was to be lord of Castle Irthing—and in order to be that he would have to cheat her of her birthright and banish her behind high, cloistered walls. No matter what Brandt might see in his dreams, no matter what his lust craved, he could not change the fact that he was Thomas's bastard, doomed to be hated by Rowanne.

So he drank in her beauty, and let his heart bleed and die for what would never be.

Bluebells, gorse oaks, and grazing herds of herdwicks cast long, distorted shadows over the heath. The party was rushing forward now, at a hurried pace, as if wolves nipped at their heels. Soon they would reach her keep, and he would be obliged to kill Geoffroi. And then he would have no more excuse to remain with her.

For one mad moment he thought of dragging her from the palfrey and riding off into the gloaming, forgetting king and country and loyal men. Brandt had become so besotted he was almost willing to abduct her to keep her with him.

Almost.

He was a knight. Honor bound him to keep his word and do his duty.

The gentle palfrey snorted and cast wild glances toward the forest of English oaks. 'Twas lambing time and the fields were alive with predators. Foxes skulked and sneaked in the long shadows. The horses blew and snorted, smelling the invaders nearby, sensing the death of the innocent and weak. Or was it Geoffroi's pending death they sensed?

And then, with the sky colored like the flesh of a salmon, they saw it—like a giant serpent slithering across England. The sight of it caught Rowanne's eye and made her pulse quicken.

"The Roman wall," she said. The sturdy stone bulwark sliced the isle in half, twining and climbing across the moors. It signaled the outer reaches of young Henry's kingdom just as it had marked the outer edges of Roman influence.

"We will reach Irthing anon." Rowanne put her heels to the palfrey's side. "I am at last home." Her voice drifted over her shoulder on the wind.

Heeding the call of a voice only she could hear, Rowanne urged her mare to more speed. Riding recklessly over the treacherous hillocks, down dales and fells, she raced east toward Irthing, toward the decision she must inevitably make.

The long black shadows had taken on a life of their own, and full darkness of night was only a whisper away when Irthing appeared against the gloaming sky. Glandamore shifted on Brandt's arm and trilled her throaty noise. The clouds suddenly sped away and the first glint of moonbeams cast shimmering iridescence on the keep. Towers, turrets, and grotesque figures appeared in the silvery light at every corner and juncture.

"Irthing," Rowanne whispered in a breathy voice. "Home."

Brandt turned to stare at her, stunned by her elegant profile, limned in the argent glow of the unholy light. Her hair had turned silver-blue, her eyes a pale echo of the moon.

"Isn't it beautiful?" She whispered. "And 'tis mine. All you see belongs to me, Brandt. I truly am the heiress of Irthing."

There was an eerie silence on the heath, broken only by the mournful soughing of wind as it swept around the stone edifice. Remarkably, even Desmond was silent as the group saw the drawbridge was down, the portcullis open and inviting. Nary a single guard or even the flicker of a fire within the gatehouse broke the enchantment of moonglow.

Brandt shifted Glandamore to his shoulder and drew his sword. Clwyd overtook the palfrey on the rocky path that split the estuary in twain, forming the fresh moat she had spoken of. The soft, lapping sound of water against stone and the breathing of the horses sounded unnaturally loud.

"Brandt?" Rowanne questioned when he pulled Clwyd up short and blocked her mare's path.

"Keep you behind me," he ordered in a rusty voice.

"Sir? I am *home.* Now all will be put to rights—"

"Nay. Something is not a'right, lady. No proper guard

sees nightfall with the drawbridge down and the portcullis up to allow entry. I have heard not one guard. Keep you behind me.'' He gave her one fierce glance and then put his spurs to Clwyd's side.

The destrier thundered across the lowered drawbridge. Desmond and Coy galloped after him, leaving Rowanne behind with Jonathan and Leopold, who was whispering Paternosters and other chanting prayers beneath his breath.

Rowanne glared at him. Since when did Thomas's hell-hound take up prayer and devotion at every eve? Or did he sense his death was nigh at hand and was wisely making peace with God?

The hair on Brandt's arms was raised on end as he rode under the raised portcullis. What kind of men-at-arms left the keep's drawbridge down, the gate unguarded? Brandt had heard more than one gruesome tale of the Scots marauders and how less of an invitation than this could result in death.

Just what sort of lord had no more care than this for his demesne? Surely Thomas's golden son Geoffroi had more in his head than porridge. Geoffroi DeLucy had been a soft youth, with spotty skin and a weak stomach, but surely the last ten years had hardened him and made a man of him. And yet, as Brandt rode through the outer bailey and beyond the lower yird to the inner gate, he saw no guard, encountered no resistance, heard no cry of halt. 'Twas as if Irthing was empty.

Brandt rode to the very steps of the great keep itself before he dismounted and urged Glandamore onto the pommel of his saddle. He held his sword at the ready, listening to the low keening wail of the wind. Moonlight skimmed over Brandt's blade like a lover's caress.

Rowanne had been right about the wind. It did not come gentle from the north. It cut raw and wild around the upper battlements, soughing with a mournful groan and skrilling screech as it whistled through narrow passages between barracks, mews, and stables. It sounded like a wailing woman.

Brandt glanced up at the grotesque statues fixed on each corner of the keep's battlements, his body tense with curiosity and anticipation.

"My lord, do you wish for us to search the castle?" Desmond asked, dropping all pretense of being strangers.

Brandt glanced at Leopold, who had finally followed them inside. He had no reaction to Desmond's words. The one-eyed brute was staring gap-mouthed at the keep before him. His eye flicked and darted as if watching specters only he could see. And now he struggled to unsheathe his sword, but the hand that gripped the hilt trembled like a reed in the wind.

"Aye, Desmond, take Coy to the outbuildings. See if any living thing bides within these walls. Have a care and report back to me anon."

Rowanne entered the bailey on her palfrey. In her blue woolen bliaut, on the gray rouncy, she appeared to be surrounded by a magical cerulean glow.

"Aye, my lord." Desmond turned and flashed Rowanne a smile that made Brandt's gorget rise.

Brandt's heart leaped within his chest at the sight of her. Then his fury at her disobedience flared and drove back his lust. The headstrong little cabbage had ignored his warning—again. She had put herself directly in harm's way by her stubbornness and refusal to do his bidding.

"By all that is holy!" Brandt had hoped to deal with Geoffroi without Rowanne seeing or hearing the bloody business. He had wished to spare her that horror, but it was also his most heartfelt wish that she should never know he was Thomas's bastard son. But when she heard the confrontation between him and Geoffroi, she would know.

She would hate him.

He could not bear that.

He was too much a coward to stand against her loathing. Jesu, she had made him a eunuch. Worry and regret had become his constant companions. Each soft, mewling emotion threatened to take the courage from his convictions. But he steeled himself against any weakness. He turned his thoughts away from Rowanne and the temptation she represented.

From the corner of his eye he saw a shape slither in the shadows near the curtain wall. Then another and another, slipping like silent death toward Rowanne's horse. He spun to face them. Brandt forgot his anger and his disgust with himself as he focused on those dark shapes. All but his desire to protect Rowanne was forgotten as he hefted his sword, catching the scent of rank fur, seeing a glimpse of feral eyes.

They melted from the shadows, moving ever closer to Rowanne. Moonlight glinted on bared fangs. He raised his sword and with a mighty battle cry launched his body into the pack of hungry wolves.

All he could think of was protecting sweet Rowanne.

CHAPTER 16

The palfrey reared and screamed in terror, her sound blending with the scream on Rowanne's own lips. Jesu. Brandt would be ripped to shreds.

Her heart threatened to leap from her breast. Rowanne screamed and screamed again, but the sound was lost among the horrific din of snapping jaws and growls. Clwyd rose up on his hind legs, pawing and kicking. She was afraid Brandt would be killed a tangle of frothing mouths and flying hooves.

"Help, someone help!" Rowanne shrieked. Leopold stood mute, his eye glazed with a strange inner fever, useless.

"Help him. Curse you, can you not see he needs help?" She addressed the one-eyed man, but he acted as though he could not hear her as he just stared dumbly at the thick oaken door of the keep, oblivious to the danger of the pack.

One massive animal almost brought Brandt down, but with a howl of rage he tossed him aside and kept his feet beneath him. There he stood with legs braced wide apart, ready to take another onslaught. The blade of his sword glistened in the moonlight. A semicircle of snarling beasts moved toward him, watching, waiting for an opening or a lapse in his concentration.

"Cymerwch ofal!" A booming male voice sliced through the night with utter authority. "Dere! Tyrd!"

The bailey went still as a tomb. Brandt's harsh breathing blended with the soughing wind. The snarling jaws of the pack snapped shut. Even the wind lessened. 'Twas as if every living thing understood the deep Welsh command that came from the shadows of the curtain wall.

But who had bellowed that command? Rowanne peered into the shadows, but the darkness was too thick, too impenetrable. Like suckling pups, the beasts made their way in a slathering, crouching, submissive group. They lay down, whimpering, whining at the feet of a tall, slat-thin shadow that separated itself from the gray stones of Irthing. The man's face was lined and weathered as the Cumbrian hills, his tunic stained and worn, his eyes deep and wise.

"Gruffudd!" Rowanne slid from the saddle and ran toward the old man. Her heart thumped a loud cadence as her slippers crunched on the stones of the bailey.

"Rowanne—go back!" Brandt took a step as if to stop her headlong flight, but she sidestepped him like a nimble hind.

"Ah, Thistledown, can it really be you?" Long sinewy arms wrapped Rowanne into a bone-crushing embrace.

"Aye, 'tis me. I have come home at last, Gruffudd."

"I ne'er thought to see you again—yet I hoped the old prophesy mightn't be true." The old man stroked her golden hair with a gnarled hand. "Let me look at ye."

Rowanne stepped away a pace. She was weeping with happiness.

"With the moonlight on yer face, ye are the image of yer mother."

"Rowanne?" Brandt was feeling confused and helpless beyond endurance. Rowanne's tears were more lethal than a battle mace. "*Rowanne?*"

She turned to him then, as if only just realizing she was not alone with the thin man and the huge predators, now cowering at the man's feet as if he were some pagan god.

"Brandt, this is Gruffudd, the houndmaster of Irthing." She wiped the back of her hand against her cheek as if the tears that fair robbed Brandt of his manhood were no more than a nuisance to her.

"Sir." Gruffudd acknowledged Brandt coolly in his thick Welsh accent.

Brandt tore his gaze from Rowanne and glanced at Gruffudd. Then, for the first time Brandt really looked at the dozen hairy bodies gathered at the houndmaster's feet. They were not wolves at all, but grizzled hunting hounds of a size and breadth that were startling. The pack was all muscle, sinew, and fawning adoration for Gruffudd. Despite their current submissiveness, Brandt was not deceived. A moment ago they were nigh ripping out his throat. They were lethal as wolves.

What manner of household bided within Irthing?

"Ah, Thistledown, now that you are home matters wi' be put to rights," the houndmaster said. His long, knotted fingers gently stroked the thick fur of the tallest dog at his side.

"Where is everyone, Gruffudd? Irthing is so quiet. Where are the men-at-arms, why is there no guard?" Rowanne asked.

"All gone, milady—all save me and the alaunts. Those that did not die of the pestilence went to live in the village. None would stay after your father died. They say that Castle Irthing is haunted by the ghost of your mother and your brothers. I have nigh come to believe it myself."

"Nay . . . nay." Leopold suddenly lurched forward. His eye was wide and white-rimmed. "The spirits of the sons *cannot* walk here! 'Tis not possible. Only the dead walk here." He spread his arms wide to indicate the bailey. The tip of his sword wobbled in his weak grip.

The pack of dogs snarled at Leopold. Their hackles bristled as he staggered near Gruffudd. A low, vibrating growl echoed through the bailey.

"The sons cannot walk as spirits!" He said again with a moan. "Rowanne's brothers cannot bide here—they are not ghosts," Leopold babbled in a voice gone high. He swung, barely keeping his balance as if he had been at the wineskin. His eye flicked and darted over the iron-studded door of Castle Irthing's hall, and then suddenly it fixed on something that was visible only to him.

"There. There! Do you see her? Do you see Rowena? For the love of God, say you see her!" Leopold made a strangled sound, stumbling backward, dropping his sword on the stones with a clatter. His face contorted as if he were in pain, and he clawed at his sightless eye with trembling fingers.

"She has come for me. Say you see her there with her arms out."

"By the Rood, he hast gone mad," Brandt said.

Leopold swung round drunkenly. As his gaze fell upon Rowanne he sagged to his knees and knitted his fingers together as if in supplicant prayer. "Oh, by all that is holy, must you devil me so, Rowena? 'Twas naught meant to happen. Please, please, Rowena, you must believe me. Give me peace, give me absolution . . . forgive me. Rowena, I beg of you. Forgive."

"By the Rood, what possesses the brute?" Desmond asked. He and Coy had returned from their search to find Leopold babbling at Rowanne's feet.

Leopold cried out and clutched his bristly head in both hands. A low, keening sound from deep within his chest made Rowanne's blood chill in her veins. Then suddenly he staggered to his feet, looking around.

"Where is Geoffroi DeLucy?" Leopold asked, casting a fearful glance at the shadows in the bailey. "Geoffroi will save me. He will know how to banish Rowena of Fontmell, wife of Etienne. He will know how to quiet the spirit of Etienne Vaudry's wife. Aye, Geoffroi is a powerful lordling; he will make her say she forgives me."

Gruffudd frowned darkly at Leopold. "Geoffroi wilt be no help to you, for he now dwells within the walls of Lanercost Priory."

"Too cowardly to remain in a haunted keep, eh?" Desmond said with a snort.

"Nay. Nay, I say. Go, bring him here. He will save me!"

Brandt watched Leopold while his gut twisted in disgust. Jesu, he hated the man, but to see him go mad was a horrible sight and one he would lief spare Rowanne. Brandt heaved a great sigh. "Desmond, take Coy and hasten to Lanercost Priory. Bring back Geoffroi DeLucy and a priest with knowledge of medicaments for Leopold. I fear he will not keep his wits nor his life through this night."

Desmond turned to Rowanne and offered her a quick smile. "Fear not, lady, for I will return anon. All will be well."

Brandt fought the violent surge of jealousy that snaked through him as he watched his men mount and thunder into the moonlit night.

Brandt's spurs echoed on the stone floor, crushing the pitiful remains of ancient dried rushes underfoot with each angry step. The scent of mildew tainted the air along with the sound of scurrying rodents. He fleetingly thought that Glandamore would soon have a feast.

Irthing was a sorry reward for the wounds he had suffered in the name of his king, but the deserted demesne was an even worse legacy for Rowanne. Brandt's thoughts slid from this tumbledown pile of stones to her.

If he was sorely disappointed by Irthing, then what pain did she feel at seeing her home reduced to a moldering pile of deserted stones inhabited by dogs and one old man? She had pinned much hope on this legacy. She had dreamed of reaching Irthing and returning to a life she remembered.

Gruffudd trundled in with gray, aged wood piled in his arms. He bent and laid the kindling in the stone hearth of the great hall. The dried logs caught quickly, but the leaping flames did little to make the hall more habitable. As light crept into the dark corners the degree of neglect and ruin was revealed.

The entire room was one ugly shade of gray owing to the thick layer of dust that covered all. What few pieces of furniture remained were draped in thick cobwebs. Tattered tapestries hung limp and tired; the odor of decay was thick in the air, and in spite of the fire, deep shadows moved and danced in the corners as if they were ghosts who refused to be banished.

'Twas easy to understand why the rumor of wraiths and hauntings had begun. Irthing had a spectral tomblike aura about it. If he were a man prone to believe in old legends and superstitions, Brandt might indeed believe that Irthing was haunted—as Leopold evidently did.

Thomas's man had lapsed into a quivering stupor, barely rousing even whilst Gruffudd and Brandt carried him before the hearth. They settled him there beside the fire, but he seemed not to notice or care where he was.

Rowanne stood staring down at him, her shoulders slumped and tired as if the sight of Irthing had laid a great weight upon her.

"It is all gone. All the laughter, all the prosperity. Where did it all go, Brandt?" Her voice was a painful whisper.

Brandt longed to enfold her in his arms and assure her that the morrow would come and she would be a'right. He wanted to soothe her brow with his fingers, to kiss her soft throat and murmur words of encouragement to her. Mayhap if he enfolded her in an embrace and told her that it did not signify that her birthright was in ruin, that he was still her champion and he would'st protect her, mayhap that would comfort her.

I will make it all right.

But how could he make such a promise when her home lay in ruins? When he himself had all along planned to put her in a nunnery, to take what remained of Irthing—to use her as a cudgel to make Thomas pay for all the pain? How could he vow to make her tomorrow bright and happy when her past was constructed on pain and sadness just as his was?

"What has brought the castle to this ruin?" Brandt asked Gruffudd, as if the knowledge of what had been might wipe away the sting of what would never be.

"First 'twas the fever. It came swiftly and laid low the strongest men of the keep. A house of pestilence was set up at the curtain wall. Soon the barracks lay empty, the boneyard full."

"Is the village outside the wall in this dire condition as well?" Brandt asked, wondering if there were even enough peasants left to provide servants for Irthing's needs if and when it was restored.

"Nay, the village is thriving, in spite of the barbarians from the north raiding it as regular as moon waning."

"The village is without protection?"

"Aye. The men-at-arms of Irthing were all the protection they had; now there is nobody to halt the bandits. Scots reivers are like a pack of hungry dogs. They are led by Lochlyn Armstrong, a bloodthirsty brute who moves like smoke. Nobody is even sure of what he looks like. He strikes in the dark and slips away to his stronghold deep in the glens. He took the sheep and the cattle. Then all the horses who no longer had knights to ride them. Etienne Vaudry's best furnishings—even the supply of woolfells was stolen from Irthing, but the village yet survives. Solway Firth in the west and Newcastle in the east keep the craftsmen busy enough to keep them from starving no matter how often Lochlyn raids."

Brandt surveyed the ruins of the great hall. How could Rowanne survive in this bleak place, without family, without a protector? Without him?

Gervais's ghostly voice mocked him with a sharper question: How would Brandt survive without Rowanne?

Gruffudd shook his shaggy gray head. " 'Tis said Rowena's spirit is against all those with DeLucy blood and the men who failed to prevent what happened to her and her children."

Brandt frowned. These changes were more recent than the bloody night when Rowanne lost her family. "How long has Irthing been deserted and completely unprotected?"

"More than a twelvemonth by my reckoning." Gruffudd scratched his bristly chin.

Brandt swung around. "Only a twelvemonth?" He tentatively nudged one of the deceptively docile hounds from his path. He stared out an arrow port, gazing at the moonlit path Desmond and Coy had taken. "Irthing's lord, Etienne, was not ill for many years before he died?" Brandt could not understand. "Etienne Vaudry was not racked and bedridden since his wife was murdered?" Brandt asked, awaiting the answer he dreaded to hear.

"Nay, milord. Rowanne's father was hale and hearty though his heart had been broken since the death of Lady Rowena and his two sons." Gruffudd scratched again. " 'Twas so grieved he never even had stones carved for the boys' graves. Only Rowena's resting place is marked. 'Tis as if the sons never lived."

"Or never died," Brandt muttered absently. Rage and impotent fury were building inside him. "If Etienne Vaudry had been ablebodied, then why did he not try to rescue Rowanne? Why did Etienne abandon Rowanne to the likes of Thomas DeLucy?" Brandt heard himself demand. "If he loved her so well, I wonder that he did he not bring her home?"

"I know not, sir. I myself urged him to ride to Sherborne and bring her back. He said he could not, that he was bound by chains stronger than iron. He refused to tell me what bound him when I had the spleen to challenge my lord and ask it of him." Gruffudd's shoulders slumped.

" 'Twas the only time I was ever 'shamed of him. But I would have forgiven him if I'd had the chance 'afore he left this earth. I had been sent to the Priory and when I returned the old lord was dead. The next morning Geoffroi DeLucy quit the keep and has bided with the brothers at the priory since."

"Geoffroi DeLucy was with Etienne Vaudry when he died? Alone?" Suspicion twined through Brandt's gut.

"Aye, it was just the two of them. 'Twas the bitterest draught of all that Etienne died with the son of his oldest enemy as his only confessor. What a sorry ending—with a DeLucy at his side."

"And you have stayed here at Irthing since, keeping the hounds?" Brandt felt a strange grudging affection for the houndmaster.

"Aye, I felt honor bound to see to the keep as best I could in case."

"In case what?" Brandt asked with a lift of his brows.

"In case the legend be true," Gruffudd said with wide, round eyes.

Brandt was about to ask the old Welshman what legend, but the sound of iron-shod hooves on the drawbridge halted the words in his gullet. With one last look at Rowanne's sad, bowed head, he strode from the keep.

Moonlight gave the inner bailey a liquid-blue patina. Every dark shadow seemed longer, more sinister, as Brandt strode forward, intent upon locating Geoffroi— killing him, to free Rowanne from Thomas's web.

"Brandt, wait." The sound of Rowanne's voice stayed his feet. He turned to find her running down the steps.

She looked like an avenging angel going into battle with her hair flying behind her like a pale pennon.

His heart hammered hard against the inside of chest. He wanted her with a heat so intense he felt scorched from the inside out.

"You are to going to fulfill your oath?" She asked breathlessly. "You are going to slay Geoffroi?"

"Aye, lady, I am your champion onto death." Did she doubt him yet? Without meaning to, he let his gaze fall upon Desmond. A shaft of lingering doubt pierced his heart. "Or did you think to have another champion your cause?"

She hesitated. In that moment a bitter river of jealousy and possessiveness flowed unchecked through Brandt's soul.

"Nay, you are my champion."

Brandt clasped the hilt of his sword, needing to feel something solid in his grip. "As you say, my lady. Then let us see about the completion of our bargain."

"If—*when* you are victorious and I am no longer bound to Geoffroi—"

"Aye?" Loneliness swamped him, but he held his ground, drinking in the sight and scent of her.

"There is another matter I would speak with you about," she said shyly.

"The freeing of your companion from Thomas?" Brandt asked softly. "I have expected as much."

She looked up at him, surprise shining in her eyes. "Aye. That and one other matter. With my birthright in ruins there is no hope any will see me as a great heiress. I no longer command wealth and position—"

"Fear not. Our bargain has been struck and I will keep my oath to you." He studied her face while a question burned in his dark mind—a question he dare not ask or even allow himself to think.

"Then draw your sword and kneel before me, good knight." She commanded, softening her words with a smile. "I pray thee to kneel before me, sir. And give me your sword," she added softly.

Time seemed to halt. Brandt could barely breathe with Rowanne so near. His heart skipped a beat.

He wanted to slay dragons for her. He wanted to rebuild Castle Irthing to its former glory, wanted to kill Geoffroi *for her*. He wanted to do it all and saw no way 'tween heaven and earth to do any of it.

"As you bid, milady." He drew the sword and handed it to her, hilt first. His mail clattered as he settled himself on one knee, catching the sweet musk of her scent with each halting breath he managed to draw into his lungs.

Rowanne needed to use both hands, but she took his sword.

"In the name of God and king and country, I name thee, Brandt le Revenant, High Protector, Captain of the Guard, and Defender of the house of Vaudry."

Rowanne raised the sword and laid the flat part on his shoulder over the blood-red material of his surcoat.

"Now rise, sir Brandt. Go with God to vanquish all my enemies."

He gained his feet and stared down at the sword pommel she thrust back into his palm. Her words, her gesture, had touched him more deeply than the deeded property and title of baron that Henry had bestowed upon him at his court in Winchester. Not since Brandt had earned his spurs had he felt so humble and unworthy. The weight of his responsibilities was keen and sharp upon his soul.

"Now, 'tis done." Without warning Rowanne stood on tiptoe and kissed him full upon the lips. He gave up his last bit of control then and crushed her to him. He kissed her greedily, hungry for her taste, eager to heft the weight of her, to commit this moment to his memory.

His tongue plundered her mouth, moving in the way he wanted to move inside her, whilst he told himself that he would have only this magic moment to last him a lifetime. When he released her and looked down into her face she was breathing in shallow little gasps.

"Brandt, when this is done—"

"Nay, say no more." He laid his finger gently on her lips. "I will keep our bargain. Then we will both do what fate and our station in life say we must. But know this, little temptress, I will carry that kiss with me all the days of my life."

CHAPTER 17

The sound of a wagon rumbling over the drawbridge shattered the bewitching silence of the keep.

"We have brought the prior and—" Desmond began only to have his words cut off by a churchman.

"I am Prior Simon of the Augustinian Canons of Lanercost," a robust monk with a bluff voice and barrel-like girth interrupted. "What is amiss? Is someone dying? Injured? In need of healing?" The prior yanked the donkey to a halt. "What has happened now within these benighted walls?" The priest raised his robe high enough to expose stout, hairy legs as he leapt to the ground to be followed by another monk, tall, reed-slender, and silent.

But there was no Geoffroi DeLucy.

"We have a man within who has gone mad," Brandt said.

"Show me where the poor soul awaits." The prior lifted his robe shin-high and took the worn stone steps at a gallop, surprisingly agile for a man as round as an oaken wine barrel.

Brandt stepped in front of the prior, blocking his way. "Where is Geoffroi DeLucy?"

Prior Simon waved his hand as if being annoyed by

a gnat. "Stand aside. There is time enough for all that later. Now lead me to the fallen man." The prior brushed past Brandt as if he were a stripling youth instead of an armored knight bristling to do battle.

"Nay, Prior Simon. You will not give medicaments until I learn the whereabouts of Geoffroi DeLucy." Brandt narrowed his eyes and placed his hand on the pommel of his sword.

The monk looked up at him and blinked in surprise. "You think to prevent me from doing God's work? By violence?" Incredulity rang in his words. "Be you not afraid of the Lord's wrath?"

"I mean no harm to you or your brother, but you *will* tell me where Geoffroi DeLucy bides," Brandt told the man in a dangerously soft voice. "Now, where is he? Is he coming? Is he riding behind you?" His blood was heavy with hatred and the need to protect Rowanne.

Prior Simon's head snapped around. His penetrating eyes skimmed the group standing there as if seeing them for the first time. From Coy to Desmond and then back to Brandt. "What is amiss, sir? Why are you battle-hardened knights here at Irthing?"

"I have come to clai—to challenge Geoffroi to combat."

"Challenge? Combat?" Prior Simon shook his head, setting his florid jowls jiggling. "Have you gone mad? 'Twould mean your soul. This is a tangled web of foolishness you speak. No man will challenge Geoffroi DeLucy, for to raise a hand against him is to invite perdition and the fires of hell."

"I am not a'frighted of Geoffroi, nor of death and damnation," Brandt said fiercely. "Now tell me where I may find the coward. We have a debt that is owing and needs must be paid this eve."

"Foolish man. Sheathe your sword, in the name of all that is holy, and show me the fallen man!" The churchman grasped the heavy cross that hung from a cord around his neck.

Brandt glared at the prior. His hand tightened reflexively on the hilt of his broadsword. The other monk moved forward and stepped in front of Prior Simon as if to shield him from Brandt's blade. For the first time Brandt spared the other monk a quick glance.

His hairline was so high that only a slender fringe of pale, wispy hair separated it from his tonsure. The eyes that bored into Brandt's face were pale, fixed intently as if to convey some silent message. Slowly, a niggling shaft of recognition and truth pierced Brandt's mind.

He loosened his grip on the hilt. "Nay, it cannot be. I believe it not. 'Tis a trick to keep me from shedding blood."

Prior Simon bustled forward, his face a stern mask. "It is no trick. There will be no combat with Geoffroi DeLucy—not this night or any other." He speared Brandt with a glare. "Brother Geoffroi is now part of our holy order. In the past twelvemonth he has given no offense—has broken no rules of our order. Any grievance you have from the past must be set aside before God Almighty. You see before you a devout man of God. He once was known as Geoffroi of Sherborne but now is Brother Geoffroi."

A bitter taste rose in Brandt's gorget as he stared dumb and disbelieving into the pale eyes of his half brother—the monk.

Brandt studied his brother. Geoffroi had changed little, save that his skin was no longer spotty. He was still lean and pale. Within the cowl he appeared young, resembling more a stripling youth playing at being a monk. But he still bore the same look of Thomas about the eyes. And yet, gone was the arrogant tilt of his mouth. In its place was a humility and genuine piousness that stripped Brandt of his lingering anger.

A monk could not do battle. And neither could he marry. Rowanne was safe from Thomas's plan to wed her to Geoffroi.

In the glare of his half brother's pale eyes the last bit

of Brandt's icy quest for vengeance melted away into the windswept night. This man was no threat to Rowanne. Even had he not been wearing monk's robes, Brandt could see he was not like his father, Thomas. Geoffroi did not deserve to die for his father's sins. And there was a poetic rightness to what had happened, for the Church would rival Thomas in grabbing land and property.

If Thomas still wanted Irthing he would be obliged to move against Rowanne openly, and that, Brandt thought wryly, was an action Thomas would never take. His father was a master at plots and intrigues. He would embroil himself in one machination after another, but he would never openly risk the king's displeasure by storming the walls of Irthing. And by now the news of Rowanne's return from the dead would be all over Winchester.

Rowanne was safe from all the DeLucy threats. *Safe.*

Brandt stared into the beseeching eyes of his half brother, and he felt a strange joy at the recognition reflected back at him. Geoffroi knew him. But now Geoffroi would speak his name and reveal Brandt's past. His lineage would be known to one and all. This would be the moment he would see hatred in Rowanne's eyes.

"Why did you not speak at once, Geoffroi? Why did you not reveal yourself?" Brandt asked, expecting his secret to be revealed in the next heartbeat.

"Lord give me the virtue of patience!" Prior Simon blustered. "Brother Geoffroi cannot answer your questions. Upon entry into our order he took a solemn vow of silence and wilt not break it. Have I not said he is an obedient man of God?"

Brandt rocked back on the balls of his feet. His brother was mute by vow to God. Brandt's heart took up a wild cadence while the impact of all that meant swept through him. *Geoffroi cannot tell Rowanne I am his half brother.*

Suddenly an unholy shriek filled the air.

"By the saints!" Coy crossed himself. "That came from the hall."

"Sounds like a man is dying," the prior said.

"Aye, 'tis Leopold," Brandt said. "I left Gruffudd to watch him in case he roused; 'twould seem that he has indeed come awake."

"Lord grant me forbearance from knavish knights," Prior Simon muttered low under his breath. "They would blather and cry for battle. The spawn of Satan, but at least they have taken up the cross to regain Jerusalem." He picked up his robe and climbed the remaining steps at a brisk trot.

When they all entered the hall they found Leopold, struggling to rise. Gruffudd held him fast to the flagstone floor. Leopold clapped his gaze upon Rowanne and thrashed as if pursued by demons.

"Rowena! Have you not tortured me enough for my sin, Rowena? Go back to the tomb!" Leopold shrieked. His hand went to his scarred face and his blind eye. Spittle ran from one side of his mouth. "Did you not exact a high enough price for what I did? Forgive me, I beg it."

"Upon the Holy Rood, he *has* lost his senses," Desmond told Coy as they flanked Brandt.

"Aye, you are right. He is mad. And 'twould seem his guilt has made him so. For the more he babbles, the more I learn he was well acquainted with Rowena, Rowanne's mother." Brandt moved a pace nearer to Rowanne. She stood motionless, the only sign she was living was the slow rise and fall of her breasts as she dragged air into her lungs. She hung on Leopold's every word as her face grew ever more ashen.

"I never meant to harm you, Rowena, I had in mind only a little bed sport and then I would have loosed you. Why? Why did you take my dagger and plunge it into your soft breast?" Leopold wailed like a child, still trying to throw off the sinewy grip of the Welsh houndmaster.

Introducing Ballad,
A LINE OF HISTORICAL ROMANCES

*A*s a lover of historical romance, you'll adore Ballad Romances. Written by today's most popular romance authors, every book in the Ballad line is not only an individual story, but part of a two to six book series as well. You can look forward to 4 new titles each month – each taking place at a different time and place in history.

But don't take our word for how wonderful these stories are! Accept our introductory shipment of 4 Ballad Romance novels – a $23.96 value – ABSOLUTELY FREE – and see for yourself!

*O*nce you've experienced your first 4 Ballad Romances, we're sure you'll want to continue receiving these wonderful historical romance novels each month – without ever having to leave your home – using our convenient and inexpensive home subscription service. Here's what you get for joining:

- *4 BRAND NEW Ballad Romances delivered to your door each month*
- *30% off the cover price with your home subscription.*
- *A FREE monthly newsletter filled with author interviews, book previews, special offers, and more!*
- *No risk or obligation…you're free to cancel whenever you wish… no questions asked.*

*T*o start your membership, simply complete and return the card provided. You'll receive your Introductory Shipment of 4 FREE Ballad Romances. Then, each month, as long as your account is in good standing, you will receive the 4 newest Ballad Romances. Each shipment will be yours to examine for 10 days. If you decide to keep the books, you'll pay the preferred home subscriber's price – a savings of 30% off the cover price! (plus shipping & handling) If you want us to stop sending books, just say the word…it's that simple.

assion-
dventure-
xcitement-
omance-
allad!

4 **FREE BOOKS** are waiting for you! Just mail in the certificate below!

BOOK CERTIFICATE

Yes! Please send me 4 Ballad Romances ABSOLUTELY FREE! After my introductory shipment, I will receive 4 new Ballad Romances each month to preview FREE for 10 days (as long as my account is in good standing). If I decide to keep the books, I will pay the money-saving preferred publisher's price plus shipping and handling. That's 30% off the cover price. I may return the shipment within 10 days and owe nothing, and I may cancel my subscription at any time. The 4 FREE books will be mine to keep in any case.

Name_____

Address_____ Apt._____

City_____ State._____ Zip._____

Telephone (____)_____

Signature_____

(If under 18, parent or guardian must sign)

All orders subject to approval by Zebra Home Subscription Service.
Terms and prices subject to change. Offer valid only in the U.S.

DN012A

Get 4
Ballad
Historical
Romance
Novels
FREE!
❖

**If the certificate is
missing below, write to:**

**Ballad Romances,
c/o Zebra Home
Subscription Service Inc.**

P.O. Box 5214,
Clifton, New Jersey
07015-5214

**OR call TOLL FREE
1-800-770-1963**

Passion...
Adventure...
Excitement...
Romance...

Get 4
Ballad
Historical
Romance
Novels
FREE!

BALLAD ROMANCES
Zebra Home Subscription Service, Inc.
P.O. Box 5214
Clifton NJ 07015-5214

PLACE
STAMP
HERE

Memory, long buried, bubbled to the surface of Rowanne's mind. She saw her mother, Rowena, laying among bloodied bedclothes with Leopold's dagger in her hand. She had begged Rowanne to take her toddling sons to safety. Then she had plunged the blade into her chest and died while Rowanne looked helplessly on.

"Rowanne?" Brandt slipped his arm around her waist. "Rowanne? What is it?"

"My—my mother. I remember now—Leopold . . . and my mother," she whispered as the full impact hit her. "He raped her. She took his eye and—her own life. How could she have done such a thing? How could she have let me *see* such a thing as her death?"

Brandt squeezed his arm tighter about her shoulders. She was so strong, so brave, so scarred by her past. He wanted naught more than to offer her his comfort, his body, his soul and his heart.

Leopold thrashed and moaned. "I have paid for my sin every day of my life. No maiden has looked upon me without gagging. Not one sunset has gone that I was not reminded of my transgression against you." He touched his scarred face. "Was it not enough?" He said all this while staring at Rowanne.

"He thinks I am my mother. . . ." Rowanne whispered. She clung to Brandt's strength, trembling while Leopold raged at her, fighting Gruffudd and the prior, who was trying to force herbs into his lips.

"I tried to make amends. Your sons live. Only I know where they are. Only I can restore your sons. Please, give me peace and I will tell you where to find your sons."

"He is quite mad," Coy said.

Something within Rowanne stretched to the limits of endurance. "You murdering bastard!" Rowanne shoved off Brandt's hand and jerked his misericorde from the sheath at his waist. "You raped my mother. I will kill you and watch your blood stain the steps of Irthing as it should have long ago," she shouted and rushed at him, startling Gruffudd and the prior so much that they loosed Leopold. He staggered to his feet, weaving like a drunkard.

"Nay. I—I let them live. Your sons, Rowena of Fontmell, Lady wife of Etienne Vaudry, I swear—they live. Your sons are alive. I swear it. I defied Thomas. I knew his plan. He wanted them dead, but he was going to say they live to use their continued safety against Etienne. While Etienne believed all three of his children were hostage he could make no move to free any of them without losing the other two." He cackled madly. "But I twisted Thomas's scheme back upon him as payment for your life. You see, in the end, I did it all for you, Rowena!"

Rowanne hesitated for a moment. "You lie. My brothers do not live."

"Nay, Rowena, not your brothers. Your sons, now grown to manhood. They live—" Leopold stiffened suddenly, clutched at his throat and fell backward. A loud crack filled the hall, echoing off the walls when his skull hit the stones. Foam and spittle sputtered from his mouth as his body jerked violently. His one eye bulged out of his head while the cords in his neck stood in stark relief. "I swear . . . they live."

"You and Thomas destroyed everyone I ever loved," Rowanne moaned in despair. She raised the misericorde high, poised to deliver a blow to his heart.

"Rowanne," Brandt spoke softly, slowly. "Give me the dagger, Rowanne."

Her eyes were wide, her face ashen and still, but her body thrummed with rage. "No. I need to kill him—I have to kill him—to avenge my brother's deaths," she whispered piteously. "He says they live, but it is a craven lie to save his life."

"You cannot have his blood on your hands—on your tender soul. Give me the dagger, Rowanne."

"But I have lived for this, dreamed of this," she said haltingly, as if waking from a dream.

"Aye, I know what 'tis like to live for vengeance. But 'twill poison you, love. I now realize how the hunger for revenge withers the heart and blackens the soul. I would spare you that, Rowanne. Give me the dagger, little temptress. Trust me. Trust me, and all wilt be right."

She looked up at him. She blinked. Slowly, her fingers uncurled. The dagger slipped from her hands and clattered to the stone steps. Then, as the last of her strength ebbed away, she crumpled, fell into Brandt's arms. He held her close, savoring the feel of her. Leopold still thrashed and frothed, but she no longer looked at him.

"Geoffroi, quickly," Prior Simon ordered, stepping around Brandt and Rowanne. "He is having a seizure of the brain." Prior Simon loosed Leopold's clothing, giving what aid he could as Leopold's body jerked and spasmed uncontrollably.

"He does not meet his death peacefully," Desmond observed. "But I wonder if any man would wish to meet the Lord with a lie on his lips? Perchance he tells the truth? Perchance the sons of Etienne yet live?"

CHAPTER 18

An hour later, in spite of the monk's valiant efforts and herbal decoction, Leopold existed in a strange, nightmarish state. He no longer suffered the seizures, but his one eye was unseeing, or perhaps it saw only guilt-producing images from his past. From time to time he would cry out, begging someone to send word to Thomas DeLucy of Sherborne that he had seen the Vaudry maiden wed.

"I have done all I can do for him here," Prior Simon said as he stood and brushed the dirt and rotting rushes from his robe. "We will take him with us to the priory. You are also welcome to come and bide with us," he told Rowanne, who still clung to Brandt.

"Nay. Castle Irthing is my home. Ghosts or no, abandoned or not, I intend to stay."

Brandt instinctively tightened his arm around her as if to drive away her fear when a tremor passed through her body.

"Ah, but the Scots reivers have not left enough for you to bide here while the king selects you a husband," the prior said.

Brandt swallowed hard. Everyone knew the heiress was alive. There were no more secrets surrounding Rowanne. Soon a husband with adequate rank and breeding would be chosen.

He must leave soon. He must leave her to be a great lady.

Simon bent and grabbed hold of one of Leopold's legs as Geoffroi lifted the other. Desmond and Coy picked up Leopold's shoulders. They hobbled down the steps toward the wagon. The prior continued to speak to Rowanne as he carried his burden.

" 'Twould be far better for you to come to Lanercost Priory and wait there in relative comfort until you know the king's pleasure about your person and your property."

"What?" Rowanne pulled free of Brandt and followed him down the steps. She looked puzzled, confused. "What say you, Prior? What husband do you speak of? Why would the king choose a husband for me?"

Prior Simon grunted with strain while they deposited Leopold into the back of the wagon. He wiped his forehead with his voluminous sleeve and turned back to Rowanne. "From what this poor man has been saying I have surmised you came here to wed Geoffroi of Sherborne." He slid a knowing gaze toward Geoffroi. "Word will quickly reach the king of what has happened here. You are the rightful heiress of Irthing, and though the hall lies in ruin, there is land to protect and control. The king will want to place a man in control of Irthing that has the skill and power to hold it. Unless you wish to make a gift of all this to the Church and join a holy order." Prior Simon smiled widely. "The Augustinians would assist you in finding a proper nunnery if you chose a life of prayer and contemplation."

"I have no desire to spend my life locked away in seclusion. I have tasted that and like it not." Rowanne quaked as the truth of his words settled over her like a fine mist. She did not wish to be a nun and she did not wish to await the king's pleasure while some cruel baron like Thomas was selected to wed her.

"I have no liking to wed a stranger." Rowanne frowned. She whirled to stare helplessly at Brandt. Her eyes were wide and full of confusion.

The prior laid a soothing hand upon her arm. "Milady Rowanne, the king should take the responsibility of your care to heart since you are without a father or guardian. This is a wild land. But if he does not, remember all I have said. You could come to God and serve him well."

"I had not expected Irthing to lie in ruins. . . ." Rowanne's voice was high and sharp, and she appeared to hear little of what Prior Simon was saying. "I had thought it would all be as I remembered. That I would have something to offer a man."

"The hall is of no import. The king will find a man with the means and ability to see all brought to rights," Prior Simon assured her.

The sound of hooves once more clattered across the drawbridge into the bailey. A horse more suited to plow than saddle appeared from the brume. A priest of indeterminate age bounced awkwardly upon the animal's back. He blinked at the small assembly as he slid to the ground.

"I heard, but I believed it not." He adjusted the rough folds of his robe and drew himself up with a measure of aggrieved dignity. "I should have been told that a Vaudry was returning to Irthing. Saints be praised, but 'twas my place to be here to greet you. Milady, Rowanne." He grasped Rowanne's hands in his own and smiled warmly.

Prior Simon smiled at the priest. "Allow me to introduce Friar Onslow, priest to Irthing."

"Ah, well, I was priest and confessor to Etienne until he died and all my flock left. But now . . . a Vaudry!" He smiled again and squeezed Rowanne's hands in his beefy grip. "You shall have my prayers and guidance, milady. I will resume my duties at once."

"Friar Onslow, I am trying to show the lady the wisdom of returning with us to Lanercost," Prior Simon interrupted, a frown furrowing his face.

"Nay, I wish to remain here in Irthing." Rowanne squared her shoulders.

The priest looked hopeful. Prior Simon's frown deepened with annoyance.

"Think of what you are saying, daughter. You are alone here. Castle Irthing no longer houses men-at-arms to protect it—and you. Scottish reivers prey upon our borders. The only reason Irthing has been spared of late is because there is little else to steal, and the rumors of spirits deter all but the most fearless. Look you, even the windlass to raise the drawbridge is broken. You need a protector, lady." Prior Simon spoke patiently, as if he were speaking to a halfwit.

"But I have a champion." Rowanne turned to Brandt. The truth of the prior's words had washed over her in a cold wave. Even though Irthing was little more than ruined stones, it was still a keep of some import because of its location. The king would surely pick a man, someone strong and battle-hardened, to help secure his borders by taking her to wife.

Unless she made her own decision.

She searched Brandt's face, trying to find some interest, some clue to his feelings. Would he rebuff her if she reached out to him? The hard, emotionless mask he always wore was firmly in place. But she thought of how he had come for her, rescued her from cutpurses, pulled her from the water. She thought of the way her heart beat faster when he kissed her. Most of all, she thought of how she felt about him.

"Then I will wed a man of my own choosing."

"*What say you?*" Brandt and Prior Simon asked in unison.

Rowanne looked at Desmond, who gave her a reassuring smile and a bold wink. Then her gaze slid to Brandt, whose expression had gone from shock to a closed and

shuttered glare. She twisted her hands within the folds
of the soft blue wool of her bliaut.

"Brandt, I would have a word with you in private."
Rowanne forced her voice to remain calm and strong.

"As you wish, my lady." Though Brandt told himself
it had always been inevitable, 'twas like salt being rubbed
in an open wound. She was going to ask him to speak
to Desmond on her behalf. She had decided to see
herself wedded before the king could bind her to a man
she did not know or love.

Love. He tried to drive the jealousy and envy from his
thudding heart, but it was pointless. Moonlight
skimmed over her slender form while he followed her
to the curtain wall. He fought the impulse to drag her
into his arms and declare himself to her.

What matter now? It was too late. Had there ever
been a chance for them, it was well and truly gone.

"Brandt. Sir. Dear friend—" She stammered, unable
to find the right address, the right tone, the right way to
begin. "I would not hurt or offend you for the world—"

"Think not to spare me, lady. Say what you must."
His voice was gruff, his words sharp with pain.

Lady Margaret's strange warning came unbidden
through her head. *Never wed a man you fancy you have
fallen in love with.* Rowanne pushed the thought from
her mind. She heaved a great sigh and looked up at
him, tilting her chin high in order to see his shadowed
eyes.

"Jesu, this is most vexing. Now that I have you here,
the words will not come to me easily." She felt the flush
of her embarrassment and was grateful the only light
was that of the moon as it played hide and seek behind
the clouds.

Brandt died a little inside. 'Twas some perverse comfort to him that she was not able to tell him easily that
she wanted Desmond. He moved a step nearer to her,
wanting to give her more than comfort and protection,
but willing to settle for that.

"Tell me, lady, what vexes you, and if 'tis in my power I will gladly see it removed from your path." He reached out and put his hands on the tops of her shoulders. He fought the urge to claim her mouth, to taste her lips one last time.

"I am fearful to let you see my boldness, sir. I would not have you think . . . less of me."

"Trust me, Rowanne. Speak freely of what is in your heart and be assured I will always think of you as a most gracious lady."

She nodded stiffly. "I have asked much of you, my champion. 'Twould seem I have much yet to ask."

"Then ask, lady, for I am forever your servant in all things." His fingers tightened on her shoulders reflexively.

"I will not be settled on some unknown man like a milch cow. I have decided to pick my own husband."

"I thought as much, lady."

"I know it is ever the way of a mercenary to hire out your sword, and—" She took a deep breath. She summoned her courage. "I would ask that you stay with me, Brandt le Revenant."

The sound of his own blood rushing through his ears grew louder.

"What did you say?" There was a roaring in his ears. "Surely I did not hear a'right."

His hand still rested on her shoulder. She put her hand over his wrist. "Help me rebuild Irthing. Be my shield and my people's protector. Stand at my side and hold this keep—and my heart—from all who would come, whether they be Scot or DeLucy or the king himself." She said in rapid rush of words.

"Wed me, Brandt."

Tell her. Tell her. The voice of Gervais screamed in his head. *Tell her now that you are Thomas's by-blow. Be done with deception!*

As Brandt thought of his DeLucy blood, a part of his soul withered under her hopeful gaze.

Nay. Don't tell her. You can have it all, his own churlish inner voice contradicted. *You can have the demesne and the maiden. Just keep your tongue between your teeth and you can hold it all. Geoffroi is as silent as the grave. She will never know you are Thomas's bastard. Take her! Take it all!*

"Take me to wife. Be my lord and husband, and I will share Irthing and all that I have—all that I am with you. The king will not gainsay this if I am wedded and bedded before he hears. You are a knight with spurs— surely he can find no fault in you. Take me to wife."

"And what of Desmond?" Brandt heard himself ask.

"Desmond du Luc has been a witty friend and companion, but you—have bid me trust you. And I do. Say aye and show me my trust was not misplaced." She smiled sweetly and tilted her head. "Friar Onslow can sanctify the wedding tonight, right here on the steps of Irthing's own chapel. Surely the king would not expect you as a knight and man of honor to leave me unprotected. As Prior Simon said, this is a wild land. Border bandits prey upon Irthing and its people. Should I fall unprotected into their hands—"

"I would never allow that." Brandt cast one more glance toward the drawbridge. Did he hope Harold would come with the king's decree and settle this matter, or did he pray he would not?

"If your answer be nay, then I will endeavor to understand and we will part friends, but if it be aye, then know I will do all to make you a good and loyal wife. I will share home and hearth and *bed.*"

Somewhere in the night an owl hooted. For a moment the moon was lost behind the clouds. Brandt used the cover of darkness to allow himself a moment to rein in the unbridled lust her words had spawned. He burned to hold her, to sink himself inside her and make her *his.*

But could he take her to wife? Could his secret be kept forever? Could he be so black-hearted as to wed her knowing that she hated any man with DeLucy blood in his veins?

"There are things you should consider, lady," he said hesitantly. "There are things you do not know about me—"

She put her fingertips to his lips to silence him. "I have considered all that signifies. You are an honorable knight. You have the might to do what is needed to bring Irthing back from ruin. I trust you. What else must I know, sir?"

Brandt beetled his brows together. Part of him wanted to take her offer, to reach out and grab at happiness, but another part of him, the part with the honor she spoke of, knew it was wrong.

"If I do nothing to insure my happiness, the king will send another man to wed me, and like as not 'twill be someone I favor as little as DeLucy scum."

Brandt cringed inwardly at her unintentional barb. Who could she ever hate more than a son of Thomas DeLucy?

"It seems to me the wisest choice is to get myself wedded and bedded before the king can choose—if I am to keep Irthing and myself safe."

"But, lady—" Brandt stammered as he glanced once more at Desmond, standing with the monks. He would be the better choice for her sake. And what of King Henry's deed of the Black Knowe and Irthing? That would be one more damning secret he would be keeping from her.

Unless he told her all right now.

Take her! Forget your damnable honor—forget truth! Take her! Reach out and grasp a bit of happiness.

"Milady, there is—" Brandt was torn by the temptation she had placed before him. She believed that she could hold Irthing with him as her husband. And 'struth was, she could, for it was already deeded to him. The document bearing the king's seal was safe in Brandt's saddlebags. If he took her to wife he would have *her*, and she would have her beloved home. De Burgh and Henry might be cross that the wedding took place without the king's permission, but likely a good bribe would soothe ruffled feathers.

Rowanne and Brandt would have their dearest desires. All Brandt had to do was silence the voice of his conscience and say aye to her proposal.

Rowanne stared at Brandt, wishing her heart would stop fluttering in her chest. What had she expected? That he would jump at the chance to take on a ruin of a keep and *her*.

'Twas not as if she were a great beauty. She chided herself for reading more into the stolen kisses than Brandt had meant. She was a fool. He was a mercenary, a man with wanderlust in his veins. She was naught but a clumsy maid with little to offer.

Irthing was a shambles, her great legacy no more than a pile of stones. A flush of shame climbed in her cheeks. "I ... I know I am no great beauty, but I am strong and would bring you sons." She remembered that Lady Margaret had said men placed great store on heirs.

Brandt stared at her in disbelief. Could she really have no notion of her worth? She was a jewel, a precious heart of light and courage. He was not worth her sweat. Did she not know?

Brandt swallowed hard, thinking of all things he should say. He should tell her the king had given him Irthing, that he held the keep and its land by royal decree. He should tell her that he had come to care for her with a passion that frightened him. He should confess he was the bastard son of Thomas DeLucy, her most hated enemy.

He should. But he could not find the words.

A night breeze lifted strands of her moonlight-kissed hair. She shivered against the chill. He longed to hold her close and warm her body with his own. He yearned to taste her mouth again, to learn every secret of her body. He hungered to get sons and daughters upon her, to insure a bit of immortality for both of them.

Had he once truly thought of her as no more than a tool of revenge? Now it seemed like a long forgotten dream. He cared nothing for revenge upon Thomas—only that Rowanne was safe and loved.

Whether in her tattered bliaut or the new gown of becoming blue, she was a goddess. And she was offering herself to him—willingly, without reservation or caveat.

He *could* have it all. But at what price? Brandt was not so young, so foolish, or so naive as to believe he could keep the secret forever. But he might have a sennight—a fortnight mayhap—until Samhain, before the bitter truth was out and Rowanne no longer looked at him with that soft glow of trust in her eyes.

He looked at her blue eyes and nubile body. A jolt of heat surged through him. Could a short taste of love be enough to risk the damning fires of hell for an eternity?

CHAPTER 19

"Aye, lady, I will wed you and bed you this night."
Brandt took the step over the precipice of his lost honor.

The chapel of Irthing was stripped bare as the rest
of the keep. Only a heavy altar of native stone and a
single threadbare prei-dieu remained among the dust
and veiling of cobwebs.

Gruffudd found a handful of crude tallow candles,
coated in dust, and arranged them so that at least the
middle of the chapel was bathed in a wavering glow of
light. Menacing shadows danced in the corners of the
room. Brandt shuddered, thinking they represented his
inevitable doom, but he turned away from them, willing
to endure what the future held for the promise of being
Rowanne's husband and protector . . . if only for awhile.

"Prior, I would ask a boon of you." Rowanne said as
he and Geoffroi followed Friar Onslow into the chapel.

"Yes, child?"

"I would ask that you do as Leopold begged and send
a message to Thomas DeLucy of Sherborne. Tell him
that Leopold has fallen ill, but that I have wed. But,
Prior, I pray you, do not say *whom* I have taken to husband—that is something I would reveal in my own time
and my own way."

Prior Simon studied her face for a long moment. Then he heaved a great sigh that made his cheeks fill like a fire-bellows. "As you wish, child. I wilt send the message with some of our brethren that are making a pilgrimage to Glastonbury Tor."

"Gramercy, Prior." She kissed his cheek lightly.

He flushed so bright that even in the muted light Brandt could see the crimson tinge to his flesh.

While Brandt and Rowanne stood on the steps the churchmen prayed and busied themselves inside the chapel.

"I am ready," Friar Onslow said soon.

Rowanne bit her bottom lip.

" 'Tis not too late to change your mind, milady," Brandt said as he took up her hand.

"Nay. I have made my choice." Then she turned and smiled one last time at Desmond. He smiled back and Brandt still felt the cold shaft of jealousy in his gut.

They knelt side by side on the cold stones of the chapel. Brandt took her hand in his own while Friar Onslow offered a benediction. Finally the ceremony had reached the point were their names would be spoken aloud. A shiver of dread shot through Brandt.

Would he have to reveal himself so soon? Before God, he could not lie, but was he to have all his dreams shattered before even one short night of bliss?

His mind raced along, grasping at something, *any- thing,* that would spare him her loathing for a little while—just a little while. He was not so foolish as to ask for eternity, but just a short span of happiness with his Rowanne.

Suddenly he had it.

"Friar, in order to properly acknowledge the great honor being done to me, I would request to take Row- anne's family name of Vaudry for my own," Brandt said softly.

"But, sir—"

"I am a bastard by birth and 'struth I have not been

acknowledged. The name le Revenant is my battle name and I would not burden my wife with a name bought with death and blood. I would be proud to take up the name of Vaudry.''

Murmurs from Gruffudd and Prior Simon filled the dreary little chapel. Brandt turned his head enough to see Desmond and Coy. They were watching him with thoughtful gazes. He knew his boon companion saw through his thin ruse, but he also knew Desmond would keep silent.

Then Brandt met Geoffroi's gaze. Geoffroi's pale eyes narrowed with unspoken accusation. For the first time in his memory, Brandt felt shamed by his older half brother. Geoffroi's silence was damning.

"Do you object, lady?" Brandt asked.

"Nay, I have no objections." Rowanne smiled sweetly. " 'Tis another debt I owe you, Brandt."

"As you will, then. From this day forth you shalt be known as Brandt Vaudry," Friar Onslow said and continued his prayers as he solemnized their wedding.

The remainder of the ceremony was over quickly. Brandt's blood was filled with a molten burst of heat when he realized that before man and God, Rowanne was now his.

His. He had done it. He had joined himself to Rowanne in front of witnesses on the steps of a sanctified chapel. He had chosen the right course, the *only* course that would bring them together.

He may have damned his soul to hell for the deception, but he had Rowanne for his wife.

"Now, sir husband, we are one—almost," Rowanne said softly.

"Aye, all that remains to be done is the bedding," Brandt replied, his voice husky with passion.

She lifted her chin and met his gaze squarely. A soft pink stain highlighted her cheeks. "Then let us be about it, for 'struth, I want no impediment to this union. When word reaches Thomas and our king, I would be your wife in all ways. I want naught left undone betwixt us. I want no possibility this wedding can be set aside."

"As you say, lady wife." He held her knuckles to his lips and lightly grazed his teeth along them. Bedding Rowanne was a task he looked forward to with relish.

"The dye is cast now," Gruffudd muttered sadly. Rowanne turned to face him. "Thistledown, I hope you do not have occasion to *ailfeddwl.*"

"I no longer understand the Welsh tongue, Gruffudd," Rowanne said softly. "Tell me in the king's English."

"I pray you will not have second thoughts, Thistledown." He said solemnly. He glared at Brandt, his bony chin jutting forward. " 'Twas hastily done, this wedding of yours. I hope 'tis not long regretted."

Brandt bristled at the barely veiled insult. "I have pledged my life and my body to Rowanne's protection— do you doubt me?"

"See that you keep your pledge, or you will have to answer to me," Gruffudd promised with a scowl. A hound sprawled at Gruffudd's feet snarled at Brandt as if in agreement with his master.

"You have a sharp and surly tongue for one who is now speaking to his liege lord," Brandt said with a wry lift of his brow, secretly touched and warmed by Gruffudd's loyalty to Rowanne.

"As you say, *milord.* But have a care about my warning. I meant it." The houndmaster nodded curtly and tugged on his tangled forelock, but there was no give in his stiff spine. " 'Tis nearing cock's crow. I will leave you to your . . . rest." Then he turned and ambled away, whistling a strange, warbling call. With barely a whisper of sound the pack of hounds padded in his wake.

Brandt's pulse thrummed in his veins. Tonight, or what was left of it, was his wedding night. He was eager to bed his bride—nay, not eager—he was *consumed* with the thought of sinking himself into her soft warm sheath, of making her his own.

"The bedchambers are no doubt in the same condition as the hall," Rowanne observed.

Brandt looked down at her golden head and felt a pang of remorse. 'Twas her wedding night and yet she stood in a pile of cold stones, with no mead with which to toast their union, no herb-scented sheets or women to help undress her for the first bedding.

"The Scots border bandits have left little to me in the way of a dowry. Like as not there *is* no bed," She said, a comely frown creasing the skin between her brows.

"Then let us find our ease elsewhere, lady wife." Brandt folded Rowanne's hand into his own. "Let us find a place of peace and privacy which we will make our own bridal bower."

Together they made their way through the ruins of Irthing Keep. They walked beyond the deserted barracks where Desmond and Coy were busy making their beds, beyond the stable where their steeds rested with Clwyd and Rowanne's gray palfrey, where Glandamore perched on a post. Brandt held her hand protectively in his, making vows that he would ever keep her safe. At the moment they passed beneath the useless portcullis, with the moon hanging low, and the faint pink promise of sunrise tinting the eastern horizon, he swore he would die before he let harm befall her.

" 'Tis safe to leave the keep?" She asked as if reading his thoughts.

"Fear naught, lady wife, I will *always* protect you from any hurt and harm." *But can I keep you from the hurt my lies wilt surely cause?*

Down moonlit-mottled lanes, up stony dales and beyond, they walked until Irthing was no more than a dark shadow on the horizon. Brandt knew not what he looked for, but the moment he spied the arbor, with its sheltering vines and thick concealing boughs, he knew he had found the perfect bridal bower. He pulled

Rowanne inside the shelter of growing things, inhaling the attar of blossoms, the thick perfume of flowers and buds.

" 'Tis not a proper bed for one so lovely, but 'tis fresh and clean and untouched by sadness and bleak memories."

"Brandt?" Her voice crackled in doubt. She felt an all-consuming panic for what she had done—for her boldness in proposing marriage to him.

"Aye, Rowanne?" He was nuzzling her neck, slowly untying the laces of her rabbit fur–lined cloak. He gently removed the alms bag where Thorn curled asleep. He allowed his hand to linger upon Rowanne's hip bone, feeling the fragile sweep of her body as desire rushed through him. His blood was hot and thick in his veins.

"Will the king be angry? Have I done a terrible thing to us both?"

Brandt raised his head and looked into her eyes. "Do you now worry that we married without royal permission? Is that what makes you tremble? Is it the king's wrath you fear, or that you have bound yourself to me?"

Rowanne's heart skipped a beat. She wanted Brandt, against fate, against the king's ire, she wanted the brooding mercenary and the fire of his kisses.

"It is the king I fear, but not for myself; rather, that he might bring reprisals against you. Are you in danger?"

Relief poured through Brandt. For a moment he had thought she might want to cry off, to have their marriage annulled while she was yet untouched—unbedded.

"De Burgh runs the kingdom in truth. Young Henry is likely preoccupied with his building projects and will give you little notice." His hand made large sweeping circles on her spine, the palm molding itself to the contour of her flank with each sweep.

"But if he does—" She felt her blood thicken and slow. A languid heaviness entered her limbs.

"Shhh." Brandt brought his fingers to her lips to gently silence her. "Forget about kings and advisors and politics. I care not what may happen on the morrow, and I have given up all my yester morns. We have now, lady wife. *Now*. 'Tis all we can hope for. Let us take this time and hold it precious to our hearts."

She moaned softly when he crushed her against him. "Aye, husband, aye." Her lips parted, inviting him inside. "Now is ours."

With a throaty groan of passion he plundered the honey of her mouth. Rowanne was sweet as new mead, and Brandt drank deeply of her. All the passion he had kept in check for the past lust-filled fortnight threatened to overcome him. His body trembled with the effort to go slow—to savor her—to bring her to passion with him.

He wanted to claim her gently and with great tenderness so that he would not frighten her. For even her fright was something Brandt swore he would keep at bay. He was her lord, her protector, *her champion*. He would feed her, clothe her, and keep her within his heart until the moment she learned the truth.

He shoved the thought violently aside. That the truth would eventually come to light he had no doubt. But he had *now*. He had Rowanne. He had his heart's desire.

"Jesu, Rowanne, you are sweeter than ale and more potent that the strongest honey wine."

"Brandt, I—I know naught what to do," she confessed in a whispery rush. "Lady Margaret made the bedding sound like the words of a troubadour's lay, but I have seen things. First my mother and then Betta—I am frightened."

"Trust me, love. What happened to your mother and your maid was not a loving thing. This bedding will be tender, slow, and gentle. I will show you the way, and I would never, ever harm you." He took her cloak from her shoulders and spread it on the turf. Wild night-blooming flowers and the blossoms from nearby gilly-flowers filled the air with a sweet perfume. It was intoxicating to him, mingled with the scent of Rowanne and the heady knowledge she was about to become his.

"Milady—*Rowanne*. Sweet temptress." He dipped his head low and kissed the bare expanse of flesh above her breasts. His tongue teased along the edge of the blue woolen gown, probing a little beyond it, a little deeper, to where the cleft of her bosom tasted musky and warm.

He told himself it did not signify if she knew who his sire was. She had chosen him—*him*—over Desmond, by the holy Rood, over whatever worthy knight the king might've chosen. He cared for her and would never play her false in any other matter. Brandt salved his conscience with that thought, that justification to his deception, while his tarse reared to life within his braies and drove all rational thought from his mind.

"Wife, *my* wife. You are mine. You will yield your maidenhead, and that precious gift will bind us forever."

Rowanne trembled with anticipation and a little fear. Each time Brandt said her name a shiver of love sizzled through her. She tried to forget what she had seen. She tried to wipe those hurtful images from her mind. And slowly, she did. Now only the swirling heat of desire filled her thoughts. It was Brandt, only Brandt who held her attention and her heart.

It was important, this bedding. It was sacred. It would bind them together in the sight of God and all men, and the act of giving herself to Brandt was rushing to meet her whether she was ready or no.

CHAPTER 20

"Say, it Rowanne. Say you are mine."

He kissed her again, plunging his tongue deep into her mouth. Widening her, opening her, whilst his hands found the bottom edge of her bliaut and slid it up her thighs.

His fingers were warm and insistent as they found the cleft between her legs. She stiffened, but he only kissed her harder, tasting, demanding, claiming. One warm finger skimmed over skin that had been the most private part of her. She gasped at the contact and jerked, but 'struth, did she jerk toward him or away?

Instead of it being a repulsive invasion, his touch was sensual, maddening, making her want more. He played and stroked, leaving that most sensitive area in lightning-quick flicks, but when he halted his hand, she thought she would go mad without his touch. Her pelvis bucked toward him as if she had no mind, no will, only her body had power—her body and Brandt.

"Ah, Rowanne, I will cherish you as no woman has ever been cherished by a man. I will protect you and see you never have cause to regret this night's work. Now say it, love. . . ."

She heard his love words and nearly wept from happiness. This was what she had hoped for but feared would never happen. Suddenly all the bleak, long days in Thomas's tower vanished from her mind.

She was happy. She was content. She was loved.

"I am yours, Brandt Vaudry. In life and unto death—I am yours."

Brandt emitted a low growl. Before she knew it, his hand was on her bare flesh and he was pushing her gown higher, seeking to look upon the juncture of her thighs.

"Open for me, love," he said as he gently but firmly pushed her legs apart.

A wash of maidenly shame stiffened her legs, but he brushed his fingers over that hot, pulsing core, and she felt her body submit to his will. Her thighs parted.

"Is there—aught I should do, milord?" she questioned.

His long fingers manipulated, caressed, and rubbed on her core again. She gasped, all coherent speech deserting her when she felt him slide one finger inside her.

"Ah, you are hot, honeyed, and *mine*. You are wet and ready."

He raised himself up on stiff arms and grinned wickedly down at her. "Show me what you pleasures you, little temptress." His hand began to do a strange exotic movement upon her flesh as he pushed himself rhythmically against her. "Does this excite you?

"Aye, I would have more."

She could feel the hard bulge of his thighs, the ridge of his hip bones and a hot, pulsing staff that seemed to make her body more hungry for his touch. Rowanne stiffened, and her back arched with a will of its own.

"That gives me pleasure," she sighed.

"Ah, as it does me. Do whatever you *feel* like doing to me, if it pleases you. Do what your body commands, love." He bent to kiss the tip of her nose. "Rowanne, know this. We are man and wife and everything we do is right and good. If you feel like touching me, then be at ease to do so, I will only love you all the more for it. Or if you feel like crying out—"

"Will I have a need to cry out?" The old terror was not quite banished yet. "What I am feeling now is . . . is wondrous, but will the rest be so painful that I will be driven to cry out?" Her voice was coming in halting little pants. She flowed over him, wet, hot, hungry, and yet there was a measure of virginal fear.

It drove him mad with passion to know she was ready, and chaste, and *his.* And yet he held himself in check and did not enter her. He wanted her to be on the brink of shattering passion when at last he took her.

Brandt chuckled deep, feeling his masculine power— and a measure of humility that God in heaven had allowed him this woman, this moment of sheer bliss. He nipped the taut point of one breast through the wool of her bliaut. "You may wish to cry out for other reasons besides pain, lady wife, but when I breech your maidenhead you will have some pain, for I have no doubts you are chaste and pure."

He was kissing her again, and all coherent thought flew from her head. When he stopped and raised his head, his eyes were as warm as banked embers. There was a fluttering in Rowanne's belly that she could not describe or control. She seemed to be tightening in on herself, needing something that had no name or form.

Needing Brandt.

And then he left her. A wash of cool air claimed each part of her flesh that was burning. She reached for him wildly.

"Leave me not."

"Have no fear, I would never leave you." Brandt unlaced the taches on his heavy crimson surcoat and spread it on the ground. "Will you help me with my mail?" He asked.

"What do I need do, milord?" Suddenly she felt very

insecure, inadequate, and filled with panic. What if he did not find her pleasing?

"Help me pull it over my head. I beg your pardon for having you act as my squire, but since we are alone—" His voice was a husky purr that rubbed over her skin.

With trembling fingers she grabbed hold of the shoulders of his heavy mail and yanked as he dipped his head and shrugged out of it. When it was free of his body she could not hold it. It fell with a clank at her feet.

"Jesu, milord, how do you endure such weight?" She looked at the iron mass in wonder.

" 'Tis better to carry the weight than to feel the prick of a sword," Brandt said as he removed his linen sherte.

Rowanne's eyes were drawn to him like iron to a lodestone. A network of scars lay randomly here and there along his sculpted body. His torso was well-favored, heavy-muscled. A hot coil twined in her belly. She reached out but halted her curious fingers inches from his skin.

"Touch me, Rowanne, never be a'feared to touch me." He took her hand in his own and drew it to his chest. With gentle strokes he guided the tips of her fingers over his collarbone, down the light curling hair of his chest, along one ragged white scar that ran along the outside of his ribs . . . and lower.

He dragged her fingers along the line of hair that disappeared into his hozen. She swallowed hard, feeling weak and feverish, fearing her heart was going to leap from her chest.

"I would never harm you," he said as he gently urged her to her knees and then slowly back on his surcoat that padded the turf and vines.

"I know, milord."

"Brandt. I wouldst hear my name from your lips, wife."

"Brandt," she complied, surprised at the breathy timbre of her own voice. "Husband. Mine."

He smiled his approval. With sure, deft movements he drew her bliaut over her head.

And then her shift.

She was naked before him.

A fire burned in his warm amber eyes as he lowered his head to claim her lips. On muscular arms he lifted himself over her, positioning himself between her legs. With one hand he balanced, while the other hand resumed its deliciously maddening exploration of her tender core. Expert fingers rekindled the banked fire in her blood. She writhed and moaned, arching into him, feeling a strange, driving need that she could not explain or control.

It was like falling from a great height for Rowanne. She felt sensations that took her breath, startled her, and made the invisible coil within her tighten ever more. She felt tense, rigid, as if she would break into a million pieces of craving want if Brandt did not *do* something.

His hands were magic, they were probing, exploring, opening her for his entry. She should have been ashamed, she knew, but she was not. There was something beautiful and wild in his touch. There was something potent and irresistible in the feelings that sprang to life. Mewling sounds came unbidden from her own lips and then suddenly—

There was pain.

He broke through the barrier of her virginity. It sliced through her, taking her breath. She froze, her body torn between rampant desire and the shock of Brandt somehow hurting her after he had sworn not to. She felt a stab of betrayal. She curled her fingers into the caps of muscle on his shoulders.

"Trust me. Only this once will you suffer," he said, and then drove hard and deep. "Rowanne, prithee forgive me." His voice was rough and strained. "Open your eyes, love, look at me. Now you are truly mine."

She dragged in panting little breaths, not realizing

that her eyes were squeezed tightly shut until he mentioned it. Slowly, she opened her eyes.

" 'Tis only the first time that causes such distress. I swear to you, Rowanne, 'twill ease anon since I am beyond the silken barrier of your maidenhead.'' He searched her face with an expression so tender that she felt a lump growing in her throat.

He held himself tightly in check, feeling a wash of concern for her. He slipped one hand between them and found her hot moist core. Slowly, gently, he stroked her until he felt her bones go liquid and saw a glaze of desire flood her eyes.

"Don't weep, love, I pray thee."

She had not realized she was weeping, but then she felt a tear snaking its way down her temple into her hair. "I am not weeping because I am in pain, Brandt."

"Why then?" he asked as he stroked the hot center of her, supporting his weight away from her on his elbows.

"Because—because . . . you and I are wed. I asked so much of you and . . ." Her voice trailed off.

"Rowanne, I am proud to be your husband, proud to have taken your name. From this day forward you are my family, my home, my future."

He moved, withdrawing slowly. Then he slid back into her. Her body tightened around him, drawing him deeper.

"That's it, take me deep, wife."

By inching degrees the pain left her lower body and was replaced by something different, something feral and hungry that would be answered in kind.

She was on the edge of a great precipice. Each time Brandt withdrew she was lured closer to the edge, and then . . . she was falling. Tumbling down an invisible cliff of pure sensation. Her body had no form, no substance. Shivering convulsions of pleasure rippled through her. Quivers of passion too intense to describe rolled over her.

Brandt suddenly stiffened above her. She saw a look of pain, or mayhap intense concentration, flit across his face. His eyes burned as if from an inner fire. The morning air was rent with his husky cry of ecstasy.

Rowanne felt *something* more in that instant. 'Twas beyond pleasure. 'Twas more a deep, abiding satisfaction and a humbling sense of closeness. It deepened in the next moment when her husband leaned his head against her shoulder and sighed her name in contentment.

"Ah, Rowanne, I am yours unto death and beyond."

CHAPTER 21

Rowanne woke with a start to the harsh call of rooks. She blinked, trying to remember where she was—what had happened. It came to her in a flood of sensation and a dull ache between her legs.

She was a wife now. Somewhere betwixt Betta's coarse rape and Lady Margaret's fanciful stories Rowanne had learned the truth, at the most expert hands of her lord and lover, Brandt Vaudry.

"Good morn." Brandt's husky voice purred at the nape of her neck against the backdrop of morn on the glen. Birds chirped and called, there was the sound of bees droning in the blossoms around them, and the small scraping noises of insects moving in the leaves and grass beneath their bodies. The world was awake and alive.

She turned her head and looked at him, lying next to her. He grinned. She had used his warm-muscled arm for a pillow, sleeping close and intimate. They were still together, legs entwined, his dark hair tangled amongst her light strands. His face was shadowed with a fresh growth of beard that he would have to scrape away.

She had never seen him thus. On the journey he had

risen early and taken care of his ablutions without her knowing. He had always been stern, armored, and somewhat distant by the time she saw him.

This other side of him was intimate, private, and arousing. He seemed younger, more touchable and approachable, as he grinned at her. There were a few fallen blossoms that had taken up residence in his hair and she gently removed one, seeing him tense slightly at the invasion of her fingers.

Brandt was somewhat stunned to find he wanted her still. He had told himself that once he had slaked his lust and discovered the secrets of Rowanne he would be more in control of his desire. Now he realized, as the blood surged to his groin, that he had been fooling himself. They had consummated the marriage as was required, but he *wanted* her now for the pure lustful purpose of feeling her beneath him.

She blushed prettily and his tarse turned solid as stone.

"Nay, do that not, wife," he said with a wider grin.

"What, milord?"

"Blush so appealingly," he said and chuckled, sending chill bumps skipping over her bare flesh. "For if you do so, then I am a'feared I will be forced to ravish you once again."

Her cheeks turned to flame at his words, at the reminder of how they had been together, and could be again. He laughed, a deep and throaty laugh, and he kissed her, driving his tongue deep into the recess of her mouth in a gesture of complete possession. But at the moment she felt her blood warm and her bones turn liquid he pulled away and was on his feet.

"Husband?"

"Fear not, love. I would not take you again so soon."

Had she feared? Nay, she did not think the emotion had been fear, but he was up and occupied, so the matter was over—for the moment.

In the clear, bright light of morn she had her first

glimpse of all of him. He was tall and well-made, and the manly part of him that drew her eye stood hard, erect, pulsing a little in the nest of dark hair at his groin. It jutted from his flat, corded pelvis like a well-wrought sword blade. She knew then why she had felt herself cleaved in twain.

"Cease, Rowanne." His voice was stern and hard.

Her eyes snapped up to his face, expecting to see a frown, but his face was a blank mask, his eyes clouded. "Cease what, my lord husband?" she squeaked, feeling somewhat chastened for having been caught appreciating him so boldly.

"If you continue to study me with such intense regard then I mayest not be able to control myself. I would not have you sore and hurting but, Jesu, I can feel your eyes upon me like a hot wind." He speared her with a look that was rife with passion and longing. "I am your slave, wife . . . but have mercy on me."

Rowanne felt herself warming deep in womanly places. 'Twas a heady power she wielded over her new husband, and she held it close to her heart in happiness at realizing it.

"Come, you minx, get you dressed so we may quit our bridal bower," he teased as he handed her the blue wool gown she had no memory of removing—and her shift. When had she undressed to the skin?

Brandt grinned wider and waggled his brows as if reading her mind, knowing her confusion. "I am now the lord of the manor and have many duties to attend. I cannot play the swain all morn."

She was momentarily taken aback, until she saw his teasing smile widen.

"You are jesting with me." She pulled the shift over her head and tied the strings. Then the soft wool tunic followed. She squirmed and lifted her arms, trying to reach the laces in back.

"Turn round, wife," Brandt ordered as he took her shoulders and spun her away from him. She felt the

cloth tighten as he tugged on her laces, drawing the
bliaut against her form.

"I am jesting, but that does not alter the truth. Our
home is in shambles, and though I find the prospect
of lying with you among the fells and dales more than
pleasing, I think a proper bedchamber need be secured
for the both of us. Lest that Scots bandit Lochlyn come
slit my throat as we sleep." He pulled her back around
to face him. "There, now that I have played the part of
a lady's maid, you must repay in kind by playing squire
once again."

He bent at the waist and effortlessly scooped up his
heavy mail. Then with a wink and another teasing grin
he proceeded to show her how to dress a knight.

When they returned from the wooded glen, Rowanne
was shocked to find the previously deserted and silent
Irthing now teeming with activity. She found her hand
reflexively tightening on Brandt's strong fingers as they
walked over the drawbridge, under the portcullis, and
through the now crowded bailey.

"Who are all these people?" she mused, speaking
more to herself than to Brandt. Wagons laden with
goods, armored and mounted knights filled the outer
bailey. A crew of brawny men were already at work
repairing the broken windlass that would raise and lower
the drawbridge.

" 'Twould seem, Rowanne, that my men have
arrived," Brandt said lightly as he searched the faces,
marking each one.

Rowanne lurched to a stop so quickly that her arm
was nearly wrenched from its socket before Brandt could
check his long, striding pace. He turned back to her,
his face a mask of confusion.

"What is amiss, wife?"

She stared at him gape-mouthed. "*Your* men?" She
asked.

"Aye. My men ... my soldiers and men-at-arms ... and goods." He grinned at her but 'twas no longer the teasing smile of a bridegroom but the guilty look of a man caught at some misdeed.

"Where, pray tell, husband, did you acquire men—and goods?" Rowanne moved quickly out of the way before she was run down by a team of four pulling a huge wagon loaded with chests and casks. She saw Coy and Desmond in the thick of things, supervising the unloading of fine, well-wrought furnishings.

Hardy peasants were spilling through the gate. One was shepherding wooly herdwicks and a good-sized flock of four horned Jacob's sheep toward the half-ruined and hastily repaired enclosure at the far end of the outer bailey.

Brandt frowned at the procession of men, horses, and carts. He should tell her the truth—*all the truth*—and this was the perfect time to do so.

"You were not a landless knight when I asked you to take me to wife," she whispered. Suspicion clouded her blue eyes but only for a moment. Then the light of complete understanding blazed in blue depths. "And Desmond and Coy were not mercenaries looking for a new lord to serve, were they?"

He wanted to tell her truth. Deep inside the need to tell her the truth clawed at him, wanting to be freed.

"Nay ... aye. They are my men—were my men when they met with Leopold and pretended to ply their sword for his purpose." He dragged his palm down his face, searching for the right words. "Rowanne, come here."

Brandt pulled her into a bend in the curtain wall near the postern gate. He stepped in front of her, hoping he could block her view of the busy, crowded bailey, hoping he could erase that cloud of doubt and anger in her eyes.

" 'Tis time you learned a bit more about the man you have taken to husband. I *am* the bastard son of a petty baron who refused to acknowledge me. My battle

name of le Revenant is the only name I have ever had
. . . until now.''

"Until now," Rowanne repeated with a tremulous
smile.

"Aye, until now." A burst of pride shot though him.
"I have earned my own way in the world by my strength
and my sword arm—"

"It has evidently held you in good stead," she interrupted, scanning the rich furnishings and hammered
tin and copper household items she saw.

He ignored her pithy observation. "Recently it has
earned me some worldly riches, as you can see." He
cupped her face in his hands. "But your happiness and
contentment are the most precious things to me. To be
your lord husband means more than all of this." He
gestured blindly behind him. "If aught about this dis-
tresses you, then I will give it away—to the priory—I
trow Prior Simon would take it in a nonce."

"No doubt."

"Or to the needy in the village. Say the word and it
will all be gone in the blink of an eye."

She rose on her tiptoes to look over his shoulder.
Fine thick rugs in long bound rolls were being stacked
on the steps of the keep. She thought of the putrid
rushes in the hall.

She saw fine carved tables and thought of the vacant
rooms, of the cobwebs, of last night and sleeping out
in the open with her most virile husband.

"If the rest of Irthing is in the same rotting decay as
the Great Hall, I believe *we* may be the most needy pair
in the shire."

His lips kicked into a crooked smile. "You are not
angry with me? I did not tell you at first because it was
of no import, and then I chose not to see censure in
your eyes because I was not what you had thought me
to be." *And yet I am still not* who *you think me to be.*

She wrapped her hands around his neck, feeling the
strength and warmth of him. "As a new bride I would

be foolish not to be happy that you are wealthy. Being chatelaine of a castle with furniture and bedclothes would be much more preferable to sleeping on the ground or being chatelaine of a wooded bower."

"You did not feel so last eve," he teased and placed a kiss on her forehead.

"Last eve I was not in my right mind, and I might remind you that we did little sleeping, milord." She found one more errant bloom behind his ear and plucked it free.

He picked her up and held her tight against him. "Rowanne, my Rowanne. Truly all the angels in heaven have smiled down upon me this day."

He whirled her around and deposited her on her feet, facing the wagons and the men. "Come my love, see what I own—what *we* own. You may use it any way you wish to make our home more comfortable. The sooner we set Irthing to rights and have secured your safety the sooner I mayest be on my way."

She froze. "On—on your way? You would leave me?"

"Aye. There is the little matter of your companion at Sherborne. I believe you named her Lady Margaret?"

A feeling like a crashing wave hit Rowanne in the chest. She blinked and blinked again. "Aye, Lady Margaret. I am shamed to say that in my happiness I forgot her."

"I would see you completely happy, goodwife, and I know you will not be so until I have freed your friend. As soon as I am assured that Irthing is fortified and there is no danger from the Scots bandits I will go to Sherborne."

"To face Thomas DeLucy?"

"Aye. To face Thomas DeLucy."

Rowanne's mind was spinning with all that had happened and continued to happen at Irthing. Women from the village had cleaned the kitchens, buttery and ovens. Now the smell of baking bread drove away odors of disuse and mildew. Dried and decaying rushes had been removed, and new ones were being scattered over the stones. Fragrant gillyflowers, ox-eye daisies, thistles and cowslip bouquets appeared in every corner.

Gruffudd's hounds had been banished outside to the kennel, much to the chagrin of Gruffudd, who alternately scowled and smiled at the chaos around him whilst the mews were cleaned and freshened for Glandamore and a few other hawks that some of Brandt's men possessed.

"William," Brandt's voice rang out, drawing Rowanne's eye. He snagged the arm of a passing youth.

"Aye, my lord." A stout lad with snapping black eyes nodded at his liege lord and managed a tottering bow. He appeared no more than ten and five summers, but his lean build was already hard muscle and sinew.

"Take my armor and roll it in a barrel of sand."

"Your armor, my lord?"

Brandt frowned and adopted that frosty, stern look Rowanne knew so well. "Aye, that is usually what a squire does for his master, is it not? Clean his armor in sand?"

William's face burst into a sunny smile. "A squire, my lord? Aye, my lord, 'tis the best way to clean armor. I have seen it done—that is to say, I can do it. When I finish you will be able to see your face in it, my lord."

Brandt winked at Rowanne, and she felt a wave of admiration for him. Obviously she had just witnessed the young man's promotion and, in a manner of speaking, his coming of age. She smiled at Brandt, feeling a strange jolt of possessive happiness. He was her husband, her lord, and already he was working miracles to restore Irthing. From the lowest to the highest, she had no doubt Brandt would touch their lives for the better.

Lady Margaret surely must have been wrong about her dire warning. 'Twas not a tragedy that she had wedded a man she loved. Already Rowanne could see the rightness of her decision.

Mayhap Lady Margaret's experience had been tragic, but Rowanne was sure Brandt was destined to be her lord and master of Irthing. Indeed their wedding night had been the most wondrous and magical thing in the world.

Brandt surveyed the bailey with pride. His men, having long experience with using what was available to survive and erect a quick efficient campsite, had worked wonders in a short time. The barracks were now airing, and holes in the thatch were being patched by shirtless knights and village peasants. The bowers for the animals, if not pretty, would nevertheless protect them all from predation. And low spots in the battlements were being filled with rubble and re-stoned.

"My lord, Brandt." Renal appeared, sweat dampening his brown hair to his forehead. "All that remained of the furnishings within the castle has been removed, as you ordered."

"Good. Pile it up and burn every stick of furniture, every scrap of linen and any bedding that survives. And when that is done, instruct the village women to wash down every inch of the castle with lime sulfur."

Renal's wispy brows rose in a question. "My lord?"

"There has been a pestilence here, though a year and more has gone by, and I would know the keep is clean and free of contagion. I would not have my wife or my household endangered by a lingering fever."

"Aye, my lord." Renal called out to other men. Within moments, several descended upon the ragtag pile of broken, cast-off furniture with torches blazing.

'Struth there was little to set fire to. The Scots had fair gutted the castle. Brandt was almost amused by the boldness of the reiver known as Lochlyn—almost but not quite. The man had stolen from Brandt as surely as he had stolen from Rowanne. When the keep was set to rights, Brandt intended to ferret out the churl. He held no enmity for deeds past, but he would make certain Lochlyn and all northern barbarians understood that Irthing and its village was no longer unprotected.

"I would never have thought it possible, had I not seen it for my self." Desmond du Luc drew Brandt's eye. He lounged against the curtain wall with one boot hitched up behind him. Though he looked as if he had spent the day composing pretty rhymes, Brandt knew differently. Only an hour ago Desmond had been perched on the roof of the buttery, working fresh thatch into a good-sized hole. Now he used his dagger point to clean dirt from under his nails, looking like the veriest gallant.

"What are you babbling about?" Brandt asked. There was still a cold runnel of jealousy and suspicion in his heart when he looked at Desmond. He told himself 'twas foolish. Rowanne had chosen him. She could have chosen Desmond if she had wanted to. But still Brandt regarded his old friend with wary eyes.

" 'Tis amazing to see." Desmond grinned again and continued to preen and clean his nails.

"What are you prating about, Desmond?" Brandt cocked his head and frowned at his friend.

"Brandt le Revenant, the *Ghost*, the scourge of the Holy Lands is truly in love."

"You speak nonsense," Brandt said as he lifted a small coffer from a pile nearby. Chests, caskets, and coffers were all stacked neatly, ready to be placed in the keep where Rowanne directed.

"Nonsense, you say? All morning long your eyes have returned again and again to the keep. You nearly lost your head 'neath that chest that was moved by Coy and Gadwin, and yet you say I speak nonsense?"

"I have taken a wife—'tis my responsibility to see to her care. And, my fine friend, you will be thanking me when evensong comes and you have bread and ale for your belly."

"Ah, I see. You consider Rowanne your responsibility . . . . Is that what we are calling it now, my lord?"

"Have a care, you bold knave, or my first duty as lord of this castle will be to see you soundly whipped," Brandt said. Was Desmond jesting with him, or was there another reason for his words?

"Do you intend to tell her who you are?" Desmond focused all his attention on removing a splinter from his finger.

"You speak boldly." Brandt stilled, all his attention focused on Desmond. "She knows who I am, Desmond. I am a mercenary, a knight, and the man who has taken her to wife. I have honored her and her family's memory by taking their name. What else is there for her to know?" Brandt's voice was dangerously low. "Or is there some truth you would impart to my lady wife?"

"Do not snarl at me, Brandt. I have known you too long and loved you too well to shake with fear and dread. I but wonder if you court disaster by keeping the truth from her. Tell her, Brandt, tell her and wipe the slate clean so you and your bride may start your lives fresh.

"I cannot."

"She will learn of your secret, Brandt."

"Are you threatening to tell her, Desmond?" Brandt adopted a stance with his feet wide apart. Instinctively his hand went to his sword.

Desmond's gaze flicked to Brandt's hand. "You know me better than that. All I am counseling is that secrets have a way of making themselves known. It would trouble me to see the lady's heart broken by deception."

"Then guard your tongue, old friend. For if she is not told, then she cannot be hurt by what is long in the past and cannot be changed."

"Tell her, Brandt." Desmond sheathed his dagger and pushed himself off the wall.

"Desmond, I love you as a brother, but in this I'll not tolerate your interference." Brandt frowned. "This benighted secret will lay between us forever, Desmond, for I will take no chance or risk to lose the treasure I have found."

"Are you referring to the lady or the land, my friend?" Desmond asked curtly. But before Brandt could find an answer, his friend had turned his back and sauntered away.

The morning disappeared in a flurry of activity. Brandt's part in the reclaiming of Irthing dwindled as castle folk resumed their duties. More and more he found himself leaping out of the way before he was unbalanced by a bucket or scowling village woman. Finally he decided to take a half dozen men and ride to the village to see the lay of the land. He had ridden less than a league before he saw the plumes of smoke. Putting his spurs to Clwyd, he drew his sword and thundered to the village, only to find he was but moments behind the bandit Lochlyn.

"My lord, shall we give chase?" Gilbert asked, his eyes glittering with anticipation.

"Aye. Send a man back to Irthing to alert the guards, and let us hie after this scrapper." Brandt nodded his head and flipped his metal visor into place over his face. Clwyd's iron-shod hooves struck sparks on the rough stones of Cumbria as he headed north in pursuit of the Scotsman known only as Lochlyn the Reiver.

CHAPTER 22

They rode hard all day, playing hidey-hole with shadows in thick woods and rocky ravines. The land was wild and offered a hundred places for the bandits to hide. Brandt was frustrated beyond endurance when he finally pulled Clwyd up and halted his men.

"This is futile. We are chasing smoke. Let us return to the castle. From now on we will post guards at the edge of the village and on the ramparts of Irthing. I want men stationed at the gatehouse and cauldrons of boiling fat readied in case the portcullis is breached. The next time Lochlyn comes calling at Irthing, I will give him a warm welcome."

By the time Brandt spurred Clwyd up the stone causeway toward Irthing' s drawbridge, a steady stream of peasants crowded through the gates and jammed tight, all struggling to get under the raised portcullis. Sheep, a few shaggy reddish cattle with lethal-looking horns, and herds of swine were being poked and prodded into Irthing.

"What is this?" Brandt cried out to the man on the ramparts.

"Tribute, my lord. They started coming at midday. Grateful they are that you are going to put an end to the thieving raider, Lochlyn," the man shouted down with a wide grin splitting his face.

When he dismounted and left Clwyd to be tended by William and an eager village lad that was clearly hopeful of gaining a like position, Brandt discovered several village craftsmen had decided to take up residence within the high stone walls as well. The blacksmith, Gilliam Trask, a barrel-chested man with a wide gap between his front teeth, was unloading his anvil and tools at the newly thatched forge. A fire blazed in the round stone hearth, and the smell of hot metal permeated the area.

" 'Tis tired I am of fighting to keep what I earn from being taken by that black-hearted Lochlyn Armstrong," Gilliam said as he spat upon the hard-packed earth. "I'd lief as live within the walls of the castle and let your soldiers handle the bandits when they come. I give ye me word, Lord Vaudry, I will keep your armor well mended, and I forge a strong blade. You' ll not want for weapons." Gilliam tugged on his forelock and nodded.

"You are well come and well met, Gilliam Trask," Brandt said, swallowing around the lump in his throat. This fealty, this gratitude and willingness to take on responsibility, took him by surprise. He had long been able to lead and tend his men, but the realization that an entire village was looking to him for protection was a sobering one.

"It appears you and your lady have your work laid out for you," Desmond said with a wry smile. "The villagers are placing all their trust in your ability to keep them safe."

"Then I will not disappoint them," Brandt replied dryly.

"Aye, I am sure you will do your best," Desmond said soberly and Brandt wondered if he was jesting again or if he truly meant what he said.

Brandt looked at the massive keep. This was what he had craved all his life, this feeling of acceptance, a home and community. But with all those riches came a weighty responsibility. If crops were poor and the people hungered 'twould be his fault. If the northern bandits raided and pillaged, that also would be due to his lack of might.

If Rowanne was unhappy and lost faith in him, 'twould be his ruin.

He made himself a silent vow that he would never let her or the village down, for the most important thing to him was that Rowanne be proud of him.

Gilliam Trask's bellows worked furiously, driving bright embers and sparks into the night sky as he hammered out straps that would strengthen the ironworks of the now closed portcullis. Six men walked along the battlements, silhouetted against the setting sun. The sight gave Brandt a sense of satisfaction.

While the local folk agreed the northern bandits were not overly bloodthirsty, their greed had seriously endangered the lives—or at least the quality of life—of the folk of Irthing. At least half of the villager's flocks of sheep, goats, and cattle had been taken over the last year by the border raiders. There would be some changes now, Brandt thought grimly. Changes and reckonings.

Then, over the steady clang of Gilliam's hammer Brandt felt the rhythmic thud of hoofbeats. He heard the guard call out and an answering voice. He knew that voice.

He strode across the bailey and stood at the portcullis while the windlass was turned. Slowly, creaking and groaning like an old man roused from his bed, the iron-studded wooden gate rose to admit the rider. Brandt watched the cloaked figure, hunched in fatigue as he clattered over the drawbridge and into the bailey.

"My lord," Harold Potts called out.

"Harold. I had begun to grieve for you, thinking some misfortune had come upon you, so long did your journey take." A tendril of unease snaked through Brandt' s belly. For though he had told Rowanne the king would not bother with one maiden' s marriage, he did not feel quite confident of that. Indeed, the displeasure of the king could mean his death, and a new husband for the comely widow he left behind.

"My lord Brandt," Harold said as he dismounted from a heavily lathered horse. "I was not here and waiting for you as I had promised. Forgive me." Harold's steps were stiff and short, revealing that he had spent long hours in the saddle without rest.

"From the looks of your horse, your time was not spent idly." Brandt slapped a hand to Harold' s shoulder. "How did you find the king's court?"

"Slow and infuriating." Harold grimaced. "De Burgh made a show of authority. He kept me cooling my heels for a goodly time before I was granted audience with our king. Henry sends his greetings."

Brandt gestured Harold to the stables. "And what else?" Before Harold could answer Brandt turned and called out to his new squire. "William. Bring a skin of wine."

The lad scurried away and was back quickly. Brandt took the skin and passed it to Harold, who quaffed deeply of the restoring drink.

"My thanks," he said at last, dragging his hand across his mouth.

"Have you brought me King Henry' s will about the heiress?" Brandt asked when he could wait no longer.

"Aye." Harold pulled a parchment from inside his tunic.

"Take your ease in the barracks, Harold. I would be pleased to have you sit with me at high table this eve," Brandt said.

"Gramercy, my lord." Harold eagerly took his leave, striding across the bailey toward the barracks and the noise of his fellows in arms.

After Harold had left Brandt broke the royal seal and

unrolled the vellum. His brows beetled tightly together whilst he read the tight rows of inked verse.

"What has vexed you now?" Desmond peeled his body away from the shadows. He plucked a fresh straw from a newly stacked rick and began to nibble at one end.

"You are becoming as stealthy as a thief, Desmond," Brandt observed wryly, his fingers tightening on the vellum.

Desmond shrugged. "Does the king make his wishes for Rowanne known?"

" 'Twould appear the king, or at least Regent De Burgh, cares more for his damned border than for Rowanne's fate," Brandt said caustically. "What would have become of her had I not happened along?"

Desmond's tawny brows shot up. "What indeed? You speak in riddles, my friend. I have not the gift of future sight, so cannot say what would *have* happened, but obviously something *has* happened to darken your mood."

Brandt thrust the parchment toward Desmond. "Read for yourself." Brandt turned away with a blistering oath for men and politics. Then he whirled back, his long cloak rustling about his hozen. "Our king is young, aye, but his advisors should be taking more care with what goes on in the land. Do they have such a cavalier attitude about every maiden without a male relative to protect her?"

Desmond read in silence. "Well . . . my lord, Brandt. It appears the king did give you a choice in the matter."

"A choice? You call that a choice?" Brandt asked with narrowed eyes. "That Rowanne be made my ward to do with as I saw fit—to put her in a nunnery if she did not please me or if—"

"You were not of a mind to marry her." Desmond rolled the parchment. "It seems your mind and the king's have run a similar course. Why are you not happy?

With this decree you are safe from the ax-man's block. Or do you now regret taking her to wife?"

"How could I refuse her offer?" Brandt asked, his eyes narrowing to slits.

"How indeed?"

"Stop saying that, Desmond, for I vow our friendship will not save you from a sound drubbing. 'Struth, I owe you one anyway for the way you fawned on and flirted with Rowanne on the journey."

Desmond's smile flashed. "Ah, so that is why you have been in a black mood for days. I see jealousy in your eyes, my friend."

"Nay, not jealousy. I just think 'tis unseemly for you to have made so close a friendship with my . . . wife." Brandt scowled and snatched the parchment from Desmond's hands.

"She was not your wife at the time, Brandt." Desmond frowned. "And since you see fit to point out that friendship, I ask again, when will you tell her the truth?"

Brandt's grip tightened on the scroll that had saved him from a royal execution. "What truth would that be, Desmond?" Brandt asked in a soft voice.

Desmond's smile bled away. "Any truth would be a start in the proper direction. Brandt, I know that Rowanne has no notion that the king had given you the Black Knowe and Irthing long before you met her. Does she even know you sent word to Henry's court about her fate? If you will not tell her who your sire is, then will you at least tell her that you were lord of Irthing *before* you took her to wife?"

Brandt turned to Desmond. Guilt over his own deception rose bitter and hot in his gorget. "Desmond, you tread in deep water and are speaking of matters that are none of your concern."

"No need to look so fierce, milord. 'Tis only my curiosity that bids me ask if you intend to tell her." Desmond said lightly, as he executed a half-bow. "And as you remind me, I am the lady's friend."

Desmond du Luc, adopted and spoiled son of a proud and noble family, cared for Rowanne Vaudry. The truth burned into Brandt's mind like a hot coal. But how much did Desmond care?

Rowanne slung her thick braid over her shoulder. She wrung the dirty water from the scrubbing cloth into a wooden bucket.

" 'Tis finished." Still on her knees, she put her hands at the small of her back and stretched upward, arching her spine to relieve the strain of her cramped muscles. The floor of the chamber was shimmering wet, scrubbed clean at last.

"Ye work too hard, milady. Ye should be lettin' us do such heavy work at this," Maeve, a plain-faced woman from the village said. "The lord will nay be pleased to find ye here wi' us on your knees when you should be sittin' at high table a'waitin' his pleasure."

" 'Tis so late?" Rowanne glanced at the arrow slit. Stars twinkled against a night sky where but only moments ago the sun burned. "Oh, by the Rood, I had no notion of the time." She yanked her fingers through the woolen strip holding her hair and combed her fingers through the strands as she gained her feet. "Were the goose, crane, and duck sent to the kitchens as I asked?"

"Aye, my lady. They be roastin' with a haunch of beef."

Rowanne nodded and made a mental note to thank Gruffudd. He had taken his hounds and the hawks out hunting early and brought back a bounty for the hungry castlefolk, going so far as to "find" a bullock haunch.

Rowanne brushed the front of her bliaut as best she could as she flew down the narrow spiraling staircase. The great hall was ablaze with rush lights and torches when her foot reached the stone landing. Cressets lamps had been hung from the iron rings along the walls. The smells of succulent roasting meat wafted through the hall. Rowanne cast a glance around the room, searching for a glimpse of Brandt among the many new faces. Would he appreciate her efforts as chatelaine, or would he find her lacking?

She nearly laughed at her foolish worries. Only a few fortnights ago her mind had been trained on thoughts of revenge and survival only. But Brandt had changed all that. Now she was like every other new wife, trying to please her husband and create a pleasant home for him.

Brandt was standing in the great archway listening to Coy and Renal list the repairs needed on the smithy, the mews, and the barracks. He had been momentarily shocked to find the previously grim keep now a model of cleanliness and hospitality. With his new furnishings placed here and there, the keep had the solid feel of a . . . *home.*

He listened with half an ear, nodding from time to time, until he felt the burn of eyes upon him. He turned and searched for the source.

Across a score of tables, freshly scrubbed and filled with laughing men, over the rush-sweetened floor, his eyes slid to the raised dais beneath a painted scene the cleaning had revealed.

There was Rowanne.

She stood with her hands gripping one of a pair of ornately carved chairs Brandt recognized as part of his plunder from the Holy Wars. Her cheeks were pink, flushed in a dusky wash of color that made his loins tighten. Her hair rippled in a cascading skein over her shoulder. She looked slightly mussed and infinitely beddable.

"It appears your lovely lady has been as busy as you, Brandt," Desmond said with a smile, suddenly materializing at his elbow.

Brandt offered his most intimidating glare, but Desmond was already threading his way through the knights and the tables. Straight toward the dais where Rowanne stood.

Brandt felt his feet moving and was only dimly aware of Coy and Renal's voices trailing off. He realized, with half-a-mind, he was leaving without giving more instructions about the keep's repairs, but Rowanne was more important.

He cut a swath through his men and reached the dias at the moment Desmond did. He took hold of Rowanne's hand in a completely possessive fashion but he could not silence Desmond.

"Milady, how pleasant you have made this hall." Desmond bent gallantly at the waist, glancing up at Brandt from under his brows. He grasped Rowanne's free hand and brought it within a whisper of his lips.

"That, Desmond, is an observation best made by a husband and not a knight who is in danger of losing his head," Brandt said without a trace of humor in his voice.

Rowanne glanced at him wide-eyed. "Your compliment is appreciated, Desmond."

Desmond laughed. "Ah, I was going to compliment you on other improvements as well, my lady, but as you see I best hold my tongue or I may'st lose it."

Rowanne felt heat climbing to her cheeks. She was surprised to see Brandt act thus and was further shocked to see him wearing a killing frown as he glared at Desmond.

"Brandt?" she asked, withdrawing her fingers from Desmond's light hold. "Is something amiss?"

"Nay, no more than having to suffer this dullard's wit," he said between clenched teeth.

Desmond only shrugged and flicked a bit of imaginary dust from his velvet surcoat. "You see what a gloomy creature he is? It is my goal in life to make him smile, but now I gladly pass that burden to you, milady. Or better yet, I shall play the part of your fool and make you laugh—lest Brandt make you cry."

Brandt' s grip on her fingers tightened. "Desmond—" he warned.

"You are teasing, Desmond, just like you did on our journey." Rowanne leaned into Brandt's chest and to her delight, he drew her nearer. "Brandt needs no amusing stories to make me laugh. He has made me *happy*."

Desmond' s brows shot upward. "Indeed? Then you truly are a wonder, milady."

"Sit down, Desmond." Brandt felt a flock of butterflies in his gut. Rowanne's gentle, heartfelt declaration had done something profound to his innards. He drew out one of the big chairs and guided her into it. 'Twas all he could do to keep from threading his hands into her glorious hair, yanking her head back and claiming her mouth to prove to one and all that she was *his*.

Or is it myself needing reassurance?

"You have wrought miracles with the hall, milady," Desmond said.

"Women from the village have toiled all day."

Desmond reached out and took hold of Rowanne' s hand. Her knuckles were rough and reddened, her nails chipped from the day's labors.

"Not just the village women," Desmond observed.

She pulled her hand away and glanced at Brandt. He was staring at Desmond with his eyes narrowed.

"I see your handiwork everywhere I look," Brandt said under his breath. He sat down beside her. Sprays of wildflowers, arranged with spiky purple thistles and Michaelmas daisies were placed at the dark corners of the room. They brightened the stark bareness of the stones and brought the clean scent of springtime inside. His groin tightened as he thought about his bridal bed. Would that he could take her there now.

"Are you well pleased?" Rowanne asked.

Brandt nodded, unable to find his voice as he fought

to control the surge of lust. If they were alone he would show her how pleased he was, but now they were the center of attention—the lord and his lady—and he fought to maintain his dignity.

Desmond, however, felt no such constraints and proceeded to lavish compliments on Rowanne. Brandt picked up his goblet and quaffed deeply. Was it Desmond that truly rankled, or was it his own prickly conscience?

Serving girls began bringing in savory meats. A trencher of hollowed-out bread filled with bits of roasted meat and seasoned juices was placed between Brandt and Rowanne.

Brandt drew his dagger and speared a bit of meat. He offered it to Rowanne. For a moment she simply stared at the meat. This was the first time in her life she had shared a trencher with a man, and though 'twas right and proper to do so with her husband, the newness of it, combined with the closeness of Brandt, the smell of fresh air and flowers, and the lingering memory of her wedding night, nearly undid Rowanne.

"Is the food not to your liking?" Brandt asked, feeling awkward and randy and unsure.

"Nay, aye. . . ." She took the offered meat between her teeth. She swallowed it nearly whole and came nigh to choking.

Brandt brought his goblet to her lips. She sipped the wine, taking a much bigger gulp than she intended. Tears sprang to her eyes and she sputtered.

"Rowanne?" He held her hand, still wrapped around the goblet in his own, covering her small, pale fingers with his wide, calloused ones. "Are you ill?"

" 'Tis strange. So many people—the noise—I feel their eyes upon us. I cannot eat or swallow for it."

He popped a bit of meat into his own mouth, barely chewing before he took up the goblet and drained it, grinning at her as he rose and pulled her from her chair. "We have finished our sup. Let us quit the hall and find a quiet corner."

Her hand snaked out and grabbed his forearm. "We cannot." Her eyes were white-rimmed. "Brandt, if we were to leave now they would all think—they would imagine—"

"That the new couple has need of some privacy?" He grinned at her crimson blush.

"Aye. Prithee, Brandt, sit." She dragged on his hand in vain. "We must stay and enjoy our meal."

He sighed and touched her cheek gently. "I would lief as enjoy the taste of you, wife." Just looking at her, knowing what pleasures awaited, was a slow torture. How could she have come to mean so much to him?

"Brandt," she gasped. "All are watching us."

"Pray, milord, at least pretend to be hungry . . . for food," Desmond said, loud enough for the entire hall to hear. A moment of stark silence was followed by raucous laughter and bawdy cheers. Rowanne was sure her face would burst into flames before the good-natured jests and helpful suggestions ceased.

Brandt shrugged and eased himself back into his chair. In a nonce his goblet was filled and he was drinking deeply of it, trying to assuage the rampant heat in his braies.

Rowanne found herself desperate to get a conversation going so she could forget how many people were observing her and Brandt.

She turned to Desmond. "Tell me, sir, a little more about your life and your home."

Desmond speared a leg of roast duck. "Ah, sweet lady, my life has been such a tangled and sad tale," he said in mock misery. "I am the unnatural son of Basil du Luc."

"Unnatural?" Rowanne asked, unfamiliar with the term.

"A foundling—an orphan. Basil and his good wife, Alys, took me in. They adopted me as their own. They did their best to put my feet upon the right path. For a time they were hopeful that I would take the cowl."

"You were not agreeable?" Rowanne nibbled on the bit of meat that suddenly appeared in front of her mouth. "The vocation of churchman is much respected."

Desmond shrugged and grinned wickedly. "I like wenching, hawking, and fighting. I would make a poor priest. Someday I will find a willing maiden and will submit to the shackles of wedlock. In fact, I may have to amend my opinion of marriage, for it does not seem to be causing my good friend Brandt too much pain, however—"

"I have listened to enough of your foolish prattle. Desmond, you twist the truth in a hundred knots trying to wring sympathy from my wife. Listen not to him, Rowanne. His parents doted on him and spoiled him shamelessly. He is the heir to a fine keep and title. Desmond may be an orphan, but he has led a charmed life."

Brandt rose from his chair so quickly it nearly fell backward until he caught it with one hand. The hall quieted a bit, and he nodded toward his men. "Stay, eat, and drink your fill, but remember our day begins at cock's crow."

Then he turned to Rowanne. "I would have you to myself, wife." With that he gently urged Rowanne from her chair. "Come, milady, let us find a bit of privacy."

Desmond lifted his cup in salute. "If I did not know you so well, friend, I would think you are jealous and anxious to take your lady wife from my presence." Desmond leaned back in his chair and rested one arm carelessly over the back. His eyes danced with mischief.

"Tread lightly, friend," Brandt warned with a dark scowl. "Lest you wake the beast in me."

Then he turned back to Rowanne and the transformation of his dark and scowling face was amazing. He smiled warmly at her, erasing the dangerous look, becoming boyish and vulnerable.

"I have a surprise for you, milady, one I hope you will like." Brandt yanked a rush light from the wall and pulled her along beside him up the stairs at a brisk trot. His men cheered and crowed their appreciation.

CHAPTER 23

Within moments the noise and crush of the Great Hall were forgotten as they strode across scrubbed floor tiles of russet and amber. Rampant dragons and griffins had been painstakingly painted on each one before they had been baked. 'Twas a treasure underfoot and one Rowanne had not remembered from her childhood until with her own hand she washed away dirt, debris, and years of neglect.

Much like Brandt had reclaimed her soul from the years of neglect by her father.

Rowanne let Brandt lead her through the many empty corridors and up the spiraling stone steps. As they reached the upper floor she stiffened. She had not come this far into the deserted keep.

"Brandt—milord," she stammered, gently pulling her hand from his.

"Wife, what is amiss?" He held the light aloft, creating a small halo of gold around him.

"I toiled in the Great Hall all day and in the solar. I—I neglected to make arrangements for our—for our—rest," she finished in a whisper and with a flush of heat rising in her cheeks.

"Ah. So you think I will be angry and disappointed

with you?" He stopped and pinned her to the stone wall with a hand on either side of her face.

"Aye." She refused to look at him. "I would not have you think poorly of me so soon after our wedding, my lord."

"Rowanne, I couldst never think poorly of you, but I have a need for you anon. I cannot wait to find a wooded bower tonight," Brandt said sternly.

She sighed. 'Twas her duty as wife to submit to her husband's needs and wishes, but it did sting that Brandt could command her so easily.

"As you wish." There was nothing but resignation and sadness in her voice.

"I am pleased you are going to be sensible," Brandt said as he released her. They continued down the hall. Rowanne tried to swallow around the hard lump in her throat while she allowed him to tug her along in silence. When they reached the thick oaken door of the chamber that had once been her parents' sleeping chamber Rowanne paused. She expected a dark maw, but now there was a golden glow around the frame of the studded door.

"Rowanne, why do you hesitate? Is this the part of the castle where your mother died?"

She could only nod.

With his boot Brandt shoved the door wide open. "Enter and be at ease, wife, for no ghosts linger within." He drew her forward with a reassuring smile. "I have vanquished them all for you."

Her breath caught fast in her throat for 'twas not an empty, filthy chamber with the rotting remains of that terrible night. 'Twas transformed. Sorcerer's magic had been wrought during the day, and no connection to the past remained in that room.

Gone was any trace of mildew or decay in the air. Dozens of beeswax candles illuminated the corners of the chamber, filling the room with the subtle scent of warmed honey. Fine silken tapestries covered the walls from ceiling to floor, which was covered in thick, exotically colored rugs, both bright and muted, rugs that invited Rowanne to kick off her slippers and curl her toes into them.

A staved oaken tub of water was waiting between two deep brass braziers. The bath was big enough for Rowanne to climb into.

"How? When?" She drifted toward the biggest bed she had ever beheld. Awash in bolsters, plump cushions, and fine sleeping furs, encased in semitransparent bed curtains, the bed sat on a wooden frame supported on all four sides by intricately carved posts. It was both thrilling and intimidating to think of lying in that bed with Brandt. She turned to see him standing tense, watchful.

"It was a challenge to keep it secret from you. Does it please you?" Brandt asked. His eyes were alive and hot with desire.

"It pleases me." She turned away and trailed her fingers over ornate carved chests of a dark exotic wood as she moved about the room, suddenly restless, needing to put some distance between herself and the man that she had chosen to wed.

"When did you purchase all this finery, my lord?" Her gaze fell upon a pair of carved fluorite goblets, nearly opaque, with a tinge of milky green in the stone.

"Most of what you see was payment for my sword arm. Will you drink our health and happiness tonight? I have made sure we have the finest mead."

She picked up one goblet. 'Twas cold and solid in her hand. The glow of mead glistened in its translucent depths.

"Do you believe in the power of mead, my lord husband?" She held the goblet out to him.

He took it into his hand. "I would not be unhappy if the legends of fertility proved true and I got a babe on you this night, but I have no doubt we will be blessed with children in the fullness of time."

Heat climbed her neck. She picked up the goblet's mate. "To our future. May we have happiness and children enough to fill all the chambers of Irthing."

"Aye, wife." He gazed at her, mentally stripping her bare, exploring her soul with his eyes.

Rowanne was pleased but oddly shy. She warmed deep in her womanly places. Restlessness made her quickly tip up her goblet and drink too deeply of the mead. It was rich, heady, and warmed her inch by inch as it trickled down her throat like a molten river.

Brandt drained his goblet and set it back on the table. "Now, wife, I shall bathe you."

She nearly choked at his declaration. "Nay, 'tis a wife's duty to bathe her lord husband." Rowanne swallowed hard, already feeling the tingle of her body as the mead began to do its work.

"Tonight I will play lady's maid once again, and you will allow me this boon. Now drink your mead, wife, before the water grows cold." He wrapped his arms around her and pulled her close, but then his nose wrinkled and his brows rose.

"My lord? Brandt?"

He stepped away and grinned. "Rowanne, it touches me that you are so enamored with my gift that you wish to keep it with you always—but *it* has a disagreeable odor." He nodded toward her middle.

She looked down in horror at her gown. Did she reek? Were her labors now evident in her scent? A new fiery blush stole up her face as she rubbed her fingers over new stains. "I—I had not time to wash it."

"Nay, wife, 'tis not your bliaut that offends but what lies in your alms bag." Brandt inclined his head meaningfully.

"Ah." She grinned knowingly. "You mean Thorn." Rowanne lifted the flap on her bag and looked at Thorn. The little hedgehog was uncurling himself, peering at her with beady black eyes.

"Let me find Thorn a proper home." Brandt strode

to a large chest with a curved top. Rowanne let her eyes roam over the breadth of his shoulders as he rummaged within and suddenly brought out a wooden casket about a rod in length. Brandt removed several scrolls with huge seals dangling from them and dropped them into a large chest of tunics. The lid slammed shut with a hollow thud.

"A fitting home for the lady of the manor's favorite pet." He handed her the casket.

She gently withdrew Thorn, being cautious as she did so both for his comfort and her own finger's safety. He curled tight as she deposited him inside. Brandt moved the casket to a stone ledge built into the wall.

"He will be warm by the brazier. I will wedge the lid so it will not slam shut on the little sod."

It was heartwarming to see Brandt's gruff gentleness, or mayhap it was the mead that made her feel overly warm as she watched him. His hand was nigh as large as the coffer he had made Thorn's new home. He crouched on one knee, diligently seeing to Thorn's comfort with a boyish look of concentration on his face. The longer she watched, the more she was consumed by a scalding restlessness.

Rowanne glanced toward the tub. Suddenly the water appeared as a refuge—a place she could cool her burning flesh.

Brandt turned and caught her studying him. Knowledge, understanding, and pure animal lust arced across the space separating them.

"Ah, wife, when you look at me thus, I am pleased and enchanted." He rose to his feet and moved toward her. "I am also on fire."

With deft fingers he stripped her bare. She shivered as he trailed his nails over her sensitive flesh.

"Your touch is magic," she sighed.

An almost feral moan escaped Brandt's lips. In a nonce he had stripped bare himself. Rowanne stared at his manhood, standing rigid and erect, and a strange drawing tightness invaded her middle.

"I will once more play lady's maid and bathe you." He whispered as he nipped the lobe of her ear. Then he picked her up, the hair on his chest abrading her hypersensitive flesh, and strode to the tub. "Then we will see if the bed is well woven and adequately sprung."

Brandt took up a scrubbing cloth and rubbed the slightly roughened texture over Rowanne's turgid nipples. The shock and pleasure of the contact made her arch her body spontaneously. His eyes became smoky pools of lusty satisfaction.

"Aye, wife, show me your passion." His voice rumbled over her, causing her loins to tighten and pull. The heated core of her throbbed, and as if he knew her better than he knew himself, Brandt's fingers sought out that hungry flesh. He rubbed and teased his hand across her cleft. When he made contact with a part of her she never knew existed before her wedding night, a sharp intake of breath marked his arrival.

"Brandt, what are you doing to me?"

"Showing you pleasure, teaching you the ways of love," he said softly. Then he picked her up from the tub and held her, dripping wet, against him, letting her body slide down his. Slowly, relentlessly, she finally settled upon his staff. The sensation of being filled, stretched, and possessed jolted through her. Rowanne clung to Brandt's shoulders, scoring his flesh with her nails as he stiffened and his head snapped back. Their combined cry of ecstasy echoed through their chamber and out onto the moors of Cumbria.

Rowanne woke the next morning in a tangle of sleeping furs, twined in Brandt's arms, him tickling her nose with a strand of her own love-mussed hair.

"Slugabed," he purred. "You slept the sleep of the just."

"And you husband? Did you sleep like the just?"

Brandt squirmed under her open gaze. He had slept like a man sated from extraordinary coupling with his wife, but he could not honestly say his slumber had been without guilt and worry. Strange, prophetic dreams came to him in bits and pieces. He had woken during the night feeling his heart pound like war drums, a sense of loss overwhelming him. In those moments when he felt a panic unknown to a warrior he had reached out for Rowanne, finding a measure of calm reassurance when he felt her silken skin.

His deception was becoming a constant pain, like a sword wound that would not be healed. 'Twas more than Desmond's taunting, 'twas his own sense of honor that jabbed at him daily. By keeping the truth from one so true, he was betraying her. And he knew he should tell her, but in the dark of night Brandt had come to realize his greatest weakness: He loved her. And he could not do the thing, say the words, that would bring a look of loathing to her eyes. Because he loved her, he had to continue to deceive her. He flung back the sleeping furs and rose abruptly, his conscience nipping at his heels.

"Come, you must rise. The maids will be here anon," he said.

"Maids?" Rowanne asked with a yawn, stretching and feeling infinitely fine after a night of pleasure at her new husband's hands and other body parts. "But why would maids come to our chamber without being bidden?"

"You are my lady wife, chatelaine of Irthing. You needs must have a new wardrobe that befits your station." Brandt pulled on his smallclothes.

Rowanne frowned. "Has my appearance been an embarrassment to you?" She thought of the fine blue gown he had given her. Had the gift been from a warm heart or was it simply a result of Brandt's chagrin at seeing her in near rags?

"Rowanne, whether you be as God made you or in fine fur, I am never shamed by you." A part of him wanted to return to bed, to hold her close and feel the quivering of her thighs as he pleasured her, but another part of him was being relentlessly hammered by guilt. His lies and his cowardice were becoming difficult burdens to bear. He knew he was tasting the first bitter harvest of the seeds he had sown, and that eventually, in the full measure of time, he would see hatred in Rowanne's eyes. While he had a short space of time of happiness, he was going to fill it as best he could.

'Twas inevitable that she would learn the truth. But he fought against that realization. For now she was his. For a tiny moment in time she was content to be his wife—unknowingly the wife of a DeLucy bastard.

He turned and felt a stab of pure longing. "I will be gone from Irthing today. The fields that lie southwest of the keep are being planted. The Scots bandit Lochlyn will no doubt see this as an opportunity to harry my villagers. Wait not for me to sup with you this eve, for I may be very late."

"Brandt? Is there something amiss? Your manner . . . have I done something foolish to cool your ardor?" Rowanne twisted her hands together before her. He was reminded of those sweet hands upon his body last eve.

Tell her, a nagging voice chanted through Brandt's head. *Tell her the truth of your sire.*

But he could not. He had made the mistake of letting his bride claim his heart. Now, to keep her, even for a while, he needs must keep his black secret.

"Nay. I must see to my duties as lord of Irthing—'tis all that occupies my mind."

Within the hour a few village women came carrying ells of bright fine silk from the East, warm wools and handwoven goods from Cumbria itself. As Rowanne allowed her fingers to skim over the rainbow of colors, she thanked God for her good fortune. Not only was her husband fine and strong, he was gentle and kind to her and evidently rich as a king.

She smiled inwardly, congratulating herself on the fine bargain she had struck with her mercenary.

And so the newlyweds settled into a routine within the walls of Castle Irthing. Each day Brandt rode Clwyd to the outer reaches of his territory. Occasionally the faceless Lochlyn swept down, burned crofts, stole animals, and melted back across the border to hide in the rough terrain of burns and dales.

He was the only blight upon the couple's idyllic existence. And as if toil could cleanse his soul, Brandt worked like a demon to reinforce Irthing.

"I will not go to Sherborne to free your friend without knowing you are safe here within these walls," he explained to Rowanne when she commented he worked too hard.

Day after day she watched him strip off his mail and gambeson and then sweat and strain, bare-chested alongside the peasants. They shored up the weakening eastern wall and put huge cauldrons of boiling animal fat on the parapets and above the hole that looked down upon the drawbridge.

The lower bailey was turned into a training ground for any and all who wished to learn how to wield a sword. Stripling youths practiced under the tutelage of Coy and Desmond, and Brandt encouraged his own seasoned men to hone their aim on the quintain, using lances and swords from horseback. The bailey fairly rang with the sound of blade on blade and the dull thud of strong oak meeting yew.

Rowanne sometimes would climb to the upper parapets, leaning against the rugged stone effigy of a winged creature, watching her husband, feeling such a burst of pride and happiness that she feared she must surely die from it. Then one day, while she watched him sweating beneath a cheerful sun the color of a disk of bronze, an unsettling melancholy swept over her.

She was too happy, too content. Rowanne had never known such bliss, never had such peace and security. She was a' feared it could not last. And she was constantly plagued by worry about Lady Margaret.

Twice Brandt had escorted her to Lanercost to see Prior Simon even though she took confession with Onslow in Irthing's chapel. Both times Leopold still lay insensible in the healing building. The prior had confirmed he had sent a messenger to Sherborne to tell Thomas that Leopold lay ill and that the maiden Rowanne had married. But not to whom.

Still her trepidation was not assuaged. Then, one morning she rose feeling more fretful than ever. Brandt was in the bailey practicing with his men. Hoards of workers were busy with the daily tasks required to house and feed and clothe such a throng of people. Rowanne went into the hall and found it empty, save for Desmond.

"Ah, Lady. The brewmaster has just finished his first batch of beer." Desmond raised his wooden staved tankard as proof. "Come have a jackmug with me." He quaffed deeply of the brew, gaining from it a small, foamy moustache. "I trow the castlefolk of Irthing are well gifted. 'Tis the best beer I have ever drank."

" 'Tis the water," Rowanne said absently.

"Eh?"

"The water—'tis cold and fresh and flavored with the peat from the mountains and dales above in Scotland. Gruffudd told me that makes the best brew."

"Ah. I see, but what I do not see, lady, is why the brewing technique has you nigh onto tears." Desmond laid a comforting hand on her arm.

Though Rowanne fought valiantly, she could not hold back the flood of foolish tears that came forth.

"Lady?" Desmond set aside his beer and tipped up Rowanne's chin. "What makes you weep?" His face hardened slightly. "Is it Brandt?"

"Brandt?" Rowanne sniffed back a strangled sob. "Why would you think 'twas Brandt that makes me weep?"

Desmond narrowed his eyes for a moment, then he shrugged. "No reason, lady, other than you are a bride. I thought that you and your husband might have had sharp words."

"Nay. 'Tis just—I know not. The strangeness of being happy—the worry over my friend yet at Sherborne."

"Ah, I begin to see. But even now your husband makes preparations to ride to Sherborne. Be at ease, lady. All that delays him is his desire to see you safe."

"I know." Rowanne wiped at her damp cheeks and smiled. "I am being foolish, but I thank you for not saying thus." She reached out and lightly rubbed her knuckles along Desmond's jaw. 'Twas a gesture she meant strictly in friendship, for 'struth that was exactly what she felt for Desmond du Luc.

"Desmond—" Brandt's voice was colder than ice. "And my lady wife."

Rowanne turned to find Brandt standing in the doorway, Glandamore on his cuff. Both the bird and her husband scrutinized her with hunters' eyes.

"Brandt!" She rose from the bench and flew to his side. "I thought you were training your men."

He tilted his head and looked down at her. His expression was a mixture of affection and suspicion. "Did you?"

"Aye." She stroked Glandamore's breast, earning a trilling purr.

"And you, Desmond? Did you think I was occupied elsewhere as well?"

Desmond glared defiantly but said nothing.

"Rowanne, would you take Glandamore and find Coy? He is of a mind to fletch some new arrows and believes that Glandamore's discarded feathers make the best."

She studied her husband for a moment. Then she smiled. "Of course, husband. As you wish."

He shifted Glandamore to her arm and stood motionless until she quit the hall. Then he turned and advanced upon Desmond.

"Desmond, 'tis time you and I spoke."

Desmond arched one brow and picked up his tankard of beer. "Of what, my lord?"

"Of your feelings for my wife," Brandt said coldly.

"As if you had to ask, Brandt. I love her—of course."

CHAPTER 24

"You love her?" Brandt repeated in a strangled voice. "You have the stones to say you love her?"

"Aye. I love her—as my liege lord's lady wife—as I would a sister," Desmond said with a brittle edge to his soft voice as he set his tankard aside. "What did you think my feelings were, my *lord*?"

When Brandt did not reply, Desmond rose to face him. "What do you imply about the lady and me?"

"I imply naught, I am but asking." Brandt's gauntlet-covered hands were squeezed into fists. He was loath to reveal his relief at Desmond's answer. For a moment—he had but thought . . . she had touched Desmond . . . but no.

"She is a comely lady, the wife of my liege lord. On our journey I found she has a quick mind and sharp wit. The lady is a treasure, Brandt, and I wouldst hope you appreciate your luck."

"And . . . . ? Speak plainly, Desmond du Luc."

Desmond stared at Brandt for a full three beats of Brandt's heart. Then he tipped back his golden head and loosed a laugh. The sound echoed off the thick stone walls and sent a chill down Brandt's spine.

"As you bid, then so wilt I do. The reason you have

been growling and scowling by turns is your guilt—and the fact that you have truly lost your heart. You are jealous, Brandt. Jealous of any who smiles at your lady wife."

Brandt flinched at Desmond's words. He was possessive, protective, and undeniably, he was insanely jealous.

"She is my friend, Brandt—your wife. I would give my life for her, as I would for you."

"Not more?" Brandt still felt a need to be reassured. It galled him, stung and burned, that he had this need, but he gave in to it anyway.

"Nay, not more. I feel a strange kinship with her. We talk, that is all. I would not have you cast a suspicious eye upon me and forsooth, if you were not my oldest friend and my overlord, I would draw my sword and demand satisfaction for the insult you do my honor and the lady's honor." The last trace of humor faded from Desmond's face. "Do you think I am so low a cullion that I would betray you? Do I appear the kind of man who cuckolds his oldest friend?"

Brandt shook his head. In his heart he did not think thus, but when he had walked into the hall and saw Rowanne's fingers against Desmond's cheek something hot and bitter had loosed itself inside him.

"Nay . . . nay, Desmond, I trust you with my life. 'Tis just that . . . I know not. I am consumed with—"

"Guilt?" Desmond provided.

Guilt. Desmond had said so a moment ago. But was that why Brandt's belly gnawed at him? Was that why he looked at Rowanne and felt a shaft of grief pierce him? Was that why he worried that each sunrise the truth would be revealed and with it her loathing?

"Come, Desmond, let us see to the back curtain wall. There is still an area that could easily be breached. I would know Rowanne is safe from the border bandits before I hie to Sherborne to free her friend from that bastard Thomas."

* * *

Gruffudd warned that the border bandits would attack with the ripening of the fruit. He also predicted that long before the first harvest was in, Lochlyn would sweep down to take the year's crop of lambs and calves. Brandt did not doubt the man's ability to see the future. He felt the unseen threat of Lochlyn on each gust of Scottish wind that soughed through the bailey.

He drove himself like a man possessed. By night he pleasured his wife, reveling in her innocent passion, and by day he worked as hard as a man could work, but still he was plagued by the certainty that his days as a happy man with a loving wife were numbered.

Desmond gave him no peace, for he would find his friend watching him with cold eyes and each time feel another stab of his conscience. Or worse, he would enter a room to find Rowanne laughing at some silly jest of Desmond's, only to see her face become sober when his hard, accusing gaze swept over her.

" 'Tis as though you are seeking penance, my lord," Desmond observed one day when Brandt had nearly broken his back helping a farmer remove an oaken stump that stood in the way of planting a field of rye.

" 'Twould surely be easier to tell Rowanne the truth than to endure this torture you heap upon yourself."

"What care you, Desmond?" Brandt glared at Desmond, feeling jealousy rise like bile in his gorget.

Desmond narrowed his gaze. "I have a great regard for the lady. If you were not consumed by your own guilt you would never dare to ask me such a question."

They stared at each other for a full minute, neither blinking or giving ground while the tension betwixt them built like a heavy, dark rain cloud. Brandt hated himself for his suspicions but he could not completely banish them.

"I love you like a brother, Desmond—"

"Better than a brother, I would hope, since you were

ready to see your blood brother Geoffroi to an early grave," Desmond interrupted.

"Aye, better than *my* brother, 'tis true, but in this you have clearly set yourself against me. Have a care that you do not go too far."

"Do not think to growl and spit at me, Brandt. I know you are an honorable man, but what you do now is without honor and will surely bring you—and the lady—to grief." Desmond gave Brandt one last hard stare. "I would spare Rowanne pain."

Then he mounted his horse and turned in the direction of Irthing without so much as a backward glance.

Brandt stared after him knowing that Desmond was right and that no good would ever come of his lies to sweet Rowanne. But what could he do? he asked himself. He had been doomed the moment he drew his first breath, for he was Thomas DeLucy's bastard—and Rowanne Vaudry had been fated to hate him.

Sun flooded the solar, warming both the floor stones of Irthing and Rowanne's flesh. She stood contemplating her new life. 'Twas time to confront some of the demons from her past.

Rowanne and Brandt had spoken little of the DeLucys since the night they wed. But by look and deed he had made it plain to her that if Thomas's plan had been to gain Irthing through the marriage then she was truly safe, for Brandt would hold what was his. Each day the fortifications and men-at-arms grew stronger. Brandt left nothing to chance, no weakness undefended.

Geoffroi was truly a devout monk, she had finally decided as she watched him at Lanercost. Yet, though she prayed that God would forgive her for her hard heart, she could not forgive him for being Thomas DeLucy's son.

The only task left undone was to gain Lady Margaret's freedom. And that, she was sure, would be accomplished by Brandt in the manner he did all else—by might and sheer determination. She had asked much of him, and he had never disappointed her. Each day that dawned and set she found some new trait in him to admire.

"Ah, lady wife." Brandt's voice rippled over her, sending a chill down her spine. She turned to see him. He stood flushed from some endless labor, his dark eyes scanning her face for the answer to some question he had yet to ask.

"I was just thinking of you," she admitted.

He strode into the solar, pulling his gauntlets from his hands as he went. The weather had been fair, and of late Brandt had taken to wearing sleeveless jerkins that drew her eyes to the heavily corded muscles of his shoulders and forearms. "What were you thinking?"

"That I am the most fortunate of women—that I chose the right champion."

He tossed his gauntlets down and drew her to his chest. She molded her form to him. "I hope you never have cause to feel differently."

"Why would I?" she breathed as he nibbled kisses down her bare shoulder, nudging the cloth of her bliaut aside as his tongue dipped toward one peaking nipple.

"Mayhap you will find I am not the man you believe me to be," Brandt said softly as he stared into her cerulean eyes.

"Ah, a mystery. Well, for now, husband, I would content myself to learn more of your mystery. Take me to our chamber and tutor me in the kind of man you are."

Her bold words inflamed him. His tarse reared to life, nudging against the confinement of his braies and hozen. He picked her up and strode from the solar, determined to do all he could to show her that he loved her—no matter what blood flowed in his veins.

Brandt shouldered open the door to their chamber and kicked the door shut behind him with a booted foot. Gently he set Rowanne upon her feet and began the deliciously slow process of getting her bare.

"I went to Friar Onslow today," she murmured.

He pulled her bliaut over her head. Now only a thin layer of finely woven linen separated her breasts from his hungry eyes. He teased one nipple with his fingers as he drew the end of the slender cording free from its knot.

"About what?" he asked absently.

"I have bid him light candles and say prayers for us."

Brandt sobered slightly, looking into Rowanne's blue eyes for understanding. "I know not why."

Did she know?

"I have asked him to pray we might be fertile, Brandt. I would be breeding a'fore you leave for Sherborne."

He flinched as if she had slapped him. "Think you I will not return to you?"

She touched the side of his cheek with her palm, cradling his jaw lovingly. "Nay, 'tis not so much that, as my desire to give you sons."

Would she feel so eager if she knew she were praying for Thomas DeLucy's grandchild to be planted in her belly?

"Come, lord husband, get a son upon me," she said in a throaty growl. "Plow me deep and plant your seed in me."

Though plagued by doubt and guilt, Brandt felt his passion flare. He scooped her up and deposited her within the shelter of the bed. In a nonce he was stripped down to his smallclothes.

"A wise man in the Holy Lands once cautioned me to be mindful of what I wished for." He warned as his gaze skimmed over her taut breasts and the tangle of golden hair splayed out on the pillow.

"I wish to please you, husband." She lifted her arms in welcome.

With his own blood surging through his ears, Brandt climbed over her. His tarse was hot and heavy with lust. He slathered his tongue over the peak of one nipple as he settled himself between her open thighs. While his stiff manhood nudged against her, he suckled from her breast, imagining Rowanne with a babe inside her—his babe. He closed his eyes, and a picture of her cradling an infant, suckling it as Brandt suckled, floated into his mind.

"Ah, wife, you please me in all things."

With one hand he reached down to fondle her flesh, readying her for his entry, but he found she was already moist—waiting. One thrust and he was tight inside her, feeling her body contract in sensuous welcome. He thrust hard and rapidly inside her, spilling himself as she arched, moaned, and cried out his name.

And yet even in that most delicious instant when passion ran so high and his pleasure threatened to squeeze the life from his body, Brandt felt guilt.

"William, I want you to take a message to Desmond du Luc." The squire's head snapped up, his brows beetled in concentration over the intricate braiding he was doing to make a headstall for one of the Irthing horses.

"Tell him to meet me at the postern gate after the nooning meal." Rowanne was of a mind to give Brandt a special present and had decided to enlist Desmond in finding the perfect gift for a former mercenary.

"Aye, milady," William said obediently.

"I will be gone when you return—I have an errand to attend to," Rowanne said as she pulled on her cloak.

"Gone, milady? Shall I accompany you?" William looked at his half-finished braiding with obvious distress.

"Nay, stay and ply your thongs. I am only going as far as the Roman wall. 'Tis time to set Thorn free. He is no longer a helpless orphan. 'Struth he has nearly outgrown the fine home Brandt provided." Rowanne chuckled as she glanced at her fat, round pet.

"I canst not say I'll be sorry to see him go, milady. He has a powerful ripe odor." The squire wrinkled his nose.

Rowanne smiled. "I never minded—he was ever precious to me. But 'tis time for the little lordling to go out into the world to make his own way. I have grown tired of capturing grubs and beetles." *And I hope soon to have a babe to keep me busy.*

"Aye, milady."

Rowanne found the Great Hall nearly deserted. Yestermorn a feral hog had been shot by one of the archers on the wall. The butchering had been done immediately, and today the time-consuming process of melting tallow to make candles for the keep was occupying most of the castle folk.

Irthing was no longer a haunted-looking place, for Brandt ordered that many arms of candles, including the metal cresset lamps on the wall, be kept burning at all hours. Rowanne was sure 'twas another way he kept the shadows of her past at bay.

The sun was bright and warm as Rowanne made her way through the inner bailey, wrinkling her nose a little at the sharp bite in the air from the midden. 'Twould soon be time for the castle folk to lime the garderobes, cover the old midden, and dig a new pit, she thought, making a mental list of the tasks she now attended as chatelaine. By the time she reached the stables William had readied her horse.

"Shall I find an escort to go with you, my lady?" he asked, his youthful face puckering with worry.

"Nay, stay and help with the tallow—or see to your lord Brandt's armor if you finish your braiding," she said, seeing a barrel of sand in readiness. William took his duties seriously, and Brandt's armor ever gleamed now, cleaned regularly whether it needed it or not.

"Aye, my lady." The lad's face was a study in relief.

As Rowanne mounted her palfrey, taking care with Thorn, she realized she had another purpose in mind as well as loosing the hedgehog. She had been avoiding the spot where Leopold had found her hiding with

her poor brothers, Phillip and Armand. Now, with the
security Brandt had provided, she felt she could finally
look upon the place and face her past. Knowing she
needs must put her fears of childhood aside before she
became a mother herself, Rowanne put her heels to the
palfrey and hurried north.

With the wind in her hair, she was swept with a feeling
of happy expectation. Desmond would receive her note
and give her aid. She would exorcise her demons without involving Brandt, and then together they would be
free to embrace the future.

Brandt spent the day guarding the fields, but his eye
wandered north toward Irthing more than once. He
was a tangle of emotions. In his black heart he knew
that he did not deserve Rowanne. He had played her
false, deceived her, and he lived in dread that God
would visit retribution upon him.

And then there was Desmond. Had he fallen in love
with Rowanne? Brandt shifted uncomfortably while the
question played through his head. He trusted his wife—
and his friend, but the poison of his own guilt was eating
him alive.

By the time the fielders were finished and he could
at last rein Clwyd toward Irthing, he had worked himself
into a fine fever of suspicion and jealousy. The sun was
a red-gold disk over Brandt's left shoulder when he
thundered over the drawbridge. Castle folk were still
stirring great cauldrons of swine fat and hide, pouring
off the liquid tallow for candles.

"William?" Brandt snagged the lad. "Go tell my lady
wife to prepare a bath."

"She has not returned, milord," the lad said in a
rush.

"Returned?"

"Aye. I saddled her palfrey and she rode out. She left

before nooning—to set the hedgehog free. And she took no guard with her."

"By the saints!" Brandt rubbed his palm down his face, trying to control his anger. "Find me Desmond, we will begin searching for her immediately."

"My lord, I cannot find Sir Desmond," William said softly.

"What did you say?" Brandt's voice had dropped to a stunned whisper. Terror rose in his squire's eyes as he advanced upon him.

"I—I cannot find Sir Desmond. I haven't seen him since I delivered my lady's message to him. I thought he could tell me where she had gone after they met but 'twas not the case."

"What message did you deliver to Desmond?"

"My lady requested Sir Desmond meet her at the postern gate after nooning, my lord."

"At the postern gate?" he repeated dumbly, wanting not to see the images that washed through his mind. But they came anyway. Rowanne with her argent hair blowing free, Desmond smiling as they met for a lovers' tryst.

Brandt roared his rage into the night only a moment before William cowered at his feet.

Twenty armed knights rode at Brandt's back toward the Roman wall. The sound of their hooves was like thunder in the gloaming. Never in his life had Brandt felt such a lust for blood as he did now. And he lusted for the blood of his best friend.

He did not know if he would kill Rowanne for betraying him, but he would surely open Desmond up like a roasted pig. He prayed to God that he would find them soon, for he was not sure if he could keep his rage to kill under control for much longer.

Brandt drew his sword the instant he clapped eyes

upon the ghostly gleam of Desmond's flaxen hair. He put his spurs to Clwyd's side and roared his battle cry.

"Vaudry men, to me! To me!"

The men thundered behind him, led by his battle cry. But when the red wash of fury thinned a bit, he realized that Desmond was dismounted, leading his horse.

He looked up at Brandt with amused astonishment. "My lord, do you make war on thistles and gillyflowers— or upon me?"

"Draw your sword, you disloyal knave," Brandt hissed through his clenched teeth. "I'll not slay you with your weapon still sheathed."

The amusement bled from Desmond's face. He dropped his horse's reins and drew his blade. "Have you gone mad, Brandt?"

"I am your liege lord. Address me as such until my blade silences your duplicitous tongue forever."

The bulk of Brandt's men looked on in confusion as they watched the bizarre scene unfolding. Before them was their boon companion and liege lord, swords drawn as if enemies instead of bosom friends.

Brandt slid from the saddle and approached Desmond on foot. "Where is she?" he asked, the air hissing from between his clenched teeth. "Does she await you in some broken-down croft?"

"Does *who* await me? By the Rood, have you lost your wits? *Who are you talking about?*" Desmond shouted.

"Rowanne. I know you met her for a tryst, now where is she?"

Shock washed across Desmond's face. "Truly you are a man driven mad by his conscience, Brandt, for I tell you upon my oath as a knight, that I have not seen the lady this whole day."

"But she sent word . . ." Brandt felt a measure of his rage being replaced by icy terror. "William said you were to meet her at the postern gate."

"Aye, she sent word to meet her, but she did not

show at the postern gate. I came in search of her, riding
out many miles, but my horse has taken a stone. The
bruise is deep, and I have had to walk my mount."
Desmond inclined his head in the direction of his gray,
who was barely putting any weight on its injured hoof.
The animal's head hung dejectedly as if it were in pain.

"Then she is not with you?" Brandt's voice trembled.
"She has not been with you?"

"Nay, and if she has not returned to Irthing I suggest
you sheathe your sword and curb your thoughts, for the
lady is not faithless, as you well should know. If she is
not yet returned to Irthing, then she is lief to be in
need of your protection and not your suspicion."

Desmond's rebuff stung. But even those harsh words
were a gentle scolding compared with the vile names
Brandt mentally called himself. His guilt and suspicion
had endangered Rowanne. He had been quick to lay
his own sin of lies and deceit upon Rowanne's slender
shoulders. She had never lied to him. All the deception
and falsehood lay only on his side. She had told the
truth, though painful and sordid, from the moment
they had met.

He was the liar—the bastard—the *DeLucy*.

Disgust for himself made his breath hang heavy in
his throat. "Desmond, I—" Brandt extended his hand
palm up.

Desmond stared at it for but a moment. Then he
shook his head and lowered his voice so no one else
would hear his words. "There is no need, my friend. I
forgive you, for I know that your doubts are born of
your own guilt and shame for keeping your secret from
Rowanne. I urge you again, Brandt, find your wife and
tell her the truth, before it destroys you utterly."

CHAPTER 25

Rowanne tried to move, but her body felt as if 'twas weighted with sheets of lead.

"Dinna try to move, lass," a gruff voice warned. "Ye have done yerself a grievous injury, ye mustna try to move."

Pain and dizziness swamped her. Nausea rolled through her middle. Rowanne was content to do as the disembodied voice bid. She slowly opened her eyes and tried to focus.

'Twas dark—too dark. It took a moment or two for her mind to register that there was a cooling cloth on her brow, covering her eyes.

"What happened?" Her tongue felt thick and her words sounded slurred as she spoke.

"Ye took a nasty fall from yer horse," the voice said, and a work-roughened hand removed the cloth.

"But my head—it feels like thunder is inside it." She could see blurry shapes of light and dark but no more.

"Ach, and I dinna wonder why, lass. Ye struck yer head on a great gnarled stone. I found ye lying there with blood all about ye. Strands of yer golden hair and bloody gore still cling to the stone."

"Who are you, sir?" Rowanne' s mind was like a hive

of buzzing bees, thoughts swarming and flying about, but where they were going she could not say.

"I be called Rowby, Rowby Armstrong of the clan Armstrong."

"Where am I?"

"Ye be safe, lass, here in the Black Knowe where the laird Lochlyn Armstrong will protect ye."

Lochlyn Armstrong. The name rattled around in Rowanne's aching head. She should know that name—she had heard Brandt say that name. *But when?*

Desmond, on a fresh mount, rode with Brandt and the Irthing men until there was not enough moonlight to show the way through the rough, rocky stones of the north. They had brought rush-light torches, but the terrain was steep and treacherous. Fearing that he might send man and horse plunging to their death at the bottom of a rocky glen, Brandt called a halt to the search.

"We will make camp for the night and begin the search again at first light," he told his men, maddened by the feeling of helplessness that cloaked him. His men were silent as monks, whether from worry or fatigue or the scene they had witnessed betwixt him and Desmond, he did not know.

"Where are you, Rowanne?" Brandt asked the stygian sky as he tied Clwyd and removed the bit so the stallion could clip grass among the rough heather.

"Mayhap she lost her way and has returned to Irthing," Coy offered, bringing a skin of wine to Brandt.

He drank deeply while the thought swirled in his mind. He handed back the skin. "At first light, take two men and return. If 'tis so, then send word back to me as soon as a rider may leave."

"Aye, my lord. And you?" Coy asked, his brow furrowed.

"I will not return to Irthing until I have found my lady," Brandt said.

"Then," spoke Desmond, "we had best try to sleep, my friend, for we will both need our wits and strength on the morrow, as I will not let you search alone."

Rowanne screamed in her dream. Like being caught in a whirlpool she was dragged to the spot where her brothers had died. She fought the weight of the dream, but it held her fast. She could not escape it this time, and Brandt was not here to help her.

Her mother had taken Rowanne and the boys to search for old coins, shoes, and bits of iron at the fortifications that sprouted like mushrooms every mile or so along the serpentine Roman wall. It had been a place of mystery and enchantment to a young girl.

Until that night.

"Easy, lassie, easy." The big, rough hand held her fast. Rowanne fought against the pressure, needing to flee, needing to run faster and farther than she had been able to that night.

"Nay! Take me, but leave my brothers. I promised my mother—I swore to protect them."

" 'Tis a dream, lass. Nobody wi' take your kin."

Rowanne's eyes snapped open. She blinked unseeing at the man holding her down with one great, gnarled hand splayed upon her chest.

"Who are you?" she asked. Her eyes flew to his other sleeve, hanging empty at his side. "Do I know you?"

"I be Rowby Armstrong. There, there, now, lass. Ye're safe here." The seamed and lined face looked upon her kindly, and a small bit of memory intruded upon her terror.

"I must return to Irthing." Rowanne saw shadows of other men in the corners of the stone building. "My husband—"

"Ye are from Irthing? Are ye from the village, then?" The man looked at her with sympathetic eyes.

"Nay, my lord husband has rebuilt the keep. He will be searching for me, I must return to Irthing."

"Ye canna go, lass. Gi' me the name of your husband and I wi' send word ta 'im." Rowby stood up and stared at her for a long while. He rubbed the stump of his missing arm with his fingers, looking thoughtful.

"I am Rowanne Vaudry. My husband is the lord of Irthing—Brandt Vaudry. Send word to him that I live."

"Vaudry? Ye'r Rowanne Vaudry?"

"Aye." Rowanne gingerly touched her head where it hurt the most. She felt soft wool, and beneath that a good-sized lump.

" 'Tis said Rowanne Vaudry died with her mother," the man challenged.

"As you can see, I am yet living, sir, though the pain in my head makes me wonder if death is not preferable." She tried to rise from the pallet where she lay, but the effort exhausted her.

"I see ye need yer rest, lass. Sleep, and I wilt watch over ye," the rough-edged voice commanded.

When the sky was streaked with the first gray and salmon rays, Brandt rose and saddled Clwyd. He refused the bread and ale Desmond offered, jumping into the saddle with an oath against the borderlands and whatever power had allowed harm to befall Rowanne. He put his spurs to Clwyd, recklessly galloping over stones and hillocks.

'Twas still early morn when he found the blood on the big stone.

"The ground is churned from her palfrey's hooves," Desmond observed darkly as he bent on one knee to read the signs of what had happened.

Brandt set his back teeth, refusing to think the worse, yet unable to banish thoughts that chilled his blood.

He silently bargained with God, promising all manner of things if He would but restore Rowanne.

The sound of a whistle had Brandt spinning on his boot heel and jerking his sword free. A man stood staring. He was a Scot with a wild, full beard tinged red with the light of the rising sun. His powerful body was wrapped in a rough plaid over-sherte and brown leggings. He stood on the Roman wall, waving his sword in the air.

"Could be a trap, my lord."

"Could be a challenge. He is a free and bold one. Methinks 'tis the border bandit Lochlyn."

"Mayhap Rowanne is being held for ransom," Desmond said.

" 'Tis of no matter, trap or ransom, I care not." Brandt sheathed his sword and mounted. He put his spurs to Clwyd, caring not if he rode to his death. Within moments he was staring into the cold, glittering gaze of a blue-eyed Scots reiver.

"Be ye the new lord of Irthing?" He was bold and brash and spoke proudly to Brandt, as if he were a lordling himself.

"Aye, I am Brandt Vaudry."

The Scot looked him up and down, openly taking his measure, openly holding him in contempt. Finally, with a cold smile he said, "The lass has been callin' for ye."

"Rowanne?"

"Aye, the same. She is fair mournin' to see ye."

"Is she harmed?" Brandt' s heart pounded a rapid beat in his chest. He silently vowed to cut out the Scot's heart if she had been touched.

"She lives, thanks be to Rowby. Struck her head on a stone," the Scotsman said. "Leave your man, follow me." He turned away, boldly exposing his back as if he had no fear of death or treachery from any man while he walked in this heather- and boulder-strewn land.

"Nay, Brandt, it may well be a trick," Desmond cautioned.

"I care only for Rowanne. I will go alone as he says, but if any harm has befallen Rowanne I will reduce all of Scotland to nothing but a blackened cinder."

The Scot turned back and flashed a defiant smile. "Ye may try, but ye wilt fail."

Brandt felt as if he were stepping into a dark pit when he crossed the threshold of the large, stone hunting lodge. Even though the interior of the building was lit with several tallow lamps that cast a warm glow and filled the air with the pungent smell of burning lard, the room seemed dark.

His heart was beating heavily inside his chest with worry for Rowanne and the knowledge that he was going to lose her when he told her the truth. For while he had been bargaining with God, he had realized that Desmond was right. She deserved the truth, and he had resolved that she would have it all—today.

"Brandt." Rowanne reached out to him the moment he neared the curtained-off bed. He was struck by how finely made were her fingers, how pale and soft her flesh, how small and delicate her bones. Not that long ago he had reveled in the feel of those hands upon his manhood. Probably for the last time.

He came to her and kneeled beside the cot. She was covered from chin to toe with a light wool blanket crafted into a soft tartan plaid. Her hair was like a pale banner around her face.

"Rowanne, I have been near madness with worry," he confessed.

"Prithee, I would like to sit up," she said.

He flexed his hands, wanting to touch her, afraid to do so for fear he might cause her pain.

"My head no longer pounds. Rowby gave me ale with herbs in it for the pain. But I am weak. I would rise with your help, Brandt. I am not so badly injured, but verily I feel foolish, husband, for I can tell by your face that you have worried for me."

She scalded Brandt with her gracious words. More and more the weight of his sin pressed down upon him.

"Nay—'twas not your fault—do not speak of it. All that matters is your safety."

"I seem always to be in peril, and you, being my protector and my champion, always come to rescue me."

"I will always come for you, Rowanne. *Always.* Have no doubt of that. No matter what the future may bring, remember I will always be your champion in my heart and soul."

"Husband, do not speak so or I will think I am truly injured and you are readying my funeral pyre." She tried to smile but her expression was full of pain.

Brandt glanced over his shoulder at Rowby, the man she held responsible for saving her life. "Is she able to travel?"

"Nae as far as Irthing Keep."

"Lanercost Priory lies betwixt and between. Can she make it that far?"

"Aye, I dinna think will harm the lass if you go easy. The lass tells me yer name be Vaudry—how can that be?"

Brandt frowned hard at the one-armed Scot. "For the care you have given my lady I bid you gramercy and will answer your question. I have taken the lady to wed, and as a mark of my regard for her, I have taken her family name." Brandt gently scooped Rowanne up into his arms. "I was not born a Vaudry as Rowanne was, but now 'tis the name I defend with honor."

Rowby glanced at the tall, defiant Scot who had fetched him. Brandt had yet to hear his name spoken, but he felt in his bones he was staring into the hard eyes of Lochlyn Armstrong.

"Then ye'r nae claiming to be a son of Etienne Vaudry?" Rowby asked softly.

"Nay, I am no son of Etienne Vaudry," Brandt said bitterly. "I bid you farewell now, Rowby. And know this—I owe you my lady's life. I repay what is owing. On that you have my word." Brandt nodded at the one-armed Scot and at the taciturn reiver who glowered from his position by the fire.

"Someday ye may gain the chance to repay the debt," Rowby said with a frown. "I wilt hold ye to be a man of yer word when that day comes."

The sun was low, burnishing the grounds of Lanercost Abbey into a reddish glow when Brandt rode through the outer gate. He had escorted Rowanne here before, but tonight the priory looked different, *felt* different, for he intended to unburden his soul and reveal the truth within these hallowed walls. The place radiated peace, or mayhap 'twas finally that Brandt felt a measure of solace in coming to terms with his own deceit. Come what may, he had to be honest with Rowanne. She was too fine to have anything less than honesty.

"I am glad we have arrived, for I fear I was more weary than first I thought," Rowanne said softly as Brandt slid to the ground and scooped her from the saddle.

When he looked down upon her he felt a fresh stab of melancholy and loss. He had carried her before him on his horse, cradled between his arms all the way, loath to relinquish the feel of her for even a moment. And now, he feared, with his confession he was going to lose her.

He stared at the gate of the priory and fought the urge to mount Clwyd again with his lady love, and flee like a coward to Irthing, take her to their bedchamber, to cosset her, bathe her—spend his life making amends and loving her.

But he could not live another day with the unspoken lie between them. As soon as she was settled comfortably and Prior Simon had assured him she was whole, he would speak. He could no longer keep the terrible truth from her.

Prior Simon had seen to everything necessary to make Rowanne comfortable. She was put to be in a clean-smelling room with fresh linen and a small brazier to keep the night chill at bay. The bed was wide enough to accommodate two, and there was even a strong bar for the door to insure privacy.

"Rest well, child." Prior Simon glanced at Brandt. "If you should need aught in the night, simply call out. One of the brothers will hear you." Prior Simon rose and patted Rowanne's hand. He smiled as if he truly understood Brandt's need for privacy. Then he quit the chamber, his sandals whispering on the ancient sandstone as he strode into the corridor.

"Pray do not look so grim. 'Tis only a bump on my head." Rowanne smiled tentatively, wishing that Brandt's strange pensive mood would depart. His intense gazes and brooding silence frightened her.

"Rowanne, there is something I must tell you."

She smiled up at him and opened her arms. "Not yet. I have craved your touch, husband."

"But, Rowanne . . . "

"Nay. Speak later. Right now I would have you show me that I was truly missed. Love me, Brandt," she whispered.

He was lost. Her ardor was like an iron shaft shoved through his innards. He could not resist—did not want to resist. For 'struth, this might be the last taste of heaven he would know.

His hands moved with a mind of their own. Soon he had them both naked. Mindful of the injury to her head, he was careful as he slid into bed beside her. The length of his body touched her silken skin from thigh to toe, setting him aflame.

"Ah, Rowanne, you are like water to a thirsty man,"

he murmured as he took one nipple in his mouth and tugged, gently, insistently, as it peaked and hardened. She moaned.

"Did I hurt you?" he asked with a start.

"Nay . . . aye . . . give me the pain that 'tis pleasure, husband."

A growl bubbled up from his own chest, and he raised himself over her, sipping, nipping, tasting. He wanted to remember every bit of her body—to sear it into his memory.

The skin on her belly contracted, and a fine tracery of chill bumps rose as he licked and kissed his way lower. She bucked and arched against him when he kissed her above the tangle of honey-colored curls.

"You are sweet with musk, my love," he said the moment before he laved his tongue over her sensitive flesh.

"Brandt." She lurched, shuddered.

For a moment he thought she would withdraw, but then she pushed herself against him—hard.

"Aye, husband . . . make me yours."

He drove his tongue deep inside her, drinking her in, tasting her nectar, burning the scent and flavor of her into his soul.

She arched and shoved her fist into her teeth, muffling her cries of pleasure, her head thrashing from side to side with each tremor as he plunged his tarse into her—deep—hard—claiming her, branding her, in a way that would never be broken—regardless of what happened on the morrow.

"What makes you so serious, husband?" Rowanne said a few hours later as they lay twined and sated in each other's arms.

"Do you recall, I told you I was a bastard by birth?"

" 'Tis of no import to me." She reached up and swiped a strand of dark hair from his brow. "To me you are all that is good and strong—I would bear sons that look like you, act like you."

He rubbed the pad of his thumb over the downy, velvet texture of her lips, silencing her, wishing he could take her one last time. He leaned over and settled for a kiss, pulling her near and crushing her to him. He knew this could very well be the last taste of her sweet mouth he would ever have. He wanted it to live in his memory forever.

"I am a bastard, Rowanne, but I know my sire." He drew air into his lungs and forged on as if facing a mighty foe in battle. "I am the by-blow of Thomas DeLucy of Sherborne."

CHAPTER 26

Rowanne's eyes grew wide with disbelief. " 'Tis not a matter to jest about, husband." She stiffened in his arms, and he felt the first deathblow to their love.

" 'Tis no jest," Brandt said sadly. "Would that it were, but I can't keep the truth from you any longer."

Her eyes darted across his features like cold lightning. She studied his face, his eyes. Her gaze probed, questioned. He could feel her searching his countenance, looking for any telltale sign of Thomas in his face.

Was his nose not the same breadth as Thomas's? And the brown eyes—did they gleam with cruelty? Brandt endured her scrutiny in silence and knew the moment she found some echo of his sire in his countenance. In that bitter moment she judged him and, for the first time in their acquaintance, found him sadly wanting.

His soul withered and died inside his chest.

Rowanne moaned softly and turned her face away from him. "Dear God, 'tis true."

Brandt bolted from the bed and looked down upon her, unsure of what he should do or say. "Rowanne, I had to tell you the truth. You *deserved* the truth."

"Nay, speak not." Her head snapped around.

"Would that you had been so nobly truthful before you made me your wife."

He balled his hands into fists and forced them to his side. Her rejection was hot as a wasp's sting.

"So, husband, you are the bastard son of Thomas?" Her eyes hardened to blue ice. "Aye, I see it plainly now."

In that moment something tender and precious between them shattered, died, withered like a new bud born to a hard and killing frost.

"Damn you. Damn you for the DeLucy you are." She began to tremble from head to toe as she pulled the sheeting up to hide her body from him, as if she could cover what they had shared, blot it out and obliterate it from memory.

"Rowanne . . ." Brandt took a step toward her, lifting his hand. He would plead, he would beg if—

"Nay, touch me not, you swine. To think I have lain with you . . . given myself to you . . . prayed for *sons!* Tell me Brandt *DeLucy*, was this all part of Thomas's scheme? Where does Lady Margaret figure in this game you have been playing?"

"Rowanne, I know not of Lady Margaret. Indeed, when I came upon you that morning in the forest I had no notion of who you were, only that your life was threatened by brigands."

"A likely story," she hissed.

"I swear it." He flinched as if she had slapped him.

"You just happened to be traveling the same road, happened to be going in the same direction as Irthing . . . just as you *happen* to be a DeLucy . . . but with no purpose?"

" 'Tis true, Rowanne, but 'twas a purpose that set me on the same road. I would have you hear it—I would have you hear it all."

"Ah, now you tell me there is another truth I must hear? Jesu, I wonder that you do not take the cowl like your bastard brother, so full of truth are you." She was shouting and sobbing. Brandt could hear the pounding of sandaled feet coming down the stone corridors toward their chamber

"I would have you hear it all from me, wife. Then judge me if you must."

"Call me not your wife, you swine, for I was tricked and betrayed into this marriage. I will petition the king to set the wedding aside."

For the first time Brandt felt a spark of his own indignation. He had not tricked her into asking *him* to wed her. In her fury she was now lashing out, laying more sins at his feet than he deserved, though Lord knew he had earned a lifetime in hell for his own dark deeds.

"The king will do naught to change your wedded state, lady wife." A flare of anger brought Brandt lurching to her bedside. "For he long ago gave your fate into *my* hands." Brandt stabbed himself in the chest with his thumb. "Just as he deeded Irthing and the Black Knowe to me long before I met you."

"You lie! Craven brute, you lie."

"Nay, about this I do not lie. I was lord of Irthing long before I ever clapped eyes upon you. The king had deeded me the keep and the forests of the Knowe, thinking all Vaudrys had perished. Then when I petitioned him to decide your fate as heiress of Etienne Vaudry, he put you in my keeping. *Mine.*"

She fell silent for a moment. Then her eyes snapped like blue flames. "So you let me grovel at your feet, bargaining for a holding that was already yours? How you must have laughed. What humor you must have seen in me. What pleasure you and your sire must have had plotting, threatening Lady Margaret's life to insure my obedience on our journey. Tell me, husband, what other plots have you hatched with your sire?"

She was shaking now with injured fury. Prior Simon was pounding upon the door, demanding admittance.

Brandt fought the urge to shake her more, to force her to listen, to see that he cared. "Never have I plotted against you with Thomas. 'Twas quite the opposite—I wanted to see Thomas foiled. I wanted to make him pay. I wanted to have *reven*—"

Too late he heard his own words, heard himself belittle the love he had for Rowanne. Brandt's mouth snapped tight, but 'twas too late to call the word back. *Revenge*. It hung, half-uttered, in the air and echoed off the walls.

"Revenge?" Her voice had dropped to an icy whisper. " 'Twas for *revenge?*" Pain and misery spiced her question. "My fate, Lady Margaret's fate, Irthing, our wedding—all for revenge against your hell-spawned sire?"

Regret was a bitter taste in Brandt's mouth. "Nay, Rowanne. In the beginning, but not after I knew you—"

"Say no more."

Brandt watched in bleak horror while the color bled from Rowanne's lovely face.

"All for revenge. All a ruse, and I, like the foolish girl I am, fell headlong into your trap," she said softly. "Go. Take yourself from my sight. Return to Irthing, for it is truly yours now, bought with lies and trickery and the will of a fickle king. Go. I will look upon you no more, Brandt *DeLucy.*"

Fists continued to pound upon the door behind Brandt. "What is amiss?" Prior Simon's voice rang out. "Open the door. Lady, my Lord Vaudry, are you well?"

Brandt pulled on his smallclothes and jerked on his gambeson and hozen. His jammed his feet into his boots and threw the bar from the door. A half dozen monks rushed in, Geoffroi among them.

"Lady?" Prior Simon's wide eyes raked Brandt and Rowanne.

"I have just learned that my husband is the brother of your silent monk, Geoffroi," Rowanne accused as she stabbed a finger toward Geoffroi. "Did you know of this, Prior?"

"Geoffroi and your husband, brothers?" he mumbled. "Nay, lady, I knew none of it." Prior Simon turned and studied the men, obviously confused. "Is this true, Geoffroi?" Prior Simon asked.

Geoffroi looked at Brandt, then at Rowanne. With a heavy sigh he nodded once. Then he turned and quit the chamber.

Rowanne reached out and clutched at the prior's robes. "Sanctuary, Prior. I beg you, give me sanctuary."

Prior Simon frowned and glanced once more at Brandt. "My child, Brandt is your wedded husband. Surely his paternity has not changed your feelings—"

"I will not dwell in *his* keep another hour. Prithee, I beg you, give me sanctuary." She paled even more and for a moment Brandt feared she would swoon.

"Rowanne—" Brandt began. "You are not well."

"I pray you, Prior," she pleaded.

With one last hopeless look in Brandt's direction, the prior nodded. "If you want sanctuary, then you will have it."

Within the hour Brandt mounted Clwyd and rode away from Lanercost, but his heart, rent and stained with the bitterness of his lies, remained behind him in a small chamber with his sobbing wife.

As the next sennight passed, the folk of Irthing continued about their duties as if all was right with their lord and lady. But the lord of the keep drank too much ale, ate too little food, and was seen walking along the ramparts long past midnight like the Irthing ghosts of legend.

Castle folk whispered about what might have happened betwixt the lord and his lady who had seemed so happy. Some speculated she could not breed, others whispered he could not bed. But none knew the real story. All they knew was that the lord of Irthing no longer cared what happened to himself and that the lady was now living in Lanercost Priory with the monks. Each night Brandt lay alone in his bed tortured by the memory of Rowanne's sweet body, her fresh scent and sensual touch. There were times when he actually thought she was with him, but when he reached out it was to take hold of air.

He had ridden to Lanercost and tried cajoling and then employed outright threats to force the prior to bring him Rowanne, but the man had refused, making the sign of the cross and openly praying for Brandt's benighted soul.

Brandt supposed he could lay siege to the holy place, but there was apparently yet a small shred of dignity and honor left in him, for as a knight he was loath to take up arms against the Church.

Even for Rowanne.

One morn, after drinking himself into a haze, he called for Clwyd and rode drunkenly to Lanercost. He more or less fell from his destrier and staggered about the courtyard roaring Rowanne's name until he grew hoarse. Desmond and Coy finally came and yanked him back onto his horse. He glared at them through bleary eyes but was too miserable and brokenhearted to resist their aid.

He was going mad. He knew it. He welcomed the oblivion, for in madness there lay peace—peace and surcease from his wanting Rowanne and from the guilt of his tainted blood and his lies.

Rowanne spent her days in prayer or hovering outside the door of the room where Leopold lay. Twice daily, between sunrise and sunset, Prior Simon would bid her eat. She did so without ever tasting any of what was put before her or caring what it was she spooned into her mouth. She walked around like a wounded animal, feeling nothing, hearing little, caring not if the sun rose or set. She thought of Lady Margaret's admonishing words over and over again and knew she should have heeded them. *Never wed a man you fancy you love; 'twill lead to utter ruin.* The sad advice ran through her head. Would that she had taken those words to heart.

How sure she had been when she swore she could never care for a son of Thomas. Had she not taken a vow? Had she not said her slain brothers would walk the earth before she would love a DeLucy man?

Well, they must surely have left their graves, for she cared for Thomas's son. She had learnt to care indeed for a dark-eyed deceiver who passed himself off as a mercenary. And now she was reaping the bitter harvest of her foolish mistake.

"More the fool I for allowing myself to love him," she whispered to herself. Then she tried to deny her heart.

"I love him not." But she did.

"I hate him." But she did not.

Her feelings ran hot, then icy cold from one minute to the next. Tears forever burned at the back of her eyes, threatening to spill forth at the least provocation, and she had trouble keeping down the bland meals the monks prepared.

In fact, on more than one morning she had risen to find herself ill, green as a lizard's spleen, groping for the chamberpot as she emptied the contents of her stomach.

She was going mad—she was ill—dying. Loving a DeLucy was a curse, and she the most accursed of women. Her battered and betrayed heart welcomed the surcease from the agony of losing the only man she had ever loved—the only man she would ever allow herself to love—and the man she had sworn to hate until the end of time.

'Twas a curse, a puzzle without solution. She had *once* loved Brandt—but no more. He had betrayed her, played her false, cruelly abandoned her at Lanercost just as her father had abandoned her to Thomas's care.

She had grudgingly forgiven her father after hearing Leopold's version of events. After all, her father had been kept in check, unable to lay siege to Sherborne because Thomas told him that his sons lived and they would be slain if he tried to rescue Rowanne.

But Brandt had no such excuse. He was a knave and worse. She would be an utter fool to love him!

Yet another, more sensible voice, a voice of reason and calm, did not let Rowanne off so easily. This taunting voice reminded her of truth. Since their first meeting, Brandt had again and again shown her nothing but kindness. More than once he saved her life.

I will always be your champion and I will always come for you. And he had. Even when she ignored him, shut herself away and refused to see him, he had come. He had sat atop Clwyd and bellowed her name like an injured beast in the courtyard of the priory.

Her own inner voice called her faithless and cruel. The whole world had no rightness from the bottom to the top. *She* should be in Irthing. Brandt should never have left her here. But what choice did Brandt have but to leave her? When she pled for sanctuary from the church and ordered him out of her life, should he have drawn his blade and forced her home?

There had been such anguish in his voice that she had very nearly gone to his side when he had returned to try to claim her. Very nearly—but she had not. She had remained locked in her small chamber, cursing him for the blood that flowed in his veins. Her wounded pride told her that he had used her to gain himself a demesne and at the same time avenge himself against a sire who would not acknowledge him.

She could not face him—not yet, not now, not when the truth of his blood was stamped upon his face. Why had she not seen it? How could she have overlooked his resemblance to Thomas?

Because you looked at him with love's eyes, that same obliging voice in her head supplied. *Because he was kind and good and did all he could to aid you. Because he was selfless and true and never once did you wrong. Because he was the answer to your heart's dream . . . .*

"But he married me for Irthing and its lands." *Ah, yes, the lands. Would that be the same hides of land you held before him like a tender carrot? The same keep you hoped would make you irresistible to him? Tell me, oh innocent and deceived Rowanne, who was the more duplicitous? Brandt did not ask for your hand. You offered yourself, body and soul, and yet now you revile him for taking what was offered.*

He could not have wedded you if you had not begged him before God and man to do so.

And so the argument went, back and forth, day and night. She both loved and hated him, missed and reviled him, and the hours of her torment were ceaseless until the day that she met Geoffroi in the cloisters.

He stared at her without rancor in his eyes. Even when she cursed him, he continued to stare at her in silence, with an expression of compassion and pity on his face, a face that was less like Thomas's than Brandt's, but still close enough for her to see the DeLucy blood-line in every sharp feature.

"Go away," Rowanne said as she turned and walked the other direction, but he only quickened his pace and matched her stride. "I said, go away. Leave me in peace, all of you damned DeLucys make me sick to look upon you." She glanced at him from the corner of her eye and saw that he was writing something on a slab of slate. He held it out to her.

"I want nothing from you." Again she turned and walked the opposite direction in the sun-dappled cloisters. He stepped in front of her, blocking her path. Once again he held the slate out, encouraging her to take it. Finally she took hold of the slate and glared down at it. In precise lettering the single word leaped out at her: FORGIVE.

She dropped the slate to the paving stones beneath her feet where it shattered into a hundred pieces, making the word disappear from sight, though not from mind.

"I will *never* forgive you or your father or your hell-spawned brother. Thomas took seventeen years of my life—ordered the death of my family. Brandt took my heart—my hope—my love." She picked up her skirt and ran around him, wanting only to find peace in the chapel.

"You must eat, Brandt." Desmond frowned at his overlord while he wrinkled his nose in disgust. "And 'twould be a boon for the castle folk if you would also bathe."

Brandt's lips pulled back in what could only be called a feral snarl as he took the tray of bread and ale from Desmond's hands and flung it across the room.

"I do not wish to eat." The wooden trencher landed hard against the wall, the fine manchet thumping onto the exotic rug while the ale ran down the stone wall. An amber rivulet was rapidly falling toward the chest of new gowns he had ordered for Rowanne.

Desmond raised a brow and folded his arms at his chest. "Ah, so now you have taken to destroying your wife's clothing in your wrath," he observed wryly. "Very valiant, my liege."

That comment brought Brandt's head up with a snap. He untangled himself from the sleeping furs and bounded from the bed. His fingers latched onto the wooden chest. He yanked it from harm's way an instant before the ale reached it.

"So, you still have a brain and a perchance a heart," Desmond said with too much satisfaction for Brandt's taste. "You still care about the maiden, what she thinks and how she looks."

"Leave me in peace, Desmond. Why must you devil me?" He moved the coffer of bliauts and shifts to another corner in the huge chamber.

" 'Tis only my natural curiosity, milord. Tell me, do you intend to starve yourself for her? That would surely impress her, to see your gaunt body laid out in the chapel with Friar Onslow saying a prayer for your benighted soul. Or mayhap we could hang you from the portcullis as the martyr you evidently feel yourself to be. The monks could come from Lanercost to gaze upon you, a lesson in sacrifice whilst they flail themselves and offer up prayers in your sainted name." Desmond tented his fingers in a parody of prayer.

"Grant me a boon and go straight to hell, Desmond, old friend—straight to *hell*," Brandt growled as he flung himself face down on the disheveled bed.

Desmond's lips twitched at the corners. His liege lord was more alive than he thought. There was still a little fight left in him. He still had a streak of Satan's own temper, and he still had a heart. That heart was battered and bruised, but perhaps if Desmond prodded him a little harder, Brandt would snap out of this mire of sadness.

"You have lands to care for. Peasants that rely upon you," Desmond reminded him sharply, kicking a discarded garment across the room. "A king who expects fealty from you as well. 'Tis time for you to end your self-indulgence, *my lord*."

"And are they in need? My people, my responsibilities, or my king?"

Desmond could not help but smile at the indignant tone in Brandt' s voice. "Nay, as a matter of fact the harvest is in, and a rich one it is. Several new hides of land have been cleared for barley. The cots are all in good repair, and the reivers have not attacked since . . . the day you went in search of Rowanne and found her in that hunting lodge within the Black Knowe."

Brandt turned slowly. His tortured gaze locked on Desmond's face. He stared through a tangle of dirty, long, uncombed hair. "Must you remind me? Must you make me remember that day—how she looked—"

"Dying won't bring her back, you know," Desmond said as if reading his thoughts.

"Tell me then, oh wise counselor, what will bring her back?" Brandt roared. "Should I go again to Lanercost and call out her name like a mewling pup? Mayhap I should find a dragon to slay? What would you suggest? That I cleave my heart from my breast and present it to her? How do I demonstrate my regret?"

Desmond shrugged. He had ridden to the priory several times and spoken to Prior Simon about the tangle the lord and his lady had gotten themselves into. 'Twas plain that Rowanne was as miserable as Brandt, but she had begged sanctuary and the stubborn prior would see she got her forty days as prescribed by the Church. She and Brandt both were behaving like spoiled children.

"Mayhap if you behaved as a man—" Desmond snapped impatiently.

Brandt was off the bed and across the room in two angry strides. "Act like a man?" He had actually raised his fist before he checked himself. He blinked several times and then heaved a great sigh as he stared at his own closed fist.

"Nay, Desmond, I will not fight you. And if your game is to provoke me to violence in some mad effort to take my thoughts from Rowanne, then grant me the boon of sodding off."

"If you will not fight me, then battle yourself, or the reivers, or Thomas—do something to heal yourself of this love sickness," Desmond shouted in frustration.

Brandt relaxed his hand and let it drop to his thigh. Then he turned and stalked to the arrow port. "I am weary of battle, Desmond. I have fought all my life, and what has it gained me?"

A knock on the door brought Desmond and Brandt both turning toward the sound. The servants had cut a wide berth around Brandt. Only Desmond was brave enough, or foolhardy enough, to risk his lord's anger.

"Enter," Brandt growled. He raked his fingers through his hair.

A maid from the village timidly opened the door and peeked around the edge. "Milord—there is—there be a . . ."

"Damn, woman, stop cringing like a mouse, and speak up," Brandt shouted.

"In the Great Hall—from the priory—a visitor." The maid shrank away before the last word was out.

"Here? Now?" Brandt's voice had gone soft and hopeful.

"Aye, milord." The woman's disembodied voice drifted into the open door.

"I will be down anon." The air in the chamber nearly crackled with Brandt's excitement.

Here. Now.

Desmond frowned at Brandt. "What are you thinking?" He asked as he watched Brandt fly around the room grabbing clean sherte, hozen and boots. He pulled on his smallclothes and splashed water from a ewer into a bowl. With a shaky hand he began to scrape the beard from his jaws.

"Did you not hear? From the *priory*. The *priory*, Desmond."

"Brandt, you do not think it is—"

"Of course, it is her. Who else but Rowanne would come from the priory?" He poured the remaining water from the ewer over his head, scrubbing his fingers into the tangled mess. Then he yanked savagely at his tangled hair with a comb carved of bone and decorated with bits of shell, tearing out knots and clumps of dark strands in an effort to make himself presentable.

"God be praised, she has forgiven me."

CHAPTER 27

Brandt negotiated the narrow spiral stairs at a near run. Several times he near lost his footing in his haste. His hair was still damp, his scalp still stinging from the brutal grooming. It occurred to him halfway down that he was a different man than the one who had haunted the keep for many sennights: he was older, wiser, *repentant.*

He made another bargain with God, promising that if the peace and harmony betwixt himself and Rowanne could be restored, that he would refurbish the chapel inside Irthing's walls. He promised to give God the gold and silver plate he had brought back from the Holy Lands—if only Rowanne could love him fully again. He promised God that he would . . .

"What do you want—*brother?*" Brandt strode to the high table and poured himself a goblet of ale, determined to hide his disappointment at finding Geoffroi waiting and not Rowanne.

Jesu, his hand was shaking as he brought the fluorite cup to his lips. He quaffed deeply of the ale and poured himself another, wanting nothing so much as to be drunk beyond thinking—beyond feeling and wanting

Rowanne. Beyond the heart-crushing realization that she had not come.

The silence in the hall was like a living thing as he gulped down the third goblet of ale. Then he heard strange scratching sounds. When his curiosity forced him to look, he found Geoffroi scribbling on a slab of slate with a chunk of chalk.

"Ah, so the good brothers have taught you to read and write," Brandt sneered, remembering Thomas's disdain for lettering and ciphering. "And to think I was sure the secret of my birth would remain a secret because you chose not to speak. If I had but waited you could have written it out and spared me the trouble of speaking the damned truth myself." Brandt loosed a hollow bark of laughter. "At least then I could hate you and not myself.

" 'Tis amusing, is it not, Brother, that I betrayed myself? I told her, you know. I told her I was the bastard son of Thomas DeLucy. Do you not find that amusing? I did what was right, and it has cost me dearly."

Geoffroi stared at Brandt in self-imposed silence. His expression was anything but amused. Then there was a harsh snort and a curse from the doorway.

Brandt followed Geoffroi's gaze to the door. Gruffudd entered the hall with a hound flanking him on each side.

"Ah, loyal houndmaster." Brandt raised his goblet in salute. "Have you come to carve out my liver and feed it to your pets?"

"Like as not, 'twould put them off their appetites," Gruffudd snarled in kind. He glared at Brandt, then shook his shaggy head. "And I thought you a man of honor, a man capable of making the legend come true."

"What legend, Gruffudd? Pray sit and amuse me with your tales and superstitions. I am in sore need of a diversion since my lady wife has gone to live with the monks of Lanercost."

" 'Tis no superstition, you foolish dolt. 'Tis written

on the ogham stone by the Roman wall. The dead will walk again if the lord of Irthing has but the courage to face himself.''

"Ah, courage, honor—those noble traits are in short supply in the present lord of Irthing. I am feared you shall have to look elsewhere for your miracles.''

Geoffroi was scratching on his slate with a chunk of chalk. He had one brow arched. 'Twas a mannerism so like Thomas it chilled Brandt's soul. Brandt drained the goblet and refilled it. "Come, houndmaster, have a cup of ale with me.''

Without warning Geoffroi's hand clamped onto Brandt's shoulder. Brandt shivered as he realized how his life had turned bottom side up. This was the brother he had come here to slay, and now they stood together in the hall.

"Appears the monk has something he wants you to read,'' Gruffudd observed as he moved nearer to Brandt.

"Fine, I will read your scratching, brother, if 'twill hasten your departure.'' Brandt jerked up the slate. It was evident that Geoffroi's knowledge of lettering was new and unpracticed. As Brandt read the awkwardly formed words, his mind and his heart refused to acknowledge what they said.

"You expect me to believe this?'' Brandt challenged. He flung the slate down on the long table. It settled with a clatter. Gruffudd picked it up and scanned the precise letters.

"By the green man. By Old Queen Mab.'' Gruffudd glanced up at Geoffroi and then back at the slate. " 'Tis true—must be true.''

"You cannot be dim enough to believe. If this information came from Leopold, as Geoffroi says, then 'tis the rumblings of a dying man—a madman who is bent on easing his conscience.''

Gruffudd glared at Geoffroi. "Do you swear you heard this, exactly as 'tis written?''

Geoffroi nodded and poked a finger at the slate. He nodded again.

"Leopold has spoken thus in the presence of Prior Simon?" Gruffudd asked.

Geoffroi nodded again and pointed at the slate once more.

"By the gods of the woods, I say 'tis true. 'Tis as the ogham stones promised." Gruffudd's normally taciturn face was split by a broad smile. "It is you, Brandt. You are the one, Brandt DeLucy—Vaudry. *Le Revenant. The ghost.* You are the one whispered about since the time of Queen Mab. By all that is holy, you must find them."

"You are both mad. I know nothing of your fairy queen Mab or your foolish legends and whisperings. What I do know is that Leopold is guilt-ridden and knows his end is near. This can be nothing more than his effort to absolve his conscience before he meets his Maker." Brandt studied his hands, showing by the gesture he was refusing to listen to such lunacy. "He claims thus so Rowanne wilt forgive him."

"Nay, 'tis the legend, I say. 'Tis Leopold's fate that he has finally revealed the truth," the houndmaster pressed.

"Truly, you try my patience, Gruffudd." Brandt toed a stool out and sat down, gesturing for Geoffroi and Gruffudd to do likewise.

Gruffudd set his back teeth and glared at Brandt for a long moment. Then, with an oath muttered in guttural Welsh, he sat down and tented his fingers before him on the scrubbed yew table. He took a deep breath. It was evident he was fighting the urge to shout at Brandt.

"Leopold was guard to Rowena of Fontmell," Gruffudd spoke in slow, even tones.

"Rowanne's mother?" Brandt asked. "He was in service here in Irthing?"

"Aye. But before that at Fontmell. It lies only a few leagues from Sherborne. Thomas developed a desire for Rowena, who was then a ward of King John the

Lackland. King John had an eye for beautiful young maidens, and 'twas thought he was grooming Rowena for himself, but then Thomas DeLucy met her—at the same time Etienne Vaudry did. 'Twas said Thomas was sure the king would choose him and give him Rowena for wife. He offered John a settlement of jewels and gold, but Etienne Vaudry doubled it. The king betrayed Thomas's trust, and Rowena was given to Etienne for the higher bride price."

"But Thomas married another woman." Brandt glanced at Geoffroi. "He sired an heir—my brother here was got upon Thomas's own wife."

Gruffudd shrugged. " 'Tis said he tried to forget Rowena. In fact, it is whispered he took another to wife even after his first wife, Geoffroi's mother, died. I have heard stories about a young, innocent maid that married him shortly before the birth of Etienne and Rowena's firstborn.

"Rowanne?"

"Aye, Rowanne, the firstborn child of Rowena of Fontmell and Etienne Vaudry. The wagging tongues say Thomas was driven by greed and his wounded pride. Whatever his reasons were, the tale soon reached Irthing that his second wife had perished, succumbed to a fever shortly after taking residence in Sherborne."

"What has all this to do with Leopold? You repeat no more than the usual castle tittle-tattle," Brandt snapped impatiently. "Gossip this old is of no import."

"Ah, but mayhap the threads of the story all bind together. You see Rowena and Etienne Vaudry dealt well together, and soon theirs became a marriage of true respect and deepest love." Gruffudd frowned at Geoffroi. "Mayhap all would've been well if Geoffroi's mother had lived—or if the next bride Thomas took had not died. But Thomas began to once again think of Rowena and her demesne and how best to plot revenge."

"I understand not what part Leopold plays in the

mystery." Brandt sipped his ale, mentally nursing his own hurts as Gruffudd talked.

"Etienne cared nothing for what Rowena brought to the marriage. Leopold had been left in charge of Fontmell, since it lies far to the south. 'Twas Lackland's way of soothing Thomas's ruffled feathers."

"Evidently it did not work. for Rowanne told me the account of her capture," Brandt sneered.

"I believe that Leopold and Thomas struck a bargain. Thomas was soon in control of Fontmell and did all he could to affront the honor of Etienne."

Gruffudd swallowed hard as if the memory pained him. "Etienne turned a blind eye, feeling that he owed Thomas something for John's fickleness. Enough time had passed that he had two toddling sons, Phillip and Armand. Etienne Vaudry felt he could be generous since he had Rowena and a family. He had an heir, a daughter, and a second son to dote upon."

"A dangerous sentiment to entertain when dealing with a man like Thomas," Brandt said softly.

"I fear you are right, for his plotting soon bore fruit. Leopold, being trusted by some of the lady's former guardsmen, gained entrance into the keep of Irthing. The rest has become legend. Rowena died, and the children were thought to be dead. But now I see the truth. Etienne Vaudry put the tale out that *all* his children had perished. Only now do I ken why he would not ride to Sherborne and lay siege to the castle."

"What are you babbling about?" Brandt roared. "Even this weak ale will not drown out your voice."

"Etienne Vaudry's children were *all* being held hostage. Open your eyes and see."

"You cannot believe that because Rowanne has returned alive from Sherborne, there is any hope for the lost sons. You know Thomas's plan was to marry her to Geoffroi and win control of all of her lands and property. He had no such inducement to leave the sons alive."

Geoffroi squirmed on his stool as if the thought made him uncomfortable. He tilted his head and squinted one eye.

"I have long wondered if you were willing to let that fate befall my lady or if you would have taken steps to prevent it," Gruffudd said with a snort.

" 'Tis an answer you will never be sure of." Brandt's lips kicked up into a mirthless smile. "Since Geoffroi had taken the cowl, the question is moot—I did not have to slay him."

"That he is alive now is not the question—" Gruffudd said softly.

"Cry off, Gruffudd," Brandt snapped.

Gruffudd swept up the slate and held it before Brandt's nose. " 'Tis here, my lord. If only you will have eyes to see. My lord Etienne would not ride against Thomas to rescue Rowanne. Why?"

"Because his spirit was broken?" Brandt offered, understanding for the first time in his life how such a thing could paralyze a man.

"Nay. He could not free Rowanne, for a threat existed against his son's lives. Phillip and Armand were not dead. They were being held to insure no move be made to assist Rowanne. And Rowanne was the guarantee that he would make no effort to free the sons! You see, one threat makes pressure on the other. He could only sit. Any attempt to save one or any of his children, and they would all be put to the sword." Gruffudd slammed the slate down and slapped himself in the head.

"Why did I not see it a'fore now? 'Tis so simple and yet so cunning. Thomas DeLucy is wily."

Brandt frowned and cupped his goblet. "It does sound the very kind of tangle Thomas would invent. Etienne would have had jagged rocks at his back and the open sea in his face. If he tried to save the sons, the daughter would perish or the other way 'round. 'Twould have been an unsolvable problem for a man who loved all his children equally." Brandt drew his brows together and felt his mind wrap itself around the problem.

"But, Gruffudd, even if the tale is true, then the trail is nigh onto two decades cold. It would take a miracle—nay, a handful of miracles—to find the sons after so long a time. They would be grown men, much changed—perhaps with different names. If their lives were in jeopardy, their identities must surely have been kept secret."

"The sons of Irthing live," Gruffudd said stubbornly. "And if they live, *you* are fated to find them." He poked a bony finger into Brandt's chest. "It is your destiny."

"Think you they are still being held by Thomas?" Brandt frowned, trying to fathom which way the mystery might run.

"I know not, only that the ogham stones foresaw your coming. You must do it, Brandt. You must be the one to find them and restore the lost sons of Irthing."

"I cannot," Brandt said softly.

Gruffudd grabbed the front of Brandt's surcoat in his gnarled hands. "If you will not do it for any other reason, then do it to win back Rowanne!"

Hope and disbelief mingled in Brandt's chest. Under other circumstances he would have cleaved off the bony hand that held him. Now Gruffudd's words rang in his ears, galvanizing him with desperate hope.

Hell's fire and brimstone. He *would* walk over hot cinders if there was a glimmer of hope it might soften Rowanne's heart. Still, a part of him was skeptical.

"If all this is true, then why have you not told Rowanne?" Brandt scowled down at Geoffroi, who had watched the amazing confrontation with mild surprise.

Geoffroi took the slab of slate. He rubbed his roughspun sleeve over the words until they vanished. Slowly, with his tongue poking at the corner of his lips like a child in deep concentration, he dragged the chalk along. He thrust it back toward Brandt.

"Ah, you tried to tell her, but she would not listen to a son of Thomas." Brandt smiled at the thought of his lovely Rowanne slicing Geoffroi to ribbons with her tongue.

Geoffroi nodded and sighed meaningfully.

"She hates us, you know. Because of our father," Brandt observed softly.

Geoffroi nodded sadly.

"I don't suppose you can change your blood any more than I can alter mine." Brandt grimaced. "Well, Brother, perchance it is time I tried to see you for who you are and not as a reflection of Thomas." Geoffroi had come to him with this information, he reflected. He could have simply remained silent.

"You openly defied Thomas by taking the cowl, did you not?"

Geoffroi shrugged as if the argument had been a long ago event he no longer cared to remember.

Brandt kicked back his stool as he stood up. "By the Rood, Gruffudd, such a feat is madness. I will do it. I will take up the challenge. Where should I begin to look after so long a time?"

Geoffroi grabbed the slate and rubbed it clean with the sleeve of his robe again. The eager scratching on the slate was like the screeching of butcher birds to Brandt's ears. Finally Geoffroi held up the slate and pointed to the lettering with one long, slender finger.

ASK ROWBY ARMSTRONG TO TELL YOU THE TRUTH ABOUT THAT NIGHT. Brandt stared at the words and felt the hair on his nape rise.

"Rowby Armstrong? The Scotsman who helped Rowanne?"

Geoffroi nodded and rose. He gave Brandt one last smile and then he took his leave as silently as he had come.

"I must be mad as a stoat to consider this, but I am going to do it, Gruffudd. I will go in quest of the lost sons of Irthing." Brandt dragged his palm down his face, feeling his heart quicken at the thought of doing *something* to regain Rowanne.

Gruffudd rose to his feet, startling the hounds that had fallen asleep nearby. "What can I do, my lord?"

Brandt did not miss the new tone of respect in the houndmaster's voice. "Tell me what you know of Rowby Armstrong," Brandt said.

Gruffudd frowned darkly. " 'Tis said he is the father of the Scots bandit Lochlyn. 'Tis also said in his youth he associated with a man named Gruenwald—a man who traded slaves to the markets in the East."

"A slaver?" Brandt mused. He remembered the one-armed man that had saved Rowanne's life—and his arrogant nameless companion. If that blond giant 'twas Lochlyn the border bandit, as Brandt suspected, then he could understand why they did not reveal his name.

"William." Brandt's voice echoed through the hall. He was already striding up to stone steps to don his armor. "Ready a pack of bread, cheese and ale— enough for a sennight. See to Clwyd. Gruffudd, you find Desmond du Luc. Tell him to prepare himself for a ride into the Black Knowe, but say nothing of our purpose. If 'tis faery smoke we follow, I would not have others know."

CHAPTER 28

Rowanne rode under the raised portcullis as the last golden stream of sunlight vanished. Her eyes swept over the outer bailey, marking even more changes, more signs of the effort to strengthen Irthing.

She had spent many sleepless nights trying to make sense of what had transpired between her and Brandt. Now, finally, she had summoned the courage to face him. Even though she doubted much of his explanation, there were questions his words had raised.

If the king *had* deeded him Irthing, then he had no need to marry her—unless he wished to. That truth had nagged at her, battered against the icy wall of her pride until she had been driven to ask the prior for the use of a rouncy in order to return to Irthing.

Gruffudd greeted her in the lower bailey. Two hounds trailed behind him. His face broke into a wide smile of surprise. "Thistledown! It does my heart good to see you."

"And mine to see you as well. I have heard tales that Brandt has made you steward of Irthing. 'Twas a wise choice." The news had both pleased and puzzled her, as the two men had been wary of each other since their first meeting.

"You are finally here where you belong," Gruffudd said gruffly, helping her from the palfrey. "And nigh about time."

A group of laughing children shot by her, chasing fowls and poultry toward the rebuilt mews and dovecotes where they would roost for the night, safe from winged predators and four-footed thieves.

"I have come to discuss a matter of some importance with my lord husband," she said stiffly. "Pray tell him I am here."

Gruffudd reached down to curl his gnarled fingers in the closest hound's fur. He cleared his throat with a low, rumbling sound not unlike a growl. "Lord Brandt is gone."

"Gone? Is he hunting?" Rowanne's eyes were drawn to the forge. Black smoke belched from it as two robust men beat hot iron for sword blades. In a basket nearby a dozen finished blades awaited hilts.

"Nay. Lord Brandt and Desmond rode out of here more than three days ago, my lady."

Rowanne drew her cloak tightly around her, suddenly chilled. "Gruffudd, when will my lord husband return?"

"I cannot say."

"What are you keeping from me? I would know why Brandt is gone and where."

" 'Tis a story you must hear from Lord Brandt alone, Thistledown." Gruffudd stared at her with a stony gaze. "I gave my word to say nothing. Do not bid me break my oath."

A hard, cold weight settled in Rowanne's belly. She turned and stared up at the castle. 'Twas her home by birth, but Brandt had made it his by word and deed. Even Gruffudd was now his man.

"Then I will await his return here at Irthing."

Brandt asked much of Clwyd, and as usual the horse did not fail him. Desmond rode beside him on his dapple-gray stallion, his stone bruise fully healed. Brandt knew Desmond was curious, but his friend asked no questions, evidently satisfied to see Brandt in the saddle regardless of what mysterious task had put him there. Together they followed the winding ribbon of the river of Irthing. It twisted and turned like a serpent, a skin of ice glittering on the top in the weak sun as it plunged deeper into the thick woodlands of the Black Knowe. 'Twas a place of wild beauty, thriving with fat, noisy capercaille, Scottish deer and grouse. A paradise in 'struth, but the farther Brandt rode, the more he realized that this land would be difficult to keep safe and even harder to hold from Irthing Castle.

The Black Knowe lay deep in the border forests, among the bandits and the reivers and far from the king's court and England's justice. The heath was shrouded in fog, and the crashing noise of fast-running burns erupted from ancient rock, giving a perfect cover for thieves and bandits to launch an attack.

On the morning of the second day of travel a light snow began to fall. Soon the ground was dusted white, and Clwyd's breath hung before him like an earthbound cloud. Brandt's fingers were chilled beneath his gauntlets. The tip of his nose stung from the cold air he drew inside his helm.

Now that summer was gone, the sun set early each day. And with the pewter clouds overhead, the countryside was soon bathed in ebony. As fog rolled in and blanketed the heather, gorse, and bracken, the land lost its familiarity. 'Twas not long after dusk that the footing on the mountainside became treacherous, the rocks slick with dew and heavy frost.

Several times Clwyd's shoes struck sparks as he struggled to maintain his footing. Soon the destrier's head was drooping from weariness, and though Brandt was loath to admit it, he as well as the horse was cold and tired. He began to cast an eye about in search of a place to make camp for the night, confused by the sight of the white-dusted landscape.

" 'Tis a light on yon hill," Desmond said, rising slightly in his stirrups and pointing to the crest of a wooded dale. Fog and snow hung between the rocky clefts in two dales. Brandt squinted, trying hard to find the light Desmond had seen.

"You have the eyes of Glandamore, my friend." Brandt blinked and wiped at the moisture on his face. Finally he saw the flicker of light.

"Think you this is near where you found Rowanne?" Desmond asked.

"Perhaps." Brandt squinted into the stygian night. " 'Tis hard to tell with the night and the snow." Then his heart leapt in his ribs. "Aye, 'tis the hunting lodge where Rowby took Rowanne." A jab of sorrow pricked him at the memory of that meeting.

They rode cautiously toward the hunting lodge. The attar of smoke filled the air with the smell of roasting meat. Knowing that Rowby was likely involved with the border bandits and perhaps even had a hand in the treachery surrounding the Vaudry family abductions made Brandt's scalp prickle.

"Mayhap our host will have a haunch to share, eh?" Desmond muttered.

"If he does, it is likely my meat we would be eating in the house of a reiver. But I would have a story before food," Brandt said.

Both knights dismounted, with a light, metallic clank of their armored joints. They walked on the frozen crust of thin snow, leading their mounts slowly toward the lodge. When they were within a pace of the door, Brandt stopped and wrapped Clwyd's reins around a low bush, shaking a cascade of dry, light snow from the bare branches with each movement.

"Ah, my lord Brandt Vaudry. I dinna think 'twould be so long a'fore ye returned." A familiar voice crackled the air. Rowby spoke from the slit of light at the open door. "Enter, and well come."

Desmond stamped snow off his sollerts and went straight to the hearth. He stripped off his gauntlets and flexed his fingers. Brandt tugged off his helm. The hot air singed his lungs while his cheeks burned from the sudden change of temperature.

"You have kept my lodge well," Brandt commented dryly as Rowby gathered trenchers and cups to put upon the table—household goods that once were no doubt part of Irthing's wealth.

"I wondered that you dinna ha' me leave the lodge when you came to claim your lady, my lord." Rowby scanned Brandt's face.

Brandt shrugged. " 'Tis useless for the lodge to stand empty. At the time my concern and gratitude was for my lady's health and care, not for a one-armed vagabond who had set his boots 'neath the bed in a Vaudry lodge. Besides, it occurs to me you were not alone that day— or now." Brandt did not turn, but he slid his gaze to the thick shadows of the room.

Desmond's head snapped around. He drew his sword. "By the Rood, there is a man there—hiding in the shadows like a craven coward. Declare yourself, knave."

Brandt raised a restraining hand. "Hold, Desmond. I owe Rowby for the care of Rowanne. I always clear my debts."

Rowby cocked his head and scratched a spot somewhere deep inside his empty sleeve. "I wondered if ye would keep yer word."

"I will. Now invite your companion to come from the shadows and join us. His eyes burn my back and make me uneasy—and as you can see, Desmond would be much more sociable if he were properly introduced to your faceless friend," Brandt said mildly.

"Come join us, Lochlyn," Rowby said. "There wi' be matters ye should hear this eve."

A whisper of sound brought Lochlyn Armstrong forth.

He stood a full head taller than Rowby, and a good bit wider at the shoulder. His coloring was far lighter than the man reputed to be his sire. From what Brandt could see within the tangle of longish, pale hair and the thick tawny beard, he was a young man—very nigh to Desmond's age. He was dressed in the usual Scots fashion with a long tunic, a thick belt at the waist, and leggings with cross-garters.

Lochlyn glared defiantly at Brandt and then sat at the table. His crystal blue eyes were hard. His jaw set in a determined angle that gave no doubt as to his attitudes.

"I have come to hear the tale of Irthing's sons, Rowby." Brandt slid into a bench and took a sip of ale, wondering idly if 'twas from Irthing's own fruit. "I am told you know much on the subject."

Rowby squinted his eyes and rubbed the stump of his missing arm some more. "I was certain sure 'twas the reason ye ha' returned. I been lookin' fer ye to come again and ask this very question." His accent slipped in and out, not totally Scots but neither English. Brandt wondered who this man, Rowby Armstrong, really was.

"When I saw yer lady close up and realized who she was, I knew 'twas only a matter of time until you or someone came to ask for the truth. She has much of the look of her mother about her. Has anyone told you that?"

"Aye, people have remarked she is her mother's very image."

Rowby heaved a sigh. " 'Tis time the truth came out. The whole truth—not parts and pieces."

"What truth?" Desmond asked as he sheathed his sword, still keeping a sharp eye on Lochlyn.

"The truth about Etienne Vaudry's sons," Rowby said. He shivered. With a steady hand he tipped up his cup of usquebagh and downed it all in one gulp. He wiped his hand across his mouth, the right sleeve of his sherte flapping empty at his other side.

"I was in the household of Etienne Vaudry in my youth. I had both arms then. Would that I could go back to those days," Rowby cackled. "I was a foolish young pup. Greed and Gruenwald's glib tongue turned me from my duty—for a time."

"What happened that night?" Brandt put his hands palms down on the table. He found himself leaning forward, eager to hear the tale.

"Leopold, Thomas DeLucy's trained hound, got inside Irthing's portcullis. He was supposed to take Rowena hostage. Lord Etienne was out chasing bandits in the Black Knowe. When he returned he was supposed to be held at bay for fear Rowena 'twould be slain. The wee bairns were to be taken from the nursery at the same time."

"Bloody hell," Brandt said under his breath. He shivered in sympathy for what Etienne Vaudry must have suffered—for what Rowanne had suffered. "What went wrong with the plan?"

"Ransom was all I ha' in mind, ye ken, but Leopold and Thomas of Sherborne had plotted further with Gruenwald, that bloody butcher. I tried to save Rowena. I received the wound that led to this empty sleeve, but the lady died with courage and by her own hand. She gouged out Leopold's eye for a measure of revenge after he ha' his way wi' her." Rowby spat into the hearth. "The filthy pig raped her."

Lochlyn Armstrong made a sound low in his throat. Brandt glanced at him. There was something familiar about his eyes. . . .

"English dogs are forever taking lasses against their will." Lochlyn's deep voice rumbled over Brandt. Clearly he was hearing this story for the first time. "What kind o'man is the filthy bastard?"

"Nae a man, Lochlyn, an animal. The lady turned Leopold's dagger on herself in shame. The children and their nurse got away . . . ran to the Roman wall for safety."

Rowby stared at the flickering fire as he reached back in time. "That's where I found them, huddled together, but Leopold and his thugs were on me in a nonce." Rowby rubbed his index finger and thumb along his jaw.

"Guilt nipped at me heels. I couldna save Rowanne, that was plain. The wee lass was to be taken to Sherborne, but I could save the lads. I found Gruenwald. I made a bargain with the swine. He had paid Leopold for the bairns, expectin' to sell them to fat Eastern pashas that raise them up and use them like wimmin."

Lochlyn snorted at the notion. "Soddin' bastards, one and all."

"I offered to pay Gruenwald twice what he would get. He had other plans. One boy was sent to the Abbey of St. Giles, on the eastern coast. 'Twas a stroke of fate that the Abbess is a kinswoman of mine."

Rowby rubbed his eyes with the heel of his hands, as if looking into the past pained him, then he smiled grimly. "But God handed me a chance for redemption. We contrived a canny plan, my kinswoman and me. She found a childless couple to take the youngest bairn, and I saw to the safety of the older Vaudry son."

"You expect me to believe such a thread of lies?" Brandt scowled. "Surely Gruenwald did not just hand them over."

"He did when he lost a finger or two." Rowby grinned evilly. "He was glad to gi' them up. Thomas has received messages about the sons for years—written by my kinswoman, o'course. It has kept him satisfied tha' the sons are close a' hand if he needs them for his wicked purposes, but in truth the lads have never been within Thomas's greedy hold."

"All it took was the occasional message from the abbess, reporting the lads to be in good health, and he was able to continue his plan?" Brandt shook his head as the simplicity of the complicated plan washed over him. "But by keeping your silence, you condemned Rowanne to seven and ten years in his bleak care."

"Ah, I didna know that. We heard the lass had died, I swear to ye. If I had but known she lived I woulda gone to Etienne myself and told him the truth." Rowby frowned hard at Brandt. "Ye canna believe I woulda let the innocent lass suffer."

"I require some proof." Brandt stared at Rowby through squinted eyes. "All you have given me is a story. I want more, Rowby. I want some solid evidence the Vaudry sons live."

"Ye understand the Vaudry sons were no more than bairns? Wee, toddlin' lads, they were and fair to look upon. My kinswoman, the abbess, found a noble family to give the younger lad a home. Perchance ye've met him in your travels—" Rowby looked hard into Desmond's eyes. "His name is Basil du Luc. His wife is Alys du Luc."

Desmond shot up from his seat. "Knave, that is my father's name! *I* am the adopted son of Basil du Luc."

"I know, lad. I knew ye the moment I saw ye. Vaudry blood breeds true both in the daughter and the sons. Where Rowanne is the image of her mother, you and your brother are the image of Etienne Vaudry."

Brandt's head swung round with a crack. He studied Desmond's face, the sharp blade of his nose, the crooked smile, the icy blue eyes and the cloud of flaxen hair. Realization hit him like a bolt of lightning.

He thought of Rowanne and Desmond, heads bent together in conversation, of how they laughed and seemed so comfortable with each other.

Brother and sister!

"There is more than a passin' resemblance." Rowby grinned wickedly. "You have much of the look of your sister, Rowanne, if one has eyes to see."

"By the saints' teeth," Brandt hissed through his own clenched teeth. "Her brother—Desmond is one of Rowanne's missing brothers?"

"Aye, I warrant ye see it plain enough now. He is the manly image of your lady wife." Rowby cackled a dry laugh. "Even these old eyes could see the true Vaudry blood the very moment I saw 'im."

"And the other?" Desmond asked in a voice that was a bit unsteady. "If 'tis true, then where is my brother?"

"Have ye nae guessed? Have ye nae seen him? Though he hasna been raised with fine clothes and soft manners, I warrant the Vaudry blood runs as deep in him. Open yer eyes and look, lad."

Rowby paused and then slowly, like a man in a dream, he turned to face Lochlyn—the Scots reiver.

"And since he is the older of ye two, he is the true and rightful heir to Irthing and the Black Knowe—and the very lodge ye be sittin' in now," Rowby said with a smug grin. "So if he has taken a ram or a bullock or silver, 'tis his own inheritance he has."

Lochlyn rose, all fury and denial in his blue eyes. "Nay! I'll nae hear any more of this, old mon. I'll nae sit and listen to yer daft tales. I canna ha' a bloody damn Anglish sire and dam—no matter how ill used the lass was, she canna ha' been my mother. Nae one drop of blood in my veins is anythin' but pure Scots. Nay. I tell ye, this is too much for a mon to bear. I am a Scot! Ye ha' raised me to be a Scot!"

"Aye, lad, I raised ye Scot, but ye were born an English lordling. You are the eldest Vaudry son, the heir to the fine keep."

Lochlyn and Desmond assessed each other with cold, hard eyes. They were of a size, now they were standing. The width of their shoulders clearly marked them as kin no matter how Lochlyn railed and might wish otherwise. As Brandt watched them he could imagine that beneath the tangle of Scots hair and beard Lochlyn's facial structure would be nearly identical to Desmond's. 'Struth, they resembled each other far more than Brandt and Geoffroi, but, then, the Vaudry sons shared a common sire and mother, not just a father as Brandt and Geoffroi did.

Lochlyn uttered a blistering Scots oath and turned his fierce gaze on Rowby. "Why? Why di' ye lie to me, old mon?"

Rowby shook his head, his face a mask of grief. "I should've told ye sooner, Lochlyn. 'Struth, I suppose I had come to think of ye as my own son. But now that your sister has returned whole, and I see Irthing like it was a'fore, when your father was still alive—'tis your rightful legacy. 'Tis yours to hold and govern. Ye can have it all, Lochlyn. Ye can ha' the fine manor and the servants. Ye can take yer rightful place. No need for you to flit over the border and live the life of an outlaw."

Lochlyn made a strangled, choking sound and then he sank like a felled stag onto a stool. His shoulders sagged under the weight of his hated bloodline. "I nae want it. I never wanted *it*. I only want to be of pure Scots blood."

"If 'tis any comfort to you, Lochlyn, I know how you feel," Brandt said softly. "All my life I have wished the blood in my veins to be cleansed, scoured away. Since I took Rowanne to wife, I have lied about that blood, but truth cannot be denied any more than blood can. I have finally begun to make peace with myself in that area," Brandt said with a grimace. "But by making my own peace I have driven your sister from my life."

"Here now, what do ye mean? When you left wi' her, there was naught but love and happiness in her eyes," Rowby declared. "How could storm clouds have gathered? What ha' you done?"

Brandt drained his tankard of ale. "Like you, Rowby, I have kept a truth of my own secret for many years—too long by some opinions." Brandt glanced at Desmond.

"Desmond is one of a handful of men that know who my sire was. He urged me to tell Rowanne early on, but I was . . . a coward. I kept the secret and tarnished my honor in doing so."

"Now dinna tell me *ye* are a bloody missin' heir to some great fortune." Rowby adopted a skeptical expression.

"Nay, 'tis not so noble a tale nor so pretty an ending, Rowby, for I am part of your tangled legend of Irthing. You see I am the bastard of Thomas DeLucy, the man responsible for destroying the Vaudrys."

Lochlyn rode with them back across the border, silent and brooding. The only time he opened his mouth was to tear off a chunk of brown bread, take a few bites of yellow cheese, and down it all with a draft of strong beer that Rowby had sent. Desmond was almost as silent as they rode south toward Irthing.

Two brothers who been raised to be as different as fish from fowl. And Brandt, the bastard son of their parents' most bitter enemy. What a strange trio they were to find themselves companions.

They set a punishing pace, pushing both Clwyd and the other horses hard. And for what? Brandt asked himself. For now that he had found the missing sons of Irthing, it seemed a sad and torn blessing. He had no great hope that Rowanne would view him any differently. The only bright spot Brandt had found in the whole of the strange business was that now all traces of jealousy at the easy comradeship that existed between Rowanne and Desmond had been erased. 'Struth, he felt sheepish as he realized the truth: they felt a natural kinship of blood. Remembering the many times he had been driven mad to see Rowanne and Desmond laughing together, he felt a flood of shame. Mentally he recoiled as he recollected his vile thoughts. When Desmond had given Rowanne a ring of woven posies, he had been tempted to draw steel. When Rowanne had favored Desmond by filling his goblet, Brandt had wanted to jerk her to him, to brand his possession on her body with his lips—and bury his tarse deep inside her.

What a fool he had been.

Clwyd floundered in deep drifts, plunging with his great hooves to find purchase on the rocky incline.

"Mayhap we should find a sheltered glen," Desmond shouted over the din of the south-bound wind that pushed at their backs.

"Nay. We must push on." Brandt stared into the murky whiteness. "Irthing cannot be far now. Where are we, Lochlyn?"

Lochlyn turned and glared at Brandt, his pale blue eyes banked with smoldering hatred. " 'Tisna' far."

"Then let us be about it." Desmond drew his cloak tighter around himself and urged his horse onward.

Brandt wondered how they felt about each other. Lochlyn and Desmond were full brothers. As second son, Desmond would inherit nothing. Lochlyn, the elder, was the true lord of Irthing. But Basil du Luc considered Desmond his son in every way. Each man would receive his rightful due, and it would be plenty. The house of Irthing was restored to wealth, and du Luc held property and power that would pass to Desmond.

With a start Brandt realized that he cared little for the loss of Irthing. Being lord of the Black Knowe or Irthing had not brought him happiness. Only Rowanne had made him smile, had brought a measure of peace to his benighted soul.

He needs must see her safe and happy—after all, he had been dubbed her champion, and her champion he would always be.

But with her brothers restored, she would have family and protection. All the things she had longed for. She would never forgive him for his DeLucy blood, but at least he would know she was well cared for when Desmond and Lochlyn returned to Irthing.

* * *

The snow on the stones of Irthing changed the appearance of the stark gray walls, softening them, rounding the sharp edges. The atmosphere inside the bailey became charged with anticipation of the coming All Saints Day. Rowanne tried to join in festivities with her castle folk, she tried to smile and look forward to the feasting, but her heart was empty without Brandt.

She had developed the habit of wandering along the rampart walls, staring off at the white expanse and the fog-shrouded mountains in the distance. And always the same question rang in her head. *Is my pride worth this misery?*

She remembered Lady Margaret's warning, and she told herself that she didn't love Brandt DeLucy. . . Brandt *Vaudry* a voice corrected. She had sworn her dead brothers would walk again before she fell in love with a DeLucy. She had meant that vow. Rowanne could no more allow herself to love a man with DeLucy blood flowing in his veins than Brandt could resurrect her dead siblings. So each eve she wrapped her cloak tighter about herself and trod on the frozen stones of Irthing. Her heart was nearly as hard and as cold as the winter weather that had come early and gripped the land with a tightening fist.

CHAPTER 29

The hall was ablaze with torchlight and buzzing with voices when the three men came clattering across the drawbridge that had been lowered at Brandt's command. The runnel in the moat had a thick crust of ice and glittered hard in the twilight.

"Go on and find Gruffudd," Brandt told Desmond. "He will make the explanations to the castle folk. Tomorrow we will ride to Lanercost and petition the prior to allow you to see your sister." Brandt's frosty breath hung before his face like a dragon's vapor. "Go. I will see to the horses. You and Lochlyn have much to speak of and more to settle betwixt you."

Desmond nodded. Lochlyn turned a quelling gaze on Brandt, but after a moment he uttered an untranslatable oath and dismounted. They made an incongruous picture, the English knight in his armor and the Scots bandit in his snow-crusted kilt and cross garters. Family bonds were prickly and treacherous things, Brandt thought as he watched the brothers climb the snow-covered steps. Not even the most prodigious liar could have created such a web of lies as the tale of the Vaudry family and the DeLucys.

Geoffroi a monk, Brandt a titled mercenary, Desmond both a first and second son, and Lochlyn—what of Lochlyn, the tall Scots reiver? His hatred ran deep and hot. The young blade would have hard choices to make. Would he keep his family as his enemy, or would he find forgiveness?

Rowanne could not find forgiveness in her heart. Was Lochlyn, her brother, forged from the same unyielding iron as she? Were all the Vaudrys content to live with their pride and loneliness?

Brandt walked the three exhausted animals to the stable and unsaddled them. He gave them a measure of grain and cast an eye for William or another lad to rub them down. The stable was empty. Brandt frowned, but 'twas not his place any more. If it had been, he would have given the lads in charge of the stable a severe scolding. But now that duty fell to Lochlyn.

When he was finished he glanced once more at the emblazoned hall, wishing he could turn back time. But would he have done anything differently? Would he have revealed himself to Rowanne at the risk of never having had her love?

He couldn't say. For a few glorious fortnights she had been his. He smiled sadly. The memory of Rowanne's love was sweetness, and he held it close within his numb heart.

Nay, if time were turned back he would still lie to her and keep his secret for the pleasure of her company. He would lie to know her love for even a short measure of time.

Tomorrow he would go to Lanercost and see Rowanne. He would see her restored to her brothers, and then he would leave her to the happiness she craved and the brothers she had mourned for so long. It would be his last gift to her: his leaving her in peace.

Rowanne wrapped her cloak tightly about her and made her way down from the parapets. She had lost track of time, staring out at the jewel-dotted snow in the moonlight.

A cheer rose up from the Great Hall below her. She had ordered extra wine and sweet cakes for the castle folk, to celebrate the good season and their full larders.

"I am glad they have happiness once again in their lives," she said aloud, watching her breath make a billowy cloud in the icy air. She shivered and flexed her numb toes. 'Twas time to go inside, though she knew the loneliness of her chamber offered little more warmth than the silvery night.

The room smelled like her, Brandt thought the moment he shoved open the door. In the soft glow of a beeswax candle he let his eyes linger on every feminine reminder. There was a bit of ribbon there, a length of cloth over here that was being worked with silver and gold thread.

Had he taken that cloth from her chest in his grief and left it here when he went to find Rowby? He did not remember.

His hands opened and closed into fists as he recalled the way her skin felt beneath his touch. The silent room echoed with the mewling sounds of her passion. She was a fever in his blood.

Roughly, Brandt tore off his armor and hozen. He had snagged a skin of wine from the empty kitchens on his way to the chamber. Now he tilted his head back and let the numbing liquid trickle down his throat.

He flung back the sleeping furs on the bed, stripped off the remainder of his smallclothes, and fell into the welcoming softness. This had been their room, the place where she had welcomed him into her.

He drained the skin of wine. With his damp fingers he snuffed out the last the beeswax candle. He shut his eyes and let the lethargy of the grape steal over him.

On the morrow . . . he would find strength and courage enough to leave Rowanne.

Rowanne descended the stairs to her sleeping chamber. There was a bit of a moon, enough to slant a cool gray light into the corridor from a pair of arrow slits. When she opened the door she was confronted by darkness, the only illumination the dull reddish glow from the dying embers of an earlier fire in the brazier. She made no effort to light a candle.

Rowanne kicked off her slippers and began to unlace her bliaut. Her cold fingers were clumsy. It took several tries before she had the laces open. She shivered in her shift while she groped her way in the partial darkness. When her fingers felt the silken hangings, she parted them and slipped into the curtained bed where the sleeping furs were thrown back. Her maid must have come and prepared her chamber, she thought numbly.

Rowanne lay back and closed her eyes, finding sleep waited like a hungry beast at the edges of her mind. Hovering on the perimeter of wakefulness and blessed slumber, she turned and flung her arm out across the bed.

And found a warm, hard chest beneath her arm.

Her eyes flew open as her breath lodged hard in her gullet. *I know this body—the measured breathing, the feel of each muscle and sinew. . . . 'Tis Brandt.*

"Rowanne?" His deep voiced rubbed over her skin, awakening all her senses. "Jesu, is it really you? Have I gone so mad that I now conjure you from the darkness?"

She stiffened and made to leave the bed.

"Nay. . . stay, wife. Stay, sweet specter, or ghost, or imagining. Stay near me for just this small space of time. I would ask no more than that. Let me have one night of peace in this room."

There was something in his request, something raw and needful—something that called to her deep in her torn and betrayed soul. Though Rowanne told herself she should not, her body relaxed of its own accord. She felt the mattress beneath her give, heard the leather straps groan and creak as she allowed her rigid body to sink into the bed.

"I was going to come to Lanercost tomorrow," he said softly. "I thought you were there, seeking sanctuary with the monks. But of course, in truth you are. This is just my wishing."

There was a dreamy, soft quality to his voice that Rowanne had never heard before. It held her, mesmerized her. She could not speak. She could not find her voice as his leg lightly brushed against her own.

" 'Tis good you are here." His breath smelled of wine, and his voice had a soft, breathy timbre to it. She had never seen Brandt in his cups before. He truly did not know if she was flesh or fantasy.

"Rowanne, your brothers live," he whispered into her hair as he turned toward her. "I know 'tis impossible, but they do—they did not perish. Desmond is your brother, and Lochlyn Armstrong, though I think Lochlyn wishes it were otherwise. I have restored your dead brothers to you, Rowanne."

She took a deep breath, intending to demand an explanation for this madness, this crazy tale he was spinning, but then suddenly he was there above her, holding his weight on stiff forearms. The dying embers cast a reddish shadow on his face as he stared down at her, bleary-eyed, his face taut with sorrow and loneliness.

It was a face full of pain and regret. Her heart cried out to erase that look of sorrow.

"Rowanne . . . give me your body. Let me bathe in the honeyed sweetness of you. Even if it is only a dream, let me dream, my love. Let me have this night."

Then his head was descending, searching out her mouth, claiming her. A voice in her head wanted to gainsay him, but she ignored it.

She did not love him. She could not love him. He

could tell all the fanciful lies about her brothers living that he wanted to, and still it would not change the truth.

He was a DeLucy. . . . He was . . . he was doing strange and wonderful things to her body. His hand slid upward, taking the shift with it. And his DeLucy blood did not signify when he squeezed a taut and peaked nipple. And she never even considered who was his sire at the moment when his tarse, heavy and throbbing with lust, slid into her wetness. Nay, Brandt was not a DeLucy at this moment, he was simply her lover.

Rowanne's body was warm and soft. A low groan issued from her lips as he slipped his hand between her thighs and began to massage her nubbin of flesh as he moved against her. One slender hand was against his chest near his collarbone, in a last feeble gesture of restraint. She had surrendered her body to him even if her heart was still locked and shuttered.

They kissed deeply. Brandt fancied he could taste the pungent mixture of honey, wine, and *Rowanne* on his tongue. How real his mind had conjured her.

He moved against her in an old familiar rhythm that increased his pulse and sent his blood surging through his veins. And then a strange thing happened. He opened his eyes and found Rowanne staring up at him. The expression in her eyes was a mixture of hesitance and anticipation. She was real, solid, and not a fevered imagining.

"I should hate you, Brandt DeLucy," she whispered. "I *need* to hate you."

"Aye," he said simply. "I know."

"I should hate you, but at this moment I cannot." She slid her arms along his neck and looped her hands behind his head. "Dear God in heaven . . . I *cannot.*" She shuddered as he plunged deep inside her. Once, twice, three times.

"Take me, Brandt le Revenant, the *ghost.* Tonight you are neither DeLucy nor Vaudry. For tonight make me

forget that we are enemies. Be a ghost on the wind—
a phantom lover with no past and no future. Take me
to heaven in your arms."

When he drove into her deeply, she raised her pelvis
and met his thrust. As his teeth grazed along the tender
skin of her throat, her nails dug into his buttocks, driving
him deeper inside her, mixing pain with pleasure. Their
coupling was so intense that he nearly cried out when
her muscles gripped him tightly and she stiffened, pulling him in, drawing him toward her core.

A deep, guttural growl bubbled up from inside him.
A chunk of his heart bled and grieved, for he knew that
this would be the last time he would hold Rowanne,
and yet . . . she had asked him to love her. 'Twas
enough, and so much more than he ever hoped to have
again.

"Aye, milady, I am yours to command, and if 'tis
passion that you yearn for, then 'tis passion you shall
have." He dipped his head and claimed her mouth
once again. A flame ignited in his chest, a fire he knew
would burn forever. "For I am always your champion."

This was joy and heartbreak, lust and love. This was
all the things that the troubadours sang of. It was light
and dark and pulsing flesh. It was a bittersweet mating
between two hearts that could never find peace and
love with one another because of their blood and their
past. Only in the night, only in dreams would they be
together.

The inner bailey was deserted as Brandt strode across
the crust of ice covering the snow beneath. He readied
Clwyd and then went to the mews to see Glandamore.
She was still sleeping, her head tucked under her wing.
He stared at her for a long moment while he thought
of his future.

A mercenary had no home. Indeed, mercenaries

never knew if they would live to see another sunrise and sunset or if death would take them in the next heartbeat.

Glandamore was a lady, and like Rowanne, deserved the best life had to offer. She was a grand bird, a noble bird, and he loved her well.

"Stay, my beauty. Stay with my lady and serve her all the days of your life." He smiled and then turned on his heel. The snow muffled the sound of his boots, but he thought he heard a familiar trilling as he left the mews.

He lowered his visor. Then he led Clwyd out of the inner bailey and through the portcullis that he had repaired and raised with his own hands. A man from the village was on the wall as Brandt rode through, the whine and creak of the windlass whining through the clear air as the drawbridge dropped into the thick drift of snow on the opposite side of the moat.

When Clwyd's iron-shod hooves sunk into the soft powder, Brandt turned and allowed himself one last look. The first rays of dawn slanted into the arrow port of the lord's sleeping chamber. He closed his eyes and pictured how Rowanne had looked with her hair splayed across the pillow.

A cold, hard lump of emotion lodged in his throat as he mouthed a farewell, then he turned and galloped south through the untouched snow and out of Rowanne's life forever.

CHAPTER 30

"Rowanne, mayhap you would prefer to go to your chamber?" Desmond lightly touched her sleeve, his gesture of affection touching, and still a bit unexpected. "You look as if you did not rest well—again."

She read the concern in his eyes. He had aged a little since Brandt had left, she thought. There were now lines of worry bracketing his lips, and a strange melancholy clouded his expression when he thought no one was watching. Where he had once been the laughing troubadour, now he was the concerned brother.

They sat together at the high table, wearing the same false smiles for the castle folk that they had worn for many sennights. Advent was nearly over, Hogmanay would begin tomorrow, and because of Lochlyn the holiday was being observed at Irthing.

The hall gleamed with candles, and the fragrance of fresh-cut boughs filled the air. And yet Irthing found no happiness in the joy of the season.

"You miss him too," she said softly.

"Aye, but then he was never my enemy as he was yours. I have always loved him like a brother and my lord. I understand what you have endured at the hands of Thomas DeLucy. I don't hold you responsible for Brandt leaving, sister, but I love him still.''

"Would that Lochlyn had your forgiving nature," she said. "If so, mayhap he would have bided at Irthing a while longer ... given it more of a chance. I would know my brother if he would but let me."

Desmond stiffened, his eyes becoming more shuttered and unreadable. "Perchance in time he will come to regard us as his family and not bloody damned English invaders that deserve only his ire." Desmond shook his head as he repeated Lochlyn's most oft used phrase. "Bloody damned English invaders—does he not realize he is English?"

"Not in his heart, and perhaps that is where it matters most."

Lochlyn had quit Irthing one morn after breaking his fast, soon after Brandt had vanished. Lochlyn had politely, if icily, explained to Desmond and Rowanne that he was a Scot by choice if not by blood. His eyes had glittered like shards of blue ice when he told them he had no intention of renouncing his Armstrong name or clan or allegiance. With a sneer he advised them that hell would likely freeze over twice before he would lay claim to Irthing or anything on the south side of the Roman wall.

The blow had been hard for Rowanne, but worse for Desmond. Now the responsibility of Irthing and her and the babe she carried in her womb was all upon Desmond's shoulders. She pitied him for it.

In addition to that, he had taken up the cause of freeing Lady Margaret, since Brandt had disappeared before Desmond could ask for his aid. Before the snows had fallen Desmond had sent a messenger to Sherborne with an offer of ransom, hoping that Thomas's reputation for greed would prevent any more bloodshed, and sorrow. But they had received no reply to his offer of ransom. In fact, there had been no word at all of Sherborne.

" 'Twill be a'right, I promise. All will be well.'' Desmond smiled and patted Rowanne's hand, hoping he could manage to deliver what he promised. "I am looking forward to being an uncle, and surely Thomas will see the wisdom of releasing the lady and fattening his purse. His plans are in ruins. Geoffroi was his last hope. Now with the story revealed, he will see reason. 'Twill all come a'right," he said, with a wink that held little confidence.

"You are a sweet liar, Desmond. Thomas is unpredictable as a snake, and I know you would much rather be tearing around the countryside having adventures and flirting with comely wenches than dealing with the tedious duties of Irthing while I breed." Rowanne sighed, feeling fat and useless and more lonely than she had thought possible.

"No good comes from wishing for what cannot be, sister." Desmond said. "I am a man of responsibility now. You can depend on me."

"I hear your words and understand they are meant for me. You are right, of course, but I cannot forgive myself, for I drove him away." *If only I had told him that I loved him that night.*

Desmond tilted his head and frowned at her. "I have known Brandt le Revenant for a long while. Never have I known anyone to *drive* him away. I believe he left with a purpose in mind—though we may never know what that purpose was."

Rowanne blinked back the sting of tears. She rose awkwardly from her chair, her belly making her balance awkward. If she stayed, she would weep, and poor Desmond could not deal with her tears. It was the one area he had never mastered and probably never would. She pitied him, for if he had the misfortune to wed a woman that would use tears as a weapon, the war would be lost before the battle began.

"I am going to walk along the battlements," Rowanne explained, trying to hide the unshed tears as she turned away.

"Wear your heavy cloak," Desmond said, sounding

more like a nurse than the lord of Irthing. "I will have your maid accompany you."

"I would rather be alone."

"But you will have the maid." Desmond motioned to a girl to follow Rowanne to the upper battlements of Irthing.

Clwyd floundered, nearly going to his knees in the deep drift. Brandt halted, stiffly dismounted, nearly falling himself as his numb feet touched the frozen ground. His joints and the long wound in his leg had since ceased to ache and had finally grown numb from the cold. The only pain he felt was in his heart. That steady ache never ceased.

He trudged through the icy whiteness to his companion's horse. 'Twas too cold to speak, but the vapor escaping from the huge cowled hood assured him that the person within was still alive and breathing.

When he left Irthing and Cumbria he had thought to make his way to the eastern coast and find a ship going to France. But as if Clwyd were being guided by an unseen hand, his course had pointed true south. South—straight as a lance for Sherborne's gates.

Clwyd whiffled into Brandt's palm and nudged at his master.

"Anxious to go, eh?" Brandt rubbed between the liquid brown eyes with his gauntlets. "Would that I was as sure of my course as you seem to be, old friend. But then, I have trusted you to guide me before, and I will trust you now."

With a gritty determination that belied his own torn feelings, Brandt mounted Clwyd and pressed on through the thick, paralyzing drifts toward his destiny.

Heavy snows blanketed the hillsides, River Irthing was frozen nearly solid at its banks, and travel had become impossible for over a fortnight. In a strange way Irthing had become a prison to Rowanne as surely as Sherborne had ever been.

This morn gray anvil clouds threatened more snow, and the wind from the north soughed around the parapets with a mournful howl. Tomorrow the high holy season would begin. Gifts would be exchanged, songs sung, prayers offered up. But the only thing that Rowanne ever prayed for now was that Brandt would return so that she might throw herself into his arms and tell him how much she loved him.

She had come to realize what a cold and bitter companion her pride was. On the day that Lochlyn left, with his chin held high and his back as rigid as stone, she realized how futile all of her hatred had been.

Her own brother by blood now considered her an enemy, and beneath her breast beat the heart of a child that carried DeLucy blood. What a tangle the Vaudrys and DeLucys were. God and all the saints had conspired to teach her a bitter lesson from all that had happened.

Desmond appeared in the bailey below with Glandamore on his cuff. He glanced up at Rowanne and gave her his half-smile. He was wearing a bright red cloak with the du Luc arms blazoned on the front. Even Desmond was not wholly comfortable with the blood in his veins, she thought wryly. A part of him was more Basil du Luc's son than Etienne Vaudry's.

Glandamore took flight, spiraling upward until she was high above the curtain walls of Irthing. Then the bird cried out and flew south like a bolt shot from a crossbow.

Rowanne watched her go, wishing that the bird had the ability to find Brandt, to take him a message, to bring him *home.* She shivered against the cold, drawing her cloak tighter about her body.

"We must go in, my lady, the snow is coming." Her maid's teeth were chattering.

"You may go, I want to stay a little longer, just a

little longer." Rowanne squinted out over the diamond-bright landscape. She could not say why she clung to her hope, but daily she remained on the wall, searching for *him*.

She wriggled her toes farther into her rabbit fur-lined boots, ignoring the way her cheeks were beginning to sting. There was something out there . . . something she must see . . . something that had drawn Glandamore's attention.

Then, on the far southern horizon at the edge of a thickly wooded forest, she saw them. Two dark dots in the snow.

She blinked. Perchance it was a pair of stags, or two boulders that were free of snow. She stared at them unblinking until her eyes stung and tears ran from the corners in the cold. Her tears made her face feel as if it were being sliced by a dagger's edge.

The two dark dots were moving. 'Twas only the barest change in their position, but Rowanne was sure they were coming toward Irthing.

"Quick, fetch Lord Desmond at once," Rowanne commanded.

"Oh, my lady, be it the babe?" the maid asked, her eyes round with apprehension.

"What?" Rowanne asked in a moment of confusion. "Oh, nay, nay, I am in fine fettle, but there are riders on the horizon." Rowanne lifted her arm and pointed at the mere specks of dark.

The maid whirled and squinted into the white expanse. "Oh, I see them, lady, I do see them." With a muffled cry she hitched up her skirts and ran toward the stairs, throwing up little rooster tails of snow with each step.

"They are too well wrapped to see much," Desmond pronounced as he stood squinting into the glare of the snow. "The only thing for certain is there are two and they are on destriers."

"Knights?"

"Mayhap, or freelancers seeking shelter from the coming storm." He frowned as if weighing the possibilities. "Though what knight of any sense would choose to travel in such weather, I cannot imagine."

Rowanne felt a moment of disappointment. For some untold reason she had hoped ... prayed that it was Brandt or mayhap lady Margaret. But of course that was a foolish thought, for Brandt traveled alone, and no man alive would be bold enough to travel with a lady in this weather.

Not even her bold mercenary.

"We needs must have patience, Rowanne, for they appear to be coming straight for Irthing. Whoever they be, we will know their identity by evensong."

"Then let us prepare a feast for Twelfth Night and our unknown visitors. Let us try to make merry this season and hope those who are not with us will also enjoy a fine feast and a warm fire," Rowanne said with a catch in her throat, "wherever they may be."

The afternoon was filled with tasks to busy the hands and occupy the mind while the castle awaited the unknown visitors. Rowanne found herself becoming excited by the laughter and whispers of the castle children. Gruffudd and his hounds sat clustered around the main hearth in the Great Hall and at his feet dozens of round-eyed youngsters listened to tales of past Twelfth Night visitors.

Rowanne smiled and rubbed her hand over her belly. 'Twas only slightly rounded, but by spring, when the flowers bloomed again, she knew she would be heavy with child.

"That is a sight to warm my heart," Desmond said

as he reached out and took one of the golden, sweet biscuits she had brought from the kitchen.

"What? All these sweet biscuits?" She asked, still smiling, thinking of her babe.

"Nay, Rowanne, your smile. I have not seen you smile thus since—"

"Since my husband left," she finished for him. "I have been a trial for you, I know. You gain a sister and a millstone all in one day."

"Nay, never say it, sister." Desmond reached for another sweet biscuit, but she slapped his hand.

"These are for our visitors. Have they come yet?"

"I have left orders with the gatekeeper that I am to be informed at once," Desmond said as he glanced up. His face changed, first going ashen but soon a secret smile split his face.

"Rowanne," he said softly. "If you could have your heart's desire this Twelfth Night, what would you wish for?"

"You know the answer," she said as she placed the tray of sweet meats on the long table next to plates of honeyed almonds, tarts, and jellied pears. Her eyes idly scanned the children at Gruffudd's feet. "My only desire is that Brandt return so that I may tell him the truth."

"And what truth would that be, wife?" Brandt's voice cut through the din like a sword.

Rowanne spun around so quickly that for a moment the room blurred. Her bliaut swirled around her ankles and she reached out instinctively for support. Brandt's icy-cold gauntlet closed over her wrist.

"Jesu, you are near frozen," Rowanne gasped. Crystals of ice spiked his lashes. There was a bluish tint to his lips. Her heart lurched painfully within her ribs. And then she saw the red stain of frozen blood on the greaves and sollerts of one leg.

"Tell me your truth, wife, for I am of a mind to listen." His eyes rolled back into his head. In a heap he collapsed at her feet.

CHAPTER 31

"Gruffudd, clear the way, make room for Lord Brandt," Rowanne shouted. In a nonce, with Gruffudd and Desmond barking orders, Irthing erupted into activity. Hot tubs of water were brought, steaming possetts and mulled ale readied. Warm furs were hauled down from the upper chambers. Frozen layers of first armor and then icy clothing were pried and peeled from Brandt's body. Rowanne worked with frozen taches and buckles until the tips of her fingers pinked from cold and effort.

"Clwyd . . ." Brandt murmured.

"Have no fear, he is being rubbed down and placed in a stall with fine, thick bedding," Desmond said from somewhere behind Rowanne. "He will have an extra measure of grain this night."

"And my—companion?" Brandt coughed and choked. "What of the lady who rode—?"

Rowanne's head snapped up. A sharp pain cut through her. She had seen no lady—Jesu, she'd had eyes only for Brandt.

"She is presently being bathed and warmed as you are, my lord," Desmond assured Brandt.

Rowanne swallowed hard and forced herself to concentrate on the task of freeing Brandt's clothing. After he was warm and dry they would talk. Until then she would blink the tears from her eyes and think of nothing more than that he had come.

He had come back to Irthing.

He had come to her once more.

Surely the fact that he had returned meant there was hope. That is what she would cling to: *hope.*

The blood began to flow freely as soon as he was sufficiently warmed. It trickled down his thigh and over the frame, staining the carpet beside the bed a bright red. It did not pool, did not thicken, but ran.

"Gruffudd, do you have the skill?" Rowanne asked as she took the last of Brandt's smallclothes and tossed them into a pile.

"I need herbs, a needle, silken thread from your sewing chest," Gruffudd rattled off a list, and people flew from the chamber to bring what was needed. "Plenty of hot water and the Scots drink, *usquebagh,* from the oaken cask. Bring much of that, for he wilt need it to fortify his blood . . . and for the pain."

Rowanne twisted her fingers. She was not needed, but she was loath to quit the chamber. Seeing Brandt weak and vulnerable had astounded her. At some point in their association she had begun to think of him as invincible. But as his blood dripped and puddled on the carpet, she knew he was not immortal.

He was flesh and blood. And in danger of dying.

"Rowanne." He called weakly, looking at her over the foot of the bed. "I confronted my . . . father." The word choked from him painfully. His eyes closed, and he lapsed into sleep, too spent to say more.

"Oh, my love," she whimpered, unable to reach him for the wall of bodies between them, including Gruffudd, who was bent over stitching closed the deep, bleeding rent in Brandt's thigh.

"You can't die now. You cannot die and leave me

alone to raise your son without you," she railed at him, suddenly angry with him for leaving, furious that he was wounded.

"He will not die, Rowanne, we will not let him leave us."

A familiar female voice brought Rowanne around. She blinked unbelievingly at the person in the open door. Lady Margaret stood there, looking nearly as pale as Brandt. Blue gray smudges lay beneath her eyes.

"Brandt would not stop, would not rest until he had brought me to you. Not even when the wound broke open for the second time. I think the cold is all that saved him, else he would have bled to death out there in the deep snow. We have traveled for days without rest."

Rowanne stared dumbly at lady Margaret. Her face blurred, her vision shrank. The world turned dark as pitch, collapsing into a spinning vortex.

Rowanne was once again in the tower of Sherborne. Lady Margaret was there. The room was warm, but Rowanne was lonely. She craved to be at Irthing, and she craved something else she could not name. . . .

Rowanne's eyes flew open. She was breathing harshly. Her heart pounded while she fought to break the hold of the dream. She sat up quickly, but her stomach churned. She swallowed back bile as she threw her feet over the edge of the bed.

"The garderobe—I need the garderobe." Rowanne vaulted from the bed and ran to spill the contents of her stomach. When she finished she felt a little better.

"Rowanne?" Lady Margaret's soft voice washed over Rowanne.

"I am well. 'Tis only breeding that makes my stomach churn and lurch with alarming regularity. Is Brandt—?" Rowanne could not finish the question.

"He yet lives," Lady Margaret assured her. " 'Tis no

wonder you fainted dead away. The sight of all that blood on Brandt's armor—and you with child. Rowanne, you must lie back down and regain your strength, or you will be of no use to your husband when he wakes."

"Husband," she murmured as she sat heavily on the edge of the bed. She collapsed into the bolster and realized she was in one of the nearby chambers that she had readied for the babe.

Margaret brought a tankard of water. "Drink, and no arguments."

"Lady Margaret, how did you get free?" she asked awkwardly between gulps.

Margaret turned and looked at Rowanne. The dying rays of the sun slanting through the arrow port turned her hair a bright ginger. "Your husband, of course. He rescued me." Margaret smiled tenderly.

"He said 'twas a debt of honor, that he was your champion," Margaret added as she sat on the edge of the bed. "He risked great peril, Rowanne. I want you to know that."

"And . . . Thomas?"

"Dead."

She had expected to be ebullient when she heard those words but instead waves of misery folded over Rowanne. She had hated Thomas as much as Lochlyn hated all English, but now the impact of all she had asked of Brandt hit her.

She had bid her husband slay his own father. And if he did not yet hate her for that request, then in the future he surely would hate her . . . and the babe.

"Rowanne, you must regain your strength so you can go to him. He has been calling for you throughout eventide."

"Oh, Lady Margaret, I cannot face him," Rowanne moaned into her hands. "I am so consumed with guilt."

"But why, child?"

"He will loathe the sight of me—for I bid him slay

Thomas. I begged him take the life of his own father. Oh, merciful heavens, what have I done? What have we both done?"

Lady Margaret smiled at Rowanne, then turned to the maid serving them. "I smelled something wonderful in the kitchens awhile ago. Would you bring some of whatever it was for your lady? Mayhap we can tempt her to eat."

The freckled girl bobbed a curtsey and quit the chamber. When she was gone Lady Margaret gathered Rowanne's hands in hers.

"Child, you must listen to me now and believe what I say. If Thomas's death is what troubles you, then be at peace."

"But how can I?"

Margaret stroked Rowanne's loose hair. She sat on a stool, her soft gray bliaut pooling at her slippered feet. "Brandt did not take the life of Thomas DeLucy."

Rowanne stopped sniffling and studied Margaret's face. "You would not be so cruel as to tell me false?"

"Nay, Rowanne, I speak truly. Brandt risked much and endured plenty to bring me away from Sherborne, but he did not end Thomas DeLucy's life."

"Then . . . who?"

"I did," Margaret said softly. "And would do so again, for I told you once before that the only way my captivity would end would be with the death of one of us. It was Thomas's. I am happy 'twas not mine." Her face was devoid of emotion as she spoke.

Rowanne was struck dumb. The cool, elegant woman before her seemed as incapable of violence as a dove was incapable of defending itself against Glandamore.

Margaret smiled sadly. "Perhaps it is time for you to learn who I am, Rowanne, and why I shared the tower with you at Sherborne."

"You were another heiress, kept for ransom or to marry off so Thomas could control a holding—"

"Nay, Rowanne. Thomas already had control of my

property. The time is long past for me to unravel the tangle of my life and let you see how our fates were twined like the web of a spider."

Rowanne watched as Margaret closed her eyes and took a deep breath. Then she began to speak in a low, monotonous tone that Rowanne knew was a defense against tears.

"I was born to my parents late in life." Margaret's slim, pale hands jerked in her lap. "My father was an Earl, well liked by all. My mother was taken by a fever in my fifteenth year, and my father, fearing he might follow, became anxious to see me wed and settled with a caring husband and protector."

"Your father must've loved you very much to have been so concerned with your happiness." Rowanne said, remembering her own father as she spoke, understanding his actions now that the truth about Desmond and Lochlyn had been revealed.

"Ah, just so. As a child I was protected and pampered. Within the walls of our castle I lived a perfect life. I had little to prepare me for the harsh realities of the real world. But I am ahead of myself in my tale." Margaret smiled sadly.

A knock on the chamber door stole her attention for a moment. "Enter," Margaret spoke.

The freckled maid entered carrying a wooden tray. She bobbed awkwardly, clearly in awe of Lady Margaret.

"The cook prepared hot bread and mulled wine, milady. She has made puddings and tarts from dried apples. I hope you will find it to your liking, milady."

Margaret sat in silence as the eager serving girl positioned the tray and quit the chamber. Lady Margaret passed a full goblet of warmed, mulled wine to Rowanne and took one up herself.

"Several men bid for my hand, but only one made the journey to my father's keep at Letchworth. My suitor was gallant and very handsome, a widower with a small, delightful son who stole away my heart. The man knew how to woo and spoke love words to me that flattered my foolish young heart. Within a sennight I was begging my father to arrange the banns. Within another fortnight I was wed. Then my father took ill, sickened, and died. All that he owned passed into the hands of my new husband."

"Oh, Lady Margaret—"

"Hush, Rowanne, and let me speak." She raised her hand and fluttered it through the air in a gesture that betrayed her great emotion and heartbreak at a loss suffered so long ago. Unshed tears shimmered in her green eyes.

"I was grief-stricken, but I had my wonderful husband to shelter me, to help me. And I had a bright child to comfort and nurture." Her smile was melancholy.

"My husband took charge of affairs at my father's castle, had my dowry packed and loaded into wagons, and together we made the long trip to Sherborne to begin our life together."

"Sherborne?" Rowanne nearly choked on a sip of mulled wine. "Nay, lady, I misheard you."

"Aye, to Sherborne. The wonderful man who wooed and won my love was Thomas DeLucy."

Rowanne could only blink as memories of her years in the tower room came swirling back through her head.

" 'Twas why you would never tell me who you were or why you were held in the tower."

"Thomas was a dangerous man, Rowanne. I knew the less you learned about his machinations, the safer you would remain." Margaret smiled again, and Rowanne's eyes were drawn to the fine network of lines across the lady's brow.

"He imprisoned his own *wife?*" Rowanne gasped in stunned outrage.

"Aye. And it is not so uncommon. Many a highborn wife has found herself a prisoner by order of her husband. Thomas was a strange man with a stranger dream. He had suffered a heartbreak as a young man that twisted him somehow. Geoffroi became his obsession. All Thomas wanted from life was a son he could be proud of, a son who led men, and commanded respect. A son who would marry well and avenge his father's wounded pride.''

''But I understand not why he locked you away.''

''Thomas was afraid he might get a child upon me. Or, if he was able to deny his own urges, that I might take a lover and get a child from another man. He had one legitimate heir and that was all he desired.'' Lady Margaret patted Rowanne's hand. '' 'Twas the reason he so shunned Brandt and 'twas the reason he locked me away and put out the story that I had died from a fever.''

''You see, Thomas never bedded me, Rowanne. He never made me his wife in deed. His fear was that another child would be a threat to all his dreams for Geoffroi—and the twisted revenge he had so carefully plotted and planned for you as the last survivor of the Vaudrys.''

''Oh, lady.''

''Now, now, no pity for me, I pray thee.'' Margaret's lips curled up at the corners. ''I warned you not to wed a man you thought you loved. Now you understand why. Thomas never wanted a wife. He had Geoffroi—he had my rich dowry, all my father's lands. I believe he murdered my father by poison after our wedding so there would be none to champion me.''

''How cruel he was. All this time I thought I had reason to hate him for my sorrows, but I see now they pale when compared to the cruelties you and Brandt endured,'' Rowanne whispered.

''Aye, he was cruel and greedy, and he lived with fear. Thomas's one great fear was that I should cuckold him and get myself with child. His foolish pride would have forced him to acknowledge the child as his own or let the world know he had never bedded me himself. He was far too prideful to consider allowing it. He had two choices, though I wonder now that he did not take the easier route and kill me."

She stared thoughtfully down at the liquid in her goblet. "He did keep me alive after all. Perhaps there was a drop of kindness in him."

"How lonely you must have been, Lady Margaret."

"Aye, lonely. Until you came." She looked at Rowanne and tears shimmered in her eyes. "I secretly rejoiced when Thomas brought you to me. To have a girl, a lovely child to share my days with . . . . 'Twas an answer to my prayers."

She smiled. "And you eased my confinement. I have come to think of you as fondly as my daughter."

"And I you as a second mother," Rowanne admitted softly.

"Mayhap Thomas did not injure me so deeply as he thought." Margaret swiped at her cheeks with the back of her hand and managed a shaky laugh.

"Wh-what happened—when Brandt came?"

"He is clever, that husband of yours. He bribed guards and found his way to my prison tower, but Thomas discovered us before we could make good a clean escape."

"Did—did Thomas know Brandt was his son?" Rowanne asked, even though a part of her did not want to hear the answer.

"Not at first. Thomas thought Brandt was merely a mercenary who had somehow learned my identity and wished to free me for a ransom."

"H-how did he react?"

Margaret tilted her head and smiled. " 'Tis almost impossible to believe, but for a moment I would swear I saw the glint of pride in his eyes when Brandt announced his identity and told Thomas of his intent."

Rowanne set her goblet aside and rose from her stool. She paced the rush-covered floor while emotions rippled through her. Thomas had been driven and shackled by his stubborn pride. *But am I less guilty of the same sins?*

"Poor Thomas. He had been nearly mad since he learned that Geoffroi had taken the cowl. All his dreams and plans went up in smoke." Margaret took a sip of wine, and Rowanne saw the trembling of her hand.

"All his years of plotting—all the misery he had wrought. All was for Geoffroi, and then to find everything he wanted was right before him in the form of Brandt. Brandt was strong and noble and the kind of man anyone would be proud to acknowledge as their son, legitimate or no. 'Twas a bitter blow to Thomas, I think. In that last moment I am sure I saw regret in his eyes."

"But Brandt's wound, Thomas's death . . . how?" Rowanne sipped at the mulled wine, grateful for its numbing effects.

"Thomas was like a crazy man. He was shouting about Rowena and Etienne. He lunged at Brandt, intending to kill him, I am sure. Brandt would not raise his weapon against his father—and he told him as much."

Rowanne whirled around to face Margaret. "Jesu! Was he willing to be killed by Thomas?"

"We will never know." One tear snaked its way down Lady Margaret's cheek. "Thomas was not looking at me. I darted forward and I shoved him over the edge of the parapet. The stone was old and crumbling, as you know. The battlements were treacherous. He fell to his death." Margaret tipped up her goblet and drained it in a long gulp.

"I know I have committed a mortal sin but surely after all that Thomas has done—I pray God will have mercy," Margaret said softly. She drew herself up and looked into Rowanne's eyes. "And now to hear that Leopold has been felled dumb—destined to spend the rest of his days being cared for by the monks of Lanercost Priory. It is divine intervention, and I wonder what awaits me." She shivered.

"There is little comparison to Leopold's black sins and what you have done, lady. You did what anyone would have done to save a life. There is no similarity."

"Mayhap and mayhap not. I have petitioned the monks of Lanercost, and Geoffroi among them, to pray for Thomas's soul. The accident that led to his death was a tragic mishap, the stones of the upper battlements of Sherborne had become unstable. 'Twas only a matter of time before someone fell, or at least that is the story Brandt told. He walked from Sherborne Hall without a limp, though I saw the pain in his eyes, and died a little inside knowing how he suffered to protect me." Margaret stared at Rowanne for a long moment.

"It was the only way we could leave and I could avoid the ax-man's chop, or a lifetime in Sherborne's dungeon. May God forgive me for risking Brandt's life."

Rowanne set her goblet aside and knelt at Lady Margaret's side. "And God will forgive, I am sure of it. You have suffered mightily for too long. 'Tis time to put this all behind you."

Margaret reached up and stroked Rowanne's cheek lovingly. "And now you are free—forever free of the DeLucy threat."

"What will you do?"

Margaret smiled. "I have not only my father's lands restored to me but all that Thomas possessed as well. When your husband recovers I will petition him for an escort—or should I ask your brother, Desmond, the new lord of Irthing? I intend to travel the breadth and length of England restoring some of what Thomas has taken, beginning with your brothers."

"Desmond and Lochlyn?"

"I knew them as Phillip and Armand. I am going to give them each a portion of lands—if they will agree to take them. After all, Thomas stole their family and their birthright for too many years."

"And you have restored it all," Rowanne whispered.

"Nay, I did little. Brandt le Revenant, the bastard

son of Thomas DeLucy, has brought it all to rights."
Margaret rose from her stool and wrapped her arms
around Rowanne, pulling her to her feet.

"Do you remember when I warned you not to wed a
man you thought you loved?"

"Aye." Rowanne's stomach clenched.

"Do you remember your answer? You said you could
not love a man of DeLucy blood until your dead brothers
once again walked the earth." Lady Margaret stroked
Rowanne's cheek. "I think the time has come to keep
your vow, Rowanne."

Brandt was once again in the Holy Land. The sun
shimmered off sand dunes in hot waves that burned his
eyes and choked the back of his throat with dust.

Jesu, he thirsted. His body ached from a hundred old
and forgotten wounds and a new one in his leg that
burned with the fires of hell. 'Twas as though a Saracen
tortured him with a hot branding iron on his thigh.

He wanted nothing more than to lie down and give
up the ghost, but he was a knight, a Crusader. He forced
himself to push on, to gain ground, to get nearer. . . .

What? What was he fighting for?

Jerusalem?

Nay.

The Holy Faith?

Nay.

The Grail, the Ark, some relic of faith?

Nay.

'Twas something more, something sweeter than land
or faith. Whatever it was, the illusive treasure refused
to let him simply die in peace. The thing he desired
beyond all reason nagged at him, nipped at his heels
like a harrier hound, driving him onward. Brandt stared
across the endless expanse of sand, searching for the
answer.

Then he saw her.

She was lovely as England in spring. Her golden hair fluttered behind her like a shimmering gilt pennon. A bliaut of soft blue clung to her curves with each desert gust. His heart beat with love.

'Twas Rowanne he lived for. She was England. She was icy clear becks, green lush fells, and loamy dark-leaved forests. She was mysterious secrets and laughing sunlight. She was warmth, lust, and unspeakable pleasure. She was everything he had ever wanted and feared he could never have.

He hungered for her, thirsted for her. He would easily give his life for her, but he realized that what he needs must do was live for her.

Live. Live for Rowanne.

He cried out to her, hearing his own words drift over the sand and disappear into the endless wind of the desert.

"I am here, Brandt." A smooth palm caressed his burning forehead. "I am right here beside you."

"Rowanne!" Brandt's agonized roar echoed off the chamber walls and into the hall. "Rowanne."

Desmond opened the door. "Is he worse?"

"I think he is rousing," Rowanne said as she bathed his face with a cooling cloth.

Rowanne stared into the face of her husband. His flesh was pale and his cheeks were gaunt, but there was still a strength that rippled from him, even now as he lay fevered and out of his mind with pain.

"Brandt, you must live. You must open your eyes and promise me that you will live," she demanded.

His eyelids raised a little. He stared at Rowanne with a glazed and unfocused look. "Come nearer, Rowanne. If I am dying I want your sweet face to be the last thing I look upon."

"I will come closer, but I will have your promise that you will not die."

He managed to curve his dry, cracked lips into a semblance of a smile. "Little tyrant—little deceiver and temptress." Then he flopped back onto the bolster and became silent and still as death.

As the sun rose on Christmastide, Rowanne continued to cool his brow with a damp cloth. The braziers were burning brightly, keeping the room warm and well illuminated no matter the hour. Throughout the lonely hours of the night she had mentally cataloged all Brandt had done for her and how little she had done to balance out the debt.

Guilt and shame for her pride and her foolishness kept her company, but a bitter draught it was, for she could not be sure that Brandt would live and thus allow her to make amends.

"Brandt, I love you. I think I have loved you from the moment you protected me from the bandits and Leopold," she said in the silence of the chamber.

"And then when you took control and brought Irthing back to its former prosperity, I admired you more than I could tell you. The harvest is good, and there are no more hungry, cold peasants shivering in their cots."

She dipped the cloth and ran it across his noble brow.

"Only because of you do I have my brothers back. And though Lochlyn's hate for all that is English runs deep in his heart, 'tis enough for me to know that he lives."

She sniffed and swiped at a tear, feeling her child flutter and kick within her belly.

"You must live, Brandt. You must regain your strength and take your place here at Irthing. Poor Desmond does not want it. He worries about properly caring for the folk and what will happen when he must take up the du Luc lands. He is torn by two birthrights. He does not need the burden of Irthing. We need you."

Her voice cracked, and she could say no more. Her heart was heavy with love and hope.

"Rowanne," Brandt moaned. "Rowanne, where are you?"

"I am here." She cradled his beard-roughened cheeks in her palms and placed a kiss on his forehead. His skin was dry and papery. His eyes were glazed with fever and pain.

"I am sorry I deceived you, Rowanne." His words were slurred and slow, but each one wrenched her heart in a painful grip. "I—I have to tell you."

" 'Tis all in the past. Shhh . . . speak no more of it." She dipped the cloth in the cooling herb-water the monk had prepared and washed Brandt's face and neck. He was bare beneath the sleeping furs, his mighty chest heaving and falling as he labored to inhale each breath.

"Must—tell you . . . if I die—you needs must know that I—"

"You cannot die, Brandt. You have a child." Rowanne choked out. "Do you hear, Brandt DeLucy? You have a child that grows within my belly. Is that not enough to keep you fighting for your life?"

"Child?" Brandt coughed. The effort he spent to remain conscious was etched into his face. "A babe? My babe?" Then a grimace of pain contorted his face and he slipped into the black abyss once again.

Brandt woke to the sound of revelry. Laughter, music, and the squeals of delighted children rent the air. He felt a weight on his chest—looked, and blinked.

'Twas Rowanne, her golden hair spilling over him like a silken fall. He smiled and lifted a strand to his face, rubbing it against his flesh. She roused slowly, yawning as she came aware.

"Brandt." She started to rise, but he held her to his chest.

"Is it true, Rowanne, is there a babe?"

"Aye, 'tis true," she said softly.

"And how do you feel to be carrying a child that

bears DeLucy blood?'' His eyes bored into her like agate daggers, allowing her to speak nothing but the truth.

"The child is ours, Brandt, conceived in love. I care naught about sins from the past. Who among us can claim no sin?"

A slow, satisfied smile crept across his face. And though he had been ravaged with fever and illness, and he badly needed a shave, his was the most handsome face she had e'er beheld.

"I have waited an overly long time to hear you say that."

"I love you, Brandt DeLucy. I care not who sired you; I care only for the man you are."

"And I love you, wife. Now come here and kiss me and give me a proper gift as befits the season." He crushed her to his chest, and the walls of Irthing were heard to sigh in contentment. Below, in the Great Hall, Vaudrys, Armstrongs, and Lady Margaret, the DeLucy widow, made merry, talking and laughing, each trying to decide if the match of Rowanne and Brandt had indeed been foretold on the ancient ogham stones that Gruffudd held so dear.

AUTHOR'S NOTE

You Anglophiles will, of course, have instantly recognized that all the locations in the story are real. One of the most fascinating, and indeed the one that inspired this story, is Cumbria. Lanercost Priory is there, as it has been since 1166, when Robert de Vaux laid the first cornerstone and began to erect the priory for Augustinian Canons. Since Hadrian's Wall was conveniently nearby, most of the stones for the construction were taken from that great barrier that split Scotland and England's border. Even today graffiti etched by Roman soldiers may be seen in some of the walls at Lanercost.

The patron saint of the priory is St. Mary Magdalene, and a statue of her was given by King Edward I, better known as Longshanks. That statue now resides over the west door, where it has been for 800 years.

Since Lanercost lies on the borderlands between England and Scotland, it has long been prey to raids by border bandits and patriots like the fictitious Lochlyn Armstrong. In 1297 William Wallace, the Scots hero, organized a raid into the north of England and rode as far as the gates of Newcastle. Lanercost was pillaged and burnt, later to be restored by the Canons.

Lanercost was also visited by King Edward I and his

beloved wife, Queen Eleanor, in 1280, and again in 1300 on his way to lay siege to Caerlaverock Castle, over the Solway Firth in Scotland. Six years later they visited Lanercost again on their way to Carlisle, with a retinue of around 200. Edward was relentless in his persecution of the Scots.

With the dissolution of the monasteries in 1536, the buildings were given over to Sir Thomas Dacre, who converted part of the monastic buildings into a home for himself. Around 1740 the Nave was restored.

Today Lanercost Priory is a living church with a roll of some 600 parishioners scattered over a wide rural area encompassing Cumbria, North Brampton, and Carlisle. It is well worth a visit if you are able to make a trip to northern England. Though it is much smaller than it once was, the foundations of its walls and cloisters are easily visible, and the cemetery is amazing. Nearby you can climb Hadrian's Wall and feel the bite of the cold Scottish wind; but beware, this section is the breeding ground of the Scottish viper.

When you are on the wall, standing in the teeth of the wind, think of Brandt, Rowanne, Desmond, and Lochlyn—and listen for their whispered voices in that weathering sound.